CRITICAL ACCLAIM FOR MICHAEL KORYTA

A WELCOME GRAVE
Nominated for a Quill Award

"Edgar-finalist Koryta stakes a claim as one of today's preeminent crafters of contemporary hard-boiled mysteries. . . . Despite Koryta's youth . . . his haunting writing and logical, sophisticated plotting rival that of established stalwarts like Loren Estleman."
—*Publishers Weekly* (starred review)

"If you haven't already discovered Michael Koryta . . . now's the time. *A Welcome Grave* is his best book."
—*Toronto Globe and Mail*

"The Rust Belt never looked so scary . . . a nightmare chess game."
—*Rocky Mountain News*

"The story is graced by Koryta's humor and style . . ."
—*Cleveland Plain Dealer*

"*A Welcome Grave* . . . is proof that after only three novels it is possible to become a 'must read' in crime fiction . . . one of the best PI-against-the-world books I've read in a long, long time. Koryta's dialogue remains vivid and his characters sharp as a diamond drill bit."
—*Crimespree Magazine*

"In his third efficiently plotted mystery, Koryta lands most of his punches . . ."
—*Entertainment Weekly*

"Koryta's storytelling is enhanced by a fluid prose style. . . ."
—*Milwaukee Journal Sentinel*

"An exciting novel with carefully rendered characers, even secondary ones, who will remain with the reader long after turning the last page."
—Bookreporter.com

MORE...

"This is the book that will put Koryta on everyone's 'must read' list. . . . The action is relentless." —*The Kingston Observer*

"The best entry yet in the Lincoln Perry private-eye series."
—*Library Journal* (starred review)

"It's time to stop referring to Koryta as a boy wonder and just focus on the sheer wonder of his storytelling. . . . *A Welcome Grave* is a nuanced, mature novel that proves both the depth of Koryta's talent and the vitality of the PI genre."
—*New York Times* bestselling author Laura Lippman

"For a while now Michael Koryta has been called one of the rising young talents in crime fiction. I say enough of that. *A Welcome Grave* proves the promise. Koryta is one of the best of the best, plain and simple. With stories like this, his Lincoln Perry is going to be around for a long, long time."
—Michael Connelly

SORROW'S ANTHEM

"Koryta's impressive second hardboiled mystery is a worthy successor to his debut, *Tonight I Said Goodbye*, an Edgar and Shamus finalist. . . . The 22-year-old author, who works for a PI and for an Indiana newspaper, displays credible insider knowledge of those professions as well as a gift for creating both sympathetic characters and a fast-moving, twisty plot."
—*Publishers Weekly*

"[A] work of rare profundity. The multi-layered and labyrinthine plot is worthy of Raymond Chandler or (more aptly, perhaps) Ross MacDonald. And that's more than mere hyperbole; Koryta is that good. *Sorrow's Anthem* is so good it'll bring tears to your eyes. And it's good on just about every level; as a crime novel, as a hardboiled mystery, and as a mainstream exploration of choices, consequences, and of individual responsibility. In the end, and as far as 'anthems' go, this one never misses a beat."
—*Mystery News*

TONIGHT I SAID GOODBYE

2005 Edgar Award Nominee for "Best First Novel by an American Author"

ALSO BY MICHAEL KORYTA

Sorrow's Anthem

Tonight I Said Goodbye

AVAILABLE FROM ST. MARTIN'S PAPERBACKS

A WELCOME
GRAVE

MICHAEL KORYTA

St. Martin's Paperbacks

This is a work of fiction. All of the characters, organizations and events portrayed in this novel are either products of the author's imagination or are used fictitiously.

A WELCOME GRAVE

Copyright © 2007 by Michael Koryta.
Excerpt from *Envy the Night* copyright © 2008 by Michael Koryta.

Library of Congress Catalog Card Number: 2007011379

ISBN: 0-312-94751-8
EAN: 978-0-312-94751-4

Printed in the United States of America

St. Martin's Press hardcover edition / July 2007
St. Martin's Paperbacks edition / June 2008

St. Martin's Paperbacks are published by St. Martin's Press, 175 Fifth Avenue, New York, NY 10010.

10 9 8 7 6 5 4 3 2 1

For my sister, Jennifer,
who read my first "book" many years ago
and managed not to laugh

ACKNOWLEDGMENTS

Peter Wolverton and David Hale Smith continue to display an astounding talent for remaining patient and positive during the ugliest of drafts, and, as always, I'm in their debt.

No one has waded through more drafts and mistakes with me than Bob Hammel, who probably has read ten times more Lincoln Perry pages than have ever been published. Thank you, Bob.

Lending a set of helpful, colorful, and decidedly unique opinions were Laura Lane and Gena Asher. One left wine stains on her copy of the manuscript, the other fell asleep on it, but they were key contributions nevertheless.

Deepest gratitude to those at St. Martin's Press and Thomas Dunne Books for all their work and support—Thomas Dunne, Andy Martin, Katie Gilligan, Rachel Ekstrom, Matthew Shear, and the rest of the team.

It has been a true pleasure getting to meet the owners and employees of bookstores around the country, who are always gracious hosts and seem to truly love their jobs. Thanks for all the support.

I write because the work of others has entertained and inspired me over the years. Those writers continue to be a constant source of motivation—on and off the page. It is a true and valued privilege to receive advice and encouragement from the writers who led me into this business, and I'm most grateful.

And, of course, thanks to my family.

PART ONE

FAMILY BUSINESS

CHAPTER

1

Sometime after midnight, on a moonless October night turned harsh by a fine, windswept rain, one of the men I liked least in the world was murdered in a field near Bedford, just south of the city. Originally, they assumed the body had only been dumped there. That Alex Jefferson had been killed somewhere else, dead maybe before the mutilation began.

They were wrong.

It was past noon the next day when the body was discovered. A dozen vehicles were soon assembled in the field—police cars, evidence vans, an ambulance that could serve no purpose but was dispatched anyhow. I wasn't there, but I could imagine the scene—I'd certainly been to enough like it.

But maybe not. Maybe not. The things they saw that day, things I heard about secondhand, from cops who recited the news in the distanced way that only hardened professionals can manage . . . they weren't things I dealt with often.

Jefferson was brought from the city with his hands and feet bound with rope, duct tape over his mouth. A half mile down a dirt track leading into an empty field, he was removed from a vehicle—tire tracks suggested a van—and subjected to a systematic torture killing that was apparently quite slow in reaching the second stage. Autopsy results and scenarios created by the forensic team and the medical experts suggested Jefferson remained breathing, and probably conscious, for fifteen minutes.

Fifteen minutes varies by perspective. The blink of an eye, if you're standing in an airport, saying goodbye to someone you love. An ice age, if you're fighting through traffic, late for a job interview. And if your hands and feet are bound while someone works you over slowly, from head to toe, with a butane lighter and a straight razor? At that point an eternity isn't what the fifteen minutes feels like—it's what you're begging for. To be sent to wherever it is you're destined, and sent there for good.

The cops were preoccupied with the basics for most of the first day: processing the crime scene, getting the forensic experts from the Ohio Bureau of Criminal Investigation involved, identifying the body, notifying next of kin, and trying to piece together Jefferson's last hours. The locals were interviewed, the field and surrounding woods combed for evidence.

No leads came. Not from the basics, at least, not from those first hours of work. So the investigation extended. The detectives went looking for suspects—people whose histories with Jefferson were adversarial, hostile. At the top of that list, they found me.

They arrived at ten past nine on the day after Alex Jefferson's body was discovered, and I hadn't made it to the office yet, even though I live in a building just down the street. Below my apartment is an old gym I own and from which I occasionally make a profit. I've got a manager for the gym, but that day she had car trouble. She called me at seven thirty to say her husband was trying a jump start, and if that didn't work, she might be late. I told her not to worry about it—no rush for me, so none for her. I'd open the gym and then leave whenever she made it in.

I'd gone downstairs with a cup of coffee in hand and unlocked the gym office. There's a keycard system that allows members to come and go twenty-four hours a day, but Grace, my manager, works the nine-to-five in the office and at the cooler. We make most of our money off energy drinks and protein shakes, granola bars, and vitamins, not the monthly membership dues.

There were two women on treadmills and one man lifting weights when I opened the office, our typical crowd. One nice thing about working out at my gym: You never have to wait on the equipment. Good for the members, bad for me.

I checked the locker rooms to make sure there were fresh towels and found Grace had taken care of that the previous night. I was on my way back through the weight room when I saw the cops standing just inside the office. Two of them, neither in uniform, but I caught a glimpse of a badge affixed to the taller one's belt, a glint of silver under the fluorescent lights that made my eyebrows narrow and my pace quicken.

"Can I help you?" I stepped into the office. Neither one was familiar to me, but I couldn't pretend to know everyone at the department, especially now, a few years since I'd last worked there.

"Lincoln Perry?"

"Yes."

The one whose badge wasn't clipped to his belt, a trim guy with gray hair and crow's feet around his eyes, slid a case out of his pocket and opened it, showing a badge and identification card. HAROLD TARGENT, DETECTIVE, CLEVELAND POLICE DEPARTMENT. I gave it a glance, looked backed at him, nodded once.

"Okay. What can I help you with, Detective?"

"Call me Hal."

The taller one beside him, who was maybe ten years younger, lifted his hand in a little wave. "Kevin Daly."

Targent looked out at the weight room, then back at me. "You mind shutting that door? Give us a little privacy?"

"My manager's late. Don't want to close the office up until she gets here, if that's okay."

Targent shook his head. "Going to need some privacy, Mr. Perry."

"That serious?" I said, beginning to feel the first hint of dread, the sense that maybe this had nothing to do with one of my cases, that it could be personal.

"Serious, yes. Serious the way it gets when people die, Mr. Perry."

I swung the office door shut and turned the lock. "Let's go upstairs."

To their credit, they didn't waste a lot of time bullshitting around without telling me why they were there. No questions about what I'd done the previous night, no head games. Instead, they laid it out as soon as we'd taken seats in my living room.

"A man you know was murdered two nights ago," Targent said. "Heard about it?"

My last contact with the news had been the previous day's paper. I hadn't seen that morning's yet, and I get more reliable news from the drunk who hangs out at the bus stop up the street than I do from the television. I shook my head slowly, Targent watching with friendly skepticism.

"You going to tell me who?" I said.

"The man's name was Alex Jefferson."

It was one of those moments when I wished I were a smoker, just so I could have something to do with my hands, a little routine I could go through to pass some time without having to sit there and stare.

"You remember the man?" Daly asked.

I looked at him and gave a short laugh, shaking my head at the question. "Yeah. I remember the man."

They waited for a bit. Targent said, "And your relationship with him was, ah, a little adversarial?"

I met his eyes. "He was sleeping with my fiancée, Detective. I spent two hours working my way through a twelve-pack of beer before I beat the shit out of Jefferson at his country club, got pulled over for drunk driving, got charged with assault. Pled the assault down to a misdemeanor but got canned from the department. All of this, you already know.

But, yes, I suppose we can say that my relationship with him was, ah, a little adversarial."

Targent was watching me, and Daly was pretending to, but his eyes were drifting over my apartment, as if he thought maybe I'd left a crowbar or a nine-iron with dried blood and matted hair stuck to it leaning against the wall.

"Okay," Targent said. He looked even smaller sitting down, as if he weighed about a hundred and twenty pounds, but he had a substantial quality despite that, a voice flecked with iron. "Don't take it personally, Mr. Perry. Nobody's calling you a suspect. Now, if I can just ask—"

"Were you there when she was notified?" I said.

"Excuse me?"

"Karen. His wife. Were you there when she was notified?"

He shook his head. "No, I was not. Lots of people are working—"

"I can imagine. He was a very important man."

Targent blew out his breath and glanced at Daly, whose eyes were still roving over my apartment, looking for any excuse to shout "probable cause" and begin tearing the place apart.

"I was out with a friend till about eleven Saturday night," I said. "We had dinner, a few drinks downtown. I've probably got the receipts. Came back here, read for an hour, went to bed. No receipt for that."

Targent smiled slightly. "Okay. But you're getting ahead of us."

"Like he said, nobody's calling you a suspect," Daly said.

"Sure."

"Just covering bases," Targent said. "You were on the job not long ago, you know how it goes."

"Sure."

He leaned back and hooked one ankle over a knee. "So you had an admittedly adversarial relationship with Mr. Jefferson."

"Three years ago."

"And had you—"

"Seen him since? No. The last time I saw him he was on his back in the parking lot, doing a lot of bleeding, and I was trying to make it to my car."

That wasn't true. I'd seen him twice after that, but always from a distance, and always unnoticed. Once in a restaurant; he'd been standing at the bar, laughing with some other guys in expensive suits, and I'd walked in the door, spotted him, and turned right back around and walked out. The other time was the day he and Karen were married. I'd parked across the street and sat in my car, watched them walk down the steps as people clapped and whistled, and I'd thought that it was all kid stuff, really, the marriage ceremony, and that when people like Jefferson—nearly fifty years old and trying a third wife on for size—went through it in public, it was pretty sad. Pathetic, even. Almost as sad and pathetic as being parked across the street, eighty-eight degrees but with the windows up, watching another guy marry your girl.

That was during my bad phase, though. Fresh out of the job, shiftless and angry. Time had passed, things had changed. Alex Jefferson, while never really gone from my mind, no longer weighed on it, either.

"You're wasting time," I said. "I understand you've got to go through the motions, but this is a dead end, gentlemen. I hadn't seen him, I hadn't seen her, and I didn't kill him. Happy he's dead? No. Sad? Not particularly. Apathetic. That's it. He and his life were of no concern to me and mine. Not anymore."

Targent leaned forward, ran a hand through his hair, and looked at the floor. "They took their time on him."

"Pardon?"

He looked up. "Whoever *did* kill him, Mr. Perry? They took their damn sweet time doing it. Slow and painful. That was how he went. With forty-seven burns and more than fifty lacerations. Burns from cigarettes and a lighter, lacerations from a razor blade. Sometimes the blade was used to cut deep, like a knife. Other times, it was used like a paint scraper across his flesh. He had duct tape over his mouth, and at some point, trying to scream, maybe, or maybe just going into convulsions from the pain, he bit right through his own tongue."

I turned and stared out the window. "I don't need the details, Detective. I just need you to scratch me off the list and move on."

They lingered for about ten more minutes before finally clearing out. They would check out my history with Jefferson now, try to prove that our contact hadn't stopped when I'd said it had, probably verify what they could of my activity the night he was killed. If things went well, went the way they should, I wouldn't hear from them again.

When they were gone, I left the gym office locked, walked up the street, and bought a newspaper. I sat on a bench outside the doughnut shop, a cool breeze ruffling the pages as I read. Jefferson made the front page, of course, but it was brief. A rewritten police press release and a note that the attorney's wife, Karen, was unavailable for comment. They'd gotten the tip late—classic police public relations. We might have to leak the news eventually, but you can be damn sure that when we do it'll be as close to your deadline as possible.

I didn't recognize the name of the reporter who'd written the story. I could call my friend Amy Ambrose at the paper, see if she knew anything more—but what the hell for? At the end of the day, why did I care? I threw the newspaper away and walked toward my office.

I came to the corner and crossed the street, went up the stairs, unlocked the office door, and stepped inside to be greeted by silence. My partner, Joe Pritchard, was out indefinitely, had been for a couple of months. Right now he was probably at physical therapy, where he went three times a week, trying to regain as much use of his left arm as possible. A bullet had gone in his shoulder not long ago, and although it came out, it left behind plenty of damage. And an empty chair at the desk beside me.

I turned my computer on and sat behind my own desk,

staring out the window. Maybe I should call Joe, let him know what had happened. Hell, he probably knew already. Joe always seemed to. He hadn't called me, though, and that was surprising. Unless, as usual, he was a step ahead of me and a hell of a lot smarter and realized that, despite the police reaction, this thing wasn't personal to me.

"It was a long time ago," I told the empty office.

I pulled the stack of case files on the desk toward me and flipped the first one open. There was work to do, and nobody else would be coming in to do it for me.

Karen's call came at ten in the morning on the day after her husband was buried. I was in the office again, alone again, typing up a report on a custody case. The father was my client, and he wanted proof that his ex-wife's new boyfriend was a drug dealer. Thought it would help him in the court battle for the kids. During the two weeks I spent on the case, I determined that the ex-wife had no boyfriend and that my client was a prick. Although he found time to call me six times a day, complaining that I must not be doing my job because "that bitch" most definitely did have a boyfriend, and a drug-dealing boyfriend at that, he somehow managed to miss his seven-year-old son's birthday by three days. When he realized that, he blamed the ex-wife, naturally.

I was sitting in front of the computer, momentarily frozen as I sought words that would allow me to tell my client he was an idiot without sacrificing the rest of my fee, when the phone rang. I hit the speakerphone button, a habit I'd developed only in Joe's absence, and said hello.

"Lincoln?" Voices on the speakerphone always seemed to come from a long way off, but this one put a different spin on that quality. It was coming from a long way off and a place I'd been trying to forget.

"Karen." For a moment I regretted saying her name, wished I'd pretended not to recognize her voice from just that one word, but then I realized that was a pointless exercise. I would've known her even if she'd only sneezed when I answered the phone, and she knew that.

"How are you?" she asked.

"I'm fine. Certainly better than you must be doing, at least."

"Are you free for a little while?"

I paused. "I'm working. Why do you ask?"

"It's just . . . I was hoping you could come by. I wanted to apologize, that's all. I just found out what the police did. That was ridiculous. I can't believe they talked to you. There was no reason for it."

"There was a reason for it," I said. "It's called doing a job. I didn't take any offense."

"Well, I'm sorry. I just wanted to make sure . . . wanted you to know that I didn't send them. That I wasn't the one who gave them the idea they needed to bother you with this."

Hearing her voice was surreal. I knew it so well, the pitch, the cadence, and yet in a way it felt like listening to a singer whose face you've never seen. That voice couldn't be any more familiar, yet I didn't know who she was. Not anymore.

"I understand," I said.

Silence. I leaned back in my chair and waited.

"Lincoln?"

"Yes."

"I wasn't sure if you were still there."

"I'm here."

Another pause, then, "Anyhow, I was hoping, if you had a few minutes, you could come by."

"So you could apologize?"

"Well, yes."

"You just did. And thank you, but it was unnecessary."

"Okay," she said. "Okay. Well . . . goodbye, Lincoln."

"Goodbye, Karen. Good luck."

She hung up, but only when the phone began to beep at me did I remember to lean over and click off the speaker-phone.

Ten minutes later, it rang again. Karen.

"Lincoln, I really do need to see you. I'm drained, and emotional, and I hung up before because . . . well, your voice was so defensive. And I understand that. I do. But I need to see you. In person."

"Just to apologize?"

"Lincoln . . ." There were tears in her voice now.

Shit. I pushed back in my chair, rolled my eyes to the ceiling, and shook my head. What the hell was this about?

"Twenty minutes," she said, speaking the words softly and carefully, trying to keep the emotion out of her voice. "It's important."

"Where?"

"The house."

The house. Like it was Monticello, some sort of damn landmark.

"I don't know where the house is, Karen."

"Pepper Pike. Off Shaker, near the country club." She gave me the address.

"The country club," I said. "Of course." That had been the location of my last encounter with Jefferson, but Karen didn't strike me as someone who'd appreciate that particular flash of nostalgia, so I kept it to myself.

"You'll come?"

"Like I've got no sense at all."

"Pardon?"

"Nothing. I'll see you in a bit."

"Thank you, Lincoln."

We hung up again, and, after a few minutes of swearing at myself, I got up and walked out the door.

CHAPTER

2

The house was a spectacle. A driveway that was probably repaved every year wound through a collection of tall, perfect trees shading a lawn that looked like a fairway at Augusta. Then the home came into view around the bend—Southern mansion met colonial met contemporary, but, somehow, the damn thing worked. It was a lot of white and glass and a sprawling front porch beneath second-story balconies. A stone wall bordered a swimming pool and patio. A cover had been spread across the pool, and it looked like there was a stone fireplace built alongside the patio.

A four-car garage stood to the side, styled to look like a carriage house. I pulled to a stop in front of it and waited for someone to come out and offer to provide my truck with oats and water while I went inside. When nobody did, I shut the engine off and got out. The spacious yard was still and silent, the house more of the same. I walked up a cobblestone path to the porch. At the front door, I lifted the brass handle and dropped it back on the wood a few times. A minute passed, maybe two. Someone had left a bouquet of flowers at the door. I picked them up, looked at the card. *From Ted and Nancy, with our deepest sympathies*. I kept the flowers in my free hand while I banged the knocker again, the sound loud and hollow. This time the door opened.

The sight of her shook me. She was gorgeous, sure, but

that wasn't it—she was the way I remembered her, the way I tried *not* to remember her. A new line or two on the face, maybe, the soft blond hair cut in a more expensive style, five extra pounds on a body that always could stand ten extra pounds, but, damn it, she was still the Karen I'd proposed to in the rain on a warm night in April. I didn't want her to be.

She wore loose white pants and a sleeveless shirt, no shoes, no jewelry. Her body was firm and lithe. Looking at her I saw a sudden flash of the scenes I'd missed in the last few years: the dinner parties where Jefferson's rich, fat friends had looked at his trophy wife and sworn under their breath with envy; the smug smile on Jefferson's face when he and Karen encountered one of his aging ex-wives.

"Good to see you, Karen," I said.

"So good," she said and stepped forward to embrace me. I remembered the fit of her body perfectly—the top of her shoulders sliding just beneath the rise of mine, her chin slipping alongside the bottom of my neck. Her hair smelled different, though. Expensive perfume where the hint of apples from some cheap shampoo belonged.

She pulled away but kept her hands on my biceps. "Thank you for coming. I understand—really, I do—that you don't want to be here. But I need to talk to you about something. I *have* to talk to you about something."

"Okay."

"Come in." Her eyes dropped to the flowers I was still holding. "Oh, Lincoln, thank you. You didn't need to—"

"I didn't. They were at the door."

"Oh." She let go of my arms, took the flowers, and led me inside. The front door opened into a wide entryway with a clear view of the lower level of the house—blond wood, white trim, more windows than I'd ever seen in a house before. I followed her past a room on my left that was filled with books—none of the spines cracked—and a room on my right with a desk and a fireplace that might have been used as an office by someone who actually worked at home but instead had the look of a showroom. Hell, the whole house had that look. When we went past the kitchen and into the living room, I noted that there wasn't so much as a juice glass on the counter or a salt shaker on the table. Everything felt sterile, as if it had been thrown together for a photo shoot. Flowers and cards had been delivered by the dozens, but I saw as we passed that all of them had been placed in another room on our right, tastefully arranged around a piano.

Karen moved into a living room at the rear of the house and sat on a walnut-colored leather chair with her back to the row of windows looking out on the yard. I settled into a matching couch across from it and sank about a foot into the damn thing.

"Comfortable," I said, wondering if anyone had ever actually sat on it before.

She didn't say anything, just sat and stared at me. She looked more tired than I'd ever seen her, more tired than I would've imagined a woman with her energy and life ever could. Beautiful, yes, but tired in a way that came from deep within. Better than her husband, though.

"Can I get you something to drink?" she asked.

"No." I didn't bother to mention that it wasn't even eleven. She'd already lifted a glass of wine from the table beside her.

"My nerves are shot," she said, following my look. "It keeps me calm."

"Sure."

She sipped it, and it was so early for wine that I felt like I should look away, as if she were changing clothes across from me instead of taking a drink.

"Are you alone here?" I asked.

"My family just left. My mother isn't well."

"I'm sorry to hear that."

"About the police," she said, but I interrupted.

"You already apologized, and there was no need for it then. They're just doing their job as well as they know how to do it, Karen. I would have been more surprised if they *hadn't* come to see me when your husband was murdered."

The word made her wince. She lifted the glass to her lips,

had it in her hand when the phone rang, a long, shrill chirp. She jerked at the sound, not a slight motion but a violent one, and the glass fell from her hand and shattered on the pale wood floor. The wine pooled, then found the cracks between the boards and ran down them, toward the stone ledge in front of the fireplace.

There was a phone on the table beside me. I picked up the handset and leaned forward, offering it to her. She pushed back into her chair, eyes wide, and held her hand out as if she were warding the phone off.

"No. Not now, please."

I gave her a long look, still with the phone outstretched, before dropping the handset back on its base. One ring later, it went silent, and only then did she pick up the stem of the broken wineglass and set it back on the coffee table. There was a photograph in a silver frame on the table: Jefferson and Karen kissing on a veranda, probably taken in someplace like Paris. I returned my attention to the spilled wine. Some of it was soaking into a rug beneath the coffee table that was probably worth more than my gym.

"Want me to grab some paper towels?"

"It's fine."

"Okay."

We sat and looked at each other. Her chest rose and fell under her shirt. I switched my gaze from her to the broken glass and the wine on the floor and back again.

"Karen, what the hell's going on?"

She drew in a long breath, ran her hands through her hair again, and shook her head. "My husband was murdered, Lincoln. That's what's going on. My husband was brutally—"

"There's something else."

"No."

"Karen."

She looked away, and when she spoke again it sounded as if she were on the verge of being physically ill.

"Do you have any idea what they did to him? They *tortured* him. Cut him with—"

"I've heard. And I'm sorry. What you're going through

right now . . . I can't say anything of substance to you because words aren't worth a damn. Particularly words from me, I'd imagine."

There was a long silence, and then I said, "So what is it that you want?"

She stared at me for a few seconds. "You'll be well paid."

I spread my hands. "For what?"

The big house felt empty in the way only too-large spaces can. From where I sat, I could see the steps leading up to the second floor, where a hallway crossed over the living room and kitchen. There were a few paintings on the walls in the hallway, and I would've bet everything I had that neither Karen nor Alex Jefferson had picked them out. Interior designer, all the way.

"I need help." She was leaning forward, gripping the edge of the chair so tightly her fingernails were probably cutting into the leather, her eyes fixed on mine.

"With what?"

"Alex's son."

"I've never been real good with kids."

"I need to find Alex's son."

I frowned and cocked my head. "He doesn't know his father's dead?"

"No."

"And you don't know how to get in touch? Don't have a phone number, an address?"

"No."

"Tell the cops to find him."

"I don't want them . . . It's awkward."

"Why?"

"Alex hadn't spoken to him for several years. To his son. They were estranged."

"The police can find him."

"I need someone else to find him." This through clenched teeth, her eyes hard.

"There are a hundred private investigators around, Karen. Any of them could do it."

"I need someone I can trust."

"And you can trust me?"

"Yes."

She said it immediately and with confidence. Instead of being flattered, I was angry. All the things that had happened between us, and she was still sure I'd be there when she needed me. That I'd do what she wanted, as she wanted.

I shook my head. "I'm not the man for the job, Karen. Sorry."

I was thinking about getting to my feet and moving for the door when she said, "He's inheriting eight million dollars, and he doesn't know it."

"They were estranged, and the kid's still getting eight million?"

She nodded. "And he doesn't even know Alex is dead. I need someone to find him, so I can tell him these things. And so . . ."

"What?"

She dropped her eyes. "It doesn't need to be in the paper and on TV, Lincoln."

"What doesn't?" I waited. "That Alex Jefferson was estranged from his son?"

She nodded but didn't look at me.

"Ah," I said. "Image. I see."

Her head rose, and this time her look was sharp. "It's not that."

I didn't say anything. She took her hands off the chair to lean forward, and when she did it they were shaking. She pressed them together and squeezed them between her knees. "You know what one percent of eight million dollars is, Lincoln?"

"Eighty grand."

"It's your fee. That's what you'll be paid, even if it's the easiest job you ever have. I promise you that. An accountant will write you the check the same day you find him."

Joe was probably done with physical therapy now. A two-hour session that would cost several hundred dollars. Insurance would pay a chunk, but not all of it. Joe went to therapy three times a week. Had been doing so for many weeks. The session fees stacked up on the rest of his medical bills, many of them extravagant. Last week, the only work our agency had was that one damn custody case, for a client who more than likely wouldn't pay the full bill.

"You and I would not have the ideal investigator-client relationship," I said. "I can recommend someone else. Someone better for this situation."

"No." Her voice was firm. "Lincoln, please . . . just find him. How long can that take you? To find someone?"

With every minute I sat there and talked to her, the house felt bigger and emptier, and she looked wearier. I remembered the way she'd looked on a Saturday one June when we'd rented a sailboat out on the Bass Islands, her wet hair plastered against her face and her neck, her smile so damn genuine. For some reason, that was the moment to which my mind returned most often. I'd be in the kitchen or in the car or in the middle of a workout, and suddenly I'd see her there on the boat, see her smile and the sun on her skin and her wet hair, and something inside me would break. Then I'd think of her with Jefferson and push the rest of my memories beneath his smug smile.

"Finding someone can take half an hour, or it can take weeks," I said. "I'd have to know the details."

"It's been five years."

"That's how long he's been missing?"

She nodded, then said, "Well, no. Not missing. I mean, missing to Alex."

"But not the kind of missing where you call police."

"Right."

I lifted a hand and ran it through my hair, looked at the floor. "Where's his mother? Is he estranged from her, too?"

"No. She died about two years after the divorce. Matthew was probably around fourteen at the time. She'd moved to Michigan. He came back to live with Alex until he went to college. They've been estranged since Matthew was in law school."

"His name's Matthew Jefferson?"

"Yes."

"A hell of a common name. Probably a couple thousand of them in the country. I'd need identifiers. Date of birth, Social Security number, whatever you've got."

"I can get everything by this afternoon."

I raised my head and looked at her. "The fee you quoted is ridiculous. It'll probably take me a day or two at most. Regardless, I'll bill my normal rate."

"You'll get what I promised."

Eighty grand for a routine locate. I did skip traces for two hundred bucks. At the end of the day, that's all this would really be.

"I remember when you borrowed a hundred dollars from me to cover your car payment," I said.

She looked at me, trying hard for empty eyes, but not succeeding. After a few seconds, she turned her head.

"Call me with the identifiers," I said after some silence passed. "I'll find him for you, and then we'll be done. Okay?"

She didn't answer, but she nodded. I stood up and paused for a moment, considering crossing the room, reaching out to her, an embrace, a hand on the shoulder, something. Instead, I let myself out of the house.

CHAPTER

3

Joe was on his back on the living room floor with a broomstick clenched in his hands. While I leaned against the doorframe and watched, he lifted the broomstick from his waist and raised it in an arc. A normal person would have brought the broomstick back behind his head. Joe stopped with the broomstick at about chin level and grimaced. There was sweat on his face, and when he remembered to breathe, it was a harsh gasp. He narrowed his eyes, and I saw his jaw muscles bulge slightly, the molars clenching. The broomstick inched back, but just barely. He held it there for a moment, took another breath, and tried for another inch. Didn't get it. He exhaled heavily and returned the broomstick to his waist.

"Didn't you have therapy this morning?" I said.

"Yes." He shifted slightly on the floor, then began the exercise again.

"So you come right back from therapy and start all over again? Isn't there a rest period in there somewhere?"

"You've got to work hard at it."

I shook my head, swung my body off the door frame, and moved around him and into the living room. He was pushing it hard—probably harder than any of the medical professionals who dealt with him wanted—but it was Joe. I knew him too well to be surprised, and certainly too well to try to discourage it.

He took another one of those shallow, gasping breaths, and I looked away. Almost three months of this now, and still I had to look away. That's how it goes when someone takes a bullet because of you.

"You heard about Alex Jefferson?" I said, taking a seat on the couch.

He lowered the broomstick and set it aside. Then he sat up with a grunt, wiped sweat away from his face with the back of his hand, and stared at me.

"Yeah, I heard. You aren't here to confess, are you?"

"No."

He smiled. "Had to check. What do you think of it?"

"Think he was probably a prick in all areas of his life, so not too hard to imagine a guy wanting to whack him." I paused. "Cops came to see me."

"About Jefferson?" Joe got to his feet. It took him some time, and some effort. At the start of the summer, we'd gone running several times a week, Joe breathing easily as we'd pushed up the hills, laughing at me, and at each of his sixty years. A long walk could wear him down now.

"Uh-huh."

Joe walked out of the living room and into the kitchen. I sat there alone for a second, then got to my feet and followed. He'd poured a glass of water, and now he leaned against the sink and took a sip, a few drops sliding down his chin onto his sweatshirt. He was wearing gray sweatpants and a Cleveland Browns sweatshirt. Until the last few months, I could count on one hand the number of times I'd seen him without a tie on a weekday. While he drank the rest of the water and poured another glass, I looked out the window, watching leaves scatter along the sidewalks and blow out into Chatfield Avenue.

"They give you much of a hard time?" Joe asked.

"The cops? Nah." I turned away from the window. "Karen called, too."

He lowered the glass and swished a mouthful of water around for a bit before swallowing it, as if an unpleasant taste had suddenly come upon him.

"Karen," he said. "No kidding."

I nodded. "Wanted to apologize for the police, she said. And to ask a favor."

He set the glass on the counter and sighed, as if he'd been expecting to hear this last bit. I told him what Karen wanted, and he listened quietly until I was done.

"You said you'd do it?"

"Eighty grand, Joe. For a locate. We need the money."

"Eighty grand is insane, LP."

"I know it. But if there's one thing she's got, it's money. I saw that much from the house."

"You're actually going to take it? Take eighty thousand dollars for a job that you'd normally do for under a thousand?"

I met his eyes. "I told her it was too high. But if she cuts me the check, you better believe I'm cashing it."

"She owes you that much, eh?"

"I didn't say that."

"Thinking it, though?"

I shrugged. "We could use the money, and she's not going to miss it. End of story."

"Okay," he said. "You are the boss, after all."

"Till your return, at least."

He didn't say anything to that, just dumped the rest of the water down the sink and moved back into the living room. I stood where I was and watched him. His shoulder was still in bad shape, yes. His range of motion was poor, and there was substantial pain, but his condition was much improved now. He could drive a car; he could sit at a desk and answer a phone and work a computer. Still he stayed here, doing his exercises, reading books, watching ESPN Classic. We'd never discussed a timetable for his return, but I'd always been sure a return would be made. In the last few weeks, however, I'd started to wonder.

I walked back out of the kitchen and followed him into the living room. He had settled into the old armchair in the corner and put his feet up. I sat on the couch and looked at him. I wanted to ask him, flat out, when he was planning to come back. I didn't ask, though. Maybe because I was trying to be patient; maybe because I was afraid to hear his answer.

"I don't have much of a starting place for finding Jefferson's kid," I said. "Weird scenario. He took off five years ago, apparently, before Karen married into the family, so she doesn't know much about him. No contact since then. She said she can provide some identifiers, but that's all I'll have."

"Computer databases will give you a start, once you get those identifiers."

"Yeah. We'll see how far they can take me, though." I cocked my head at him. "Not going to tell me to stay away from this one?"

"You already made the decision to step into it. Looks like a simple enough job, too." He picked a book off the table beside him and set it on his lap. I'd expected questions about my emotional response to Karen, warnings about the risks of getting involved—but the conversation, it appeared, was done.

"I guess I better head out," I said.

"Okay." He opened the book. "Good to see you."

"Right."

I was halfway through the kitchen when I heard a rustle of movement. I glanced back to see Joe pulling a blanket over his legs as he settled in with the book. I stood where I was for a moment, frozen. His gray head was bent over the book, his shoulders poking at the sweatshirt, the blanket wrapped around his legs.

Joe Pritchard looked old.

He lifted his head then, noticing me standing there, and I looked away quickly, as if I'd been caught at something, and walked to the front door. I left the house and went back to work, alone.

The phrase "missing person" carries with it connotations of kidnapping and abduction, mystery and mayhem. I work about ten missing person cases a month, though, and most of them don't fall anywhere near those categories. In my experience, the person is usually missing only to a small portion of his or her world. People travel; they marry, divorce, and remarry; they take jobs and lose jobs. Along the way, they drop out of contact with certain areas of their lives. It's my job to find the area they *haven't* lost contact with and use the resources there to track the missing ones down. Sometimes, they want to be hard to find. These are the people leaving problems behind—legal troubles or unpaid debts or unwanted family responsibilities. Other times, they simply fade out of sight because nobody cares enough to pay attention to where they're going.

I had no idea which category Matthew Jefferson fit into, but I was feeling good about my chances of finding him quickly and easily. He came from prestige and money; he'd have active bank accounts, cars registered in his name, maybe a mortgage. The hardest people to find are the sort whose lives are in constant disarray. They have suspended driver's licenses, no assets, no credit, and they live with family or friends or whomever they can bilk out of a free month's rent. I didn't anticipate that the son of one of Cleveland's most prominent attorneys would fall into that lot.

I was wrong. Wrong, at least, in assuming he'd be easy to find. Karen had left me a voice mail with Matthew Jefferson's date of birth, Social Security number, and driver's license number. Where she came up with that, I didn't know, but it also didn't help me. The driver's license had expired three years earlier, when Jefferson was twenty-six. He was twenty-nine now, and the last computer record I could find on him put him in Bloomington, Indiana. There were several addresses for him in that town, all apartments. Bloomington was home to Indiana University. Maybe Matthew Jefferson had gone to school there.

Amy Ambrose had once provided me with a great link to newspaper Web sites all around the country. I went to that page now and tracked down a student newspaper for Indiana University, ran a search for Matthew Jefferson, and got a few pages of results. There was a Matt Jefferson who appeared to be something of a track star, and then a reference from several years earlier to a Matthew Jefferson who'd won a few academic honors at the law school. In one, his hometown was listed beside his name: Pepper Pike, Ohio.

"Got ya, Matt."

I ran a check through the Indiana and Ohio bar associations, as well as two national databases, and couldn't find an indication that the Matt Jefferson I was looking for had ever taken up the practice of law.

Next I put his Social Security number through Ohio Department of Motor Vehicle records, and got nothing but the expired license. Surprised, but not concerned, I tried a live credit header search. Contrary to popular belief, private investigators can't access personal credit reports, but we do have access to the "headers," a portion of the credit report that includes the address and the reporting date. If you apply for a credit card, a loan, or anything else along those lines, at least one of the major credit bureaus tracks the date and the address you use. Matthew Jefferson's Social Security number generated an address match in Indiana, for a town called Nashville, reported six times in the last few years.

I pulled a road atlas out and flipped through it until I found the Indiana map. Nashville was a small town in Brown County, maybe a five- or six-hour drive from Cleveland.

"I suppose I'll make the trip," I said aloud. "There's certainly enough money in the budget."

I laughed at that, but nobody laughed with me. I was talking to myself more regularly, particularly in the office. Sometimes, like when I laughed at my own jokes and no one joined in, it wasn't that different from having Joe around, at all.

The phone rang, and I answered on speakerphone.

"Turn that thing off—it makes you sound like you're in a cave," Amy Ambrose said.

"I only turn it on for certain callers. People I know will talk so long I'll get a neck cramp if I actually hold the phone."

"Hilarious. Joe back yet?"

"No," I said, and some of the humor went out of my

voice. "No, and he's given no indication of when he thinks he will be. To be honest, today I was about to ask him if he ever will come back. I'm not sure anymore."

"You should have asked."

"Probably." It was quiet for a moment, and then I changed the subject. "Hey, what are you doing the next two days?"

"Writing great stories, per the norm."

I'd first met Amy when she was working on a newspaper story about a murdered high school student who'd been a member at my gym. After a contentious start, we'd become friends, and now she joined Joe in the small circle of people I trusted completely.

"Any of those stories crucial?" I asked.

"Not particularly. Why?"

"Take a road trip with me. Scenic southern Indiana."

"Ugh."

"Come on, corn is gorgeous this time of year. Supposed to make the ladies swoon."

"I see. So this means you're finally taking it up a notch, proposing romantic road trips instead of making sopho-moric remarks about my ass?"

"I was thinking of a package approach."

She hesitated. "Are you serious about this?"

"Absolutely. I've got a client throwing tens of thousands of dollars at me to locate a missing heir. Hell, I can probably bill you out as a subcontractor. I'll let you contribute somehow—holding my gun, maybe."

"You can hold your own gun, soldier."

"No bonus for you, then. I'm serious, though. Want to go along for the ride? Take a day down there, a day coming back."

"I guess. I've got an interview to give early, but I could probably leave by ten."

"Good," I said, and although the idea had been sponta-neous, I was glad she'd agreed. I was tired of working alone.

"Who's the client?" Amy asked.

"Karen Jefferson."

Silence.

"You're working for the woman you were once engaged to," Amy said mechanically. "She of the recently murdered husband. Same guy she left you for."

"That's her."

"Are you out of your mind? Why would you possibly put yourself in this situation?"

"Easy money. Nothing more to it."

"Oh, please, Lincoln. That's so weak."

"It's not weak if it's the truth, Ace. The cops came to question me about Jefferson; she found out about it and called to apologize. Then she asked me to find Jefferson's son. He's in line to inherit a few million and doesn't know it. Doesn't know his father's dead, either."

She didn't say anything.

"Hang on to the skepticism as long as you'd like, Amy, but the only reason I'm doing this is for the money. There's a lot of it promised to me, and the agency can certainly use it with Joe out of work, stacking up medical bills."

"Okay," she said, and then it was quiet again.

"I've got things to work on," I said eventually. "I'll see you in the morning? You can give me shit for taking this case for the entire drive if you'd like."

"See you in the morning," she said and hung up.

I sighed and turned the phone off. I hadn't expected Amy to be particularly impressed with me for this one, but hopefully she'd decide against taking my suggestion to heart and berating me for the entire drive.

I spent a few hours finishing the only case report I had to write. You can afford to spend a little extra time on polish when you've got nothing else waiting ahead of you. It's a luxury most small business owners aren't hoping to encounter, however. When that was done, I locked the office and walked back up to my building, changed clothes, and went down to the gym to work out. I lifted for an hour, then left the gym and went for a run. The air had a chill to it when I returned, the sun fading and leaving my building dark with shadows. I stood on the sidewalk and stretched, looking up at the two stories of old stone that became my home after my fist connected with Alex Jefferson's face and ended my police career. I thought about Karen in the extravagant house near the country club, and how empty it had felt that morning. I wondered if it felt emptier still when the sun went down.

CHAPTER

4

Amy came by my apartment at ten the next morning, as planned. She pulled her Acura into the spot beside my truck, came to a jarring stop when her tires ran into the parking block, and then put it in reverse and backed clear again.

"She's landed," I said. I was standing in the doorway to the gym office, talking to Grace, who was asking me to diagnose a car problem that began with a "thwackity thwak" sound and progressed to a "clankity clank" upon reaching highway speeds. I'd recommended taking the vehicle to an actual mechanic, and, when that was dismissed with a snort, I'd suggested she wear headphones when she drove.

"Hey," Amy said. She was wearing jeans and a thin jacket over a white cotton shirt, sunglasses tucked into her hair above her temples. She'd straightened her dark blond hair about two months earlier, and I still wasn't used to it. It looked great, but there was something carefree about the natural curl that I missed.

"Traveling light?" I stepped into the parking lot with her. She had a small purse over her shoulder but nothing else.

"No," she said, leaning against the hood of her car and stretching her legs out in front of her. "I don't think I'll be making the trip."

I frowned. "You have to work, or did something else change your mind?"

She gazed up at me for a moment, then away.

"Are you backing out on this just because I'm working for Karen?" I asked.

"No."

"Okay. It's not that, and it's not work, and yesterday you were up for it, but today you've changed your mind. What's the deal?"

She sighed and tugged the sunglasses free from her hair, then ran one hand through it. "Why do you want me to go along?"

I tilted my head and looked at her, puzzled. "Thought it would make the trip more enjoyable for me, and thought you might enjoy it, as well."

"Why?"

"Why would you enjoy it?"

"And you? Why would you enjoy it more because I was along?"

When I was a kid, I went to a camp once where they had a row of small platforms scattered across a pond. Some of the platforms would float when you landed on them; others would sink immediately. You'd try to cross the pond by jumping from one platform to the next. Each leap had the potential to sink you, but you didn't know which one would do it. Right now, the conversation had that feel.

"Why would I enjoy it more?" I echoed. Anytime you start repeating questions when you're talking to a woman, you're in trouble.

"Yes."

"I imagined it would make a long drive a lot more fun. Getting kind of tired of working alone."

"So you want me to be your surrogate Joe?"

"What? No." I shook my head and stepped away from her. "I imagined we'd have a good time, because we usually do. Thought it would add some laughs, a little banter, turn a boring road trip into an enjoyable one."

"I'm a source of banter, then."

"Amy." I looked at her hard. "What the hell is this about? We hang out together all the time, but you think it's odd I'd ask you to go along on this?"

"I don't want to be Sundance to your Butch," she said. "Not just on this case, or on your little trip. In general."

I gave a short laugh and spread my arms. "Where is this coming from? We've been friends for almost two years. Now you're having some sort of identity crisis with it?"

"How many lasting relationships have you had in the last two years, Lincoln?"

I dropped my arms. "Roughly? Zero."

She didn't smile. "And me?"

"You've dated a few assholes."

"Lasting relationships?"

"Zero."

"Right." She folded her arms over her chest. "Can you tell me that's unrelated? Do you think it is, at least?"

"Probably not."

She smiled sadly. "There ya go. And I know the story— you're not good with relationships, and the friendship's too important to jeopardize. But here we sit."

"So you're disagreeing with—"

"I'm not disagreeing with anything, and not saying anything other than that I need to think a few areas of my life over and maybe redirect them."

"Kind of comes out of nowhere this morning."

She laughed and shook her head. "If you think this comes out of nowhere, then your agency is really hurting for detectives right now."

Someone pulled into the parking spot beside us. It was one of my regulars, and when he climbed out of his car, he decided it would be a good opportunity to talk sports and weather for about five minutes. I smiled and nodded my way through it. After a while, Amy dropped her sunglasses over her eyes and stood up.

"I'll catch you inside," I told the guy, holding a hand up to interrupt him. "Okay?"

He went in, and I turned back to Amy. She had her hand on the door handle.

"Amy . . ."

"I've got to get to work, and you've got to get to Indiana, of all places. We'll talk when you get back, okay?"

I didn't answer. She got in the car and pulled away, and I swore loudly and sat down on the parking block. A second later the door opened and Grace stuck her head out.

"Everything okay, boss?"

I turned to her. "Any idea what it means when your friendship starts making a thwackity thwack sound that progresses to a clankity clank?"

"Yeah," she said. "It means you screwed up."

"Ah," I said, nodding. "And how to fix it?"

"Stop being scared," she said, and she went back inside.

"You're fired," I told the closed door, and then I stood up and got into my truck.

The third time my truck dipped down a steep hill and left my stomach at the top, I got the idea that this portion of Indiana wasn't what I'd expected. About five hours out of Cleveland, I'd passed through Bloomington and turned back to the east, heading for Nashville. The highway between the two towns was a winding two-lane, cutting through hills with a cruel sense of humor. One minute I'd be laying hard on the accelerator, coaxing the truck up a hill that made the motor grind; the next, I'd be hard on the brake, trying to keep from alarming the driver in front of me on the steep downgrade. The road twisted too much to let me take my eyes off it for long, but when I did, the views were spectacular. Hills rolled away from the highway across sprawling fields and into dense woods lit with colors so vibrant I doubted even the best camera would be able to successfully capture them.

After about thirty minutes of driving along a highway that was clearly designed by the forefathers of the roller-coaster industry, I ran into a backed-up line of traffic so long that I assumed it was the result of a car accident, or maybe some late-season road repair. It turned out to be the wait to get into Nashville. It took ten minutes just to pull onto the one main street that cut through the little town, which, ironically, was called Van Buren, while Main Street was a little offshoot to the side.

There appeared to be a construction code for the town, and it involved a lot of logs and old wood siding and shingles, everything having the look of a New England village at about the turn of the century. In case you missed the point, a number of the little shops incorporated the word "old" into their name, often underscoring it with an *e* at the end: Ye Olde Fudge Shoppe. Ambience.

The sidewalks teemed with people laden with shopping bags, and small public parking lots were filled and had waiting lines. I saw license plates from North Carolina, Florida, Arizona, and Ontario. I hadn't gotten around to making a hotel reservation, figuring they probably didn't fill up too often in a place like this, but now it occurred to me that could have been a mistake. I stopped at the first hotel I found, a building halfway up the hill above the town. The parking lot was jammed, so I pulled into the entrance and left my hazard lights on while I went inside and asked for a room. The question produced a smile from the receptionist.

"You don't have a reservation?" she said.

"No."

"It's October."

"So it is."

Her smile widened. "You don't know the area, do you?"

"Nope."

"You want to stay in Nashville in October, you make a reservation."

I looked around, thought about the little street I'd driven through, wondered what great draw I could have missed.

"No offense," I said, "but what brings so many people to this town?"

"Leaves."

"Leaves?"

"The kind on the trees," she said.

"People come from all over the country to see leaves?"

"Drive around a little bit. Look up. You'll be impressed. There's shopping, too."

"Of course there is." I looked back out at my truck. "Well, can you tell me where the nearest hotel with a vacancy would be?"

"Bloomington, probably. That's about thirty minutes up the road. You aren't going to find anything closer tonight. I'm sorry."

If staying near the town was going to be such a hassle, maybe I'd try to get in and out in a night. All I had to do was find Jefferson's son and give him the news, then head home. The drive wasn't that bad, and it beat bouncing from hotel to hotel, hoping to find one with a room open.

"I'm just here to pass a message to someone," I said. "He lives on Highway 135. Is that nearby?"

She nodded and pointed. "Just keep going up the hill. Van Buren turns into 135."

I thanked her and walked back out to my truck, drove to the front of the parking lot, and saw that it was going to be about a five-minute wait just to pull back into the traffic.

"All this for leaves," I said, looking around.

But, damn it, the leaves were spectacular. Crimson, orange, and burgundy splashes everywhere you looked, climbing the hills and surrounding the town. The crisp air smelled of them, too, and of rain and wood smoke. I'm not much of a country boy, and in places surrounded by pavement I've always been able to find the kind of moments of beauty that other people find deep in the woods, but I do acknowledge that if there's one season that the city really kills, it's autumn.

Matthew Jefferson lived less than a mile up the road, his home one in a cluster of four log cabins off a circular gravel drive. The mailboxes were bunched together at the end of the drive, and I didn't see any numbers on the cabins themselves. I'd gotten out of the truck and was standing in the driveway, looking for a hint to the numbering system, when the door of the largest cabin opened and a gray-haired woman walked out and headed for a Honda parked nearby.

"Excuse me," I said. "Do you live here?"

She looked at me warily. "I rent here, yeah. Don't own it, though."

"I'm looking for one of your neighbors."

"Oh." She smiled and shifted a purse that must have weighed sixty pounds from one shoulder to the other. "Most people that stop by this time of year are trying to buy the place. Doesn't matter if there's no For Sale sign, they stop. We just rent, and we still get about ten offers each year."

"Won't get one from me. I'm just looking for a guy named Matt Jefferson. You know him?"

"Matt? Sure. He lived in Number Two for a long time." She pointed at the cabin directly behind me.

"Not anymore, though?"

She shook her head, and I wanted to shake my own, having just made a six-hour drive to check out a dead address.

"You wouldn't have any idea where he went?"

"Sure. He moved into a little apartment where he works."

"What does he do?"

"Picks apples."

I raised my eyebrows. "Seriously?"

She nodded. "Up the road, near Morgantown. Big orchard there, and Matt runs the—what do you call it?—harvesting?"

"Harvesting," I echoed. "He runs the apple harvesting operation."

"Uh-huh."

When last heard from, Matthew Jefferson had been in law school, the son of a prominent and wealthy attorney, his stars appearing perfectly aligned. Now he was running the apple-picking operation in a small Indiana town? That was an interesting detour.

"Can you tell me how to find the orchard?"

She gave me directions, and after the sixth time she said

"make another left" I decided I'd better go back to the truck
for some paper and a pen.

Even with the written directions, I was almost an hour
finding the place. Intersections were spaced out conveniently
at about every six miles, so if you missed a turn, you were a
while figuring it out. Fortunately, many of the roads were
also lacking signs, so missing a turn was easy. There were no
gas stations around, either, so I took comfort in knowing that
if I didn't find the place soon, I'd have to venture ahead on
foot. I thrive under pressure.

Eventually, though, I rounded a bend in the road and
spotted a hand-painted sign that said: THE APPLE EMPORIUM —
THREE MILES, TURN LEFT. These people were wise enough not
to even bother with a street name, no doubt knowing that the
corresponding sign would inevitably be missing. I went three
miles, hung a left, and found the orchard.

The main building was a long red barn, the doors slid
open to reveal rows of barrels and crates overflowing with
apples, a stack of pumpkins on the front porch, everything
shaded by tall trees. Overhead, clouds were building, the sun
that had been out at the start of my drive now tucked behind
a thin veil of gray. I walked down to the barn and through the
big open doors. Inside, women were holding apples up to
the lights and frowning at them, checking for any slight im-
perfection. Two teenaged girls were working cash registers
at the front of the barn, but the lines were long. Surely, there
was a manager or supervisor around. I moved through the
rest of the barn, then followed a sign that said CIDER MILL
and walked outside.

Rows of late-season flowers bordered a stone path that led
down to a gazebo overlooking a large pond. Across the pond,
the trees spread over the hills, their hues somehow seeming
even brighter now that the clouds had gathered. No one else
was outside; the whole place was still and private, and I looked
down at the gazebo and thought it would probably be a hell of
a nice spot to kill an afternoon and a bottle of champagne.

Good thing Amy had decided not to come along, or I might have been tempted to do just that.

I walked around the rear of the building, still in search of the cider mill, and as soon as I rounded the corner I ran into a tall metal machine making a soft churning noise. A red-headed woman turned to me, holding a tray of small paper cups filled with a walnut-colored liquid.

"Try a sample."

"Actually, I'm looking for—"

"Try a sample," she repeated, and the look in her eye suggested she could arrange to have something bad happen if I refused—have me dipped in caramel and covered with nuts, maybe.

I grabbed a paper cup and took a sip.

"Good, isn't it?" she said, watching my face.

"My knees almost buckled."

"Day-fresh," she said. "Now, what can I help you with?"

"I'm looking for the manager, or owner?"

"I'm both. Kara Ross." She couldn't shake hands because of the tray, but she made a little bow with her head. "What can we help you with?"

"I need to speak with one of your employees. His name's Matt Jefferson."

"Really?"

"Doesn't he work here?"

"Oh, yes, he sure does. I just never see any visitors for him. Matt's a pretty quiet guy. He runs our picking operation."

"So I've heard."

"He's actually out working right now. We've had to expand to another growing site a few miles down the road. Supply and demand, you know?"

"Can I find Matt at this other growing site?"

"It would be better if you could wait an hour or two. Unless it's urgent."

I shook my head. "It's important, but I can wait. He'll be coming back here?"

"Yes, he lives here. Follow me." She walked past the cider

mill and into a dim hallway. An old dog was sleeping in the middle of the hallway, but Kara Ross stepped over it as if it didn't exist, and I followed suit. Back in the barn's main room, Kara Ross set the tray down on the counter and turned to me.

"I'll leave a note on the door for Matt if you'd like," she said. "I'll be gone when he comes back."

"When will that be?"

"He'll work until sunset," she said. "Come by around, oh, seven. He should be here by then."

She found a pad of paper shaped like an apple and held her pen poised over it. "What should I write?"

It didn't seem appropriate for Jefferson to find out his father was dead through a note written on apple-shaped stationery and stuck to his door. Finding out he was a millionaire would be a little better, but, still, I thought I'd just hold off and tell him in person.

"Just write that a man from Cleveland is here to see him," I said.

"No name?"

"The name wouldn't mean anything to him," I said. "It's family business, but I'm not family."

She wrote:

> Matt—
>   Man from Cleveland here to see you.
>   Will return tonight.
>   Family business.

"Good?"

I nodded. "Perfect."

"I'll leave it on his door. When you come back, this part of the building will be closed. I'll show you where his apartment is."

"Great. Thanks for the help."

"No problem." She smiled up at me. "You know, we sell that cider you liked so much."

"Give me ten gallons and a long straw."

I bought a quart of the cider and a bag of honey crisp apples. A wise tactical move—always keep the locals happy. Then Kara Ross took me around the side of the building again to leave the note on the door to Jefferson's apartment, which apparently occupied the loft room of the converted barn and looked out on the pond and woods beyond. Not bad.

"Man from Cleveland here . . . family business," she read aloud and then laughed. "I bet he'll be intrigued."

It was an obvious hint that she wanted to know details, but I wasn't giving them out to anyone but the junior Jefferson. It wouldn't hurt him to be intrigued for half an hour or so until I showed up.

"Sure that note won't blow away?" I said.

Kara Ross carefully applied tape all around the apple-shaped piece of stationery, until the wind could no longer work on a free edge. Then she stepped back and looked at it with satisfaction.

"No way he'll miss it now."

"Good," I said. The wind had picked up, stirring dry leaves around our ankles, and I was glad the note wouldn't end up in the middle of the pond. I wanted to be sure Jefferson's son would know I was coming for him.

CHAPTER

5

I drove to Morgantown along a road that embodied autumn the way only a painting or postcard usually will for people who live in the city. Crimson and auburn trees lined cornfields gone weathered and broken, a pale gray sky hanging over it all. The clouds had thickened even in the short time I was at the orchard, spoiling the chance for a nice sunset. The wind was cooler, but no rain fell.

Morgantown was more of what I'd seen in Nashville, only without the obvious design toward tourism. As I sat at one of the two stoplights, waiting for a green light, I thought that if you snapped a black-and-white photograph of the street ahead of me, and captured the stone buildings with their colored awnings and plate glass windows, only the modern cars would clearly separate it from the 1950s. One business sign boasted about handmade furniture; another offered shagbark syrup. It was one of those places that made you glad to be off the beaten path, away from interstate exits with seven chain restaurants and two truck stops.

I killed some time walking around the little town, checking out shops and nodding at passersby, then found a restaurant and wasted forty more minutes on dinner. Dusk settled as I drove back to the orchard, the brilliant shades of the trees fading into muted browns and casting long shadows over the road. I left the windows down, but the air coming into the cab of the truck was cold enough to make me wish I'd asked for another cup of coffee for the road.

The big barn at the orchard was dark—the doors shut, the parking lot empty except for a few farm vehicles. Floodlights near the parking lot entrance lit up displays made from dried cornstalks, haystacks, and gourds, and a scarecrow hung from a post beside the barn. I parked the truck and rolled the windows up, the windshield fogging immediately as the interior temperature warmed.

Outside, the silence made me pause next to the truck. I live in an apartment beneath which traffic passes at all hours of the night, sometimes with stereos pounding or sirens wailing. A quiet night is one where I can't hear a woman having an animated cell phone conversation in a convertible or the loud laughter of men coming out of the bar up the street. Here, the only sound was the wind. It didn't whistle or howl, just offered a quiet, constant rustle though the leaves and over the grass.

I walked up to the barn's front porch, my shoes slapping off the boards, and then went around the side of the building, the way Kara Ross had taken me earlier in the day. A moon that was about three-quarters full provided the only light on this side of the building. I knew there was a name for that stage of moon, waxing or waning or something, and it had that coppery color it gets only in the fall. I turned the corner and found the door to the loft apartment.

The note was gone, every trace of tape peeled away. I banged my knuckles off the rough wood and waited. Nobody came down to open it, and I didn't hear anyone move upstairs. I knocked again and got more of the same. There was no knob, just an odd hooked handle and a lock. I tugged on the handle, but the door didn't open. Jefferson's son had gotten the note, but he hadn't waited for me. Maybe he hadn't been as intrigued as Kara Ross had predicted.

I turned away from the door, shoving my hands into my pockets and tightening my shoulders against the chill night air. Out ahead of me, the black surface of the pond rippled as the wind passed over it. I was watching that when I noticed the figure in the gazebo.

There was no light in the little building, but the silhouette of a man was clear. He was sitting on the bench beneath the fancy trelliswork that passed for walls, as still as the scarecrow that hung in front of the barn. When I saw him, I tensed slightly, a human presence somehow seeming threatening in a spot that was absolutely desolate at night. Then I realized the man had to be Jefferson's son. If I lived in this place, I'd spend my evenings down by the water, too. The gazebo and the pond were maybe a hundred feet from the rear of the barn, and I was surprised he hadn't heard me approach or knock on the door, but maybe the wind had carried the sounds away from him. I set off down the stone path that led to the gazebo, stepping carefully in the darkness.

By the time I was halfway there, I could see he was sitting with his back to the pond, facing me. He must have seen me at the door, and yet he hadn't said a word, just sat there and watched. I'd planned on calling out a hello before I reached the gazebo, but his behavior was so odd that breaking the silence seemed wrong somehow, and instead of speaking, I just kept walking.

When I reached the gazebo, I went up the three steps and onto the main surface, only a few feet from him. I could see now he was wearing jeans and a heavy flannel shirt; thick dark hair hung over his shoulders and across his forehead, a few strands in his eyes, blending with the shadows. His chin was close to his chest, but his eyes were up, on me. There was a bottle on the rail beside him, some sort of whiskey, not much left in it. I was opening my mouth to say hello when I saw the gun.

It was resting on the bench beside him, but his hand was around the butt, and even though my night vision was still adjusting, I could tell his finger was on the trigger. The barrel was pointed at me but not raised. I stopped moving forward and looked from the barrel of the gun to hollow dark eyes that were watching me without interest or emotion.

"My father's dead, isn't he?" His voice matched his eyes.

I tried hard to look at his face and not the gun. "Yeah," I said. "He is. That's what I came to tell you."

The hand with the gun shifted, and then it was pointed at my chest, maybe six feet separating me from the barrel. It was the kind of range that took shooting ability out of the equation. Even if the whiskey bottle on the railing had started out full, he wasn't going to be able to miss if he pulled the trigger.

I stayed as still as I could. My mouth had dried out as quickly and completely as desert sand after a cloudburst, and I could feel my heartbeat picking up, the blood beginning to pound in my temples and wrists, my leg muscles trembling the way they do after a long run.

"Listen," I began, but he cut me off immediately.

"I could kill you," he said. "Could have as soon as you came around the corner."

I didn't try to talk again. I've had guns pulled on me before, and I've even talked a few men into lowering them in the past, but this didn't feel like a situation where that was an option. There was no quality of indecision to Jefferson, and also none of the boiling emotion you usually get when someone pulls a weapon. He spoke and sat like an actor trying to finish a scene alone—everyone else might have left, turned the lights off onstage, even, but he knew his role, and he was damn sure going to finish it.

"Wouldn't do any good to kill you, though, would it?" he said. "You didn't come alone."

Now I felt like I *had* to say something, although I didn't know exactly what, and with that gun pointing at me, I definitely didn't want to pick the wrong words. I swallowed, trying to still myself so that when I spoke my voice would be calm and not escalate the tension of the moment.

"At least he has a reason," he said. "You got nothing but greed."

The gun moved again, a twirling flash, and in the darkness I wasn't sure what he was doing with it, only that it was moving, and instinct forced me into motion. As I heard the clicking sound of the hammer being pulled back, I made a stumbling, awkward lunge to the right that would have accomplished absolutely nothing had Alex Jefferson's son fired at me instead of jamming the barrel of the gun into his own mouth and pulling the trigger.

The bullet exploded out of the gun with a sound loud enough to make everything else in the world temporarily disappear, and then it punched through the back of Matthew Jefferson's skull and scattered his brains into the pond. His body rocked back, following the path of the bullet, but then his shoulders caught on the railing and threw him forward. He slumped off the bench and fell, landing facedown at my feet, a pulsing crater where the back of his head belonged.

I think I tried to shout, and maybe I even succeeded. If I did, though, I didn't know it. All I could hear was the gunshot, still echoing through my head, even louder now. I looked down at Jefferson's son, blood pumping out of what was left of his skull, and then I was scrambling backward, climbing over the gazebo railing without taking my eyes off the body. I fell over the railing and landed awkwardly in the bushes below, fought my way out of them, and staggered up the hill. When I reached the barn I fell on my ass, sat with my back against the weathered boards, and stared at the gazebo.

He had not shot me. The gun had been pointed at me, held just a few feet away, and then it had been fired. He had not shot me, though. I had not been shot.

"You didn't get shot," I said aloud. "You did not get shot." I'd hoped the sound of my voice would calm me, but instead it made the shaking start. It worked its way through my hands and into the rest of my body, and I forced myself to get back to my feet and walked through the gardens to the stone path. I stood there, taking deep breaths, until the shaking stopped, and then I reached into my pocket and took my cell phone out. The first time I tried to open it, my hands weren't steady enough, and I dropped it into the grass. The second time, I managed to punch in the three numbers I needed.

I told them what I needed to tell them. The dispatcher wanted to keep me on the line until the police got there, but I hung up. I walked slowly back up to the gazebo, feeling a need to see the body again—maybe to reassure myself that it wasn't mine.

The blood had spread, pooling around the body. The gun had tumbled from his hand when he fell and lay beside him. Even outdoors, with a steady breeze blowing, the smell of the blood was powerful.

"You're a millionaire," I said to the corpse. "That's what I came to tell you. I don't know who the hell you thought I was, but that's what I came to tell you."

It got hard to look at him then, and I turned away and refocused on the pond that had swallowed a piece of his skull. The moonlight reflected on the whiskey bottle that remained where the dead man had sat, and I saw the bottle was resting on a piece of paper, pinning it to the railing. I stepped closer and saw it was that apple-shaped stationery upon which Kara Ross had written my note.

> *Matt—*
> *Man from Cleveland here to see you.*
> *Will return tonight.*
> *Family business.*

CHAPTER

6

The sheriff's department sent the first car, driven by a deputy who looked about fourteen. He shuffled around in the parking lot nervously, talking into his radio, and when I called out to him he jumped like I'd fired a shot into his car.

"There's a body down there," I said, walking up out of the shadows and into the parking lot. "And a lot of blood. You processed any death scenes before?"

He shook his head and took a hesitant step backward. The damn kid was afraid of me.

"Is there anybody else on the way?"

A swallow and a nod, and then, "Yessir. State police."

"You want to just wait on them?" I said, my voice gentle.

"Sure. Why don't we?" He realized then how this might look to the state cops, him standing up here with me in the parking lot, having not even seen the body, and said, "Well, maybe I should . . . you know, secure the area."

I nodded slowly. "Okay. Follow me."

We were halfway down the path to the gazebo, the kid stumbling in the dark, when he was saved by the sound of another car pulling into the gravel lot. We both turned, and I saw that it was an unmarked car. A Taurus, just like Joe drove.

"State police?"

"Yeah." The kid sounded relieved. He started back up to

the parking lot. A cop in street clothes climbed out of the unmarked car and walked down the slope. He met us at the corner of the orchard barn, in the glow from one of the few
outdoor lights.

"We got a suicide down there," the sheriff's deputy said,
his chest filling a bit, trying to impress the varsity.

"Uh-huh," the plainclothes guy said. "Kinda figured that,
you know, when dispatch told me to come take a look at a
suicide."

The kid's chest deflated.

"And who're you?" the new cop asked me. He was an
unremarkable man in every way—average in height and
build, not handsome or ugly, just one of a thousand guys
you'd pass on the street and hardly spare a glance.

"Name's Lincoln Perry. I called it in."

"Found the guy?"

"Saw him do it."

"Ah." He nodded and slipped a small tape recorder out of
his pocket. "Lincoln Perry. Good name. I'm Roger Brewer,
state police."

He turned the recorder on and spoke into it, giving his
name and the date and time, then stating our location and
what he'd been told by dispatch and by me. That settled, he
held the recorder against his leg and nodded at me.

"Lead the way."

They followed me around the side of the barn, and when
we got into the darkness, the state cop produced a flashlight.
I took them up to the gazebo and then stopped.

"That's him. I imagine you want me to hang back."

"Uh-huh." He walked up onto the gazebo without any
sign of trepidation, the deputy following nervously. When
they got a clear view of the body, Brewer let out a long, low
whistle and shook his head.

"Did a pretty good job of it, didn't he?"

I didn't say anything. The young deputy's face had
blanched, and he stood at the far end of the gazebo, his hand
tight on the railing, his eyes averted. The wind was blowing
harder now, and cooler, rippling across the pond and sending

a chill through me. A few leaves came tumbling down, one of them settling gently onto Matthew Jefferson's back. Brewer flicked it off with his index finger.

The woods and the pond lit up with flashing lights as another car pulled in up at the barn, this one a state police cruiser. The two cops who got out were in full uniform, right down to the tall black boots and the full-brimmed hats.

"Wait there, would you?" Brewer said.

"Sure."

I stood at the edge of the pond with the deputy while Brewer walked up to meet the new arrivals. I could hear him telling them to get an ambulance down to collect the body, and to make sure the hands were bagged. When he was done talking to them, Brewer called for me to come up to the top of the hill. I passed the uniformed cops in silence, both of them giving me hard, suspicious stares, and joined him on the front porch of the barn. He was speaking softly into his tape recorder.

"Well, Mr. Perry, I'm going to need to take a witness statement from you. Going to be a pretty important thing, seeing as how you're the only person who actually saw anything."

"Sure."

"You ever given a statement before?" The question sounded procedural, but it was also a slick way of finding out whether I'd bumped up against a criminal investigation before.

"I've given them, yes, but I've taken a lot more."

"Oh?" His eyebrows went up.

"I was a cop in Cleveland, Ohio, for several years. A detective at the end of it."

"No kidding." He nodded thoughtfully. "And now?"

"Private investigator."

"Private investigator," he echoed. "Well. The plot thickens, right? Were you down in our little part of the world on business or pleasure, Detective?"

"Business."

"I see." The recorder was still running, held loosely in his left hand. "Well, tell you what we're going to do, Mr. Perry. We're going to run through everything now, you tell me what you can, and then maybe I'll have more questions later."

"Right."

He motioned with his hand for me to begin. I told it to him as clearly as I could, and as honestly, leaving out nothing except my personal history with Karen. It wasn't relevant to what had happened, but I figured he might try to make it fit somehow, and I didn't want that headache. Instead, I told him all the details that I could think of, simply presenting Karen as a routine client. That's what she was, now. The ambulance pulled in as I was finishing, but Brewer let the uniformed cops deal with that, keeping his attention on me.

"Now that," he said when I was done, "is one hell of a strange thing to happen. I mean, the guy finishes a day of work, gets a note that you're in town, and goes to sit by this pond with a bottle of whiskey and a gun. He doesn't kill himself then, in private, but waits for you to show up. When you show up, he somehow is already aware of the very news you drove six hours to share with him. He tells you this and then kills himself."

I didn't say anything, and Brewer made a little clucking noise with his tongue and shook his head.

"One hell of a strange thing," he said again. "You got any theories, Mr. Perry?"

"Well, it seems pretty clear that he thought I was someone else."

"Someone who knew his father."

"Yes."

"Someone who was not alone, based upon the comments you say he made."

"That's right. He seemed to think there'd be someone else with me."

"And he was, what, scared of this third party?"

I thought about it and nodded. "Yes, I think he was. Well, I think he would have been, maybe."

"Would have been?"

"Had he not already made the decision to put the barrel of that gun in his mouth. That was not a spur-of-the-moment decision. He knew what he was going to do."

"But he waited for you to show before he did it."

"Yes."

"And didn't wait for this unnamed third party to show."

"Apparently not."

"He didn't know you."

"Thought he did, though. Thought he knew who I was, or knew who I was with, at least."

Brewer stood there and stared at me. I looked at the set of his face, at his eyes, and I knew he didn't like my account of things. He wasn't ready to say he didn't believe me yet, but he definitely didn't like what he'd heard.

"Mysterious," he said.

"I guess."

"No, really, it is. I mean, we'll get a psychological profile together on this guy, and maybe that'll tell us something. But at this point, it seems like a pretty unusual way to kill yourself."

"Agreed."

He shifted position, moving out of the glow of the floodlight. "That's assuming he did kill himself."

"He did."

"Says the gentleman from Ohio," Brewer said goodnaturedly. "But, unfortunately, the gentleman from Ohio was the only person present. So if we say—just for the sake of argument—that he could be lying . . . well, that's trouble. Because if he did happen to be lying, I'm looking at a homicide."

"You're not."

"Gun wasn't in the dead man's hand."

"It fell out when he fell forward. You worked any suicides before?" When he nodded, I said, "Then you know that you often find the gun beside the body. The instantaneous rigor grips happen, but they aren't the rule."

He didn't say anything, just stood there and looked at me.

"Check his thumb," I said.

"Excuse me?"

"Check his thumb for a hammer imprint. The gun was a revolver, and he cocked it right before he fired. I know, because I heard it. Then he died damn fast. No slow process on that one. The hammer spur impressions could still be on the thumb. That happens when circulation stops abruptly."

"That's a fine idea." Brewer cleared his throat and spat into the bushes beside us. "I'll be sure that the thumbs are checked, Mr. Perry."

"Great."

"It's a strange thing," he said for the third time and shook his head. "Now, Mr. Perry, as I said, I'm going to need to get that written statement."

"Uh-huh."

"When was it that you were planning to head back to Ohio?"

"The plan was for tonight."

He smiled and shook his head. "Oh, I'm afraid that's not going to work."

"I've told you everything I can possibly tell you, and I'll give you the written statement. If you need me for anything further, you'll have my telephone number."

He made a face, as if he were getting ready to break some bad news and didn't relish the task. That was a joke, though—he was enjoying it just fine.

"I'm in a position where I could really embarrass myself here," he said. "I mean, sure, you say it was a suicide. But right now, until I've done a little more investigation, that's all I've got to rely on. Make me look awful bad if I cut you loose only to have my evidence team tell me it looks like you killed the guy. Then we've got to go find your ass, and I've got to deal with a bunch of cops in Ohio who are going to shake their heads at me, whisper to each other about this moron in Indiana who let a killer walk right out of his county."

He looked at me with flat eyes. "I hate to have people whisper about me."

I met his gaze. "You've got my statement. Unless you're arresting me, I'm going to go home." Home, suddenly, was sounding very nice, indeed.

"Push comes to shove, eh?" Brewer said.

"Yeah."

"Well, I'm afraid I'm going to have to keep you here. At least for a few hours, while we get this straightened out."

"You arresting me for murder?"

He shook his head. "I'm considering this an equivocal death investigation, Mr. Perry. Suicide's an option, as is murder. As is, I suppose, an accidental shooting. That'd be the gamut, right? Anyhow, I'm going to have to look at it from a few directions, make sure—"

"I get the idea. But if you intend to keep me here overnight, you're going to have to arrest me for something. And I don't think you've got probable cause to say I killed that guy, Brewer."

He smiled sadly and nodded, as if I'd beaten him on that point.

"That private eye license of yours," he said, "is from what state?"

Shit. I saw where this was going now and shook my head.

"Well?"

"It's from Ohio."

"Oops. That's no good. Because we're in Indiana. And that dead guy out there? He's in Indiana. And here you are, conducting an investigation in Indiana, without an Indiana license? My, my. I hate to say this, Mr. Perry, but that sounds like a crime."

"Not the kind you go to jail for."

This time the smile showed his teeth. "It'll do for a night."

The jail in Brown County was brand-new. The kid deputy provided this information after Brewer assigned him to the task of transporting me. When he got the news, the kid blanched noticeably, no doubt believing I was going to jail for offing the guy in the gazebo, and thinking about the few minutes he'd spent alone with me before Brewer had arrived. Once we were in the car, he kept glancing nervously in his rearview mirror, as if he thought a master criminal like me might somehow slip off the grate that protected the front seat and strangle him with my handcuffs. Maybe five minutes and fifty nervous glances into the ride, he decided he'd talk to me. Could be I'd pass on the chance to kill him if he was friendly enough, just thump him on the head with his own gun and steal his car. That was how the kinder master criminals did it.

"Pretty fancy, really," he said of the jail. "A lot nicer than the old one. We got all electronic locks now, more space, everything high-tech."

"And to think, I was worried about finding a place to stay tonight."

"It's a nice place. For a jail."

"Lowest rates in town, I'm sure."

He kept up the stream of nervous chatter for the whole ride while I sat back and watched the dark countryside roll by. I wondered when I would make it back to Cleveland.

Brewer seemed like a hardass, the type who would keep me as long as he could, but unless they were stupid enough to actually charge me with murder, that wouldn't be beyond morning. Karen would have the news long before I made it back. They'd probably call her tonight, as I'd been helpful enough to provide Brewer with next-of-kin information for the corpse. After all, I'd been hired to facilitate a notification of death, and Matthew Jefferson had already heard of his father's murder. Hate to think I was getting paid for nothing.

I leaned back into the seat, ignoring the deputy, who was now telling me something about the perimeter security at the new jail, subtly trying to discourage me from attempting to break out of the place. Hopefully, when Brewer talked to Karen, it would loosen him up a bit. She'd support the story I had told him. Between that and the lack of physical evidence to suggest a homicide, he'd have to cut me loose in the morning. Son of a bitch probably would give me a fine for operating without a license in Indiana, though. That would be relayed to the Ohio licensing board, which would then fine me as well. Terrific.

It took them half an hour to book me into the jail. I was allowed to keep my clothes, but I had to give up my belt so I couldn't hang myself. They took me back into the bowels of the building through several heavy steel doors that shut with loud, hollow clangs. Doors in jails always make me think of hatches in a submarine—there's a sense of finality when they slam shut behind you.

I was alone in my cell, which was a plus, but there was a drunken hillbilly across from me who wanted to talk about my crimes, see what I was in for.

"Moonshining," I said, and then I rolled over on the bunk and put my back to him. Sometime in the hours before I fell asleep, it occurred to me that Amy had missed a hell of a trip.

Brewer came for me early the next morning, probably running on no sleep, the way a good cop always seems to be. Brewer struck me as a good cop, just temporarily misguided.

"Sleep well?" he said as the jailer let me out of the cell and they led me through a series of doors and into a small conference room. It had shackles attached to the walls, sure, but was a conference room just the same.

"Are we done with this stupidity yet?" I answered. "Because I'd really like to be northbound sometime before noon."

"Don't be in such a hurry."

The jailer left, and then it was just Brewer and me. He'd changed clothes, was wearing jeans and a sweatshirt now, cop casual. His face was covered with a day's growth of beard, though, so he hadn't taken much time at home before rolling back out for the second round with me.

"I've done a little research," he said. "Sounds like you were a pretty good cop. You've had some big-deal cases as a PI, too. That's good. Makes your witness testimony a little more reliable."

"Don't you wish you'd been nicer now?"

He tapped a pencil on the table in front of him. "Thing that makes me curious, though? Is why a smart detective like you would neglect to mention some damn interesting things during that witness testimony. Things like your arrest for assaulting the dead guy's father. Things like the romantic relationship you had with the dead guy's stepmother."

"Too many irrelevant details can make a statement murky."

"You think this is a game where we sit around and trade wise-ass remarks?"

"It's shaping up like that."

"Not anymore." He leaned forward. "Yeah, I'd say you neglected to mention some pretty damn interesting things last night, Mr. Perry. You told me you were here to tell Jefferson his father was dead."

"I was."

"You didn't mention that you were also here to tell him he was inheriting many millions."

"That's family business. I'm not interested in sharing anyone else's financial details, Brewer."

"Of course you're not. Now, let's review what you told

me last night, shall we?" He pulled a small notebook from his pocket and glanced at it. "You told me, and repeated this several times, that Matthew Jefferson already knew his father was dead. That this was, in fact, the first thing he said to you when you encountered him."

"That's right."

Brewer slapped the notebook down. "Now, if he knew his father was dead, it would stand to reason that he could also imagine he had just become a very wealthy man. Odd motivation for a suicide, don't you think?"

"He'd been estranged from his father. Could be he had no idea he was getting any money. Maybe that was part of his emotional problem. Not only had he lost his father, he'd lost a fortune."

"If he'd been estranged from his father, as you also indicated last night, then why had he received three phone calls from the man in the last few weeks?"

I leaned back in my chair and looked at him. He wasn't bluffing; I could tell that from his face. If he'd called a judge at home and gotten an order for the phone records, he could have had them easily enough by this morning.

"Interesting, isn't it?" Brewer said, watching me.

"I suppose." I kept my voice neutral. It was more than interesting, but I didn't want Brewer to think I cared. Hell, did I even *want* to care? Right now I just wanted to make my way through about three more locked doors and into the parking lot.

"And the money?" Brewer said. "Those millions that were supposed to go to the son? Well, now that the son is dead, it appears that money goes right back to the widow. The same widow to whom you were once engaged."

He spread his hands and pushed away from the table. "You know, if I were the paranoid sort, I'd be seriously questioning whether I could believe your description of what happened, Mr. Perry."

"I hadn't seen Karen Jefferson in years, Brewer. Call the Cleveland Police Department, ask around. Trust me, they would have checked our relationship out pretty thoroughly after her husband was murdered."

"I will indeed be on the phone with Cleveland. But right now I've got you to deal with. And I want to know why in the hell you would have taken this job. Or—and this is the really interesting question—why in the hell you would have been *asked* to take this job. You and this woman break off an engagement, you beat the shit out of her future husband and lapse into years of silence with her. Then the husband gets murdered and suddenly you're a friend of the family?"

"I'm not a friend of the family. I'm a guy who's doing a job."

"Notification of death, that was your job?"

"I had to find him, too. Nobody knew where he was."

"Except his father."

I shrugged.

"Yeah," Brewer said. "The father knew where the son lived, because he'd been in contact with the son. Or somebody from that house in Pepper Pike had been. And if the father has been talking to the son, well, shit, doesn't it seem odd he wouldn't have mentioned that to his wife? 'Hey, hon, remember that kid I lost track of for a few years? Well, the boy's living in Indiana now, works at an apple orchard . . .'"

We sat in silence and traded stares for a few minutes, Brewer tapping that pencil off the table again.

"Last night you told me the dead guy had been estranged from his father, and that turned out to be untrue. Today you tell me you've been estranged from the soon-to-be-rich widow. I wonder if that's true? I'm just thinking out loud, is all."

"As flattered as I am to be included in your thought process, I'd really like to be on my way."

"Like I said, don't be in such a hurry."

I stood up. "Release me or charge me with something, Brewer. Something a little better than operating without an Indiana PI license. Or get me an attorney and a telephone so

I can start making calls to the media about how you're hold-ing me without charges."

He sat there and looked at me, neither friendly nor un-friendly, just thoughtful. "You think we're all a bunch of hicks, don't you? Think I'm some redneck cop without a clue, bored of busting up meth labs in barns?"

"No, I don't, Brewer. I actually think—had been thinking, at least—that you're probably a pretty good cop. Pretty smart. But I hate to see a good cop and a smart man waste his time."

He got to his feet and unlocked the door, held it open for me. I was halfway through it when he reached out and took me by the arm. It was a slow motion, almost gentle, but his grip was like a pair of forceps. His slender fingers closed around my elbow, his thumb finding a pressure point there and grinding against it. He held me like that and leaned his face sideways, looking up at mine.

"Last night you suggested I check the dead man's thumbs for hammer impressions."

"Did you?"

"Uh-huh. And they were there. I found that out, and I thought, shoot, that is one smart guy we've got sitting in the jail. Started to feel bad, you know? Then I began to wonder if it wasn't *too* smart. Hammer impressions on the thumb. Hell of a thing to think of in the first hour after witnessing a traumatic event like that."

"I'm a detective, Brewer. It's kind of ingrained in me by now."

"Coroner tells me that the hammer impressions could have been left by someone placing the gun in the victim's hand and using his thumb to pull the hammer back. Said it would have had to be done very fast, immediately after the shot was fired, but that it might be possible to leave those im-pressions and then freeze them when circulation stopped."

I reached down and wrapped my fingers around his wrist, pulled his hand from my elbow, and then used my forearm against his chest to push him back. I moved just as he had—aggressive disguised as slow and gentle. He kept his eyes on me and didn't attempt to resist. I turned away from him and walked through the little hallway to the next locked door. Then I looked back at him expectantly. After a moment's pause, he walked down and unlocked this door, too.

"It's been a blast, Brewer. Damn shame we're never going to see each other again."

"Oh, we most certainly will. I intend to be present at your murder trial."

He had those eyes that never told whether he was kidding or serious.

CHAPTER

8

The sun was a smashed ball of red in my rearview mirror when I reached Cleveland. I made one stop for lunch, as I'd missed out on a tasty jail breakfast, but otherwise stayed on the road and kept the speed up, not really caring if I got pulled over. When you're a suspected murderer, tickets don't mean a damn thing. Lincoln Perry, highway rebel. I needed to get a tommy gun, be ready to go down in a hail of gunfire if it came to that.

I came up I-71 into the city, heading for the west side, and home. When I got to Brookpark, though, I pulled off onto I-480 and started east. I was wearing the same clothes I'd had on the day before, unshaven and tired and stiff, but I wasn't ready to go home just yet. After seeing a guy blow his brains into a pond and spending a night in jail, waiting for some cop to lock his fingers into my arm and call me a murderer, I had a few questions of my own. A detour to Pepper Pike seemed very much to be the order of the evening.

The house and all its windows were gleaming in the sunlight when I pulled into the drive, the glass reflecting a crimson glow back into my eyes. I got out of the truck and laid my hand against the hood, feeling the searing heat of an engine that had been driven long and hard. The longer you spend around a machine, the more human it begins to seem. Like that old Steve McQueen movie where he's the engineer on the navy ship. *Sand Pebbles,* was it? Good movie. He loved that damn ship engine. McQueen dies at the end, though. Trying to save a woman, if I recall correctly. Probably should have stuck to the engine room.

I walked up the path to the house and onto the porch with my head down, thoughts of McQueen and engines running through my head, and when I reached the door I saw it was already open, Karen looking at me with red-rimmed eyes.

"I heard you drive in."

"Yeah?" I went in without waiting for an invitation, walked past her, and into the living room. I dropped down into the same couch I'd taken on my last visit and waited for her to join me.

She came in a minute later, after shutting the front door and fastening all the locks. I heard her do it—the snap of the dead bolt, the rattle of the security chain. I listened to that and thought about the way she'd rushed to the door at the sound of my truck and how she'd spilled the wine during my last visit when the phone rang. Pretty damn jumpy.

"They told me what happened," she said. She was wearing jeans and a sweatshirt, but they were the sort of jeans and sweatshirt that you pay three hundred bucks for in a store where all of the employees have their nails done weekly and none of them has ever purchased a rock album.

"Who did?"

"The police in Indiana. They called me last night."

"Did they tell you they were keeping me in jail?"

Her eyes went wide. "No. What? No. They just said . . . the detective said that he needed to get your statement and needed me to verify that what you said was true."

I grinned. "They took their time verifying it. Thoughtful enough to allow me a comfortable cot behind bars while they sorted it out, though."

She tugged the sleeves of the fancy sweatshirt down past her wrists.

"Lincoln, I'm sorry. I didn't know this would happen. You hadn't even told me you were going to Indiana."

"For the amount of money you were throwing around, I thought I should make the notification in person."

"I understand. I just can't believe what happened." Her hands now out of sight, tucked into the sleeves, she folded her arms across her chest, hugged them under her breasts. Her eyes passed over me only in flitting glances before settling on some more reassuring, inanimate object in the room. The base of the floor lamp seemed to be her favorite.

"It was pretty surprising," I agreed, watching her with a hard stare. "The crazy bastard put the gun in his mouth and blew out a nice chunk of his skull. He was closer to me than you are now when he did it."

Her eyes rose, surprised by my description. "How awful."

"Hell of a strange thing," I said, and realized I was echoing exactly what Brewer had said to me the previous night. I'd taken his role now. We'd see if I had any better luck at it.

Karen didn't say anything, just sat there, eyes on the base of that floor lamp.

"Imagine," I said, "killing yourself just before you inherited a few million. I mean, what the hell, you know? Talk about bad timing. The really crazy part, Karen? He knew his father was dead. Told me that as soon as I saw him, sitting there with a gun in his hand and a bottle of whiskey beside him."

She pulled her head back, gave me the wide eyes. "*What?*"

"Didn't know that?"

"No, of course not. How could he possibly have known?"

I looked at her for a long time. She held my eyes, but she wasn't comfortable doing it.

"You must be pretty damn stupid," I said, "to think I wouldn't be able to tell when you're lying to me, Karen. If there's one thing I remember about you, it's what you look like when you lie. That's pretty well ingrained in my memory."

She recoiled, pulling back into the couch and releasing her arms from that squeeze she was giving herself. "Excuse me?"

"Do not lie." My voice was ice. "I watched someone die who could just as easily have shot me as himself, and maybe was thinking about doing just that. Then I spent a night in jail, and now some Indiana detective wants to throw my ass back in there for good. My temper, Karen, is going to be pretty damn easy to trip. So don't you dare tell me another lie."

She looked like she was about to cry. "Lincoln, I haven't been—"

"You knew Alex and his son had been in contact. When I told you the man knew his father was dead, you pretended to be surprised. That was stupid. First of all, because I know when you're lying, and, second, because the cop that called you would have told you already. He's a good cop, and he would have been awfully curious about that detail. He would have asked you about it. Asked how the kid might have found out. So why are you lying about it now? Because you already knew they'd been in contact. Yet for some reason you sent me to look for the son, and I'm damn lucky I didn't end up dead."

By the end my voice was rising and she was crying. I sat where I was and let her cry. The hell with her. I could close my eyes and see that gazebo again, see the gun moving in the shadows and hear the sound of the hammer pulling back, and I could *feel* the bullet heading for me, just like I had in that half second before Matthew Jefferson dispatched himself to places unknown. She wanted to cry? Shit.

My chest was rising and falling, a hit of adrenaline working through me. I sat there, watched her cry, and took deep breaths. Eventually, I spoke.

"Tell me something that's true, Karen."

She wiped her eyes. "It was all true."

"Bullshit."

"It was true! They'd been estranged. For years. I had no idea where Matthew lived. None. I didn't have a phone number for him, or an address."

"You knew they'd been in contact recently. Why didn't you just check the phone records?"

"All I knew at the time was that he had called Alex. Incoming calls don't show up on our phone records, only what you pay for."

We sat and stared at one another. The room was growing dark, but the pale hardwood floors still glowed with a faint hint of red. A clock ticked on the wall, and a mild breeze scattered leaves out on the deck, but otherwise it was silent.

"You're a very rich woman now that your husband and his only other heir are dead," I said.

The fear and apprehension went out of her eyes, replaced by anger.

"What? Surely, Lincoln, you're not trying to say—"

"I'm not. But some other people might try to say some things, Karen. The things that people say when a woman becomes rich amidst a pair of mysterious deaths. And if I believed those deaths were unconnected incidents, and unconnected incidents that you know absolutely nothing about, I'd tell you to ignore the talk and go on with your life."

"But you don't believe that," she said slowly.

I shook my head. "I don't believe it, because it's not true."

"I don't know what's true, either, Lincoln. I really don't."

"You know more than me."

"And you want to hear it?"

"I've got cops trying to pin a murder charge on me, Karen. Yes, I damn well want to hear it."

She stood up from the couch and walked into the kitchen. I stayed in my chair and watched while she took a bottle of wine from the rack on the counter. She lifted it free, hesitated, and put it back before crossing to the refrigerator and returning with a bottle of mineral water. I waited while she sipped it, her eyes on the floor.

"There's something very wrong with this family," she said.

I almost laughed. No shit, Karen? Something wrong with this family? Where in the last week of torture killings and bizarre suicides did you get that idea?

"I met Alex through work—"

"I know," I interrupted, and I couldn't keep the cutting quality out of my tone. I knew awfully well how she'd met Alex Jefferson, though, and I didn't need to be told again.

Karen had been working in records with the district attorney's office when she'd made the switch to the private sector and taken a nice salary boost to work as a paralegal for Cleveland's most prestigious business law firm. Yes, I remembered that well, indeed. I'd splurged on champagne the night she took the job, bought a bottle of Dom on a cop's salary, and toasted to her future success with Alex Jefferson.

She looked at me with sad eyes. "If you want to hear what I can tell you, you'll have to listen to me talk about Alex. I can't sit here and give you facts, because I don't know any. All I can tell you are the changes I saw in my husband."

I didn't realize I was grinding my teeth until I had to loosen them so I could speak.

"Tell me, then."

She took another drink of the mineral water, then put the top back on the bottle and set it on the table beside her.

"I met Alex when I began working with his firm. He was kind, and he paid attention to me. He took me to lunch my first week with the company, and then that became a regular pattern. I remember thinking how busy he was and being surprised that he'd make time for me every week. He asked about you a lot, and at first I thought that was just his way of reassuring me that his interest wasn't romantic. Then I began to get the idea that it was just the opposite, that he was feeling me out to see how serious we were."

To see how serious we were. Apparently, the word "engaged" hadn't meant a lot to Jefferson. Maybe in his world, though, an engagement—or even a marriage—was no indication of how serious a relationship was at all.

"I know you don't want to hear this, and I'll spare you the details. I still feel awful, Lincoln. You probably don't believe that, and maybe you never will. But the reason I'm telling you this is because I have to explain what I saw happen to my husband."

I was leaning forward, elbows on my knees, eyes on the floor. I reached out and ran my hand through my hair as she spoke, squeezing it until the roots pulled hard at my scalp.

"You, and everyone who knew us, probably had a lot of

theories as to what attracted me to Alex. I'm sure everyone talked about the money, though I'd hate to think they truly believed I was so shallow. I'll tell you what the attraction really was, though—he *needed* me. He seemed desperate for me. He used to joke about how much he enjoyed my youth and innocence, but after a while I saw that they weren't all jokes. That I represented something that he thought he needed very badly. He told me once that I healed him, and he said that seriously. As seriously as anything anyone had ever told me. And it was attractive. Compelling, somehow. Here was this man who seemed to have everything, and yet what he thought he needed was a twenty-five-year-old girl who worked in his office and had aspirations of law school."

She went quiet. I didn't want to lift my head and look at her, but eventually I did. I sat there with my elbows on my knees and my hands clasped together and looked at her while she said, "I know you loved me, Lincoln. But I never felt like you needed me."

For a moment silence filled the room, the ticking of the wall clock audible again. Karen looked uncomfortable. I probably didn't look particularly at ease myself.

"You're a very strong person," she said. "You're so comfortable with your abilities, so . . . assured. That's probably the right word. Self-assured, I guess. And independent in a way that most people aren't, either. Those are wonderful qualities, Lincoln, really they are, but . . . maybe they make you seem distanced. I knew I was important to you, I knew you loved me, but I just never had the sense that I was *necessary*. I never—"

"I thought you were going to talk about your husband."

She froze with her mouth half open, another thought about ready to spill out, and then she nodded, almost imperceptibly.

"Okay. That's fair. I'm sorry." She leaned back into the couch and pulled her legs up beside her. "There was always something beneath the surface with Alex. Something that intensified how he felt about me, but that I never really understood. I thought it had to do with his family, with his son. He told me only that Matthew and he were no longer close. It wasn't a subject Alex was comfortable with, and I didn't push. Not until we were making the wedding plans. Then I told him I wanted his son to be there, that it was important to me. He told me Matthew would never come, and he refused to talk about the circumstances at length. That was the hardest I ever pushed him for details, and it was utterly unsuccessful.

"Once we were married, the topic almost never came up. I knew it was sensitive for Alex, and, to be perfectly honest, I never thought about his son. Why would I? I'd never met him, and he'd never been any sort of factor in my relationship with Alex. Every now and then something would remind me of him, and I'd wonder, but that was it. I was happy—we were happy—and Alex seemed at peace."

"Until recently?"

She nodded. "A few weeks ago, something happened. The change in Alex was sudden, and profound. He was scared, Lincoln, and he wouldn't tell me of what. He didn't sleep; I'd find him sitting at his desk or out on the deck at two in the morning, just staring off into space, mostly. He became secretive and guarded. I know you want more details, but I just don't have them. All I saw was the change in his personality. All I saw was his fear."

"What was the response when you asked him about it?"

"He denied it at first," Karen said. "Told me I was crazy, that he was fine, just busy. This went on for a while. Until Matthew called."

"When was that?"

She frowned, considering. "The first call was two weeks ago, almost exactly. The phone rang very late, almost midnight. Alex was downstairs, and I was upstairs. I came down to see who'd been on the phone, and he said it was his son. He looked more scared than anyone I've ever seen, Lincoln. I asked him what was wrong and he just shook his head. Told me that it didn't involve me and that the most important thing for him was seeing that it stayed that way. Obviously, I was furious, because now he was scaring me, and I didn't even understand what was going on. I started yelling at him, demanding he tell me what was going on, and he got up and left the house. He didn't leave in anger, though. He was robotic. Silent."

She stared at the front door as if she were watching him walk out of it again.

"He left, and he was gone for hours. It was about four in the morning when he came back. I was still awake. He got into bed next to me, and I didn't say anything, but he knew I was awake. He just lay there for a few minutes, and then he told me that he was sorry for upsetting me but that he was thinking of my best interests. He told me that someone wanted to make him accountable for something he'd done a long time ago. 'For an old sin' was actually how he put it."

"There were no other details? No throwaway reference to something you didn't understand?"

She started to shake her head, then stopped. "Actually, there was one. He said something like 'When the phone rings at two in the morning, you know it's either a wrong number or a prank or that it's about to change your life. For me, it was the latter.'"

"He was certainly right about that."

"But that's the problem—he couldn't have been talking about the call from Matthew. It was midnight when Matthew called. I was home, I heard the phone ring."

"Maybe he misspoke. By the time you had that conversation it was, what, four in the morning?"

"Yes."

"It probably seemed like the call had come in later than it did. But I suppose there's nothing to lose by checking some phone records, seeing if there was a call that you missed some night."

"I already looked, and so did the police. There weren't any other calls that late. Not to the house or to his cell phone or his office."

"That was the first time that they'd spoken in how many years?"

"Five years. Alex told me that the night of the call. We

were done talking, both of us trying to sleep, and he said, almost to himself, 'That's the first time I've heard his voice in five years.'"

"But the specifics of this old sin? They weren't given?"

"No. He just said he was going to handle it."

"He didn't handle it," I said, thinking of what Targent had told me about the razor cuts and the burns.

"No," Karen said, and her voice was faint. "It doesn't look like he handled it."

"Did you tell the police all of this?"

"Everything except Matthew's call."

I frowned. "Why leave that out? It sounds like he knew something, Karen. Something that could have been valuable."

"I know. That's why I wanted to talk to him first. Before the police."

I stared at her, puzzled for a second, and then I got it. She was worried about what her husband had done. Worried about his image, maybe. And hers.

"You wanted a chance to do damage control before the cops and the media got to it. Wanted to make sure the right buried secrets stayed buried."

Her eyes flashed. "That wasn't it. I just wanted to know what happened. I just wanted to talk to him first."

I shook my head. "Well, it was a hell of a bad idea, Karen. Because now Matt Jefferson's not going to be telling anyone anything. If you'd played it right, and been honest with the cops, they would have gone down there and grabbed him before he had a chance to blow his head off. And, yes, I mean that they would have handled it better than me. Of course, I would've handled it differently if you'd been honest with me, too."

"You think I don't regret that? You think I'm not feeling guilty?"

I was quiet. She shook her head and blinked at tears that were rising again. She kept them in this time, though. After a minute, she turned back to me.

"I want to know what happened to this family, Lincoln. I've *got* to know what happened to this family."

"I'm not the guy to help you. Never was. Why the hell *did* you call me, anyhow?"

"The police told me they'd talked to you, and I . . ." She let her words trail off, staring thoughtfully at nothing. Then she looked back up at me. "Remember those qualities I was telling you about? The confidence, the independence, the—"

"The things that drove you away."

She seemed to wince at that, but still she nodded. "Yes. Well, even if they made you seem distanced, they bred faith in you, Lincoln. They bred trust. I'm sorry, but that never went away." She looked at me sadly. "Doesn't that make any sense to you?"

"As much sense as any of the rest of this."

"Do you understand that I need to know what happened to this family?"

"Yes. And I wish you luck with it. But I'm not going to help. I can't. I never should have let myself get involved with this in the first place, and I spent a good portion of the drive home today swearing at myself for making that mistake."

She was quiet for a long time. Then she said, "I'm sorry that's how you feel. I'm sorry for getting you involved."

I stood up. "You need to call the police and give them the straight story."

She followed me to the door. "I'll send a check. For the amount we agreed upon earlier."

I shook my head. "You'll get a bill with my normal fees. Pay that, and we're done."

She stood in the entryway as I pulled the big door open and stepped out. The sun was completely gone now, and I was greeted by chill, dark air. I turned back to her, now nothing more than a silhouette framed by the light over the entryway.

"Good luck, Karen," I said, and then I walked back to my truck and drove away.

CHAPTER
9

I made it only to the end of that long, winding driveway before a pair of spotlights lit up the darkness, blinding me with harsh beams. I winced and slowed, shielding my eyes with my forearm. When I brought the truck to a stop, the spotlights went off, and then someone's knuckles rapped on my window.

After a hard blink that sent white squares floating through my field of vision, I lowered the window, and after one more blink I was staring into the face of Hal Targent.

"Mr. Perry, how are you?"

"Tired, and going home. You want to clear those cars out of my way?"

"No, I want you to clear yourself out of your truck."

I looked away from him and leaned back in my seat, frustration building through me and threatening to spill over. I wasn't ready to deal with more of this. Not another cop sweating me over things I had nothing to do with. Not tonight.

"Get out of the truck, Mr. Perry."

"No."

"Excuse me?" He leaned in the window, and I could smell cigarettes on his breath.

"There's no reason for me to get out of the truck, Targent. What the hell do you want?"

"Just want to talk. Easier to do that if you get out here with us."

"I'm going home."

He hooked his forearms over the door, leaning his entire upper body in through the window, into my space. I felt my hands go tight on the steering wheel, but I kept my eyes straight ahead, out the dark windshield. My vision had cleared enough to show me the two cruisers parked side by side in the driveway, blocking my exit. They couldn't have followed me here, not when I was coming in straight from Indiana. That meant they were either watching Karen's house or they'd happened to stop by, conveniently found my truck in the drive, and waited to ambush me on the way out.

"Last I heard you were in a jail in Indiana," Targent said. "Came back and went right to see the widow, huh?"

"I was working for her."

"So I hear. So I hear. Pretty funny, you working with her just a few days after you told us what a bitch she was, said you hadn't seen her in years."

"I hadn't seen her in years. And I didn't call her a bitch."

Targent nodded absently. "Sure, sure. I spent a while on the phone today with a detective from Indiana, name of Brewer. Said he enjoyed some conversation with you."

"He's a lovely man."

"That was my take, as well. Has some funny ideas, though." Targent's face was almost touching my own, lit with a green glow from the dashboard lights.

"Yeah, he does," I said. The truck was in park but still running, and I stared at the gearshift and thought about dropping it into drive and hammering the accelerator, seeing if I could clip Targent's toes before he got out of the way.

"Man proposed a theory to me that was damn near wild," Targent said. "I mean, this is some made-for-TV-movie shit. He has two stars in it, a couple of old loves who reunite, secretly. Has things between them heating up again, and then they get this crazy idea to kill the woman's husband. Why? Well, he's in the way, of course, but there's more than that. Turns out the poor bastard's filthy rich, and the leading male character—in this Indiana guy's version, I think you get the starring role—he's had a hard-on for the husband for a while.

Assaulted him once before, in fact. So, the couple, they take the husband off the playing field, right? But, shit, that's only good for half the money. Other half goes to his prick kid, who was never even around. Don't seem right. But what if the kid turns up dead himself? Be damn convenient. Now, here's where the plot starts to slip away, in my opinion. Here's where it goes from feature film to the made-for-TV shit. The man and woman try to fake the son's suicide. A suicide, even though there's no apparent motive for him to do it, and even though he's standing to inherit millions. Then—and this is where the Hollywood directors would really get pissed, because the story's losing all credibility—the only witness to the suicide is the *same guy who's a suspect in the husband's murder*."

Targent chuckled and shook his head. "I mean, is that not ridiculous? A suspect in the murder, the rich widow's old love, he just happens to be the only witness to the kid's suicide? That's reaching for it, don't you think?"

"Get the hell away from my truck," I said, and I dropped the gearshift out of park and into drive.

"Now, slow down, Perry. I was just explaining the Indiana guy's theory. It's not my own."

"Away from the truck."

"No need to hurry. I'm afraid your driveway's blocked."

I took my foot off the brake and got the truck rolling slowly. Targent walked with it, his hand still on the door. Then I moved my foot to the gas pedal, and Targent stepped away from the window before I started dragging him. The cruisers were parked about forty feet in front of me. I cut the wheel left and pulled off the drive and onto the lawn. There were some ornamental bushes blocking me from open grass. I drove right over them. There's a reason I have a Silverado instead of a Toyota Prius, and it's found in moments like this. Clear of the fancy bushes, I cut the wheel back to the right and hit the gas again, felt the tires tearing up the wet grass as I drove around the cruisers, over another set of bushes, and then popped back onto the driveway.

"She's got money and gardeners," I said aloud. No need

to feel bad about a little lawn damage. Then I was pulling out of the driveway and back onto the street. An engine roared to life behind me, but nobody turned on the flashers, and I thought that was probably a damn good thing—one night in jail per week is plenty.

"What have I told you about mulch?" Joe said. "You can't just throw it down in clumps and knock it around with the rake. It's got to be smooth and even. Like a blanket."

I looked up at him from my hands and knees, sweat dripping down my face, and resisted the urge to impale him with my rake. He was sitting on a lawn chair maybe ten feet from me, wrapped in an oversized parka that he shouldn't have broken out of the closet for another two months, sipping a cup of coffee and glaring at my work.

"Listen," I said, "you already used up a good portion of my patience making me rototill the damn garden. That's something you do in the spring, Joe. Not the fall."

"If you knew anything about winterizing a garden, you'd know that's not true. You do it in the fall and again in the spring. Makes a world of difference."

World of difference, my ass. I turned away from him, shaking my head, picked the rake up again, and knocked some more mulch around. Joe's wife, Ruth, had produced the finest flower gardens in the neighborhood before she died. With her gone, he'd taken up the task, even though he'd never so much as glanced at the flowers before. Not surprisingly, Joe brought more intensity to gardening than most. Now, with his shoulder and arm far from functional, he'd recruited me to do his winterizing. I hadn't minded the idea until he'd dragged the lawn chair out and made it evident that he intended to supervise.

"Have you even been listening to me?" I said.

"Yes. But it's a lot easier to listen when you're doing the work right."

I went on spreading the mulch and talking, taking him through my experiences in Indiana and up to my encounter with Targent the previous night. His eyes implied that his focus was on the mulch, but he grunted occasionally, following along.

"So now I've got cops in Indiana and up here wanting to tie me to not one but two homicides," I concluded.

"That's a pretty solid day's work, even for you. One homicide I would've expected, but two is overachieving."

"I got the feeling the cops were pretty impressed, too."

"And Karen?"

"Is she impressed?"

"No, I mean how is she holding up?"

"Not well. Or, maybe, as well as you could ask her to, considering what kind of family she married into."

"You say that with such satisfaction."

"Did I?"

"Uh-huh. And I hate to add bad news to your . . . You know, I don't think you got those perennial bulbs deep enough."

"What bad news?"

"I told you six inches, minimum, LP. You've got to go deeper to hold them through winter. Fall planting is all about depth."

"I went six inches."

"I don't think—"

I sighed and turned around. "Joe? What bad news?"

He scowled at the flower beds again and then refocused on me. "Doesn't affect you, really, but it's not encouraging for Karen's situation."

"Explain."

"Cal Richards called me the day you left for Indiana. Seems Targent asked him about you, wanted to get his take on whether you had it in you to work someone over with a razor blade."

Cal Richards was a Cleveland Police Department homicide detective we'd worked with over the summer.

"Let me guess—Cal told them to slap the cuffs on me?"

"Nah, I think he must've been fresh off vacation or something, in a good mood, because he told them to quit wasting time looking at you. They assured him you weren't a serious option. That may have changed after the suicide in Indiana, but that was what they told Richards."

"Okay."

"Richards told me—with the required threats of what would happen if I disclosed the information, of course—that Targent and his team are interested in some conversations Jefferson had with his broker or investment planner, whoever the hell his financial guru was."

"Yeah?"

The breeze picked up, lifting Joe's thinning gray hair off his forehead and blowing the steam from his coffee off the rim of the cup, whipping it away into an overcast sky. Joe's tone was casual, but his face had changed, darkened and tightened.

"According to this guy, Jefferson was trying to determine how much cash he could put together, and how quickly. He wasn't offering reasons, and he told his financial geek to mind his own business when the guy inquired, but he was interested in liquidating as much as possible, as quickly as possible."

I frowned. "He was a corporate attorney. Could be he'd helped put something together that was getting ready to come down around him, thought his assets would be seized in the investigation."

Joe grunted, but it wasn't in approval. I've spent long enough with him to translate the grunts.

"If he was worried about some sort of investigation, don't you think that would have come out by now? Someone would have stepped forward and said they'd been looking at the guy. And I don't recall anyone being tortured with a razor blade and a lighter during the fallout from white-collar crime, do you?"

"Half of the mob's activity could be considered white collar. But I do see your point. What's your take, then?"

He shrugged and drank some coffee. "Handful of reasons for a guy to want to turn assets into cash overnight, LP. You suggested one, and maybe another is that he was planning to take off, run from something. But there's no evidence to support that. So what's left? What would you do with all that cash?"

I rocked back on my heels, hunkered down there over the garden like a catcher guarding home plate, and stared at him, getting the idea.

"A payoff," I said. "You're thinking someone was extorting him?"

He shrugged again. "That struck me as a possible motivation for the conversations with his financial guy. And if that *was* the case, well, maybe the debt wouldn't end with Jefferson. That's why I mention Karen."

I thought about it, remembering her obvious fear, her nerves exposed like the bare ends of downed power lines, jumping and sparking at the slightest shift in the wind. Was it money? Was someone pressuring her for money?

"Don't make too much of it," Joe said. "I just threw it out there, that's all. It was the only detail of any significance that Richards could offer."

I knocked mulch off my gloves and removed them. Joe stood up and folded the lawn chair by bracing it against his thigh and using his good arm.

"I'd say it would be a fine idea for you to keep your distance from all this, LP."

"A little late for that advice, but, yeah, it's my plan."

He scowled at the flower beds one last time and shook his head. Utterly unimpressed by my work but figuring that it would have to do till spring.

"You have therapy this afternoon?"

"Not till tomorrow."

"Okay. Well, I'm going to head down to the office. Might make some calls to our favorite attorneys and see if they have anything new on their plates. Sometimes those guys can stand a reminder to send some business our way."

It was something he could help with, something he could engage in, and I waited to see if he'd take the bait.

"Not calling around about Jefferson, I hope," he said.

"No, I won't do that."

He nodded and then began to walk back to the house. "Thanks for the help with the yard. And good luck, Lincoln."

I said goodbye and walked back out to the street, unlocked my truck, climbed inside, and started the engine. *Good luck.* Same thing I'd said to Karen the previous night. Before I'd walked away and left her to deal with her problems on her own. Coincidence? Sure it was. Sure.

CHAPTER

10

The day passed slowly. We had some work, but nothing that required a particularly high level of effort or thought. Computer jobs, mostly, a few skip traces and some property records research. I cut out at five, drove back to my building, changed clothes, and went down to the gym.

After an hour of work with the weights, I left and went for a run. October is one of my favorite months for running, the air cool enough to feel energizing but not cold enough to squeeze your lungs. I ran for about thirty minutes, across Rocky River Drive and down the hill into the park, then up to the bridge. I touched one of the iron arches on the bridge lightly with my hand, as I did every time I crossed it: a recognition of the time my partner almost died in the river beneath; a thank-you that he didn't. I made it back to the gym with a good sweat going, breathing hard, and rounded the corner of the building to see Amy's car in the parking lot.

I slowed to a walk, my heart thumping and chest heaving. I was happy to see her, but I was also immediately on edge, too. The last time I'd seen her she'd been angry—frustrated, at least—and we hadn't spoken since.

She must have been watching the mirrors, because she opened the door and stepped out of the Acura before I reached it. She was wearing jeans and a button-down shirt over a white tank top, looking small and trim, as always. Looking good, as always.

"Hey," I said. I've got a knack for slick opening lines.

"Hi." She was holding a piece of paper in her hand, watching me with a frown. "Sounds like I made the right call passing on the Indiana trip, huh?"

"You talk to Joe?"

"No."

"So what've you heard, then?"

"This." She passed the paper to me. It was a printout with ASSOCIATED PRESS across the top. A dateline said "Morgantown, Ind." There was no headline, but the lead sentence gave a clear idea of the article.

The only witness to a violent suicide near Morgantown Thursday night was a private investigator from Ohio who has ties to the victim's recently murdered father.

I looked up at her, matched her frown. "Where'd you get this?"

"It's on the wire, Lincoln. We're running the story tomorrow."

"What?"

She nodded. "I knew you'd be upset, but there's no way I could talk my editor out of running this. Not with Jefferson's murder being such big news. This reporter from Indiana must be in good with the cops down there, because she got a lot of information. Hell, suicides usually aren't news, unless the victim was famous or an elected official or something. It's one of the few areas where we media types have any respect for privacy."

I groaned and read through the rest of the article as we stood there in the parking lot. Yes, some reporter from Indiana was in good with the cops, indeed. There weren't any quotes, just a lot of generic "police said" attribution, but I knew the source had to be Brewer. The story named me and explained that I'd been detained overnight and cited for operating without an Indiana PI license, but that could have come from anyone in the department. The details about my relationship with Karen and my assault on her husband, though, reeked of Brewer's personal touch.

"He probably asked her to make sure the AP spread it around." I crumpled the paper. "He wants me to feel the heat. The asshole actually thinks I'm involved in this."

"What asshole?"

I sighed and rubbed my eyes. "Yeah, I've got to catch you up on all of it, I guess. Let's go inside."

We went up to my apartment, and I told her what had happened while I drank a bottle of water, leaning against the wall while she sat on the couch. She listened with interest, but she was too quiet, offering no questions when usually I would've had to shut her up just to finish my story.

"You mind if I take a shower real quick?" I said when I was done. The sweat from my workout and run was drying, and I wanted to get cleaned up and into fresh clothes.

"Go ahead."

I went. When I came back, she was still on the couch. The television was on with the volume turned off, but she wasn't watching it, choosing instead to stare at the wall.

I walked over to the couch, but there was an aura there, a kind of pulsing defense field that told me I probably shouldn't sit down right beside her. Instead, I sat on the floor and put my back against the couch, tilted my head so I could see her face.

"You all right?"

She nodded. "Yeah. I probably owe you an apology, though. I needed to let some things out the other day, but I don't know if I went about it in the right way."

"It's okay, Amy."

She shrugged but didn't say anything else.

"You need to say what's on your mind, when it's on your mind," I said. "That's the only way to live, Ace."

"Oh, yeah? Then why don't I ever know what's on your mind?"

"Because I'm a shallow, stupid man. Nothing's ever there."

She laughed. "Good argument."

It was quiet for a minute. I wondered if she was hoping

I'd take the lead, direct things back to the conversation she'd started in the parking lot the morning I'd left for Indiana. I didn't say anything, though. If there's one thing I'm worse at than handling a relationship, it's discussing a relationship. A conversationalist who doesn't want to converse about the real important things. So what did that make me? A shallow, stupid man? Uh-oh, maybe I hadn't been joking.

"Rough couple of days for you," Amy said then, probably just to fill the silence.

"Oh, yeah." I sat with my head down and took a long, deep breath. It had been a hell of a couple of days, at that.

She reached down to me, her cool fingers sliding across my neck, and began to massage the spot where my upper back muscles joined my neck muscles. I sighed gratefully and tilted my head back and to the side, feeling tension drain away. Her hands were small and delicate, but strong. Every other part of my body seemed to disappear, and I existed only in about one square inch just above my shoulder blade. That slight touch was reminding me—not for the first time, or even the five hundredth—just how bad I wanted her.

Do you know what it means when your friendship starts making a thwackity thwack sound that progresses to a clankity clank? Yes. It means you screwed up. And how to fix it? Stop being scared.

She worked on my back for a few more minutes, then stopped, running her nails gently up my neck before pulling her hand away. I twisted my head and looked up at her.

"Thank you."

"Sure. Looked like you needed it."

"More than you know."

I put the heels of my hands against the floor, pushed myself upright, and slid onto the couch beside her. She was curled up against the armrest, watching me. I looked back at her and tried to remember why I'd always avoided making a move with her, what I'd been waiting for. My basic logic had seemed sound enough at first: My track record of sustaining romantic relationships was poor at best, and Amy was too good a friend to risk losing. Maybe Grace had a point, though. Maybe I should stop worrying about what could go wrong with it and see what could go right. Maybe the moment was now.

I'd actually started to lean toward her when she said, "I've got to stop thinking of you as a relationship possibility."

I stayed where I was at first, caught in that awkward half lean, and then I pulled back and raised my eyebrows.

"I'm sorry?"

"It wouldn't work, you know? We'd be at each other's throats. We are half the time anyhow, and that's in a friendship. Too many similarities. We've made the right decision, or maybe you made it for both of us, and I just need to do a better job of being grateful for that. I apologize. Good friends are hard to find, and painful to lose, Lincoln. I don't want that to happen here."

I hadn't actually made the move to kiss her, but I felt like I had, and now I was struggling to connect with the sudden turn in the conversation.

"You have nothing to apologize for," I fumbled.

"I let some emotions get away from me the other day, that's all. The questions I asked you, like how many successful relationships I've managed since I met you, those should have been questions I directed at myself."

"Actually, I was thinking—"

"*Damn!*" Her eyes had gone to her watch.

"What?"

"I was supposed to meet a friend for coffee twenty minutes ago. I didn't realize how long I'd been here. I just wanted to drop off that article and apologize, that's all."

She was on her feet, gathering her purse.

"Let's not cut off this conversation here and forget about it," I said.

She gave me a hurried nod as I followed her to the door. "Sure, we'll come back to it, but I really do have to run out of here. Sorry, Lincoln. I'll talk to you soon."

"I hope so," I told the door as it swung shut.

A minute later, I went down to the parking lot as if to catch her, even though I'd heard her drive away. The lot was empty, none of the night owls hitting the gym tonight. I stood with my hands in my pockets, braced against the October wind, and stared at nothing for a while. It was cold, but I didn't want to go back upstairs. I closed the door and locked it, then walked around the corner of the building and started west down Lorain.

I'd known Amy for a year and a half, spending more and more time with her with each passing month, and I'd never instigated anything beyond friendship. Then, the night she explains that she's accepted that as a permanent—and appropriate—situation, I'm ready to make a move. Perfect. I'm a master of timing.

I hung a left on Rocky River, went down to Chatfield, and then walked east, taking as close to a circular route as you can get in a city where everything's laid out in rectangles. A car swung in beside me and parked at the curb in front of a house with a giant inflatable witch on a broomstick, her face glowing a bright electric green under the pointed black hat. Halloween was one week away. I was headed for Joe's house, but unintentionally. He'd probably still be up, watching whatever old game was being aired on ESPN Classic tonight, but I didn't know if I really wanted to drop in on him and hit him with this news. Maybe because I didn't want to bother him so late, and maybe because as the weeks stacked up he was starting to feel less like my partner and more like a guy I used to work with.

Several other houses along Chatfield were decked out in the holiday spirit, grinning jack-o'-lanterns in the windows and gleaming skeletons hanging from the trees. All holidays are bizarre when you think about where they started and what they became, but Halloween may be the strangest.

My breath fogged out in front of me as I walked, moving quickly, my hands still in my pockets, keeping my arms pressed against my sides for warmth. My wet hair soaked in the chill, made me shiver a bit. Just begging to catch a cold. Maybe that wouldn't be the worst thing, though. I'd have to stay home, stay in bed, stay out of the world and all of the twists it could throw at you.

The attacker ran through the grass instead of on the sidewalk, so I didn't hear his footsteps behind me until the last second. A car door had opened and closed, but I'd assumed it was the people who'd pulled up in front of the house with the witch decoration, and I hadn't bothered to glance back. I was half turned to see what was coming when he hit me, a tackle that lifted my feet off the sidewalk and slammed my shoulder against a tree before I fell heavily to the ground.

I landed on my back, which put me in the best position to defend myself against the next attack from a man I saw only as a dark shape, his face obscured by the shadows and a baseball cap pulled low on his head. I pushed myself off the ground as he swung at me, ducked, and lunged toward him as the blow missed by inches. From the sound his hand made as it passed by my ear, I knew he was holding a weapon, something with some weight to it. He stepped back deftly and quickly at my move forward and, instead of collecting himself for another swing, he simply reversed his body and momentum and threw his right hand at my head again, this time in a smooth, fluid backhand, like a tennis player. He did it so fast and so hard that I thought I tasted the blood in my mouth before I was knocked into a black oblivion.

CHAPTER

11

The first thought I had when I regained consciousness sent a bolt of pure horror through me—I was blind. I'd come around slowly, groggy, but then I was awake and alert, blinking and trying to focus and finding that impossible. There was nothing but blackness, and for a few awful seconds I knew a fear as great as any I'd ever felt, thinking that my vision was gone, maybe permanently. Then I felt the cloth on my face, and I realized there was some sort of bag over my head, fastened tight around my neck.

Someone prodded me in the ribs. "You back?"

I was starting to get my bearings now—on the ground, cool, wet grass beneath me, hands bound behind my back, not with handcuffs but one of those thin, incredibly strong plastic ties that cops use as an alternative. Cloth bag over my head, very thick, allowing absolutely no light to filter through the fabric. I ran my tongue over dry lips and winced as it touched a deep cut with a coppery flavor. There was a steadily increasing ache behind my right ear.

"Say something." Another prod in the ribs, probably with the toe of a boot.

"Take the bag off my head, asshole."

A laugh. "Ah, you are back."

"Take the bag off. I can't breathe." As soon as I said it, I began to feel as if I really *couldn't* breathe, then had to still myself before I began gasping, sucking in panic breaths.

"You don't want that bag to come off. That bag represents a nice alternative I'm providing to you, Lincoln Perry. It's a chance to do some talking. The other option is that you do some dying. So, no, I don't think you want that bag to come off."

A hand reached down and grabbed the bag, taking some of my hair with it, then jerked me upright. When I was on my knees, he released me.

"Stay up."

Sitting there on my knees, hands bound behind me, a bag tied over my head, I felt like I was waiting for execution. I tried to get to my feet, but he put his boot in the middle of my back—not gently—and shoved me back to my knees.

"No movement. Just sit still and talk. Do that, and you'll go home tonight."

I licked my lips again, and the moisture turned the dried blood to liquid, filled my mouth with the taste.

"Who are you?"

"A man who has plenty in common with you," he said. "That's one of the reasons I prefer you talking to you dying. We've got some similarities, yes, we do."

I was silent, waiting for more.

"You don't need to know about me, Lincoln Perry. I know about you, and that's the important thing. I know who you are, I know what you've done with your life, I know who is important in it. I know that you paid a visit to Karen Jefferson last night, that you worked in your partner's garden this morning, that you spent some time with that good-looking reporter this evening. She seemed upset when she left. What'd you do to spoil her fun?"

"Told her I wanted to play kinky games with my hands tied behind my back and a bag over my head."

He laughed. "Good, Lincoln. Very good to see you're rolling back into form, hiding your fear. I applaud the attempt. But don't take it too far."

There was the ratcheting sound of a round being chambered, and then I felt a hard press of metal at the back of my skull.

"Keep your fear, Lincoln. I'm a man to be afraid of, no matter what I said about wanting to let you live tonight. Don't forget that."

The gun lifted away from my head, and I realized I was biting down on my wounded lip, making the blood flow freely again.

"You're causing some problems," he said, moving around behind me, shifting to my left side. I could hear nothing but a soft wind and his voice. Wherever we were, it was someplace secluded. That realization wasn't particularly comforting.

"I believe these problems you've caused were inadvertent," he continued. "That's just unlucky for you. But now I need to address them."

"All right." My lips brushed against the thick bag when I spoke.

"What happened in Indiana? Why were you there, and what happened?"

I stayed silent for a minute, and then I realized how pointless that was. If I didn't talk, he'd go to work making me talk. That would be fine, if I had something valuable to protect. I had nothing to protect, though. There was nothing I could say that he wouldn't already know from the papers.

"I went to find Jefferson's son and tell him his father was dead and he was rich. When I found him, he killed himself, with me watching."

"How long were you with him?"

"Two minutes, tops."

"He spoke to you?"

"Yes."

"What did he say?" His voice had picked up a new intensity.

I hesitated.

"What did he say?"

"Told me your name and your game," I said. "A dozen cops are on it right now."

There was a pause, and then he hit me. It was a swift, staggering blow to the kidneys. I fell forward, and, since I couldn't put my hands out to protect myself, I landed on my face. I smelled the wet earth for a half second before his hand tightened on the bag and my hair again and jerked me back.

"Why?" he said. "Why do you say that, why do you tell a lie that there's no reason to tell?"

"Because I'm tired of the bag, dickhead."

The gun was back then, hard and cold against my skull. "I'll ask again—what did the man's son tell you?"

I could feel blood running down my chin. After giving it a long pause, I spoke.

"He told me you had a reason, and all I had was greed. He thought I knew you, thought I was with you. He said that, and then he put the gun in his mouth and pulled the trigger."

"You're lying."

"That's what you said last time. Pick one to believe."

His hand tightened on the bag, pulling my hair painfully. "We're coming from the same place. I know what you did to Jefferson, and I know what he did to you. I admire you for it, and I sympathize with you. But the score you had to settle? The wrong you suffered? Lincoln, it can't touch me. You saw him on his best day. I saw him on his worst. And I came to settle up."

"You killed him."

"Yes. I would have killed his son, too. But then you got in my way. I'm not happy about that."

"What does the son have to do with it?"

"Everything. That little shit called his daddy for help in the middle of the night and I paid the price, paid it for five years. But that doesn't concern you. None of it does, really, and I regret that we're here, but when you went down to Indiana and left a dead man behind, you created some real problems. You changed the game with that move, even though you can't see that. We're going to have to refocus our attention now, and you've *got* to remove yourself from the situation."

"Refocus where?"

"Lincoln, are you hearing me?"

I was shaking now, the wind blowing cold as I sat there on my knees, no jacket over my thin T-shirt, my mouth bleeding, my eyes blind.

"Stay away from Karen," I said. "Whatever Jefferson did to you, it wasn't Karen's fault."

He spoke with the voice of a frustrated teacher. "You don't understand a damn thing about this. Can you tell me that? Can you tell me that you don't understand?"

"I don't understand."

"Of course you don't. And that's a very, very good thing for you. Because I'm going to see that you get home. And home, Lincoln? That's where you need to stay. You know what I promised Jefferson? I promised him that by the time I was done he'd welcome death. Beg for it. I told him that his would be a welcome grave, Lincoln. I don't think he believed me. Not at first. He thought he could stop it. But by the end? He believed me by the end."

He knelt beside me and tapped my skull with the gun.

"Leave the dumb slut alone. I'm disappointed in you even for speaking to her, but I suppose that's to be expected. No more, though. No more. Another trip to that house may cause you problems that I can't stop."

There was silence for a few minutes, and then he rose, and I could hear and feel him pacing around behind me. A few raindrops were falling now, the wind blowing strong and steady, and I couldn't stop the shivering.

"What did Jefferson's son tell you?" he asked again.

I shifted forward on my knees, my body beginning to ache from holding the position.

"He didn't tell me anything. Nothing more than what I've already said."

"He knew what was ahead. That's why he did it. He'd been told what his father had been told—that his would be a welcome grave—and he didn't have his father's arrogance, or his father's stupidity. He believed me. He knew he couldn't stop what was coming for him."

It was quiet, and then he spoke again. "All right." His voice was thoughtful. "All right."

Good, I thought, *the crazy bastard's satisfied now, and he's going to let me go.* That was the last thing I thought before he hit me again, a massive blow that seemed to separate my head from my body, and then the world went away for the second time.

I woke up in the bed of my own truck, which was still in the lot behind my building. I groaned, the pain in my head seeming to spread through every inch of my body, and tried to sit up. The sky and earth reeled around me in a crazy dance, and I settled back down, licked my bloody lips, and waited.

It took me three tries to get out of the truck. The bed wall seemed impossibly tall, the ground impossibly far away. When my feet touched the pavement my knees buckled, and if I hadn't caught myself on the truck I would have collapsed. I hung there on the side of the truck for a while. Maybe five minutes, maybe ten. I took short, shaking breaths and tried to block out the bell choir that was banging away with gusto inside my skull.

My keys were still in my pocket. I fumbled them out with stiff fingers, unlocked the door, and went up the steps one at a time, my hand on the wall for support. Then I had to unlock the apartment door, which took further effort. When I finally staggered across the threshold, I felt like I'd just finished the last leg of a triathalon. If you ran a good portion of a triathalon on your skull, that is. I went into the bathroom, turned on the light, and looked in the mirror.

"Ho—ly shit," I said. There was blood on my face and on my neck, and my skin was as pale as I'd ever seen it. I ran some cold water and rinsed my face with it, then turned a white towel red with blood. When I'd gotten my face cleaned off, I saw things weren't really so bad. The cut on my lip had bled like a bastard, but it wasn't too traumatic, just one deep slice on the inside. Probably needed stitches, and I definitely should be checked for a concussion. I didn't know what he'd hit me with, a blackjack maybe, or perhaps brass knuckles, but it had rung me up like a baseball bat swung by Mantle.

I ran my fingertips over the back of my head and felt two large lumps growing there, both on the right side. I knocked a bottle of ibuprofen out of the cabinet, got the top off, and threw a few into my throat and chased them with water. I'd hardly swallowed before I felt them coming back up, and I dropped to my knees and threw up in the toilet. I curled up on the floor, gasping, and leaned my head back against the bathtub. The cool ceramic felt good on my battered skull. After a few minutes had passed, I tried the ibuprofen again, and this time I held them down. I went out to the kitchen and filled a plastic bag with ice cubes, then positioned it over a pillow on the couch, lay down, and nestled my head in it.

"Holy shit," I said again. I'd had some headaches before, like the time I ran head first into a brick building, but this was something else. Concussions were dangerous things. Skull fractures were worse. If I fell asleep now, I might never wake up.

Two minutes later, I was gone.

I woke sometime after two, rivulets of cold water from the melted ice trickling down my neck. I moved around a bit, testing my coordination. Everything seemed to function right. My head hurt, yes, but it wasn't as intense as it had been. My vision was clear.

"No hospital," I decided. That would turn into an hour or so of sitting in a chair in the emergency room, anyhow. I was walking and talking and not bleeding profusely, and in a Cleveland ER, that knocks you to the bottom of the list. Instead, I swallowed a few more ibuprofen to keep the swelling down and went to bed.

He'd told me I'd be left alone as long as I stayed away from it. What the asshole didn't understand was that I *was* going to stay away from it. Right up until he put that bag on my head.

PART TWO

OLD SINS

CHAPTER

12

I found the photograph in the morning. It was a simple print on low-quality paper, slipped into the back pocket of my jeans. I hadn't noticed it the previous night, but I'd been damn groggy then. Besides, the picture didn't have much weight to it. Not until you looked at it.

Alex Jefferson's head and upper torso filled the frame. His shirt was off, and there were two diagonal slashes across his chest, intersecting at the bottom of the picture in a way that made me think it was the top half of an *X*. The blood appeared more black than red in the photograph, and the wound had to be fresh, because the blood was just beginning to spill and coat his skin and the wiry gray hairs that covered his chest.

There was duct tape over his mouth, covering the lower half of his face, and above it his eyes bulged with pain and horror. His gray hair hung disheveled over his forehead, a sheen of sweat on his skin. Temperatures had taken a drop the week Jefferson died, cold nights and cool mornings, like the one when Targent and Daly showed up at my gym. I remembered that, and then I thought about the sort of pain that could make your body break out into a full sweat on a cold night.

For a long time I looked at his eyes. I'd swung on them that night in the country club parking lot. Connected with his nose, maybe, but when I felt my fist shatter bone and saw Jefferson's legs crumple soft beneath him, it was his eyes I wanted to change. The smugness, the arrogance, that sense he had that the world was in his palm, everything perfectly in control. I wanted to remove it, and I failed. The splash of blood on the pavement didn't disrupt his life anywhere near as much as mine. The next time I saw him, the world was still his, and his eyes showed it.

Not anymore. I looked at the photograph, and I saw that all the things I'd loathed were gone from his face. The world had risen up out of his palm, risen harsh and angry and violent, leaving a powerful man utterly powerless in the end. The world has that tendency.

Several minutes passed while I stood alone in the bedroom with the photograph in my hand. The police should have it—evidence, directly connected to the crime scene.

Evidence. The word had been running through my brain for all of my professional life. It was the focus of my work, what I pursued, what I needed. And now, what I feared. Any other day, with a photograph of a murder scene in my hand, I'd be reaching for the telephone to call the police. Today, I hesitated. Evidence.

I saw Targent leaning into the cab of my truck again, his face reflecting the dashboard lights, explaining the options he and Brewer had discussed. They were options that would send me to jail. Ludicrous options, sure. But now I held a photograph of a murdered man in my hand. It would be evidence, yes, but evidence against whom? I already knew that there would be no fingerprints on it, that the paper would be a generic brand sold across the country, that the image itself would offer nothing to point back to the killer's identity. All that would have been cleared long before it was carefully folded and placed in my pocket. Jefferson's killer was a pro.

There was my face, the bruises and damage left by my attacker. Would that be proof enough, though? Would Targent and Brewer, pinning me between two investigations hundreds of miles apart, believe my story?

I wasn't going to give them the photograph. Even while I

realized this, I marveled at it, the audacity and stupidity of such a decision. It was ridiculous. A crime, suppression of evidence. I chastised myself when I held the flame of a cigarette lighter to the photograph's edge, continued even while I sprayed water at the charred remains to drive them down the sink drain in a swirling smear of wet ash, kept the lecture up until I was in my truck and headed for Karen's. I expected the berating would scare me eventually, convince me I had made a mistake. Instead, what let the fear loose was the unshakable sense that I had not.

"Lincoln—your face!"

It wasn't the nicest greeting I'd ever heard, but I suppose it had to be expected. I tried to smile at Karen as she stood there in the doorway, but didn't put too much into it. Wouldn't want that split lip to open up again and start dripping blood all over her furniture.

"Morning," I said. "You mind if I come in?"

She stepped away from the door, her expression still horrified, and let me inside. This time, she didn't take me into the living room but just stood in the entryway.

"What happened?"

There was a mirror just over her shoulder, a huge thing with a polished brass frame that probably weighed about eighty pounds. I caught a glimpse of myself in it, and it took effort not to grimace.

"One of your husband's old friends decided to look me up," I said. "He wished to talk. The talk, I was told, was the alternative to killing me."

She lifted a hand to her mouth and then lowered it, slowly. "Who . . ."

"Didn't give me a name, unfortunately."

"Well, what did he say? What did he say about Alex?"

"That he killed him."

Her head rocked back, and more of the rest of her went with it than should have, and then she blinked and steadied herself.

"You saw the person who killed him."

I shook my head. "No. I saw the inside of the bag he tied over my head after he knocked me out and dragged me off into the woods to sit with a gun against the back of my head and answer questions."

She seemed twenty years older than me, and I wasn't feeling particularly young. Her face was pale, with dark circles under her eyes, and her expression was the weary look of someone who's been lost for a very long time and has given up on ever making sense of the map.

"You didn't see him."

"No."

"What did he sound like?" she said, and her voice had a hard edge.

The question surprised me, but I answered it without hesitation. "Like an evil son of a bitch, Karen."

She didn't say anything to that, just turned and wandered out into the living room as if I weren't even in the house. After a pause, I followed her. She watched me as I sat down, but her eyes were unfocused, distant. They stayed that way while I told her the rest of it, providing as near to a word-for-word account as I could manage. I came pretty close, too. It hadn't been the sort of incident that fades from memory overnight.

When I was finished, she was sitting quietly. She hadn't interrupted once, hadn't visibly reacted. This wasn't the Karen I knew. She'd never been able to internalize her emotions well, and I remembered that while we were together I'd thought that quality would've made her a bad cop—unable to stay distanced and unable to bluff.

"Is there anyone who has been pressuring you for money? Any unsettled debts?"

She shook her head. "No."

"No one's made contact with you about the murder?"

"The only *contact* I've had came in the form of two police officers showing up at my door to tell me Alex was gone."

"Your husband was looking into turning assets to cash

just before he was killed. Looking to generate big money, and do it fast. Why?"

"The police told you that?"

"Not directly. But I think the money is important. Liquidating assets just before he was killed could suggest extortion."

"I know. And some of it is missing."

"What?"

"According to the police. I didn't even know. But the police have looked, and they say there's fifty thousand dollars missing."

"That's all?"

"That's all that they told me about."

Fifty grand, gone. Jefferson trying to free up even more cash. A menacing presence back in his life, reminding him of old sins. Whatever Jefferson had done, it must have been serious. The fifty grand hadn't made a dent in his debt, apparently. Neither had his life.

"We'll start with a phone call," I said.

"Who are you going to call?"

"Nobody. But this all began with a phone call, and we need to find out when it happened. You told me that the one night your husband talked to you about what was happening, he made a comment about getting a call at two in the morning."

She nodded. "He said he knew it was either going to be a wrong number or it would change his life."

"Right. And last night the bastard who attacked me made a similar comment. He said that Matt Jefferson called your husband for help and that he—the guy who attacked me—paid the price. He said he paid it for five years."

"I have no idea what that means."

"I didn't expect you would. But you should be able to get phone records. You're the spouse, after all—I think they'll have to honor that request. If we get those records, if we go back and find this phone call that came in the middle of the night five years ago and changed your husband's life, we'll have a starting point. A day on the calendar, if nothing else."

"We won't need to make a request."

"No?"

"Alex almost never used the house phone, just his cell phone. He had some weird hangup with that."

It was easier to trace and tap landline calls. To be concerned with something like that was the essence of the corrupt. I was interested but didn't comment.

"We'll still need the records, though."

"The cell phones have detailed billing. He saved all the bills."

"You can go back five years or more?"

"I'd be stunned if I can't, but let me check."

"Please do. It's a place to start, and without the phone call, I don't seem to have one."

"Two days ago you didn't want one," she said. "Two days ago you wanted to get far, far away from it all."

"Uh-huh. Then I changed my mind. Credit for that goes to the guy who killed your husband, though."

She gazed at me through those flat eyes she'd seemingly developed overnight. "Well, I hope he gets all the credit that's due to him."

"Yeah," I said. "That's the goal."

CHAPTER

13

It took an hour to put together the possibilities. Alex Jefferson didn't receive many phone calls in the early hours of the morning, but there were a few. Karen was right: The bills were detailed, and they went back eight years. I found three early-morning calls in the previous month's bill and recorded all the numbers. One was from an 812 area code, which I recognized now as belonging to southern Indiana. That had been the first call from his son in many years. The other two calls were local numbers, and I noted them and moved on.

I'd gone through five years when I got another hit. On July fifth, Alex Jefferson received a call on his cell phone at 1:36 A.M., again from a number with an 812 area code. The call had lasted eleven minutes. The next call on the record, this one outgoing, had been placed at 1:52 A.M., to a number with an area code from northeastern Ohio, between Cleveland and Pennsylvania, the Ashtabula area.

I went through the rest of the bills, just because they were there, and found five additional calls that had come in around one or two in the morning. While I recorded each number, I wasn't optimistic that they would matter. What was interesting, though, was the prevalence of calls from that 812 number.

"Would you have an address book or a phone list around somewhere?" I asked Karen. "Anything that would show old numbers?"

"A Rolodex in the office."

I wrote the 812 number down and handed it to her. "See if you can find this. I think it belonged to his son at one point."

Five minutes later she returned with confirmation. "The Rolodex says that was Matt's cell phone number. I just tried to call it, and I got some woman who had no idea who Matt was."

"I bet he stopped using it several years ago. The last number he called from is different. All I needed to know was that it belonged to him at one time."

"So you're getting somewhere?"

"I don't know, but I've got a list of numbers and call times that I can check out. It's something to do. There are other places to look, too, and I'll be working on them soon." I paused and then added, "Hopefully, with some assistance."

Joe was on his way out of the house when I pulled into his driveway. He was wearing jeans and that big parka again, holding his car keys in his hand. He stopped walking as I put the window down and glanced in at me.

"Bad timing, LP. I'm on my way to physical therapy."

"Skip it," I said.

He tilted his head and peered in the car, looking at me with surprise. "What?"

I turned to face him, making sure he could see my black eye and battered lip as I shut off the engine. "I need you for a minute, Joe. Is that okay?"

He managed a nod. "Sure. I guess we better go inside."

We went in and sat in the kitchen. Or I sat, at least. He poured himself a glass of water, drank a little, and then leaned against the counter.

"Well," he said. "What's up?"

I told him what was up. He didn't say a word. Just stood there and drank his water and refilled the glass once. I was in a chair at the little kitchen table, everything in the room so damn neat and ordered and so . . . *Joe.* When I was finished with the story, I met his eyes.

"I'm starting to drown in it a little bit, Joe. I'm starting to feel a little overmatched. Maybe I shouldn't. Maybe I should be good with all this, be all collected and focused and calm about it, everything that you'd be if you were in my shoes. But, damn it, I'm used to working with a partner. Used to working with *you*. Then this shit keeps stacking up, and I've got cops talking about murder charges, and guys putting bags over my head and guns against my skull, and I turn around and look in my corner for you, and you're not there." I softened my voice, leaned back in my chair. "I don't see you there, at least."

He stared at me, no clear emotion on his face, and then he finished the rest of his water and set the glass aside. He shook his head.

"I'm sorry to hear you say that. But you have to admit, I didn't know about most of this until five minutes ago."

"Right," I said. "Because you haven't been around. Don't misunderstand me—you getting healthy is the most important thing. But did you have to go so far away to get healthy?"

"I've been right here."

"Did you have to go so far away to get healthy?" I repeated, and after a pause, he nodded, getting it this time.

"All right," he said. "That's fair enough."

It was quiet for a moment.

"I'm not blaming you for anything," I said. "Shit, Joe, you took those bullets for me. Because of me. If I can realize that and somehow be pissed at you for all of this, then I'm pretty damn self-absorbed. I'm just saying that . . ."

"What?"

"That I could use you right now. That I need some help. Okay? I need some help."

He ran a hand through his gray hair and nodded. "Then I'll help. Of course I'll help. Damn, LP, you had to know that."

"I did. I do. But you have to understand the kind of distance you've been keeping lately. It's my fault that you're gone—"

"It's not your fault."

"The hell it's not. It's absolutely my fault, and I under-stand that. But do you think that makes it easy for me to ap-proach you, ask you when you're going to come back?"

Something changed in his eyes then. Something a stranger or casual acquaintance wouldn't pick up on, but that I couldn't help but notice after years of working so closely with him.

"Are you coming back, Joe?"

He picked up the empty glass and rinsed it. Rinsed water out of a glass with more water, then set it back down as if he'd accomplished something.

"Look," he said, "the issue of the day is what's happening with Karen. Right?"

"Right."

"Okay. Then let's get focused on that, LP. You aren't go-ing to need to worry about having a partner if they send you to prison." He paused, then smiled slightly. "On second thought, maybe having a partner is exactly what you *will* need to worry about if they send you to prison."

I was laughing then, and so was he, and it felt damn good. Shit, when was the last time Joe and I had laughed over anything? I couldn't think of it. We laughed about the prospect of me in prison, a real howler of a subject, and then he pulled up a chair and sat down across from me, resting his bad arm on the edge of the table.

"So what have you got? Other than a beat-to-shit face, what have you got?"

"A vague reference to an old sin, a list of late-night phone calls, a missing fifty grand, and that's it. Had a photograph of the murder victim, but not anymore."

He frowned. "I don't like your decision on that one. You could have guessed that, I'm sure. That's *evidence,* LP."

"Same word I used to motivate myself when I burned it."

He sighed and drummed his fingers on the table. "Well, we aren't going to accomplish much if we stay in this kitchen, are we? Better get down to the office."

I looked at the clock. "How long was the therapy session supposed to go?"

"An hour."

"Would they let you start late if you told them you got held up with something important?"

He shrugged. "Probably."

"Then go to your physical therapy," I said. He started to shake his head, but I held up my hand. "Joe, go to it. I said you getting healthy is the most important thing, and I meant that. But come on by the office when you're done. Come on by, and give me a hand."

He hesitated before nodding. We left the kitchen and walked outside. I paused at the door to my truck, and he slowed down and looked back at me. I said, "Thank you," just as he said, "I'm sorry," and then we both just nodded at each other. I climbed in my truck and started the engine, then drove to the office, feeling better than I had in a long time.

Good enough that I could almost forget about the question he'd left unanswered.

I'd been in the office for fifteen minutes before Targent and Daly showed up. All I'd accomplished so far was to boot up the computer and crack the windows, let a little of the Indian summer day bleed into the room. I heard their steps on the stairs as I settled back into my chair behind the desk, and for a moment I thought it was Joe, deciding to pass on therapy after all and get an early start on this. Then someone knocked on the door, and I had a bad feeling I knew my visitors.

I pulled the door open, and Targent greeted me with a cheerful smile.

"Good afternoon, Mr. Perry."

They came inside. Daly was carrying a black leather bag, and he walked past me and sat on one of the old stadium chairs that occupy the center of our office, relics from Cleveland Municipal Stadium. Targent came in, too, but he stayed on his feet.

"What are you doing here?" I said.

"Well, you drove off in such a hurry the other night I didn't have a chance to wrap up our chat."

"I wrapped it up, Targent. And I'm busy. So this better be damn important, because if you're just visiting, I'm going to have to ask you to leave."

He nodded, looking at me with a curious expression. "Speaking of visiting—you been doing any in places where you're not wanted?"

"Nope."

"Because," he gestured at his own face, pointing to his eye and then to his lip, "you're a little banged up there."

"Uh-huh. That's a souvenir from the guy you *should* be arresting." I knew where we were headed, and it wasn't going to be good. I should have reported the attack. I'd waited because I hadn't talked to Karen yet, and my chances of getting an honest answer about any extortion attempts seemed better if I went alone. Now that was about to blow up in my face.

"The guy I should be arresting?" Targent's eyebrows arched.

"I was interrogated about some things last night. Rather vigorously. The guy put a bag over my head and asked me what had happened with Jefferson's son, in Indiana."

Targent turned and looked at Daly. Then he looked back to me, and when he did all that was left on his face was anger.

"You were interrogated about Jefferson's son."

"Yes."

"Well, someone is in trouble," he said. "Whoever failed to get this police report to me and point out that it has a direct impact on my murder investigation, they are in some kind of trouble. We must have an incompetent asshole in our midst. Because I'm quite sure you had a police report made, and yet that report never made its way to my desk."

I held his eyes while I shook my head.

"You didn't," Targent said, and now that low voice had the full force of his rising fury behind it. "You were approached— no, attacked—by a man you had every reason to believe was involved in a homicide, and you didn't feel it necessary to inform the police? Is that what I'm understanding?"

"I wanted to talk to Karen."

"She's running the homicide investigation?"

"No."

"So you are?"

"No." I paused but spoke again before he could jump in. "The last time we talked, you were full of shit, Detective. You blocked me in the driveway and gave that entertaining speech about the movie plots and generally wasted my time. You think I was in a hurry to sit down with you again?"

"I'd like to think you would be *in a hurry* to see this crime solved. Holding back information like this is not a help, Perry. It's a crime. You were a cop, you know that."

"Look, Targent, if I'd come to you last night it wouldn't have helped. The guy was gone, and what lead would my story have given you? Nothing. All he left me with was vague talk and a collection of bruises."

"You held back critical information in a homicide investigation—"

"I'm giving it to you now. You think you would've broken this case if I'd called you at two in the morning? Come on. I'm giving it to you now, and that's enough. We can spend the rest of the day arguing about it, but if you're so interested in getting this case closed, like you say, you'll be smart enough to realize that's not going to help. If you're more worried about winning some sort of macho pissing contest with me, then go ahead. We can waste as many hours as you like."

"Okay," he said. "We won't argue about that, but I'm not ready to leave yet, either. There's a matter I think you're going to want to discuss with us."

"You don't have anything I want to discuss."

"No?" His eyes had changed, the anger replaced by the hard glint of a poker player sitting on a hand he was sure the others at the table weren't anticipating.

"No."

"Not even a Russian by the name of Thor?"

I looked at him for a long time, trying to keep my face impassive and hoping nobody could hear the thudding increase in my heart rate.

"You don't know a Russian named Thor?" he said. "I'd try the last name, but there's no chance I'd even get in the ballpark. Too many consonants. Or maybe it was vowels."

"What's he got to do with this?"

"So you *do* know the man?"

"I didn't say that. Just tell me why you're asking about him. Tell me that or get the hell out of here."

Targent smiled, enjoying the tension he heard in my voice. "After Jefferson's body turned up, we searched his vehicle and pulled some prints. There were several different sets there, but only one turned up a match on our computers. Two fingers of the right hand of a Russian mobster named Thor. A gentleman who's been charged with four crimes and investigated in maybe thirty others and convicted of none. Word about this guy is that he's a hitter. Serious protection for Dainius Belov, and I'm quite sure you know who *he* is."

His words slid in and out of my brain. I couldn't focus on anything other than a Russian with the palest blue eyes I'd ever seen, eyes that belonged to some ancient glacier. Did I know Thor? Targent had asked. Proof of that acquaintance was standing in front of him. Thor had saved my life once. Saved it while taking the lives of a few other men, sure, but when you're the one who comes out alive you tend not to worry about the other side of the equation so much.

"We were pretty intrigued by this guy, right from the start," Targent was saying. I blinked hard and stared at him, struggling to pay attention, to look calm, and not like I'd just been kicked in the stomach.

"Yeah?"

"A guy with that sort of reputation, you kidding me? Looked like a good fit. Problem was motive, Perry. All we had connecting Jefferson to this guy were those two fingerprints in the car. Nothing else. Not a phone record, not a mutual acquaintance, nothing. Then we learned something very interesting about you."

He motioned at Daly, who reached into his bag and pulled out a sheaf of papers. Targent took them and shuffled them for a minute, then spoke again.

"We're acquainted with a homicide detective named Swanders. That one familiar to you?"

I nodded.

"Right. Turns out you two were working the same case about a year ago. Guy named Wayne Weston got whacked. Trail ran back to the Russian mob, Belov's crew. You played a pretty heavy role in the way everything shook out on that one. Dangerous stuff, is how they wrote it up in the papers. The interesting thing about the newspaper articles was that they were filled with loose ends. I hate unanswered questions, you know? So I threw a few of those questions at Swanders. The way he remembers it, right around the same time this Weston case was going on, the Russians had a bit of an internal shake-up."

I sat down on the chair behind my desk, leaned back, and gave him indifferent, as bored an expression as I could muster. It wasn't much.

"We asked around about this shake-up. There are a couple guys with the department and a few more with the FBI who keep a tight watch on the Russians. They remember the situation. Seems about three of the Russians who were affiliated with Belov just disappeared." He snapped his fingers. "Poof. One day they were here, wreaking havoc on the city, and the next, they were gone. Then there's you, a guy who by all accounts should have been viewed as a major pain in the ass by these Russians, and yet . . . you're still here. Some of the cops who work on these guys? They find that pretty damn incredible."

"If you've got prints from this Thor, and he's got such a history, seems like you should be talking to him, not me."

"We've talked to him," Targent said. "Tried to, at least. He lawyered up right away. I'm wondering if maybe we asked the wrong questions."

"I wouldn't be surprised. None of your questions seem particularly bright to me."

"You've got the motive. Thor didn't, not that we can see, but you do. And when we prove you're connected to him, Perry? Shit's gonna turn pretty damn interesting, I'd say."

I leaned back and smiled at him. "Targent?"

"Yeah?"

"Get the hell out of my office. Immediately. You've been crowding the line with me, and today you jumped over it with both feet. I'm done tolerating your stupidity."

I stood up and went to the door, opened it, and stood there looking at him expectantly.

"You don't think we'll be able to connect you to him?" Targent said.

"You're done. Leave."

"I'm guessing we can make that connection," he said, starting for the door. "I'm guessing you and this guy have some serious history."

They brushed past me and went outside, and I slammed the door behind them. When I heard their car start up in the parking lot, I looked at the clock, wondering when Joe would be done with therapy, hoping he'd have some advice about how to handle a ghost with a Russian accent and translucent blue eyes.

CHAPTER

14

Joe's natural expression falls somewhere between grim and gloomy. To see him look troubled, then, is to see the kind of look that belongs only on the face of a man in a foxhole who is running out of ammunition and has an entire enemy battalion headed his way. It doesn't bolster your confidence, is what I'm saying.

"Thor," he said, hunched forward at his desk, flexing a thin metal ruler in his hands as if he were testing its strength, expecting to need it as a weapon at any moment.

"Yeah."

"Shit."

"Yeah."

"You didn't pay him to kill Jefferson, did you?"

"Um, no."

"Shit," he said again, and he pushed the ends of the ruler closer together, straining the metal's flexibility, and stared at me with that look of impending doom.

"I think we've agreed on that point," I said.

He dropped the ruler on the desk. "This development is more than a little disturbing, LP. This isn't a small town. The odds of Thor being brought in as a total coincidence are not good."

"Could it be a bluff?"

"You mean Targent is looking for ways to make you sweat and decided to push that button?"

"It's possible."

"Hell of a good guess on the right button, then. If he looks hard enough, he might find that his theoretical connection between you and Thor is a very real one. And that's going to raise some problems."

"If it's not a bluff, then what the hell *was* Thor doing in Jefferson's car?"

That question made Joe's frown deepen, and he reached for the ruler again, went back to bending it. "Any chance the guy who grabbed you off Chatfield the other night was Russian?"

I shook my head. "His speech was pure Midwest."

"Maybe it's simple. Jefferson defended Thor in court, something like that."

"Targent said they'd been unable to find any connection between Thor and Jefferson until they found me. If it was something as obvious as Jefferson handling work for Belov's crew, they would have turned that up right away."

Joe didn't say anything. I sat with my feet up on the desk and stared out the window. Someone had parked beneath us and left the stereo running, rap music thumping loud enough to make our windowpane tremble slightly.

"I suppose I could look Thor up."

Joe looked at me as if I were pushing on a pull door. "Brilliant, LP. The cops are looking to pin a murder on you based in part upon your association with that lunatic, an association that you denied, and now you think you should go *look him up*?"

I shrugged. "He could answer some questions, maybe."

"Or slit your throat, maybe."

The last time I'd seen Thor, he'd stabbed a hunting knife into another man's thigh. Perhaps Joe raised a valid point.

"So we push on as if we didn't even know this little detail?"

Joe scowled. "I don't like it, either, but I have to say that seems like the brightest option. You've got to remember that you're a suspect, LP. That's going to have to change some things about the way you operate."

We sat in silence for a few minutes, the rap music still booming beneath us, Joe still flexing that metal ruler.

"If I found Thor, got just five minutes with him for some questions," I began, but Joe cut me off with a groan.

"There are other things we can do, too. We still haven't checked out those phone calls."

"Joe, come on. With Thor involved, I think it's gone beyond worrying about phone records."

"Why? An hour ago you insisted those calls were significant. Now, because Thor's name is mentioned, you're wild to grab a gun and go after him? Do some *detective* work. That's how you get answers. Did you accomplish anything while I was gone other than getting your ass chewed by Targent?"

"I was waiting for your great wisdom."

"Good, because I'm ready to parcel some of it out. First thought is that you need to stay away from the Russian angle. Far away from it. You start nosing around with those boys, and Targent will catch wind of it. Second thought is that those calls in the middle of the night mattered. Don't give up on them just because Targent threw you a curve."

I nodded and retrieved the list of numbers. Seven total, from calls spaced over a five-year period. I gave the three most recent numbers to Joe, kept the three earlier numbers for myself. The seventh didn't matter—I already knew it was Matt Jefferson's cell phone.

It took us less than twenty minutes to break all the numbers. Some were easy, using a basic reverse lookup, and two others—pay phones—required our more sophisticated search databases.

"Both of the recent calls were made from pay phones," Joe said. "Not surprising, if those were the calls that freaked Jefferson out, this guy stepping back into his life. What do you have?"

"Two of the calls he received came from Fairview Park Hospital. They're four years old, though, and my guy last night made some reference to five years ago. I'm more interested in a number Jefferson called."

I explained the sequence to Joe: At nearly two in the

morning, Matt Jefferson had called his father, who then immediately made another call.

"And you got a match on the number he called?"

"Yeah. It returns to one Paul Brooks, of Geneva-on-the-
Lake."

"Mr. Brooks would seem to be our best option, then. Nobody at the hospital is going to talk to us about a four-year-
old phone call, and the last time I interviewed a pay phone it
didn't go well."

"You really are dispensing wisdom today, aren't you?"

"Geneva-on-the-Lake is a long drive. Let's hope the
guy's around. If not, we can wait on him."

"You want to drive out there? Don't think we should call
first?"

He shook his head. "Harder to blow us off in person."

"True."

He got to his feet and picked up his car keys. They belonged to a new Ford Taurus. His old Taurus had suffered a
little body damage back in the summer. A little body damage
of the sort a car can suffer when an assault rifle is unloaded
into it. True to form, Joe simply purchased a newer version
of the exact same car, in the exact same color. Word from
Ford was that the Taurus would soon be reaching the end of
its line. I didn't want to break that news to Joe, though. He's
a strong man, but news like that . . . no sure thing that he
could handle it.

"You driving?" I said.

"Yes."

"Wouldn't it make sense to let the guy with two good
arms drive?"

"Not when the guy is you. Besides, I need to put some
miles on the car, break it in. Still haven't hit a thousand."

"You've had the car for two months, Joe. How have you
not hit a thousand miles?"

"Haven't had to go anywhere. It's been two months since
you got yourself into trouble."

"A new record," I said, and then I followed him out the
door.

* * *

An hour later, Joe pulled onto 534 north as it became the lake road and led into the village of Geneva-on-the-Lake. In the summer, the place would have been buzzing, filled with families and tourists, but here in late October things were quiet. We drove through the village and onto a winding country road, glimpses of Lake Erie showing through the pines occasionally.

"We should be coming up on it," he said. "I hope the damn place has a mailbox with numbers. Drives me nuts when the mailboxes don't have numbers."

Turned out he didn't have to worry—the numbers were two feet high, painted on a huge wooden sign that proclaimed Paul Brooks's residence as BROOKS'S NORTHSHORE WINERY. Joe turned the Taurus into the drive and pulled into a long parking lot filled with cars. Behind the parking lot was a large log building, and behind that was the lake, looking hard and gray.

"Thought you said the number was residential," Joe said.

"That's what the computer told me."

"Well, let's go in and ask."

We got out of the car and walked into the building. Racks of wine lined one side of the room, with coolers of chilled wine on the opposite side and bins full of fancy cheeses and other gourmet items in the middle. In one corner, about a dozen people were gathered together, glasses in their hands, listening intently as a woman with red hair explained the "full-bodied richness" of what they were about to sample. A young, attractive girl in a black skirt and blouse approached us then, smiling.

"Do you gentlemen need any help?"

"It seems we're a bit confused," Joe said. "We thought this place was a private home. We're looking for Paul Brooks?"

She nodded. "Mr. Brooks owns the winery. And there is a private home—you just needed to go right when you came through the gate instead of left. It's tough to see with all the pine trees."

We thanked her, walked back out to the car, and followed her instructions. The house was maybe two hundred yards down the drive, a good distance from the winery, and the girl was right: The pines screened it from the parking lot completely. The construction matched the winery, though; it was a big log home with a green-shingled roof, looking every bit the perfect lakeside retreat. We walked up to the front porch, past a black BMW that was parked in the drive, and knocked on the door. About ten seconds later, a good-looking young guy opened it. He couldn't have been much past thirty, wearing a white dress shirt untucked over blue jeans and leather moccasins. Between the outfit and the perfect face and the thick brown hair that hung down almost to his collar, he looked like he should be a model for one of those "outfitter" catalogs that pretend they're marketing clothing for outdoorsmen but really sell only to men who live behind computers.

"Can I help you?"

Joe and I passed him our licenses. He didn't show either the distrust or the childish excitement that most people give you when they see the PI license, just nodded.

"Are you Paul Brooks?" I asked.

"Yes. What do you need to talk to me about?" He had noted the damage to my face but immediately looked away. Manners.

"A five-year-old phone call," I said.

"Excuse me?"

"We're looking into the background of a man who was recently murdered. Five years ago, he called this house at two in the morning on—"

"The Fourth of July," Brooks said. "That's what you're talking about, isn't it? It would be five years now."

Joe and I exchanged a glance while I nodded.

"That's it. The call was on the fifth, but it was basically the night of the fourth."

Paul Brooks sighed and pushed the door open wider. "I think we ought to sit down for this one."

CHAPTER

15

He took us out to a cedar deck that overlooked the woods and a private beach on Lake Erie. The water banged gently against the shore, and out beyond it the clouds were thickening. It made my own beautiful view of the stoplight on Lorain and the small-engine-repair shop across from it seem inferior.

"So, Paul, what can you tell us?" I asked.

He shook his head. "Let's not get in such a rush. I still don't know what interested you in the phone call to begin with."

I gave it to him as concisely as I could, saying simply that we'd been employed by Alex Jefferson's widow to look into the circumstances surrounding his murder and his son's death, and that those circumstances had landed us here.

"I'd heard about Alex Jefferson being killed," he said when I was through. "Didn't know about the son, though."

"Haven't been reading your paper."

He smiled. "Guess I'm a few days behind. But what makes the phone call significant to you?"

"Matt called his father before two in the morning, and his father then called your house. We're wondering why."

"You're going to love the reason."

"Yeah?"

"The calls were made because someone was murdered on my father's property and Jefferson's son saw it happen."

It was quiet for a few seconds then, Joe and I waiting on Brooks, who was staring out at the lake. The beach in front of his house seemed to continue all the way up to the winery. Voices and laughter were audible, but we couldn't see any people because of the pine trees.

"Can you provide a little more detail than that?" Joe said.

"I assume you know of my father?" Brooks asked in response.

Joe and I looked at each other, then shook our heads in unison. Brooks frowned at us, slighted.

"Fenton Brooks? Brooks Biomedical? That mean anything to you?"

"Stents," Joe said.

Brooks nodded. "Yes, the company makes stents, although we also manufacture many other medical products."

"But your father made his money on the stents, right?" Joe said.

"A good portion of it, at least." Brooks looked annoyed, as if he found Joe's question in poor taste. "The company has gone on to much greater things, though. My father passed away a few years ago. Cancer."

"I'm sorry."

For a moment it was silent, and then Brooks cleared his throat.

"Okay, so now you understand the situation. My father owned a large company, had lots of employees, attorneys, advisors. He bought this winery as a side venture and liked the location enough that he built this house as a summer retreat. He used to have parties in the summer for friends, colleagues, that sort of thing. Five years ago, he held a Fourth of July party. There were about one hundred people out here, maybe more."

"Including Matt Jefferson."

"Yes, he was here. Alex Jefferson was, too, although he went home much earlier in the night. He was one of my father's attorneys, you know."

"We did not."

"Well, he was. His son was in law school then, I believe. A

few years younger than me? That sounds right. At any rate, he was here, and I gather he felt a bit out of place. The crowd began to thin out around twelve, but the man Matt Jefferson had come with was drunk and hanging around, and so he had to stay, too."

"Who was that man?"

"Another one of the company's attorneys, James Simon. Matt was working for him, some sort of internship."

"So what happened?"

"Okay. Well, a few people stayed late—you know how that goes when you've got an open bar. Simon was drunk, and Matt got bored or annoyed or something and went up the beach, back toward the winery. We'd had a catered dinner up there earlier, so Matt knew where he was going. Found a guy and a girl up on the deck, apparently engaged in a little late-night illicit behavior. Matt figured they were entitled to their privacy and turned around and started back up the beach. But then he got the impression that the girl was resisting. Heard her shout or something. So he decided to go back in case there was a problem. When he got there he couldn't see the girl, and the guy was booking around the corner of the building. Matt ran up onto the deck and found the girl. Clothes half off, and dead. She'd been strangled."

The clouds had made the temperature dip, and Paul Brooks wasn't wearing anything over his thin shirt, but he looked warm enough, sitting there watching our faces with a hint of satisfaction, a storyteller pleased with his ability to capture the audience.

"So what happened?" Joe said again.

"What do you think happened? The cops were called, obviously. Interviewed Matt and everyone else. Matt was pretty upset by it, I guess, and that was understandable. He wanted to talk to his dad. I think maybe he took the police questioning the wrong way. He called his dad, and his dad told him just to answer the questions and try to help. Then Alex called the house and asked for my father, making sure Matt had been honest about the situation."

"That's more than we were bargaining for with that phone call," Joe said.

"Pretty intriguing stuff, but I don't see what it could possibly have to do with Alex Jefferson's murder or the son's suicide," Brooks said. "I'd have to say you're grasping for straws on that one."

"Who was the victim?" I said. "Did she belong with your party?"

"In a way. She worked for the caterer my father had hired for the party. She was only twenty years old, I think. A girl, really. They'd been going back and forth between the house and the winery, and she was left to clean up there alone. Not a good decision."

"And the guy who killed her?"

Brooks hooked one moccasin-clad foot over his knee. "Someone she'd gone out with a time or two, then tried to dump. He was a real loser, criminal record nine miles long. Lived in a trailer maybe three miles up the road from the winery. Easy for him to come down that night."

"He was arrested?"

"Arrested, tried, convicted. He's still in jail."

"You know his name?"

"Andy Doran. The girl he killed was named Monica Heath."

"Quite a story," Joe said.

"Quite a story," Brooks agreed. "I imagine that answers your question about the phone call. What I can't imagine, though, is that it will help you with the current problem."

"You never know."

Brooks looked skeptical. "I guess not. The whole situation was quite an embarrassment to my father. I mean, Andy Doran was certainly not an invited guest, but still . . . the girl was working at our party, you know?"

"Nobody else saw or heard anything?" Joe said. "No other witnesses except for Matt Jefferson?"

"None."

"So Matt Jefferson gave a positive ID on this guy, Doran?" I said.

Brooks started to nod, then frowned and shook his head.

"To be honest, I can't remember. I feel like he recognized a car, but not the actual guy? I'm not sure."

"Pretty tough to convict someone with nothing but one eyewitness."

"They had a lot more than that. Turned up hard evidence at the guy's trailer, and then he got himself into all sorts of trouble lying to the cops. Changed his story six times before the trial, or something like that."

"You said Matt called his dad because he took offense to the questioning," Joe said. "What exactly did you mean?"

"Him being the only witness, I think maybe the police were more aggressive with the questions than he thought they should be. What I mean is, I think he felt—for a little while at least—like he was a suspect."

"No kidding," Joe said. "Like *he* was a suspect."

Brooks saw where he was going and grinned. "Don't get ahead of yourself, Detective. The right guy went to jail. Check the case out yourself, but I'm pretty sure you'll agree with the jury."

"How well did you know the Jeffersons?" I asked.

He shrugged. "Casual acquaintance. My father knew them better."

"What did you think of the two of them? Alex and his son?"

"Didn't know them well enough to make any sort of a judgment, really. But it would appear they were ill-fated, don't you think?"

CHAPTER

16

We drove back down the winding road without seeing another car.

"And you wanted to give up on the phone call," Joe said. "Go chasing Thor around the city, waiting to be killed."

"The phone call was a good idea. I'm glad I thought of it."

"Thought of it and then decided to forget it."

"That's why I need you around—to keep my own genius focused."

He smiled and shook his head.

"It feels like something," I said, "but it could be nothing."

"What's that?"

"All of this—the girl's murder, the cops questioning Jefferson's son."

"Be a hell of a surprise to me if it's not worth something. Jefferson and his murderer both referenced this phone call from the son. We trace the call back and find the kid was a murder witness? That matters."

"Okay, but how? Sounds like this Doran guy was good for the crime. Hard evidence against him, a story filled with lies, and the kid putting him at the scene. Where does Alex Jefferson come into play there?"

"No way to know until we get into the old case, see what really happened. The obvious guess is that they set him up."

"Looking at Jefferson's kid as a murderer might be a bit overzealous."

He shot me a quick glance before looking back up the road. "You're the one who told me the kid was front and center in this thing, and your boy from last night came with a grudge."

"Indeed he did. But Doran's still in prison. So scratch him from the list of grudge suspects, and who do you have left from this scenario?"

"Maybe the guy who came after Jefferson's family is connected to Doran. A brother or a close friend or something."

"Someone who cares about Doran enough to kill for him but is restrained enough to wait five years before moving into action?"

Joe sighed. "Okay, the time lag is a problem. Still, it's something to consider."

"And we'll consider it. I'm just saying we don't know much yet in the way of facts."

"We should try to get in to see Doran. Most of the guys doing time for crimes they pretend not to be guilty of will talk to anyone looking at their case, let alone the guys who *really* aren't guilty."

"Not a bad idea."

It was quiet for a minute, and then I looked over and saw that Joe was grinning.

"What?"

"Sign of the apocalypse," he said.

"Huh?"

"You just cautioned *me* against getting overzealous. Told me to slow down, get some more facts."

He was still laughing at that when we made it back to the highway.

We got back to the office just after five. Joe pulled into the lot and shut off the engine and reached for the door handle. He went across his body with his right arm, which told me that his left arm had to be aching from driving.

I'd just closed my own door when I heard another one open and turned to see Targent climbing out of a Crown Victoria that was parked on the street just up from our building. He was talking on a cell phone, but he lifted his free hand in a congenial wave.

"Shit." I pointed at Targent. "Doesn't this guy have anybody else to talk to?"

Joe and I waited beside the car while Targent wrapped up his conversation, snapped his phone shut, and walked over to join us.

"Should we go upstairs?" he said.

"I don't think so. You spend any more time in our office and I'm going to start charging you rent."

He gave me a wan smile and nodded at Joe. "Mr. Pritchard. How you doing?"

"Fine."

"Where you guys been?"

"Nowhere exciting," Joe said. "Now I'd like to get some dinner. Didn't have lunch, and I'm hungry."

"I hear that. Hate to stand between a man and his stomach, too, so I won't take up much of your time. I just thought I should drop by after my last conversation with Mrs. Jefferson. She indicated that you were now, um, investigating on her behalf?"

"That's right," I said.

"I'll go ahead and tell you I'm not real enamored with that idea."

"Didn't figure you would be."

"I'm torn on how to handle it. Part of me would like to cut you off at the knees, tell you this isn't going to happen. Another part tells me it's not worth fighting you."

"Listen to that voice."

Targent had his eyes on the ground and was using the fingers of his right hand to rotate the wedding ring on his left. That impenetrable calm surrounded him again. Even today, when I'd told him about the attack and admitted to not calling him when it had happened, he'd been cool, or at least he'd gotten the cool back quickly. In my experience the unflappable cops always made suspects the most uncomfortable, giving off the sense that they were a hundred chess moves ahead. Joe was one of that breed. I wasn't close.

"Okay," he said. "Maybe you're right. Maybe I should just let you do your thing. We'll stay out of each other's way, right? Share information when we get it? A regular team."

I stood and stared at him, wondering what he was really thinking, why he was here, going with the friendly act.

"Sure, Targent. We'll do that. A team, like you said."

He nodded. "That's real good news. Damn neighborly offer on your part."

"I thought so. Now are we done?"

"Well, not quite. I'm going to need another minute, I'm afraid. Got a call this afternoon from Lieutenant Brewer of the Indiana State Police. Man had a strange tale to share."

Targent reached into his back pocket and withdrew a piece of paper. He took his time unfolding it, then smoothed it against his leg and handed it to me.

It was a booking sheet from the Brown County Jail, where I'd spent the night on my visit. The photograph was of a middle-aged man with a poorly trimmed mustache, nobody I'd seen before, and the charge was interference. He'd been booked about six hours earlier.

"Stan Meyers." I looked up at Targent. "This guy supposed to mean something to me?"

"You mean a lot to him, at least."

"How?"

He took the booking sheet out of my hand, folded it, and slid it back into his pocket. "Mr. Meyers is a private detective in Indiana. Does that jog your memory?"

"Nope."

"He was arrested yesterday. Tried to bribe a records clerk with the state police into releasing closed reports." He paused a beat. "Reports concerning the Matt Jefferson death investigation."

"Suicide," I said.

"Death investigation. Results inconclusive as of the last time I spoke with Lieutenant Brewer."

"Okay. I'll give you that. What does this Meyers guy have to do with me?"

"Kind of surprised to hear you ask that question," Targent said. "Considering you hired him."

I didn't issue an immediate denial. Maybe that made Targent think I'd admit to it; his eyes narrowed and he looked excited for a moment.

"You remember now?" he said. "Temporary amnesia fading away?"

"I didn't hire this guy to do anything. I've never heard of him."

"You have any proof that Lincoln hired him?" Joe said. "Or is everybody just taking his word for it because he seems so damn reliable?"

"Meyers named him immediately. Told Brewer and another detective that Perry called him the day after Matt Jefferson's suicide and attempted to employ him to watch the investigation, monitor the cops."

"So the answer to my question is—"

"Not yet. That's the answer. No proof yet, but Brewer's working on it."

Targent turned from Joe back to me. "He said you stressed that his efforts be hidden from police, and when he heard that he declined. Said then you called back, repeated the request, and told him you'd put ten thousand cash in the mail if he just tried to get the latest reports. Old Mr. Meyers doesn't sound like the finest of investigators; Brewer said he moonlights as a ten-dollar-an-hour security guard. So the ten grand convinced him, is what he said. That was a bad decision, of course—the dumb bastard's probably going to lose his license now."

My throat had tightened around the most unpleasant of dry tickles, as if there were a blade of grass caught there.

"You know this is a lie," I said. "You have to know that, Targent."

He held his hands up, spread them wide. "You shouldn't be telling *me* that, you should be telling Mr. Meyers. He's convinced that he's working on your behalf. Brewer wants you back down there. Says he's going to throw the same charges at you. I cautioned him that with the cash payment, this may be tougher to prove than he realizes. I anticipated your, uh, brilliant defense of total denial. Warned him that you're less than forthright, less than cooperative."

"You have no evidence. Brewer has no evidence. You've got a secondhand account and ten grand in cash that could easily have come from Brewer himself."

"They recovered the envelope. Postmarked in Cleveland."

I was silent.

Targent smiled. "That concerns you?"

"Not really. I was just thinking that maybe you're the one who mailed the cash."

"Of course. You're the conspiracy victim, right? Sorry if I keep forgetting that."

"I don't have ten grand to spare, trust me, Targent. You want to see my bank account history, go for it."

"Ah, but Alex Jefferson had some cash, and fifty grand of it is missing. Cash withdrawal, not seen since."

"So, what, you think he paid Lincoln to kill him?" Joe said. "Makes a lot of sense."

Targent shook his head. "Remember that someone could be extorting the Jefferson family, Mr. Pritchard. Where'd that money go? Possibly to the person who laid on the pressure."

"What pressure would Lincoln have to lay on?"

"I was hoping he'd explain that."

"This is important," I said. "If someone actually hired this guy, pretended to be me . . . that's a pretty damn big deal, Targent, and finding out who it was will be—"

"Someone pretended to be you. That's what you're telling us."

I nodded. "Yeah. I didn't hire him, and if he's serious in thinking that I did, what other option is there?"

"I suppose that's it. Either someone's pretending to be you, or you're lying. Those are the options."

"You can scratch the second one."

"So what's the point? Huh? Why pretend to be you? Why pay out ten thousand dollars to a PI when there's no guarantee he'd even be caught? If he just snagged the reports and sent them on back to you—I'm sorry, back to your *imposter*—then what would have been accomplished?"

"I don't know."

He smiled at me and nodded. "Of course you don't. Of course. I'm beginning to feel sorry for you, Perry. Because if you're not lying to me, than you're the most clueless son of a bitch I've ever seen. Makes my heart ache for you. But, being a kindhearted guy, I'm going to help you out. All those things you don't understand? All those questions? I'm going to explain them. Every last one. I'm going to do that just for you."

He nodded at Joe, then turned and moved for his car, walking briskly and whistling, the sound teasing the air between us.

CHAPTER

17

You can stand on a riverbank and study the water and think it looks languid and warm, inviting even, well worth a try. Then you dive in, and things surprise you—the cold, the current, the snags underfoot.

That's how I felt now. Karen's request that I track down her dead husband's son had been a safe enough thing to accept. All that money for such a routine task. Sure, there was a clear note of warning—I was on the police suspect list, no matter how far down. But I'd ignored that over a simple tenet I'd explained to people constantly when I was a cop: If you've done nothing wrong, you have nothing to fear.

I'd done nothing wrong, but with each passing hour it felt like I should have more to fear. The latest, this discovery by Brewer, changed everything. Before, I'd been dealing with nothing more than coincidences. While they were a pain in the ass, they could be dismissed, at least in my mind. Now that was gone. Someone had impersonated me, invested ten thousand dollars into the effort.

"It started when you went to Indiana," Joe said. We were sitting on the trunk of his car in my parking lot. Targent had gone.

"Seems to."

"Cops came to see you when Jefferson died, then they went away and nothing pointed back to you. But when you went down to find that kid, something changed. You attracted someone's attention there."

"Yeah—the cops'."

"Somebody else, LP." He was rubbing his shoulder, and I saw for the first time how tired he looked. It had been a long day for him, two hours of driving on top of a therapy session.

"Go home, Joe," I said. "Get some dinner, take a painkiller, relax."

He stopped massaging his shoulder and shook his head. "Nah, I'm good. We ought to spend some time on the computers, look into this Doran guy, try to set up an interview. It's clear someone is on the offensive with you. Be a good idea if you started preparing a defense."

"Doran's not going anywhere. He'll be in the same cell tomorrow as he is today. It'll hold till morning."

Proof of his fatigue showed when he nodded and gave in. "Okay. We'll get back at it early, though."

"Yeah. And thanks again."

He waved me off and opened his car door. "Want a ride?"

"I'll walk it and see you in the morning. We'll make progress tomorrow. Already did today."

"What do you know, the day you start making progress just happens to be the same day I get involved."

"Too bad you didn't get involved a little earlier," I said. "Then maybe my face wouldn't look like it was run over by a truck."

He got in the car, started to pull the door shut, and then stopped. "Remember when I told you I didn't like your decision to burn that photograph?"

"Yes."

"I think I'll retract that statement," he said, and then he closed the door.

I went home, scrambled some eggs for dinner, and ate quickly with the intention of going down to the gym to work out when I was done. I gave up on that idea while I washed the dishes. I didn't have the energy for a workout, and I

A WELCOME GRAVE

didn't want to be alone tonight. My thoughts had been on
Alex Jefferson and Karen and Targent, but Amy was invad-
ing them regularly. I dried my hands on a dish towel,
grabbed the phone, and called her.

"You around tonight?"

"Maybe," she said. "If by 'around' you mean am I willing
to sit on the couch and drink a beer, yes. If by 'around' you
mean am I willing to go out somewhere, then, no."

"Homebody mood, I take it?"

"Already changed into comfortable clothes. No way you
lure me out into the world after that point in the evening unless it's for something damn relaxed."

"I was thinking of a toga party."

"That's what I like most about you, Lincoln. The high level
of sophistication."

She came in wearing old jeans and a sweatshirt—not the designer jeans and the sweatshirt made of pima cotton or whatever the hell it was Karen had worn, but the kind you dig out
of your closet and throw on when a night turns cold.

"I've got Beck's and Budweiser," I said. "Take your pick."

"You ever going to make it farther into the alphabet with
your beer selection?"

"Don't see the need."

"Beck's."

I handed her a beer and opened another for myself. When
I turned from the refrigerator she did a double take, and I remembered for the first time in a few hours how my face
looked.

"Oh, yeah. I haven't told you about my evening, have I?"

She reached out and touched the skin under my eye, then
winced and pulled her hand back.

"That looks *really* bad, Lincoln."

"Didn't feel much better."

"Tell me what happened."

We went into the living room and sat down on the couch,
and I drank some of the beer and told her about the past

twenty-four hours. When I got to the part about Thor, her already concerned face took on a whole new gravity.

"Thor's involved? The same Thor who makes men disappear like it's his day job?"

"Technically, I think it *is* his day job."

"Not funny."

"No."

"If the police connect you to him, Lincoln . . ."

"Yeah. It won't go well. But right now Thor's not as unsettling to me as this PI in Indiana. Somebody sent him ten grand in cash while pretending to be me, Amy. That's a sizable investment. I'm wondering what sort of a return they're looking for."

"You in jail," she said.

"Blunt."

"But true?"

"I don't know. If it involved Alex Jefferson it would make more sense. Whoever *did* kill him would want to point the cops elsewhere. But his son committed suicide."

"The two are so connected, though. If you can be made to look guilty for the son's death . . ."

"The father's takes care of itself," I said, and I felt that blade of grass in my throat again.

She stood up and went into the kitchen and came back with two fresh beers. We stayed there on the couch and talked and drank, maybe an hour of it, talked about Thor and Jefferson and Targent. I loved talking to her. Needed to do it. She'd become that person in my life now, the one I knew would be there to discuss the difficult things, providing better answers than the walls of the empty apartment—my usual sounding board—ever did. I'd gone a while without someone like that, and although I could do it again, I didn't want to. I was aware of her beside me on the couch in a way that sometimes made it hard to focus on what was being said, my mind led away by the curve of her hip against the couch and the trace of perfume she wore.

She was asking something about Targent when I interrupted.

"I was about three seconds from kissing you the other night when you told me a friendship is the only thing that can work for us."

Her eyes widened. "Wow. That was an abrupt conversation shift."

"Sorry."

It was quiet for a moment, and then she said, "Three seconds away, huh?"

"Maybe less."

"Damn. If I just talked a little slower." She laughed, but it was awkward, tense.

"I probably shouldn't have said that. You seemed pretty set on the conclusion you'd reached while I was down in Indiana. And maybe you're right."

"Maybe *I'm* right? I thought that decision was your baby, Lincoln."

"I know. But since when do you give me any credit for intelligent decision-making? You know better than that."

She started to say something, then stopped and shook her head.

"What?" I said.

"It's just interesting timing. I get upset with you for this bizarre relationship we've developed, and then you decide you're going to make a move for the first time? Damn, if I'd known that would've worked all along . . ."

"It wasn't because you got upset."

"I won't debate that with you, but I could."

"I know."

Her gaze was intense. "So you were ready to make a courageous first move, and then you chose to abort the attempt."

"Yeah, the news you had kind of killed that."

"I'll be kicking myself over that, of course."

"Listen to her lie."

"Truer words were never spoken, Lincoln."

There was a comfortable silence for a few seconds, and then I leaned over and slid my hand behind her neck and pulled her in and kissed her. She returned it, gently but passionately, and then broke away. Her eyes could have been happy or sad. Probably somewhere in between.

"Now who's not being fair?" she said.

I nodded. "It's not fair. I understand that, Amy."

Her face was inches from mine, her hair soft against my hand. "So stop it."

"Okay," I said, and then I kissed her again. She separated from me once, said, "Damn you, Lincoln," and then we were back at it, twisting on the couch so that she was above me, her body resting lightly against mine, her hair hanging down against my face.

Her fingers slid over my shoulders and up to my neck, and when her hand moved on me a quick line of electricity seemed to dance along my spine. She pushed her hands through my hair, and when her fingers crossed over the lumps on the back of my skull, a surge of pain passed through, a momentary reminder of Alex Jefferson and Karen and Targent and a nameless man with a grudge and a gun. Then I was sliding that old sweatshirt off of her, my hands gliding over her small, smooth back, and the pain and the problems and all of the rest of it faded away.

Later, in my bedroom, she lay warm beside me, her leg hooked over my knee and her head nestled against my neck. Her breathing was slow and easy, moving toward sleep, but I was awake and alert, watching shadows slide across the ceiling as cars passed along the avenue.

"Remind me why we never did that before," I said.

"I used to have standards," she said, her breath hot on my neck, and then she bit my shoulder gently.

CHAPTER

18

The phone rang, shrill and insistent. I lifted my head and blinked, searching for the phone in the darkness. Beside me, Amy stirred but didn't wake, sleeping as if she had a winter's hibernation ahead of her. I pushed myself up with the heel of my hand and reached over her and grabbed the phone from its base. Then I climbed out of the bed and walked into the hallway, squinting to make out the number in the display as it rang a third time. Karen's house.

I answered the phone just as my eyes found the clock in the living room and saw that it was ten minutes to three.

"Karen, what's wrong?"

"He called me, Lincoln. Just now." Her voice was terse and frightened.

"Who did?"

"The man who killed my husband! He asked me how much money Matthew would have inherited. I started yelling at him, I was hysterical almost—"

"Slow down, Karen." She was talking so fast I could hardly understand her.

"He told me I didn't have to die," she said, and this time the words were slow and clear.

"What else?"

"He said that all he wanted was whatever had been coming to Matthew, provided that it was reasonable. He actually said that. Provided that it was reasonable. Then he said that all further instructions were going to come through you."

"*What?*"

"He said I was supposed to tell you that you have a conference call coming on the phone in the gym. He told me to call you immediately and tell you that."

I was standing in the kitchen now, the tile floor cold on my bare feet. "He told you I had a conference call coming on the phone in the gym."

"Yes. Lincoln, what—"

"I'll call you back, Karen."

Amy was pushed up on one arm when I went back into the bedroom, her eyes bleary with sleep but concerned.

"Who was that?"

"Karen. My friend from the other night has apparently requested that I take a phone call in my gym."

Now she sat all the way up, holding the sheet to her chest. "Lincoln, do you really think you should—"

"I've got to," I said. "It'll just be a phone call. He doesn't want to kill me."

He hadn't the last time we'd met, at least, but of course I had spent the past twenty-four hours ignoring his instructions.

"I'm going down with you."

"No, you're *not*." I pulled a shirt over my head and looked at her. "Stay here, Amy. Stay here, and if it sounds like there's anything wrong, call the police."

I went into the extra bedroom and got my Glock out and checked the load. When I stepped back into the hall, she was standing in the door of my bedroom, a pool of light from the street at her feet.

"It'll be fine," I said, and then I left.

I was still barefoot, and the pavement was hard and cold as I crossed to the gym, got the key in the lock, and opened the door. Everything was still, the way it should be at three in the morning. Standing with my back to the wall, I slid my hand around until I found the light switch and got the lights in the office turned on. Then I pivoted, keeping low, and pushed inside, sweeping the room with the barrel of my gun. Empty.

The overhead lights in the gym had been turned off by the last member to leave, but a ring of low-wattage emergency lamps around the room offered a dim glow. You never want a twenty-four-hour facility to be entirely dark, even when it's empty.

I wanted to check the rest of the building, but I also wanted to remain close to the phone. The phone won out, and I sat down on the edge of the desk with the Glock in my hand, waiting.

When the phone out in the gym rang, I almost emptied my clip into the wall. I'd been ready for the desk phone, so having the sound come from someplace else caught me off guard. There's a phone on the wall in the weight room for members to use, but it's a separate number from the office line. It rang again, and I stood up and took a deep breath, rocking the gun in my hand.

"All right, asshole," I said aloud. "I'm coming."

I was halfway across the weight room when the front window exploded. Glass blew into the room, and with it came cold air and the staccato rattle of a semi-automatic weapon. I hit the ground and rolled to my left, trying to push myself behind the concrete pillar that stood in the middle of the room and supported the weight of the building. Bullets shredded the wall behind me, nicking off chunks of stone and shattering metal and glass. I got all the way behind the pillar, pressed my back against it, and ducked my head and put my forearms against my ears as the deafening rattle continued, the wail of the alarm from the broken window still not drowning out the gunfire. Bullets drilled into the pillar and decimated the paper towel dispenser attached to the opposite side, shards of plastic scattering around me. There was a brief pause, and then more bullets were emptied into the room, an east-to-west sweep that rippled past me.

Then it was gone. The alarm had stopped even before the

gunfire, taken out by one of the bullets, apparently. I lowered my arms and held the Glock with both hands, a shooter's grip, preparing to turn around. It took me a few seconds to convince myself to do it.

When I spun around the pillar, all I could see was the empty street in front of me. The room was covered with stone and glass and other debris, but with the window gone, there was nothing out there but the street. No cars, no gunmen.

The phone on the wall rang again. The waves of sound trapped in my ears from the shooting and the alarm almost kept me from hearing it, but as soon as I did I moved across the room, not caring that the last time the phone had rung it had been a prelude to the gunfire.

I picked up the receiver and put it to my ear but didn't say anything. When the man on the other end of the line spoke, I could hardly hear him, but that was probably due more to the echoing ringing in my ears than to a soft voice. Even so, I knew the speaker. He'd just left the same impression on my gym that he had on my face.

"Still alive," he said. "Good. I shot high and wide, but with all those bullets, you never know."

"When I find you—"

"Shut up, Lincoln. You're not going to find me, and if you try, you die. I've got a nasty feeling that's what will happen here, eventually, but you have no one but yourself to blame for that. You were given an opportunity to step back. An opportunity you should have taken but did not. Next time you won't even have time to regret that."

"You'll be the one talking about regrets, you piece of shit. You shouldn't have shot high and wide."

"Damn, but you get your confidence back quickly." His tone was light, carefree. "Jefferson's son was due a nice chunk of cash before his unfortunate passing. Something in the neighborhood of five million dollars, probably. Could have been more, could have been less, but we're going to be fair, in the interest of time, and ask for a mere three million. Tell the wife to get it ready to move, and we'll be in touch to tell her where to move it and when to move it. Do that, and maybe nobody else dies."

He continued before I had a chance to respond to that.

"Go ahead and call the cops, Lincoln. You disappointed me today, running to them so quickly. My opinion of you was clearly set too high. Go ahead and call them now. It's not going to stop a thing."

Then all I could hear was the hum of the dead line after he hung up, and the sirens of police on their way, and Amy screaming my name from outside.

CHAPTER

19

I called Targent myself. The CPD cops that showed up were clueless to the situation, and the more detail I got into with them, the more complicated it was all going to become. I wanted to call Karen, too, but the cops were in my face, asking questions, and I didn't have a chance. Targent arrived maybe forty-five minutes after the first squad car got there. If my shot-up gym cast any doubt on my guilt for him, he didn't show it. He just stalked around the place, growling and grunting and saying little while I gave him the scenario. His eyes took in Amy, who was standing in the corner of the gym answering questions from another officer, but he didn't ask anything about her, not even to see if she could corroborate my version of the night.

"I've got video cameras that record everything in the weight room," I said. "Have to have them, for insurance, since there's no staff here during off-hours. If you need to verify my story, make sure I didn't stand on the sidewalk and cut loose into my own building, go ahead."

I went back to the office and got the current tape out of the videocassette machine that the cameras fed into and gave it to him. He took the tape without a word, spoke in hushed tones to the sergeant who was in control of the scene, and then told me he'd be talking to Karen to verify my story.

"The good news is, I wasn't hurt," I said.

"You know what's curious?"

"What?"

"That this guy wants to go through you. I mean, I've worked some extortion cases before. You want to squeeze money from somebody, you usually just go right to squeezing them. But this guy, he calls Karen Jefferson to tell her he's going to be calling *you*? Then he gives *you* the price tag he's after?"

I stared at him and then turned back to my gym and swept an arm around it. "You see this place, Targent? You really think anyone would open up on his own business with a semiauto just to preserve a lie?"

"Depends on the individual," he said, "and the magnitude of the lie. You get the right mix, and, yes, I can believe it."

I shook my head. "Watch the damn surveillance tape. Watch it, and then you'll either believe me or give me an Oscar."

My request for Targent had only increased the curiosity of the city cops, but I told them any elaboration on the situation would have to come from him. They milled around for a while longer, taking pictures and trying to dig bullets out of the walls. Two of the uniformed guys helped me clean up, sweeping the glass and stone fragments up and dumping them into a large trash can. The free weights had survived with just a few nicks, but a couple of the stationary bikes had taken direct hits, and their computers were destroyed. The damage would be in the thousands.

The cops finally finished with Amy, and she stood in the corner, arms wrapped around herself, shivering in her thin sweatshirt. All the cold air was pushing into the gym, no window in place to keep it out. I went over and rubbed my hands over her upper arms, trying to warm her. She attempted to smile at me, but it didn't work. She looked scared.

"Go home, Amy," I said. "You're going to get sick, standing around like this. Go home and get warm. I'm sorry."

"You don't need to be sorry, Lincoln. I'm just . . ." She

shook her head. "I went to sleep and you were there, right? And I woke up and you were gone and talking on the phone, and then two minutes later I'm all alone and someone is shooting at the building . . ."

"I know. I'm sorry. It all happened pretty fast. I didn't know what to expect."

Her eyes were on the cops across from us. "This is all about Karen?"

"It's about her husband."

She took a deep breath and nodded.

"Night to remember, huh?" I said.

She managed a weak smile. "In a lot of ways, right? In a lot of ways."

"Go home and get warm."

She nodded again and reached up and hugged me hard. I kissed her once, and then she stepped away and walked to the door, pausing to say something to the sergeant, probably to ask him if it was okay if she left. She turned at the door and looked back at me.

"Hey, Lincoln."

"Yeah?"

"The fireworks that are supposed to happen when you're with someone for the first time? They work a lot better as a metaphor."

I laughed, and it was as if something inside of me had just been loosened, knowing that she could still manage a joke about all of it.

"I'll keep that in mind," I said, and then she left.

By the time they were all gone, it was past five. I found a large sheet of plastic and a roll of duct tape and set to work covering the hole in the wall where the front window had been. As I worked, I thought about Amy, and my anger toward whoever had done this grew. It should have been a wonderful night. Had been, for a few hours. But they wouldn't even allow me that. Amy had gone home cold and tired and scared. I wondered if these bastards knew that, if they'd watched Amy's lonely ride home and laughed.

Once the window was covered and as much of the debris as possible cleaned up, I sat in the gym office with my feet on the desk, drinking coffee and staring at the damage. I'd hung a CLOSED DUE TO VANDALISM sign on the door. When seven o'clock came, I called Grace and told her what had happened and that she wouldn't need to come in for the day. After dealing with her worried questions and attempts at mothering, I managed to hang up and call Joe. He listened to the story in total silence, and when I was done he asked just one question.

"You say Amy was there?"

I sighed. "Yes, Amy was there."

"Slumber party?"

"Joseph—"

"No, no, don't worry, I won't pry. I just have trouble believing it. Seems to me she'd have good taste, and your taste has certainly never been so impressive before."

"I'll see you at the office." I hung up on him, but I was smiling when I did it.

The next call went to my insurance agent. It was still too early for him to be in, but that was good—I wanted to break the news on his answering machine. Explaining that I had a claim due to an assault on my building would be tedious.

At ten to eight, I finished my coffee and walked into the weight room again, taking one last look before I went down to the office. The sleep I'd lost wasn't tiring me yet, not in the face of the anger I felt as I surveyed the bullet-riddled equipment.

I'd left the lights off to help make it clear that the gym was closed. The plastic sheet I'd spread over the broken front window let some sunlight in, but it came through filtered and gray, the plastic not being completely transparent. Now, as I stood in the middle of the weight room and stared at it, a figure developed in front of the plastic sheet. The milky cast kept any facial features from being distinguishable, but I could see the figure was a man, and he seemed to be peering through the plastic, searching the interior of the gym. For a reason I could not begin to articulate, I felt a wave of dread, a quick sense that the man on the other side of the plastic was a dangerous one.

Taking two steps toward the wall, I bent and picked up one of the curl bars. It was fifteen pounds of solid metal, and if I swung it accurately, it would make a hell of a weapon. Even as I twisted the bar in my hands, shifting it so I gripped the end like a baseball bat, the man on the opposite side of the plastic pushed hard against the edge of the sheet, and the duct tape that held it in place began to peel back from the wall. A second later that entire side ripped free, and the man stepped right through the window and into the gym.

His name was Thor. The brief, seemingly unfounded sense of danger I'd had when his silhouette appeared was not so absurd, after all. Thor—I still knew no last name— was probably the deadliest man in the city. I might have denied knowing him the previous day, but the recognition as he stepped through that window affected me in a way few things could. Although I'd met him rather unwillingly, it had been an important acquaintance for me. The kind of acquaintance I would not forget, no matter how long I might live. The kind of acquaintance that sometimes made sleep a hard thing to find.

"Lincoln Perry," he said, his voice soft and controlled and without menace, the way it always would be, no matter what the moment, no matter what the stakes.

"Thor."

His ghostly eyes took in the bar in my hands with a disinterested glance and then returned to my face. He wore black slacks and a long-sleeved black shirt, and everything about him was unremarkable other than those eyes.

"It would seem," he said, looking around the gym quickly but without missing a single disturbed item, "that you have had some trouble."

I looked around the gym again, too. "I've made some enemies."

"That is something you appear to do regularly." There was no smile in his voice or on his face, but I had the sense the statement amused him.

"We've all got talents," I said.

He ran an index finger down one of the weight benches, admiring the deep split that a bullet had left in its cover.

"Your troubles and my troubles appear to run together often."

I didn't say anything to that.

"The police have been asking me questions," he said. "In all truth, the police often ask me questions. I rarely provide answers. But yesterday, the questions concerned you."

He looked up at me, held me with those blue eyes.

"What did you tell them?" I asked.

"As I said, I rarely provide answers."

I nodded. "They've been asking me questions, too, Thor. Your name was brought up for the first time yesterday. You were in the car of a dead man, they said. A dead man they suspect I may have killed."

His face didn't change at all. "Did you kill him?"

"No."

"But you are in love with his wife?"

"No. I was once. I'm not now."

"We know some things about one another," he said, the words slow and careful, as if he had taken great care selecting them. "Things that would probably be best left between us."

"I'm not going to talk."

His head bobbed once. "There was another man . . ."

"He's gone, and he was so scared of you that he'll never talk, no matter the incentives."

This, he certainly believed.

"I suppose that is all, then." He gazed around the room once more. "At least for me. You? You seem to have some issues that need to be addressed. I wish you luck with that. I trust you will not need it."

He turned on his heel and moved back for the window, reaching out for the free edge of the plastic sheet.

"Wait," I said.

"Yes?" Half-facing me, but still leaning toward the window.

"Why were you in his car?"

When those ice-blue eyes met mine, my spine felt as cold as the metal bar in my hands.

"I do not discuss the affairs of others."

He would end the lives of others, had done so frequently, but he would not discuss their affairs. Honor.

"They're coming for me, Thor. Whoever did kill Jefferson, and the cops. They're all coming for me."

Thor cocked his head, frowning. He did not like to talk. He was a man of deeds, not discussion. He stood there and stared at me, though, and I thought that maybe he was remembering the way we'd locked eyes after he'd plunged his knife into another man's body, remembering that he'd not seen me in court after that, testifying against him. Those things that he wanted to remain between us already had, for some time.

"An offer was made," he said. "It was made out of confusion. I declined the offer, and I went on my way. That was the only time I ever saw the man."

"What offer?"

He looked at me for a long time, and just when I thought he was going to decline to answer and make his exit, he told me.

"Alex Jefferson wanted to employ me to kill a man. I do not know who the man was, because I stopped him long before he got to the details of the situation. I told Mr. Jefferson that whatever he had been told about me, it was wrong. I told him that I do not engage in activities of murder for money."

No, only murder over *money,* I thought. Didn't seem like the kind of point Thor would appreciate, though, so I didn't offer it.

"How did he find you?"

"Through an acquaintance who has represented some of my associates in legal matters."

"A criminal defense lawyer, then," I said, and he seemed amused again.

"That is of no concern to you. I have told you all I can. I would hate to think that I have already said too much?"

The question held the menacing edge of a machete blade.

"You haven't said too much."

He didn't respond to that, just nodded once, politely, and lifted the free edge of plastic and stepped over the low window frame and out onto the sidewalk.

For a long time after he was gone, I kept the curl bar in my hands.

CHAPTER

20

"*So it wasn't too* much of a coincidence, after all," Joe said. "I said earlier that the city wasn't small enough for both you and Thor to figure into this. When it comes to hired killings, though? City becomes an awful lot smaller. Tight little community."

I winced. "You're including me in that community?"

He shrugged. "Look, *I'm* not getting visitors like Thor."

I pushed out of my chair and walked to the window, looked down on the street for the third time since I'd gotten to the office. I was looking down on the street a lot lately. It's a habit you pick up when you always think someone dangerous is nearby. Just a little healthy paranoia.

"I should have pushed him harder."

"Are you insane? Men like Thor do not respond well to pushing, LP."

"Men like Thor also share only the bare minimum of information," I said, turning back to him. "He knows more than he gave me."

"If I were you, I'd just be glad he walked back out that window." Joe shook his head. "Walking through the damn window. For all his stillness and calm, that guy has a flair for the dramatic."

"If Jefferson was willing to hire Thor to do his killing, he'd have been willing to hire someone else. If whatever he was afraid of had become that serious, pushed him to that extent, then he wouldn't stop because one man declined his offer. He'd keep looking."

"Maybe."

"Thor basically admitted that Jefferson had found out about him from a criminal defense lawyer who has defended Belov's crew. If we can find that guy, maybe we can find out who else he might be connected to."

Joe looked at me as if I'd offered him a glass of milk that had been left in the sun for a week.

"Surely, LP, you're not suggesting we refocus on interviewing every contract killer we can find."

"One of them will know something."

"Right. And when we find that one, he'll kill us and consider the problem solved. I'd suggest approaching this a little more obliquely."

I ran a palm over my face, feeling the haze of a sleepless night already working on my brain.

"I know you're right. It's just difficult to pull my mind away from Thor. He's the sort of guy who can hold on to it, you know?"

"I certainly haven't forgotten him. But I think I've got something that'll refocus you."

"Yeah?"

He had a piece of paper in his hand, an excited gleam in his eyes.

"Remember the problem we had believing that someone connected to Andy Doran could be coming after Jefferson?"

I nodded. "The time lag. It seemed like a stretch."

"About ten minutes before you showed up, that problem was blown away, LP."

He slid the paper onto my desk, and I saw it was a printout from an Internet newspaper site.

"Andy Doran escaped from prison the end of September. He was back on the streets over two weeks before Jefferson was killed."

I picked up the printout and looked from it back to Joe. He had a tight smile on his face.

"Well? Think you'll be able to forget about Thor for a bit now?"

Without answering, I dropped my eyes and read through the article. Doran had been one of three inmates from a cleanup detail who'd broken out of prison by hiding in a garbage truck. The other two had been arrested within twenty-four hours. Doran had vanished.

"Are you sure he's still out? Most of these guys are caught so fast . . ."

"He's still out. There's a page devoted to him on the U.S. marshals' Web site."

I read the article a second time, then set it aside and stared at Joe. "He's the guy. Doran's the guy."

"I'm leaning that way myself."

"When he had that bag over my head, he told me that Jefferson's son called his dad for help, and he paid the price for five years. It says in this article that he'd been in prison for five years on a twenty-year sentence."

"It's a possibility," Joe said. "Maybe a strong one. But we've got to dig deeper before we throw this one at Targent. A single remark about five years of paying a price is not going to convince the cops."

I looked back down at the article. "It said he was convicted of manslaughter."

"I saw that, and I don't understand it. We're going to need to go get the case file, see how all of this unfolded."

"Case file will be out in Geneva."

"Right. Which is why I suggest we leave now."

I called Karen while we drove, asked her if she'd received any more phone calls, any more threats. She hadn't, but it was clear she was still shaken from the first, speaking in a tight voice, her words coming too quickly, her tone too uneven.

"You okay?" I said. "You get any sleep?"

She gave a bitter laugh. "No, Lincoln. I didn't feel sleep was much of a possibility last night. The police came out and spent a long time here. That was good. I was . . . It was a tough night. I was a little unsteady."

"Maybe you should go somewhere today. Get out of that house, stop being alone, spend some time around people."

"I'll be fine."

"All right. Listen, Joe and I are working on this, okay? We've got some ideas, maybe a decent lead. We're going to make progress today, Karen. I'm sure of it."

"Anything you want to tell me about?"

"Give me the day. Let us have the day to work on it, and I'll come by the house tonight, tell you what we've done and what we're considering."

"I'd appreciate that, Lincoln. I *do* appreciate it."

I hung up and relayed the conversation to Joe.

"I'd be damn careful deciding what to tell her, and when to tell it," he said. "There are a million types of grudges, and reasons for them. But if this guy really is Doran, and he really was innocent?"

"It'll make Jefferson look like one dirty son of a bitch."

He nodded. "You got it."

"I don't have trouble buying that idea."

"No. But Karen will. And having it come from you . . ."

"Let's worry about that when we get to it. All I care about now is finding out what happened to this guy."

Making the drive felt good. Joe was in the car with me, where he belonged, and we were making progress on a case that mattered. It was in that moment of satisfaction that I thought of the question I'd asked him yesterday, the one he'd chosen not to answer.

"I appreciate you coming out with me on this one, Joe. Don't know if I made that clear enough."

"It's nothing."

"When I came by your house yesterday, though . . . I asked when you were planning on coming back."

"Uh-huh."

"You didn't answer."

He was quiet. I kept my eyes on the road and waited.

"I joined the police right out of school," he said. "It was the only thing I ever wanted to do, the only thing I ever considered doing. So I joined up, and I did my thirty. Ruth died and I took a week off and went right back to work, and then it was all I had. She and I had made all these plans, right? Plans for retirement, the way we'd spend it together. But then she was gone, and what was I going to do, see Europe by myself? Build a greenhouse and plant tropical flowers? Come on. All that was gone, and so I retired and started the PI gig with you. Didn't pause for so much as a summer. Just went right back into the work. It was without the badge and without the bureaucracy, but it was the same work."

He paused for a minute, and I wanted to look at him but was afraid to, somehow, as if movement would disrupt him, stop him from continuing.

"When I got shot this summer, it forced me to step away from it," he said. "That was the first time I'd done that, LP. The first time since I was a kid that I wasn't living and breathing an investigation."

"And that was good?"

"Maybe it was, maybe it wasn't. It was different, at least. It was something different, after three decades of it all being largely the same. And it made me wonder . . . I don't know."

"What?"

"I guess it made me wonder if there's something else I want to do before I'm gone, you know? Something else I need to do, or should do. I'm running out of time—"

"You're not running out of time."

"You say that because you're young. I'm not at death's door or anything, LP, I know that, but I'm also not young. I'm old, and getting older. And all I've ever done is this sort of work."

I looked over at him for the first time since he'd started to talk. "Are you happy being away from it?"

"I don't know."

"You didn't look happy. You looked . . . kind of empty, Joe. I understand what you're saying about how long you've been in this game, but all you were doing until I dragged you back out of the house was sitting in your chair in the living room. Is that better for you?"

He shook his head. "No, it's not. I have no intention of spending the rest of my life sitting in that chair, feeling like a damned old man. There's a part of me that believes it's time for a change, though. I was in the chair only because I don't know what the change should be, or even if it should be."

I sat and watched the highway open up ahead of us, didn't say a word.

"I know you feel like I left you adrift these last couple of months," Joe said, "but if you were smart enough to consider it, you'd realize there's an unspoken compliment there. I don't have to worry about you. Don't have to call the office nine times a day to make sure nothing's going wrong. Nothing will be going wrong, because you're good. You're damn good, probably already better than I am in some ways. You've got an instinct for this sort of work that's as good as anybody's I've ever seen, and now you've matured to the point where you can build off the instinct with a cool head. You're not the cowboy you used to be, not so much of one, at least."

"I still need you, Joe. I can't run this thing by myself."

"That's not true." He shook his head. "You can run it by yourself, and you know that. You can handle any case that comes our way, handle it well. You did it alone for the last few months, and did it easily."

"You know I'll support you with whatever it is you want to do," I said. "I don't want to work alone, but I will support you if you decide to leave."

"I know. And when that decision is made, it'll be made in consultation with you, LP. You're my partner whether I'm in that office or not."

CHAPTER

21

Eight months out of high school, Andy Doran was arrested for the first time. He was in Cleveland then, a John Marshall High School graduate who got picked up for breaking into a house in Shaker Heights and making off with a few televisions and some speakers. Made it about three miles before he was pulled over for speeding by a cop who grew curious about the odd collection of used electronics equipment in Doran's backseat.

Doran managed to walk away with nothing more than probation for that first offense, and he kicked around the city for another two years before joining the Army. There he lasted four years, earning a few commendations for his physical skills and marksmanship while completing advanced infantry training, airborne training, and some specialized urban combat training. The commendations didn't mean his military career was off to a problem-free start, though—his personnel file grew thick with disciplinary actions before he was arrested for the second time. An MP investigation revealed that Doran, in connection with a couple of civilian buddies near Fort Bragg, had been selling stolen military equipment through local gun dealers and the Internet—military equipment that included night-vision goggles, guns, and grenades. A dishonorable discharge was the prelude to a two-year prison stay for that one.

He made his way, as ne'er-do-wells usually do, back home. Six months after he moved into his mother's house, she died, leaving her son a meager inheritance and a larger mortgage. Doran promptly defaulted on the loan and moved out of the house to places unknown. Eighteen months later, he turned up in Geneva-on-the-Lake, where he was arrested for assault and battery after a bar fight. Doran walked away from the fight with some minor bruises and lacerations—all to his hands, which he'd used quite effectively on the other man's face. For this offense, he served another six months in jail. The fight apparently stemmed from a territorial debate involving a redheaded waitress. While Doran won the brawl, he did not win the waitress, because he was single when he got out of jail, a problem he quickly sought to rectify upon meeting twenty-year-old Monica Heath.

By then Doran was driving a truck, albeit without a commercial driver's license, engaged in furniture deliveries and whatever other local hauling he could land. One of those jobs was driving the catering van for Heath's company. A short relationship flourished, apparently based upon a shared love of outdoor intercourse and marijuana. The couple remained together for about three months before Heath's friends convinced her that Doran was trouble and she could do better. They made out in the van one last time, split a joint, and parted on what appeared to be amicable terms.

Seven weeks later, Heath was dead with her skirt pushed up over her hips, her underwear missing. She'd been strangled with the towel that she'd used to wipe down the tables. The towel was a problem—no fingerprints, no grip marks. The police interviewed Doran after the body was discovered, then returned the next day, this time with a search warrant for his trailer and orange Camaro, motivated by an eyewitness who could place Doran at the scene. Doran was high when they came for him, with a water bong sitting in his sink, but not so far gone that he failed to put up a fight when officers found a black garbage bag tucked beneath a stack of cinder blocks near one end of the trailer—with Monica Heath's underwear inside. Doran stumbled out of the trailer spewing profanities and trying to fight the cop who'd made the find, screaming about being framed as he swung uncoordinated punches at the man's head before being subdued.

The underwear was taken to the Ohio Bureau of Criminal Investigation, where lab tests returned Heath's DNA, but not Doran's, or anyone else's. Still, the black Victoria's Secret thong made things grim for Doran, particularly when combined with his criminal history and the testimony of Heath's friends, a half dozen of whom reported that Monica had frequently stated that sex with Doran—while good—was also rough, that he was aggressive and wild and, yes, prone to the occasional hair pull or maybe even a little choking. None of them was firm in the memory of a choking reference, but two of the girls thought that, yeah, maybe, just *maybe,* Monica had mentioned it in the past.

Powerful evidence, made only more powerful by the addition of an eyewitness account placing Doran's Camaro at the scene and a man matching his description involved with Heath on the winery's deck.

That eyewitness, a Matthew Jefferson, of Pepper Pike, came forward in something of an unconventional manner. Jefferson had discovered the body and called the police. He had not, however, been able to pass along any details of the man on the deck—at least not at first. It was the following day when young Jefferson reappeared with an amended account of the night and his father at his side. In this meeting, the law student claimed that he'd been frightened by the police, who had apparently been aggressive in their questioning, and that he'd neglected to mention that he'd seen a car in the parking lot on his walk up to the winery. The car, he explained, was an older Camaro that had looked orange in the moonlight. Also, he'd had a better look at the man on the deck than he'd shared, a good enough look to tell him that the man was about six feet tall, with bristle-short hair and a tattoo of some sort along his left forearm.

Doran insisted he had an alibi: He'd spent the night with a man named Donny Ward, drinking whiskey and target shooting with a .22. When the police went to interview Ward, though, he claimed to have no idea what Doran was talking about. Said he hadn't seen Doran since an encounter at a bar a few nights earlier.

Within days of Heath's murder, Doran found himself facing an eyewitness account, hard evidence found at his home, and a useless alibi. He was broke, of course, and couldn't afford a private attorney. His public defender, a man who had worked on exactly zero murder cases, managed to get a plea offer that reduced the charge to manslaughter, occurring during autoerotic activity, *consensual* activity, mind you. Two days before his trial was to begin, Andy Doran was offered a plea agreement for a twenty-year prison sentence, which meant he could be out in ten if he didn't cause any trouble. Facing a life sentence if he was convicted, possibly even the death penalty if things really went bad, Doran accepted the plea.

Five years passed, and Doran stayed in prison. He behaved well in custody, gave the jailers no trouble, kept his mouth shut. Behaved well enough, in fact, that he was trusted with some sweet prison jobs, simple, yawn-while-you-work tasks like cleaning up after meals, mopping the floors, and taking out trash.

It was a tough fiscal year, state and federal budget crunches being felt in almost every agency, including the correctional facilities. Jobs were lost, and employees who left of their own volition were not quickly replaced. Reduced manpower was a challenge in every jail, and with that challenge Doran and the rest of his cleanup crew were given a new responsibility: running the trash compacter, a task previously supervised by a corrections officer. All trash leaving the jail was compacted both for efficiency and to ensure that any inmate hoping to escape in a garbage bag would be properly flattened before finding his way to the truck.

One day in late September, not all of the trash was compacted. Andy Doran and two others hid in a heap of refuse, were loaded into the back of a garbage truck, and were driven out of the gates and back into freedom. Within forty-eight hours, the other two were arrested at a truck stop on I-70, where they were attempting to purchase hot dogs and Red Bull energy drinks even while their pictures were being displayed on the television set just over their heads. Andy Doran wasn't with them when the cops came, though, and, according to his fellow escapees, the last time anyone saw him he was walking through a muddy wheat field, heading north.

All of this, Joe and I learned through several hours spent in the Ashtabula County Courthouse reading hundreds of pages of depositions and transcripts in Doran's case. While I went through the case file, Joe made a trip to the library and came back with a dozen more articles relating to Doran's escape from prison and the subsequent—and unsuccessful— manhunt.

"Can we really believe," Joe said, "that when this guy broke out of jail the first thing on his mind was settling a score?"

"Why not? If he'd done five years for a crime he didn't commit—"

"He might have murdered that girl. Can't be sure he didn't, not yet, at least."

"Right. But playing out the thread here, we'll say that he didn't, and that for some reason unknown to us he held Jefferson responsible. Five years is a long time to spend in prison for something you didn't do. A long time to build a grudge. Ever read *The Count of Monte Cristo*? Besides, the guy's a fugitive now. Where's he going to run? And on what cash? He needed money, and Jefferson had it."

Joe wore a deep frown as he continued flipping through documents, but he was also nodding. "Jefferson never went to the cops. He tried to hire Thor to kill whoever was threatening him. Doesn't exactly smack of legitimacy, you know? So maybe we're right. Maybe the reason he had to try to handle it with someone like Thor was because he knew Doran had him—and his son—by the balls."

"His son's testimony was absurd. Showing up with his father to change stories a day after he found the body?"

"It is weak, which is why it wouldn't have convicted Doran. The girl's underwear—"

"Which could have been planted easily enough."

"Yes, but it was still more convincing evidence than anything Jefferson's son said. Although he did point them in Doran's direction, I suppose. He got it all moving."

"That time reference . . . it's too clear. Paying the price for five years, he said—and then he comes after Jefferson and the son as soon as he gets out of prison. It's also the exact same time Jefferson and the son developed their rift. I bet Jefferson pulled the son out of the fire and then cut him off. He wouldn't want his image tarnished by a son who was a murderer, but he also wouldn't want the kid around. Out of sight, out of mind."

"Maybe you're right when you say it's too clear, LP."

"What do you mean?"

"Why would Doran make that reference to you? Seems like he establishes his identity a little too easily with that. Anybody who knew what happened with Matt Jefferson in that situation, or even looked into it on the surface like we have, would roll to the same conclusion."

"What does Doran care? It's not like he has anything to lose—the day he runs into a cop, he goes right back to prison. He couldn't give a shit if I turn more police attention onto him. He's already a fugitive."

Joe thought about that and nodded.

"If this guy *isn't* Doran, I'll be amazed," I said.

"I think I'm with you. Right now we're guessing, though. No real reason to suspect he came after Jefferson other than that remark about the five years."

My cell phone vibrated in my pocket, interrupting us. I slipped the phone out, checked the display, and saw my gym's number looking back at me. Odd, considering the gym was closed. I answered and got Grace.

"Lincoln, I think you'd better get down here. There are some, um, people here to see you."

"I'm in the middle of something important," I said, thinking that she was with the insurance company, an ordeal I didn't want to tackle right now. "Why don't you have them call me to set up a meeting instead of just showing up like that?"

"It's the police." She had dropped her voice.

"What?"

"They're at your apartment, and it looks like they've got a warrant."

CHAPTER

22

It took us an hour of fast driving to make it back, but they were still there when Joe pulled into my parking lot. I saw Targent's Crown Vic and two squad cars. The door to the stairs was open, and Targent came through it as I got out of the car, rage boiling through my veins. There was a warrant in his hand.

"This is bullshit," I said when he gave it to me.

"Judge didn't seem to think so."

"Judge is going to be regretting that when I get an attorney to go after you guys for an unfounded warrant. You've got absolutely no evidence to suggest I've done anything, Targent. And the saddest thing is that the more you dick around with me, the less you're accomplishing on this case."

"You go ahead and get your lawyer," he said, moving for the door. "And we'll be discussing that supposed lack of evidence in just a minute, Perry. Now stay out of our way until this is done."

He turned and walked back up the steps. Grace was standing inside the gym office with the door open, watching with concern.

"I came down to help clean up," she said. "They told me I could either unlock the door or they'd break it. I didn't want them to break—"

"It's okay, Grace. This is no big deal. You did the right thing."

My words were calm, but they couldn't hide the anger. Joe stopped to talk to Grace as I walked up the steps and into my apartment. Targent was speaking in a low voice to his team, offering instructions, but I couldn't concentrate on the words. There's a sense of total invasion and violation that comes with being served a search warrant, being required to open your door for a group of cops whose mission is to find something in your home that indicates your guilt in a crime. I'd exercised search warrants constantly when I'd been a cop and never really paused to think about it. Now I was getting a whole new perspective.

Daly and the two cops I didn't know were taking books from shelves and opening drawers. Targent stayed near the door.

"Let's you and me sit down and have a talk about the reason we're here," he said. "Let the boys do their job."

I shook my head. "Not a chance, Targent. You think I'm not going to watch your guys at work? I wouldn't be surprised to see a bloody knife appear under my pillow the moment I turned my back on them."

He scowled but didn't argue. I followed the searchers through my apartment, clenching and unclenching my hands at my sides. They were doing a professional job of it, checking everything thoroughly but keeping it neat, replacing items as they found them. One of the younger guys located my guns in the extra bedroom and held them up to Targent with a questioning look, but I answered before his boss could.

"Those aren't leaving with you. The warrant is for Alex Jefferson's homicide investigation, and he wasn't shot. Put my guns back."

Targent didn't tell the kid otherwise, so he replaced the guns in their case and moved on. Beneath the gun case, in the spare bedroom's closet, they found another metal box, a fireproof thing that's supposed to be used for important documents. The young cop pulled this one out of the closet and opened the lid, withdrew a large manila envelope, and shook out the contents.

The first thing that fell out was a small felt box. The cop flipped it open to reveal the engagement ring inside. Karen had mailed it back to me shortly after I'd realigned Alex Jefferson's nose. I'd thrown out the accompanying note but kept the ring, eating the cost of it because I couldn't bring myself to walk back into the jewelry store and ask for a refund—and the pitying glances of the employees. Behind the ring box were notes and letters and photographs. Targent stooped and lifted a photograph that showed Karen standing on the balcony of my old apartment, her blond hair pulled back, wearing sunglasses and holding a can of beer and laughing at something. In the half-second glance I gave the picture, I remembered that we'd just come back from a picnic at Edgewater Park along the lake. She'd had a dog back then, an ancient, fat Lab that would waddle along with us for about two hundred feet before sighing and dropping to the ground, rolling over on his back in surrender.

Targent gave me a raised eyebrow. "She looks familiar."

"I'd imagine."

"Interesting that you chose to hang on to all this." He shuffled the photographs, tapped on the ring box.

"I was engaged to the woman, Targent. I have a few artifacts to prove that. It doesn't make me guilty of anything."

I was staring at one of the items that he'd left on the floor, a letter with a Boston postmark. I remembered that she'd been gone only a week, and I'd thought it was a hell of a long time. I reached down and picked the envelope off the carpet, opened it and slid out the letter, and read the short note filled with kind sentiments and soon-to-be-broken promises. Karen Grayson, the return address on the envelope said. Grayson. The name seemed not to fit her now. I imagined she felt the same way.

"You pull this box out often?" Targent said. "Go through all the photos, think about what you lost?"

"I haven't opened the box since I put everything in it and threw it in the closet, Targent. Don't get excited."

"Most men would've burned all this shit."

"Most men are idiots."

They were at it for quite a while. I hadn't been paying any attention to the clock, so I couldn't say exactly how long it took, but they went through the place inch by inch and spent what seemed like an eternity going over all the paperwork on my desk. Nobody yelled "ah-hah" and held up a case-clinching find. I knew they shouldn't, but I couldn't help fearing they might. The guy who'd killed Jefferson had seemed pretty good. Good enough to slip past a few basic locks and plant something in my apartment, certainly. Nothing turned up, though, and by the time the cops had cycled back out into the living room, I was giving Targent hell again. He ignored me and told the two younger guys that they could go, leaving just him and Daly left in my apartment. Daly sat down at my kitchen table while Targent pulled out a chair and motioned for me to take it.

"You didn't find anything," I said. "So what are you doing sitting down in my home? I don't want you here, and if you think I'm going to talk to you, you're crazy. You guys would probably show up here tomorrow claiming I'd confessed to Jefferson's murder, and maybe a dozen others. I get the feeling you have plenty of cases that aren't closed."

Daly reddened at that, but Targent seemed oblivious.

"How close did you look at that warrant?" he asked.

"Why? You print it out on your home computer? I wouldn't be surprised."

"Should have studied it a bit. You'd notice that we're exercising the warrant in connection with a request made by the Indiana State Police."

"My old friend Brewer?"

"You got it."

"Well, they must have pretty lenient requirements for a warrant in Indiana, because he doesn't have any reason to search my property, or have you do it."

"No?" Targent leaned forward, bracing himself with his

hands on the table. "Brewer didn't get that warrant yesterday, when he arrested your PI buddy. He got it this morning,
after he confirmed something I find *very* interesting. The ten
grand in cash you allegedly sent that PI? Wrapped in two
five-thousand-dollar bundles of fifty-dollar bills. This morning Brewer got a bank in Cleveland to confirm that the cur-
rency wrappers are identical to the ones they use. That bank?
Cuyahoga Valley Credit Union, where Alex Jefferson withdrew fifty thousand dollars in cash a week before his death."

He stood above me, staring down into my face as that
blade of grass in my throat worked its way into my stomach
and bloomed large and cold, unfolding through my chest.

"And, yes," Targent said, "Jefferson's withdrawal was made
in bundles of fifty-dollar bills."

CHAPTER

23

"*There's still no hard* evidence connecting you to that money," Joe said. "That's the good news. They don't have to believe someone impersonated you, but they *do* have to prove otherwise."

We were on the steps of my building, Targent and Daly gone.

"Yeah? Well, how much circumstantial evidence do you think it'll take to produce an arrest warrant?"

He didn't answer that.

"I thought these guys helped me out last night," I said. "When they shot up my gym, I thought they actually helped. Even Targent would have to believe that I wasn't fabricating all of this. But it doesn't seem to be the case."

Joe shook his head. "It's not, and that shouldn't be surprising. Targent applied pressure to you yesterday, or at least Brewer did, with that arrest in Indiana. If you were lying, and wanted to convince him, you would have needed some kind of splashy evidence. Having a guy unload into your building wouldn't be a bad idea."

"That's ridiculous."

"Is it? The phone call about Karen's money came at the same time they shot up the place with you inside. All right. But if I'm Targent, standing back and looking at it, what I see is an overcompensated effort to prove you're distanced from these guys. And Targent's right—why *are* these guys going through you to get to Karen? It's illogical. Unless the goal is simply to pull you inside."

"Doran—if it even is Doran—he told me he had an associate who wanted to take me off the board. Gave me one chance to step away from it, and I ignored him. Maybe this is the reprisal. I passed on the chance to walk away, and now they're going to cooperate. Bring me all the way inside."

"You say anything to Targent about Doran?"

"Not yet."

"Probably not the worst thing. We need something direct to connect him to Jefferson, anyhow. Targent isn't going to be impressed with what we've got now, because it's all rooted in a comment that guy made to you, a comment nobody else can support."

I'd been sitting on the steps, and now I pushed off. Sitting felt useless. Targent and Brewer and people whose names and roles I didn't even understand were active all around me, circling, tightening nets and laying traps, and I was doing nothing. Sitting on my ass in a parking lot, waiting for them to finish their work.

"We've got to get somewhere with this, Joe. This thing in Indiana . . . what if it's not the end? There's no reason to think it will be. Once they commit to making moves like that, drawing the police pressure down on me, why would they stop? If they keep setting me up to look like a suspect, then I'd damn well better have another one to give the cops."

Joe nodded. "We'll go back to the Doran case. Make something unravel. When it does, we'll convince Targent to take him seriously."

"And if it doesn't?"

"I'll make sure your commissary account is well stocked with cigarette money."

It was a nice attempt at a joke, but neither of us laughed.

Donny Ward lived six miles from the winery where Monica Heath had died. His house had a buckling roof and a sloped foundation, and four dogs roamed the yard, slinking through grass that was about three feet tall. A thin trail of smoke rose from an old barrel that, judging from the accompanying odor, was used for the legal and environmentally friendly practice of burning trash. Joe knocked on the front door while one of the dogs, a hound with tattered ears, growled from the base of the porch.

"Good boy," I said, and he bristled and snapped his jaws.

"Nice touch with the animals," Joe said.

"You want to be the one to pet him?"

Nobody came to the door, and there was no sound from the property other than the growling dog.

"We can wait, or we can come back," Joe said.

"I'm a fan of the latter option." I was watching the dog, who had gathered the courage to inch closer to the steps.

We'd just turned from the door when a pickup truck came boiling down the lane, acrid black smoke puffing out of the exhaust pipe and rising above an old bed cover that didn't match the blue truck. The driver pulled in just behind Joe's car, and the dogs whirled around the truck with delighted yips and wagging tails. They were a mangy pack of strays, but they certainly loved this new arrival.

"This would be Donny?" Joe said.

"I'd imagine."

We waited on the porch while the driver got out of the truck and played with the dogs for a few seconds. He was a lean guy, all sinewy muscle, wearing a sleeveless shirt even though the temperature was hardly above fifty. There was an Indians cap on his head, tufts of dark hair hanging out beneath it. When he was done with the dogs, he straightened up, adjusted the cap, and squinted at us.

"Mr. Ward?" I said.

"Uh-huh." He sauntered up to the porch. "You here 'bout the dogs?"

"No."

"Good." He got a key out and unlocked the door. "Bitch lives up the road keeps calling the county, says I got feral dogs. 'Cept that's ridiculous, you know? They've all been neutered. Well, one was spayed, you know, because she's a female. But the point is, they all been fixed, they all got their shots. I have six acres here, and be damned if I'm going to lock these old boys in a kennel. You ever seen a dog in a kennel? I mean, really looked at his face? Breaks your heart, is what it does."

By now we were all inside. He hadn't asked for an introduction, just kept talking as he stepped into the house, and Joe and I followed.

"Breaks your heart," he said again, tossing his keys onto a lamp stand beside the door. The house wasn't as bad on the inside as I'd expected from the exterior. The couch had duct tape wrapped around one arm, probably to keep the stuffing in, and the ceiling showed water marks, but the place was clean enough. Past Donny Ward's shoulder, a Crock-Pot and a bread maker sat on the counter, where I would've expected to see only a pyramid of empty Busch cans. There were framed photographs on the wall in front of us, all of them featuring a girl of maybe six or seven with a chubby face and a few missing teeth. More to Donny than initially met the eye, it seemed.

"So," he said, turning to fully acknowledge us for the first time. "What are you gents needin'?"

"We're private investigators," Joe said. "From Cleveland."

Donny smiled good-naturedly. "Private eyes. Ain't that exciting."

"Sure is. We hate to impose on you, dropping in unannounced like this, but we've got some pretty important questions about a man named Andy Doran."

The smile stayed on his face. His eyes moved to the door, which was closed now, and he exhaled out of his mouth without opening his lips, a hiss of air escaping out of that smile.

"You remember Mr. Doran?" Joe said.

"Fellas," Donny took a few steps away from us and into the living room, "I'd love to help you. Really would. But I'm done talking about that."

"It seemed awful curious to us," I said, "that Doran would

claim you as a hard-and-fast alibi, when he hadn't even seen you that night. Wasn't like you two were good friends, either. You have any idea what the hell he was thinking?"

Donny shook his head. "Nah, I don't. But like I said, I'm done talking about that."

"You know he's out now?"

Donny stared at me for a minute, wet his lips, and nodded. "Yeah."

"Seems to me, one of two things has to be true. Either you told the truth to the police and Doran was just a first-rate dumb shit when it came to his alibi, or you lied to the police. And if the second is true, well, I'd imagine old Andy might want to pay you a visit. Don't you think?"

Donny crossed to the front door, opened it, and gestured with his free arm for us to step outside. Neither of us moved.

"I've talked to him, Donny," I said. "Good chance I'll talk to him again, too. And I can tell you this—the man is angry. He told me he did five years in prison for someone else's murder. One of the people he holds responsible? Man was killed, Donny. Tortured and killed."

Donny Ward removed his baseball cap and held it in his hands, flexing the bill and staring at the grinning caricature on the hat as if looking for reassurance.

"I've got to make a decision," I said. "Got to decide whether I believe that somebody set Doran up. If somebody did, then I think you're a liar, Donny. And I need to know why. That's all. Because I don't think you made it happen. I don't think you put all this in motion. But you can help me understand who did."

"I don't have anything to tell you."

"More than fifty slashes, Donny. With a razor. All over the body. Pain like you or I cannot possibly imagine. That's how it ended for the other guy Doran blamed for his prison stay."

He was still staring at his hat.

"Son of a bitch shot my dog."

I looked at Joe and then back at Donny Ward.

"Doran did?"

He shook his head, slipped the baseball cap back on, and used his heel to swing the door shut.

"Nah. The guy they sent to talk to me. I didn't even know Andy'd been arrested yet. Hadn't heard from the police. This guy, he got here first."

"Who was he?" Joe said.

"Like I got his name? Like we exchanged business cards or somethin'?"

"You don't know who sent him?"

He shook his head and walked into the living room, sat down on the couch beside the duct-taped arm.

"Man showed up in the morning. Not a real big guy, dark-looking, Italian maybe? But strong. Stronger than a damned bull. He got out of his car and came up to the porch, and I let him inside. He told me the police would be coming to ask about Andy. Told me I should say I hadn't been with him. That it'd be, you know, easier on me anyhow, not having to deal with going to court and all. I said he was shit-house crazy, thinking I'd lie like that when a man could go to jail. He got out this bag he had with him and started pulling out cash. I don't know how much. Seemed like he'd never run out. He stacked it all up on the table over there and said, 'You sure about that?' "

Joe and I were still standing, but Donny Ward didn't look like he was even aware of us. He was picking at the duct tape idly with his fingers, eyes on the wall.

"And I told him, I said, 'You get out of my house, get back in your car, and drive straight to hell.' Because I wasn't about to send a man to jail in exchange for some dollars, you know? I wasn't. And this guy, he just piled the money back up and put it in the bag, had this little smile on his face. Once the money was all gone, he reached down into the bag and took out a gun. Stuck the gun up in my eye and reached out and grabbed me by the balls. You heard that expression, somebody's got you by the balls? Well, this son of a bitch actually did it. Just reached out and took my nuts and squeezed, and I thought I was gonna die. Couldn't breathe. He kept squeezing, and he kept the gun in my eye, and he asked . . . he asked how much I love my daughter."

Donny Ward looked up for the first time since he'd begun to talk, a quick jerk of his head. His eyes didn't go to either of us, though, but beyond, to the wall where the photographs of the little girl with the gap-toothed smile hung.

"I got a daughter, but she don't live with me. Her name's . . . well, that don't matter. She's my daughter, you know? She's my daughter. And he said . . ."

He stopped talking and wiped at his eyes and looked away. His hand was tight on the duct tape; a strip of it pulled loose and clenched between his fingers, leaving a sticky sheen on his skin.

"I had a big old bluetick, best dog you ever seen. When this guy let up on squeezing me, he took his bag and opened the door and walked out on the porch. Otis was out there, waitin' on me, way he always did. When he heard the door open he'd come running. And this guy, he just lifted the gun and shot him. Shot him right in the center of his head. Turned back to me, cool as anything, and said, 'You think about your daughter, Donny.' And then he started to walk away and before he got in the car he yelled back at me, said, "You best have that dog cleaned up before the police get here.'"

Donny Ward's voice broke at that point, and he stopped talking. For a long time he sat there picking at the duct tape. Joe and I let him sit. We didn't look at one another.

"We're going to find this guy, Donny," I said.

"I wouldn't want that, I was you."

"I do want it. And if I see Doran again, if I have a chance to talk to him, I'll tell him that you weren't a part of this."

He cleared his throat. "He already knows that."

"What?"

"I did what I did because I was scared. Scared for my daughter. But that don't mean it was easy to take. I watched Andy go to prison, and I knew he hadn't killed that girl. That ate me up pretty good. Kept at it, too, didn't just go away after a year or two, you know? Well, a while back my daughter's mother moved. Went out of state, married this guy . . . He's good to my daughter. I don't know if I thought she was safer or not. I'm not about to go to the police, tell them what happened or anything. I'd still worry. Fact is, you go and get the cops and bring them back here, I'll call you liars."

He looked at us with a challenge in his eyes, but Joe and I didn't say a word. After a few seconds, Donny continued.

"Time went by, and I kept thinking about Andy, and . . . I just felt like I needed to say something to him. Make him understand? 'Course he wouldn't understand, sitting there in prison, but I had to try. So I got one of those blank cards and I wrote him a note. All I said was that I did it because they threatened my daughter. I didn't sign it or nothing, but I figured he wouldn't have trouble guessing who wrote it."

I looked at Donny Ward and thought about Alex Jefferson, about the handiwork with a razor and a lighter.

"It's probably a damn good thing you sent that letter," I said.

CHAPTER

24

It was dark when we left Donny Ward's house in the woods. The dogs circled around us as we walked to the car. Two were friendly, but the third, that chewed-up hound, kept his distance and growled until Joe had the engine going. I wondered how old he was, if he'd been around the day Donny had been visited by a man with a gun and a bagful of cash. Might a dog remember something like that? I thought he probably would.

Joe's car bounced along the rutted lane, and then we came out onto the main road, and within a few seconds Donny Ward's home was out of sight. It was raining now, a light mist that didn't make a sound against the car but appeared in thin sheets on the windshield between swipes of the wiper blades.

"We've got to give it to Targent," Joe said. "I don't believe Donny would do what he said, deny everything. He broke pretty easy with us, and I think that's because he's been breaking a little bit over it every day for a long time. He'd give it to the cops."

"Probably, but it doesn't make the bridge between Doran and Jefferson. Not alone."

"Targent needs to hear it, though. Proves Doran was set up. By somebody who had plenty of money to spare."

"Yeah. We've just got to show that it was Jefferson. I want to get that prick."

Joe shot me a hard look. "That's what this is about now?"

"You heard what that guy said. About his daughter, and the dog . . . If Jefferson made all that happen, I intend to see that people know about it."

"The man's dead."

"The people who need to know what happened aren't."

"People like Karen?"

I turned to him, but he had his eyes on the road.

"I didn't say that. I was thinking more of people like Monica Heath's family. Like Andy Doran's family."

Joe slowed, a stop sign ahead. "There's an obvious problem with Donny's story."

"I don't see it."

"This guy who was sent to intimidate him came *before* the cops. How would anyone have known what Doran's alibi was before the police?"

That was a damn good question. I didn't answer for a while, thinking of the possibilities.

"Could it be a cop was involved? Jefferson paid one off?"

Joe frowned. "Would have had to pay off more than one, don't you think?"

"That is a problem. I don't know the answer, but I do believe Donny Ward. You've done thousands more interviews than me, Joe. Did you think he was telling the truth?"

"Yes. But I still want to know how that guy appeared on Donny's front porch with a bag of money before the police had talked to him."

"We'll come back tomorrow. Talk to the cops, to the prosecutor, to Doran's public defender."

"And tonight when you see Karen? What will you tell her?"

I looked out the window at the shadowy forests around us.

"I don't know."

Targent was at Karen's house when I arrived. I laid my hand on the hood of his Crown Victoria when I walked to the door and found it was cool to the touch. Great. Targent had been alone with Karen for a while, filling her head with theories that all pointed back to me.

Karen answered the door and forced a smile that was as hollow as they come. Her face was drawn and strained, a mild but noticeable increase. It was as if a sculptor went back and added slight changes each night, a gentle buffing of tension and a few ridges of fear for display in the morning to come.

"Hi," she said. "Detective Targent is in the living room. I didn't know he would be here. I told him you were on your way, and he wanted to wait."

"Grand. I've missed his wit and charm."

She didn't respond, and I followed her into the living room.

"Thanks for joining us," Targent said. He was sitting on the low stone ledge that ran below the fireplace. Daly was missing in action.

"I've got something for you," I said. "While you've been busy getting useless search warrants, my partner and I have actually done some investigating."

"Oh?" His face didn't change. Karen looked interested, though.

"You ever heard of a man named Andy Doran?" I asked. I said it to both of them but watched Karen. The name didn't seem to mean anything to her.

"Nope," Targent answered, and Karen shook her head.

"He went to jail five years ago for murdering a girl out by Geneva-on-the-Lake. The first witness—only witness, actually—to identify him was Matt Jefferson. Matt called his father the night of the murder, then went back to the cops the next day and changed his account of the night in a way that implicated Doran, who was then arrested. Doran said he'd been set up but eventually took a plea for twenty years."

Targent wasn't looking at me. He had his head down, tracing the edge of the stone shelf with his index finger.

"So he's in jail," he said. "Makes it tough for him to wreak such havoc, don't you think?"

"He's out, Targent. Broke out of prison by hiding on a

garbage truck about a month ago. It was, in fact, immediately before Jefferson got his first disturbing phone call."

Targent rolled his head and looked at me. "So the idea is the guy was so pissed off that Jefferson's son identified him that he came after him and his father as soon as he broke out? Give me a break, Perry."

"Maybe he's not just pissed off that he was identified. Maybe there's more to it than that."

"Such as?"

I glanced at Karen. "He told police he'd been set up."

I could tell Karen didn't like this. She saw where I was going with it and shook her head.

"Doesn't *every* criminal say they were set up?"

"Exactly," Targent said.

"My partner and I have already uncovered some fairly appalling evidence of how corrupt the case against him was."

I hadn't decided until that point that I would tell them about Donny Ward. Part of me still thought it was too early, but I'd also expected to receive at least a meager amount of interest from Targent. So far, I wasn't getting that.

"Doran told police he had an alibi," I said. "Told them he'd been with a friend all night. When the cops interviewed the friend, this guy pretended to have no idea what Doran was talking about."

"He probably didn't."

I shook my head. "Joe and I interviewed him this afternoon. He had plenty of reason to lie to the cops back then, but that doesn't mean it wasn't a lie."

I explained Ward's story, but Targent's expression didn't change; there was still no trace of anything but skepticism and strained patience in his face.

"Isn't that enough for you, Targent? Don't you think this is at least worth checking out?"

"I'll check it out, because that's my job, but my perspective right now is that this is more than a stretch. You're forcing it. Even if everything you've told me is true, I don't see the connection between this and Alex Jefferson."

"It's there. Trust me, it's there. The guy who attacked me on the street told me Jefferson and his son had—"

"Hang on." Targent held up his hand to interrupt me. "This is all fascinating stuff, don't get me wrong, but I've got a few points to make before we get lost in this. What did you just say?"

I frowned. "That the guy who attacked me—"

"No. Before that. You said the connection was there, and then you said . . ." He waited.

"Trust me."

He nodded. "That's the one. That's what I was looking for. You said, 'Trust me.' As if you're a reliable source of information to this investigation. As if you're not lying to me now, haven't been in the past."

"That's right."

"Okay. Let's all keep that statement in mind while we watch a movie."

"What?"

"Mrs. Jefferson and I were about to watch a movie when you joined us. I'm glad you'll be here for the viewing. I think that's most appropriate."

Karen was seated in the far corner of the couch, tucked back into it, as far away as she could get from both Targent and me.

"Mrs. Jefferson and I have talked about last night's events," Targent continued. "We both agree that it's unusual that this, um, predator has chosen to go through you if all he wants is money from her. Why pull you off the street before he'd even contacted her? Why shoot up your gym?"

I looked at Karen, and there was a quality in her eyes that I didn't understand. Was it an apology or an accusation? More like something in between, I thought, and then I got it. She was suspicious. Targent had actually pulled that off. Karen was suspicious of me. She didn't want to be, felt bad about it—that was the touch of apology I saw in the look—but she was, anyhow.

"Karen," I said. "You know this is insane."

"I know you have nothing to do with this," she said. "I'm

just confused. I don't understand why someone is making it seem like you do. This man in Indiana who said you hired him—"

"You told her that?" I said to Targent.

"It's relevant to the investigation. I'm trying to keep her up to date."

I shook my head, disgusted. "I don't know what to tell you about that, Karen, except that it's a lie. I never hired that guy."

"I believe you."

"Back to my movie," Targent said.

"You've got to at least hear me out on Doran. There's more here than you understand."

"I'm sure there is. I find it fascinating that you'd locate this suspect with a grudge so quickly after I informed you— and Mrs. Jefferson—that Brewer had heard something along those lines in Indiana. That's a real neat trick of timing, Perry. As was that violent incident at your gym last night."

"You've seen the tape of that. You know what happened, and you know it wasn't some elaborate façade."

For a long moment, he just sat and looked at me. His eyes flicked to Karen for an instant, as if to make sure she was watching, and then back.

"I've been talking to Mrs. Jefferson about the fingerprint we found in her husband's car. This man named Thor."

Shit. That was the last thing I wanted Karen to know about.

"Met with Detective Swanders again today, as well as one of the organized crime guys at the FBI," he continued. "There are people down there who are pretty disgusted with you. People who think you withheld some very important information about the Russians. Some believe you might have interacted directly with Dainius Belov when all that was going on. This Thor guy, they told me, he probably would have been around. Sounds like he's Belov's top lieutenant. I asked the guy at the bureau to give me odds on you knowing Thor, and he said ten to one."

Karen would not meet my eyes. She was watching Targent and would not turn my way.

"You want to tell Mrs. Jefferson how you're acquainted with Thor?"

"Already told you, I don't know the man."

Targent picked up a remote control and turned to the big plasma television beside him. He turned it on and then punched a few buttons on the remote, and the screen turned to a grainy black-and-white image of my gym. It was from my own security cameras, and it showed the front of the weight room, where I stood by the blown-out window with a curl bar in my hands and Thor in front of me.

"Can you tell us who that gentleman is?" Targent said.

Now it was me who couldn't look at Karen. "You know who it is."

"Right. And so do you, Perry. We're sitting here looking at proof that you've lied to me. Remember what you told me this afternoon when we searched your apartment? You told me I needed to prove that you were lying. Consider it done. And lying to me is withholding information critical to a homicide investigation, and that can be considered a crime. You lied yesterday when I asked you about him, then lied again sitting here in front of your client thirty seconds ago."

"You shouldn't have that tape. I never gave—"

"I left an officer watching your gym today. For your own well-being. You know how guys sometimes like to drift back by the scene of a crime, check it out. Thought maybe we'd get lucky, and I guess we did. I just didn't expect it to happen the way it did."

"Your officer didn't shoot that tape. It's from my gym camera. That's illegal search and seizure."

"Perfectly legal. You gave me consent to the tapes in the presence of about five other officers."

"That was for last night's tape."

"Really? Sorry, I forgot. Called your gym manager and told her I had one tape to return and one to pick up. We agreed that it would be best not to bother you. After all, you'd had a long night." He cocked his head. "Tell me why Thor was there."

"Dropped by to ask about a membership. Wants to get back in shape, he said."

Targent's face stayed neutral, but Karen's flushed with anger. I looked at her and felt my shoulders tighten and the back of my neck go hot. Honesty matters deeply to me, and to sit here in front of Karen and lie was painful. I could tell them why Thor had been there, what information he had shared, but I wouldn't. Even if I could disregard the fact that Thor had saved my life once, decide that wasn't enough to earn my silence, I'd be a damn fool to talk. Send Targent back to Thor with the details of our conversation? I might as well start shopping for a headstone.

"I didn't kill Alex Jefferson," I said. "I didn't hire someone else to kill him. All the rest of this is external, irrelevant crap. If you want someone to be guilty bad enough, you can find something that makes him look like a possibility."

"True enough," Targent said. "But I'd like to hear you explain something. *Anything.* Why is this guy going after you? Why did Jefferson's son wait for you to arrive before capping himself? Why is Thor involved, and why are you lying about him? Can you give us *one* answer, Perry? That's what I'm asking from you. *One* honest answer."

"This is ludicrous, Targent. You really think I'm behind all of it? Karen came to *me* about finding Matt, not the other way around. Karen asked *me* to help with this. That's why I'm involved."

"He's right," Karen said.

"Terrific. She brought you into it. What does that explain? Which one of my questions does that answer?"

"That's *your* job. I'm trying to help, but you won't even hear me out on Andy Doran. Aren't you even a little intrigued by the timing of his prison break and those first phone calls to Jefferson? Or do you think it's more likely that I spent the past three years brooding and working up my nut to kill a guy for something that was such a minor offense?"

"Did you think it was a minor offense when you assaulted him?"

"That's in the past, gone and forgotten. Stop trying to make it count."

"I've seen some things that suggest maybe it isn't gone and forgotten, Perry. Your little box of keepsakes . . ."

"I kept photographs of a woman I was engaged to and you think that's evidence of some sort of obsession? Are you serious? It would be more psychotic if I *didn't* have anything like that, if I'd purged it all."

"My partner interviewed one of Alex Jefferson's colleagues. This guy said Alex saw you at his wedding, parked on the street, watching the ceremony. He didn't tell Mrs. Jefferson because he didn't want to put a damper on their special day."

Karen looked at me with surprise and sympathy, and I turned away.

"This is a cheap tactic, Targent. Throwing this shit in my face with her in the room."

"Cheap tactic or not, I'd like you to explain your presence at their wedding. That seems, Perry, like the action of a guy who has not moved on. A guy who has an unhealthy obsession."

I shook my head, not wanting to look at either of them.

"Well?" Targent said. "Can you explain?"

I laughed without humor. "Yeah, I can explain it. I missed her. Is that what you want to hear? That what you need me to say, you prick? I missed her. Was it unhealthy, to miss someone I loved? I don't know. It was just the way it went, for a while. But it stopped going that way a long time ago."

"I don't think we need to be talking about this," Karen said, and the pity in her voice wounded me.

"It's all right, Karen. He wants to lay the pressure on, and that's fine. The sad part is that it's not helping you."

"And you turning up in every corner we check, disrupting our investigation?" Targent said. "That's helping?"

"I'm not turning up anywhere, Targent. Someone's trying to give it that appearance, that's all. But since you can't recognize the truth when you hear it—"

"You know what? I'm done with you tonight. You've had your say, Perry. I'd like you to go on home."

"I came for a few words alone with Karen, thanks."

"You can have them later. I'm not through with my conversation with her, but I am through with you. Take off, Perry. You want to talk to her, you can call her later, although I will urge her not to take your call."

"It's okay, Lincoln," Karen said. "I don't know what's happening, but I do know you. Don't worry about this."

I'd been dismissed. I got to my feet with the two of them sitting there waiting for me to leave, walked down the hall, and let myself out of the house, closing the door on soft voices discussing my potential as a murderer.

CHAPTER

25

Confusion kills.

The words were written on a dry-erase board, with a marker that made a wince-producing squeak at the end of each letter, the old cop's hand moving too fast, using too much pressure.

The training seminar was called "Critical Incident Response," bureaucratic code that meant situations where people were going to shoot at us. I was one of a dozen cops in the room, listening to an instructor who'd trained SWAT teams all over the country for the better part of three decades.

Confusion kills. He read it aloud, then faced us.

"You must know your assailant, you must know your friend," he said. "It sounds simple sitting here in this room. It will not be simple when it's dark and loud and there are bullets searching for your heart. If you are properly trained, properly prepared, you will execute under fire, you will survive, you will accomplish your goals. If you are not, then the first thing those bullets will create is confusion. And confusion, gentlemen, kills."

Matt Jefferson came home from a day in the apple orchard as the sun descended. Pulled his truck into the gravel parking lot beside the barn just as he did every evening, walked up the stone path to his apartment door, and stopped short. Read my note. A man from Cleveland was here to see him. Family business. The man would return.

A few short sentences, one meaning clear to me, another meaning clear to Matt Jefferson. While I sat in a small-town diner, eating pie and thinking about Amy, Matt pulled the note off the door and went upstairs, found a bottle of whiskey and a gun, and walked down to the gazebo to wait.

What a beautiful spot. It must have been something as the sun set, that pond catching whatever muted colors the over-cast day allowed, then fading to a black sparkle as the sky darkened and the moon rose. I'd taken my time with dinner, driven slowly on the return to the orchard. He'd had some time to sit. Listen to the wind, watch the dead leaves fall to the earth, taste the whiskey in his mouth and feel it burn down his throat, the stock of the gun cool and comfortable in his hand.

When I arrived, he knew me. While I banged on his door, within gun range, he knew me. With each echoing step I'd taken over the wooden bridge that brought me face-to-face with him on that gazebo, he knew me. And when he lifted the gun and twirled it and jammed it into his mouth and pulled the trigger, then, he'd known me most of all.

Confusion kills.

Brewer was right, looking at me for murder. In a way, I had killed him. It was my arrival, the sight of me there in the gazebo, my failure to clear the surprise and fear out of my brain fast enough to explain, that made him pull the trigger.

"The son believed me," my attacker had said a few nights later. "He knew that his would be a welcome grave."

True enough. Matt Jefferson had welcomed it, sent himself to that waiting grave, because he knew that what was in store—what I represented—was worse.

So who was I? In that moment that he'd known me, who the hell had I been, and why was I there?

At least he has a reason. You got nothing but greed.

Matt Jefferson believed he knew who I was and what I was after, and that confusion killed him. Back in Karen's living room, the confusion was alive and well again, flourishing, with Targent nurturing it and some unknown participant—maybe Andy Doran, maybe not—validating it. This time, I had the opportunity for a few words of explanation, all that Matt Jefferson would've needed. This time, the words weren't going to be enough. This time, that gun was going to stay pointed at me.

I went into the gym before my apartment, the late-night check such a habit now that I didn't even think about it. The sight of the plastic sheet over the window surprised me for a second. Somehow, the damage to the gym had faded in my mind during the rest of the day.

The day. It had been just that morning that I'd stood in the gym and watched Thor step in through the window. That seemed impossible.

I locked the gym door—as if it mattered with the plastic sheet there instead of a window—and walked back through the office. The message light on the desk phone was blinking, but I didn't stop to pick it up. There would be a message there from my insurance company, a call I absolutely should return, but I couldn't make myself care about that right now. The insurance company wasn't going to disappear, and neither was the damage to my building. I, on the other hand, might need to if Targent came up with any more finds.

There were more phone messages waiting for me at my apartment, most from the gym members who knew me well enough to have my home number, calling to express their concern and pry for details. I deleted them and dialed Amy's number.

"I was waiting for some indication that you were alive," she said when she answered. "I've never dated a guy who presented that problem—the need to check to make sure he was still alive."

"I'm sorry," I said. "I've wanted to call you all day. Things got away from me a little bit. Starting with the gunfire and progressing to the cops exercising a search warrant on my apartment, then producing video evidence that I know Thor and lied about him before."

"Uh-oh."

"Yeah." I leaned against the wall and exhaled, worn out just from reciting the day's synopsis. "Any chance I could see you?"

"I was hoping so. Why don't you come here? No offense, but after last night, I'm not a real big fan of your building."

"A little late-night gunfire and all of a sudden it's a bad neighborhood?"

"Just come over."

She met me at the door, barefoot, wearing a T-shirt that was four sizes too big and her glasses, which she never wore outside of the house. I loved her in the glasses.

"Wine?" She had a bottle in her hand.

"Definitely."

We went upstairs. She poured two glasses of red wine and passed one to me, and then we went into the living room and sat down on the couch. I took a swallow of the wine and closed my eyes.

"Long day?" she said.

I laughed.

"Funny question?"

"Yeah. Just a few minutes ago I was standing in the gym trying to figure out how many days had passed since it got shot up. Had trouble convincing myself that it was really just last night."

I told her about Thor, Donny Ward, the private investigator in Indiana, and Targent's video. It took a while to tell.

"He's serious about this?" she said. "He actually considers you a suspect?"

"Considers me *the* suspect, Amy. And this thing with Thor . . ." I shook my head. "That hurts, no question. Because on the surface it does fit. It really does. This idea that it was a man with a grudge and a hired killer, well, Thor and I make a natural pairing for that. Thor showing up in my gym today makes it a lot worse, too. I can't explain that."

"Why not?"

"When a man like Thor tells you that a conversation is to stay confidential, you'd be well advised to pay attention."

"But if it would clear you . . ."

"Which it wouldn't. There's no evidence that it's true. Targent wouldn't believe Thor, and all I would have accomplished would be to anger one of the deadliest men in the city."

"So what can you do?"

"The job Targent should be handling. Finding a real suspect. If I can do that, show a strong case, they'll have to redirect. Andy Doran could be the ticket."

Amy was quiet. I looked at her and thought that this should be a good night. This moment, on the couch with her sharing wine and conversation one day after we first made love, should have been special, carefree. Instead we were talking about killers and cops.

"It has to stop soon," I said. "Targent's got to burn out with it. That's what happens when you're wrong—you run into the wall. There's no evidence, nothing left to push with."

"Well, when's he going to hit that wall?"

"It had better be soon." I reached out and rubbed her leg. "I'm sorry, Amy. We should be talking about something else. You shouldn't have had to get up at three in the morning to stand around with a bunch of cops, either."

"It wasn't exactly a traditional first date."

"I always try to provide women with something unusual. You know, stand out from the crowd."

"Mission accomplished."

I don't know when the conversation slowed, or when it stopped. All I know is that at some point we both fell asleep on the couch, and when I woke up in the night and saw she was still there I was glad.

I was back in my apartment, getting dressed and drinking coffee, when Joe called.

"You planning to show up today?"

"It's ten to eight, Joe."

"You're going to want to get down here."

"Why?"

"While you were sleeping, I was working, And you will be thrilled to hear what I learned. *Thrilled.*"

"What's that?"

"Remember my problem with Donny Ward's story?"

"How the guy got to him before the cops."

"Exactly. Well, that problem is solved, LP, and the answer is going to make your day."

"What is it?"

"Get down here, and I'll tell you."

Fifteen minutes later I walked into the office and found him behind the desk, a grim smile on his face.

"What do you have?" I said.

"That question ate at me all night, LP. I couldn't put a scenario together to explain it unless Ward was lying or this guy had been following Doran the night Monica Heath was murdered."

"You think that's it?"

He shook his head. "Nope. I got up this morning at about five and read through the case file again, looking for something I missed. Found out that Doran refused a police interview and demanded an attorney. They gave him a public defender, and Doran talked to this guy before he ever told the police his account of the night. The only person who would have known Donny Ward's role at the start was Doran's PD."

"So he had to leak it."

"Exactly. I thought I'd track him down and we could interview him. Learned he's no longer with Ashtabula County. Moved into private practice. Guess where?"

I didn't answer, just waited.

"Jefferson, Groff, and Associates," he said.

I stood where I was and stared at him, watching his smile spread.

"You're serious," I said.

"Absolutely. He's listed on the firm's Web site and with the bar association."

"He went to work for Jefferson. Sometime after he convinced Andy Doran to take a plea bargain that kept a weak case out of court scrutiny, he went to work for Jefferson."

"That's the story."

"Son of a bitch," I said. "We've got him. Jefferson rigged Doran's case from the inside and outside. Intimidated his alibi into silence and paid off his attorney."

"The fact that he works for Jefferson's firm today is not proof of any wrongdoing in the Doran case."

"But you *know* it's there. How many public defenders from rural counties has Jefferson's firm added in recent years, I wonder?"

"At least one."

"Yeah. I'm guessing it wasn't the strength of his résumé that landed him the spot."

"We'll have to confront him, but I don't know how well that will go. Tough to imagine him being as forthright as Donny Ward. The guy's an attorney; he knows what this means—loss of his license and probably jail time. If he undermined Doran's offense, he'll be petrified of us."

"So he'll deny it. Fine. It still gives us credibility with the Doran angle. Even Targent will have to pay attention."

"I also called the prosecutor in Doran's case, a guy named George Hilliard. He sounded leery, but he agreed to give us a few minutes this morning."

"You have any reason to think he was involved with this, not just fooled by it?"

"Can't say for sure, but there's been no obvious indication he played a part."

I nodded. "We'll ask him about the public defender, too. See what he thinks of the guy. I also want to know when Jefferson's firm hired him. How close it was to the Doran case."

"Karen should be able to help with that. She worked for Jefferson's firm. She can get the hire date, I'm sure."

I nodded and walked behind my desk and sat down. "Yeah. It'll take one phone call for her, and probably a court order for me. I need to talk to her, anyhow. I was chased out of the house last night."

Joe raised his eyebrows. "By Karen?"

"Targent. He played a copy of my gym's security tape that showed Thor."

Some of the good humor left his face.

"He did that with Karen there?"

"Yeah."

"How ugly did it get from that point?"

"The two of them asked me to leave so they could finish discussing the investigation. I doubt Andy Doran's name came up often in that conversation."

"So you did tell Targent about him?"

"And wasted my breath." I picked up the phone receiver. "Let me call Karen and get her in action on this public defender. What's his name?"

"Cole Hamilton."

It took Karen one ring to pick up. Probably close to the phone at all times, waiting for another call with instructions about a money transfer. Her voice was tight and unnatural when she answered, and it didn't change much after I identified myself.

"You okay? No calls, no contact?"

"Nothing. It's been quiet."

"Listen, the stuff Targent brought up last night—"

"Don't, Lincoln. You don't have to explain it."

"I felt like I should have warned you about some of it. Particularly Thor. That's my mistake."

She didn't respond.

"Joe and I are working on this, and we're getting somewhere. Andy Doran is more of a legitimate suspect than Targent wants to accept. I think we might have something that can change his mind, though, and I'm going to ask for your help. Can you contact your husband's firm for us and verify the hiring date of one of their attorneys?"

There was a long pause before she said, "Why?"

"His name's Cole Hamilton, and he could be very important to all of this."

"Why do you need this? Why is he important?"

"He was Andy Doran's public defender. We found out he's since gone on to work with your husband's firm."

"Which means what to you?"

"It could be important, Karen. That's all. Matt Jefferson was a key witness, and this attorney going to work for your husband . . . We need to connect the dots. That's all I'm trying to do."

"You're suggesting that Alex hired him because of what happened with that murderer? Doran? You're suggesting that—"

"That he might know information of importance, Karen. I just need to know the date he was hired."

"No. I want to hear what you think happened, Lincoln. It seems to me you're accusing Alex of something horrible."

It was quiet. Ten seconds passed, maybe twenty.

"Well?" she said.

"Something you need to understand, Karen. Whoever killed your husband? He probably had a reason. Okay? He had a reason."

There was a pause, a second or two in which she said nothing, and I actually closed my eyes with regret, understanding how the statement must have sounded to her.

"Do you know what they did to him?" she said. "Do you know the pain he had to have felt, the agony? Now you're telling me that it was somehow *justified*?"

"No, Karen. Damn it, that's not what I said and not what I meant. It was a heinous, terrible crime, but whoever did it had a *motive*. That's what I'm talking about."

"I should never have asked you to do this."

"Karen, I'm trying to help. I'm not concerned in the least with your husband, I'm just trying to show—"

"That's not true. You *hated* Alex. And I understand that, Lincoln, I do, but . . . I just shouldn't have asked you to help. This is my fault, and I don't blame you, but I also don't think you need to be involved anymore. It's not right. Not with the police considering you a suspect—"

"You *know* that's insane, Karen. You have to know that."

"Even so, you shouldn't be involved. It's not fair to you or to my husband. I should have understood that before, and I apologize for putting you in this position."

"You're asking me to quit? Just go away? Karen, we're close to the truth here. Closer than Targent by a mile. You don't want to shut me out of this now. Not with this guy out there and the cops ignoring him."

"Detective Targent can handle the case. I think that's who *should* handle it."

Joe was watching me, picking up on the ugly turn the conversation had taken. I looked back at him as if seeking help, even though he could only hear my side of it.

"Would you at least find out about Cole Hamilton's—"

"No, I won't. Do you not understand what I'm saying? This needs to stop. You need to stop. And, for the record? I know Cole, and he's a good, honest man. Just like my husband was."

Her voice broke, and then she hung up.

CHAPTER

26

I set the phone down and turned to Joe.

"We just got fired."

"Targent's idea?"

"He'll certainly be thrilled, but it was Karen's move. She didn't take well to the suggestion that her asshole husband could have earned the attention of the guy who killed him."

"Not a huge surprise."

"But we've got the right guy, Joe. I don't care what she doesn't want to hear about Jefferson, shouldn't this be the most important issue?"

"She loved him, Lincoln. Doesn't matter if the man is dead now, she's not going to enjoy having him maligned."

I pushed my chair back from the desk and shook my head. Karen had dragged me into this despite my reservations, convinced me to go along with her on a mission that brought me head-on into a battle with cops in two states, and I'd agreed to it because I wanted to help. Thought that I should. Now she was telling me to stop? Saying I shouldn't be *so involved*? I hadn't wanted to be so involved when some bastard masqueraded as me and hired a PI in Indiana, but where was Karen then? Sitting back in her fancy house waiting for me to help. She'd been accepting enough of that help until the moment I suggested her husband could have been anything other than pure.

"I wish she could see him for what he was," I said. "I saw him for that, and Doran definitely got a more painful picture than I did. Doesn't mean Doran's not an evil bastard, but he saw the real Jefferson. Karen's never been able to."

"She saw the side you and Doran never did."

"Saw the façade, maybe. I don't believe she ever saw the real man."

Joe's eyes were sharp as he gazed at me. "So there can't be multiple sides to the guy? He's all bastard, through and through?"

"He sent an innocent man to jail. You're saying that's just the bad *side*? That he could have been a pretty decent human being, other than that little issue?"

"We don't know all the circumstances yet. Okay? We're not done with this."

"According to Karen, we are."

"So that's it? You're stepping away, with the cops still on your ass?"

I didn't answer.

"We've got an interview set up with the prosecutor in Doran's case," Joe said. "You want me to cancel it, trust Targent to sort this out on his own?"

"What time's the interview?"

"In an hour and a half. He emphasized that it would be short."

I stood up. "Better make it count, then."

The Ashtabula County prosecutor, George Hilliard, looked less like an attorney and more like a guy who would own a Christmas tree farm and make furniture with his own hands during the summer months. He was about six-three, with a body that was a chunk of undefined muscle mass, no taper to it at all, and a full beard. He had a suit on, but the jacket was tossed over the back of his chair, and the knot in the tie was awful, the sort of thing a ten-year-old kid tries in place of a clip-on. Joe and I sat side by side in chairs that were about ten inches off the ground, leaving us to look up at Hilliard as if he were seated upon a throne. I wondered if he'd had the chair legs sheared in half to create just this effect.

"Of course I remember Doran's case," he said after I'd made my initial pitch. "I've been in this office seven years and handled just five murder cases. They tend to stand out in my memory."

"Were you aware of Doran's jail escape?" Joe asked.

Hilliard nodded. "I heard about it, yes. Nobody's contacted me, though, and I don't know why anyone would. My knowledge of Mr. Doran has been outdated for quite a while. That's why I'm a little surprised that you think I can help you."

"Can I ask why you offered the plea agreement?" I asked. "If you get only five murder cases in seven years, as you said, then it seems to me you'd want to go all the way with them when they do arrive on your desk."

Hilliard leaned back in his chair, and it creaked ominously beneath him. From what I could see it was an odd-looking wooden swivel chair, the finish seeming heavier on one arm than the other. Maybe Hilliard really did make his own furniture. His face was set in a frown, but he shrugged.

"What the hell, I guess I can say it. I offered the plea agreement because I didn't think the conviction would stand on appeal—if I could even get the conviction. The plea was a better alternative than going into court and getting my ass beat."

"Why didn't you think you could get the conviction?"

"You saw the case file. There was plenty to prosecute on, but in the face of intense scrutiny—the kind you get in court—there would have been some obvious holes, holes that I couldn't fill. Sure, they found the girl's panties at Doran's place, but they couldn't get a DNA match off them, which left the door open to say they'd been planted. Then our key eyewitness had wavered on his testimony."

"You mean between the first night with the police and the story he brought forward the next day?"

Hilliard shook his head, rolling it slowly from side to side, like a bear.

"Nope. That was bad enough, but then he sent me a letter sometime in early fall and said he wasn't going to testify in the trial. Said he'd plead the fifth or claim he didn't remember a damn thing anymore, and that we'd have to send someone out to bring him in because he wasn't going to honor a subpoena."

"That didn't put up any red flags for you? Make you think that maybe his testimony had been bogus from the start?"

Hilliard's lip curled. "Sure, it made me wonder. But the case was already under way, and we still had the panties and no alibi for Doran. Who, I might add, is one dangerous son of a bitch. Felt good about locking him up back then, and I still do."

"Even if he didn't do it?"

"If he didn't kill her, then he shouldn't have taken the plea. Look, I wasn't the one who came up with the plea idea in the first place. I was counting on going to trial, and feeling bad about my chances. Then Doran's attorney starts floating into my office every other day talking about this new scenario with autoerotic asphyxiation, saying he killed her by accident, blaming it on all the drugs and shit in his bloodstream. I ask him if that's where he's going to go with his defense, and he counters by saying that if it is, then maybe we can avoid a trial. Says maybe he could get Doran to cop to a plea agreement if I drop the murder to manslaughter. Hell, it sounded good at that point."

I looked at Joe, and he nodded. This was more confirmation. Doran's own defense attorney had suggested the plea, the means of keeping a case with large holes out of the courtroom, out of heavy scrutiny and further investigation and media attention. The same defense attorney now living large with Alex Jefferson's firm.

"Did the public defender know about Matt Jefferson's letter?" Joe asked.

"No, but I wasn't required to tell him yet. I mean, we still could have subpoenaed the kid and brought him in. I hadn't even had a chance to try to convince him that we really needed his court appearance. I wasn't positive his testimony was gone."

"When Matt Jefferson called the police to change his story, he came with his father."

"I remember him."

"What did you think?"

"That he was protecting his kid, that's all. Only problem I ever had with the father was his involvement with the victim's family."

"I'm sorry?"

"He had the family convinced that he was helping the investigation. Fenton Brooks owned that winery—he's dead now, but he had more money than Fort Knox—and Jefferson was one of his lawyers. Well, I guess Jefferson convinced Fenton Brooks it would be a good idea to talk to the family, see if he could act as liaison between them and law enforcement. Brought one of his investigators in, some ex-cop from Cleveland. Brooks felt guilty about the girl being killed on his property, at his party, I guess. I had a talk with him, told him outsider involvement could only undercut our investigation, particularly when his attorney's son was a key witness. He apologized. Said he'd been encouraged by Jefferson, for liability reasons."

"You do know," I said, "that Alex Jefferson was recently murdered?"

He scratched his beard and studied me, rocking gently in the chair, which continued to creak like an old oak tree in heavy winds. "I am aware of that. Are you suggesting that's related to the Doran case?"

"Doran's out, and Jefferson's dead, Mr. Hilliard. That's what I'm considering."

"So Jefferson was in that house? With one of his investigators?" Joe said.

"Yes," Hilliard said.

"Interesting."

"Why?"

"Well, Doran always said the girl's underwear had been planted, and it didn't have any DNA match except the girl's. Supposing you wanted to find some evidence to plant that *wouldn't* have any other match, where do you think you'd come up with it?"

Hilliard didn't answer, but I did.

"In her home."

CHAPTER
27

Jerry and Anne Heath lived in a modest ranch house at the end of a quiet cul-de-sac in Geneva. There was a flagpole in the front lawn and a big F350 diesel parked in the driveway in front of a two-car garage. Jerry Heath was raking leaves when we pulled in behind his truck, and he gave us a long look but didn't stop raking right away. He finished the stretch between the driveway and the pile he was accumulating and then walked into the garage and hung the rake up on a peg. He was a tall man, wide through the shoulders, with gray hair that hung over the back of his neck and a mustache that hooked down to touch his chin on each side. He wore a plaid flannel work shirt and olive cargo pants and boots. Joe and I were out of my truck and standing in the driveway, but he didn't say a word, just walked past us and hung the rake up and took off his gloves. Then he came back outside and squinted at us.

"You the detectives?"

We'd called after leaving George Hilliard's office.

"Yes, sir. Joe Pritchard. I spoke with you on the phone."

"Uh-huh. Well, let's go on inside. Mother's waiting. She'd like to talk to you."

Somehow it was clear that he was referring to his wife, and it didn't seem at all demeaning to call her "Mother," simply appropriate in an old-fashioned way. He took us in through the garage, walking past neat rows of tools and an old but spotless Buick sedan, and then we entered the house. He stopped and dusted his feet off carefully on the mat inside the door, and Joe and I did the same. The house smelled of potpourri, and there were handmade baskets hung on the walls. We walked through the hall and past the kitchen and out into the living room. A petite blond woman was washing windows with her back to us, spraying Windex on the glass and wiping it clean with a cloth, entirely focused on her work and unaware of strangers in the room.

"Those detectives are here, Anne."

Anne Heath turned to us and smiled, set the Windex and the cloth down in a plastic bucket at her feet, and walked across the room to shake our hands and exchange greetings. She had strong hands, and her face was creased with laugh lines.

We sat on one couch, and they sat together on another. The furniture was worn but comfortable and clean, which went for the rest of the house as well. Everything spoke not of money but of a high level of care.

Joe took the lead, since he'd already spoken to Jerry Heath on the phone, and explained again that we'd become interested in Andy Doran's background through a case unrelated to their daughter's death.

"There are some people we're curious about," he said. "People who were involved in the investigation a few years ago. I know it must be a difficult topic for you, but if you could tell us what you remember about these individuals—"

"We wanted her to go to college, you know." Anne Heath smiled at us. "Her grades were good, and she could have gone. Money might have been a little tight there for a while, but that's how it goes with college. We had some savings. But she said no. She said she couldn't go sit in a classroom again, not so soon. So we agreed that she'd take a year or two off, take a break and work and save some money, and then she'd go back to school."

She was talking more to Joe than to me, and I was glad of that. He had an ability in these situations that I'd never had, a way of talking to victims that comforted them somehow, and it wasn't through anything excessive or dramatic, no tears or hand-holding or blundered sympathies. It was just a quality he had, maybe a quality he'd always had, of looking people in the eye and letting them know that he understood.

"I'm sorry she didn't have that chance," he said now, and Anne Heath smiled again and nodded.

"Thank you. I think she would have done well with it. But God took her, and we've made our peace with that. Have to do it again each day, you know, but we do."

I looked at Anne Heath and then back around the house, and I pictured a twenty-year-old girl growing up here, nurtured and cared for and living clean, and I could understand the desire for a touch of rebellion, smoking a little pot and dating an older guy like Andy Doran and feeling like it'd never catch up in any way that really counted. In fact, if Joe and I were right, dating Doran hadn't. Not in the way her parents thought, at least. Not in the way the police had decided.

Jerry Heath put his hand on his wife's knee and said, "Who was it that you had questions about?"

"There was an attorney who came to see you," I said. "A man named Alex Jefferson."

Jerry and Anne nodded in tandem.

"He came with Fenton Brooks," Anne said. "They brought flowers, and Mr. Brooks was so kind. He told us how awful he felt about it happening at his party, and how he was going to put all the resources he could behind the investigation."

"Jefferson brought a detective," her husband added. "The attorney suggested that he could, you know, help the police out and keep us aware of what was happening."

"Help the police out," I echoed. "Do you remember this detective's name?"

"Robert Walker. He was retired from the Cleveland police. Well, maybe not retired, because he was a pretty young guy, but he'd stopped working for them."

I looked at Joe. "Know a Robert Walker?"

"Nope."

"Me, neither. Mr. Heath, what did this man look like? I'm trying to place him. Joe and I worked with the Cleveland police, too. We should know him."

Jerry Heath turned to his wife with a frown. "He was, what would you say, maybe forty?"

"Or younger. He was Italian, or very Italian-looking. A quiet man. He just listened and took notes, mostly."

"An Italian man named Walker," Joe said, and glanced at me, one eyebrow raised.

"Can I ask whether he was ever alone in your daughter's room?" I said.

Jerry Heath's face went hard and curious, but his wife answered.

"Yes, he was. The police had already searched it, but he wanted to take a look himself, make sure they'd done a thorough job. Wanted to know what they looked at, if they took pictures of anything or wrote down a, uh, what do you call it? An inventory. Said he wanted to be sure it was all being done by the book. I guess he was pretty experienced at that sort of thing."

"He was alone for this?"

"Yes. Mr. Jefferson said he didn't want to make us go through it again, you know, because it was so difficult to go in there and look at everything."

"Why do you ask about that? Whether he was alone?" Jerry Heath said.

"Just trying to understand the situation," Joe said.

The phone rang, and Jerry Heath got to his feet and went into the kitchen and answered. He talked in low tones for a few minutes while Joe and I sat with his wife, waiting on his return. When he came back into the room, his face was dark with anger.

"You fellas got about ten seconds to get the hell out of this house."

"Excuse me?" Joe said.

"That was George Hilliard. The prosecutor. Told me he just got off the phone with the police back in Cleveland. Called to ask about you boys. They told him you're working without police approval or even a client."

He turned from Joe to me, and jabbed his rough index finger at my chest. "And they said *you* are a suspect in a murder investigation."

"What?" Anne Heath stood up fast.

"Somebody killed the same attorney that came in here, trying to help us. The one they've been asking about, Jefferson. Police said this guy's trying to use Monica as a distraction. To use *our daughter* as a way to keep the police off his own back."

"That's not true," I said. "We're trying to prove what really happened to your daughter, Mr. Heath. We think Andy Doran—"

"I will go open this door for you, and you best walk through it with a spring in your step, mister. Because if you don't, I will gladly throw your ass right through it. Now get out."

When we left, Anne Heath was crying.

CHAPTER

28

Anger rode through me like water filling a hose as Joe drove us away. I had my cell phone out of my pocket before he cleared the driveway, dialed Targent's number, and sat through the rings with my hand tight on the phone.

"Who you calling?" Joe said, but I ignored him because Targent picked up.

"Yeah, Perry?"

"You're pathetic," I said. "I'm out here doing *your* job and you try to derail us like that? Tell those poor people that I'm using their daughter as a distraction?"

"I told the prosecutor that you were a suspect, not the family."

"You knew how fast that information would be relayed."

"You're damn right I did, and it *should* have been relayed, too. What you're doing out there is nothing but a hindrance, Perry."

"Somebody should be investigating—"

"Shut up. You call me to cry and bitch? That takes some balls considering I just spent an hour on the phone convincing Lieutenant Brewer not to push for an extradition order that would send you back to Indiana."

"No judge in the world would extradite me based on what he has, Targent. Don't try to pass yourself off as my protector."

"I'm not your protector. Only reason I told him not to go

for it is because you're the centerpiece of a far more important investigation back here. Told him I needed some more time with you. And that evidence you questioned? It just changed, Perry. In a big way. If Brewer wants an extradition order, he's going to get one."

"What are you talking about?"

"You have half an hour to get back to your office. I'll be waiting there. You don't show, maybe I'll reconsider what I told Brewer, arrest you myself and ship your ass back to Indiana."

"I'm an hour away, Targent."

"Well, then, I suggest you hustle."

Targent reached our office before we did. He was out of the car and sitting on a parking block behind the building with a bottle of water in hand, waiting. When Joe pulled into the lot, Targent didn't get up, just sat there and drank his water and watched us get out of the car. Only when we were standing above him did he screw the cap back on the bottle and stand up, without a word of greeting.

"What did Brewer tell you?" I said. "What's the latest bullshit I've got to deal with, Targent?"

"Inside."

We went inside the building and up the steps, and Joe unlocked the office door. Targent went in first and sat down across from my desk. I brushed past him and sat down, pulled up to the desk, and spread my hands.

"Well?"

"At my request, Brewer took the cash that was sent to the PI in Indiana and tested it for fingerprints. I wanted to see if he could pull one of Jefferson's prints, prove conclusively that it was his money."

"I don't care if it was his money, I didn't send it."

"Well, we didn't get one of his prints."

"Tough break."

"We got one of yours."

You hear people use the word "shocked" all the time. They

were *shocked* to find out the ATM overcharged their account by fifty dollars, *shocked* to learn their purebred Shitzu was actually a mutt, *shocked* to discover HBO wasn't included in their deluxe television package. Those people are full of shit. They're surprised, not shocked. Shock is what you feel when you're told something that can't possibly be true, then assured that it is true. Shock is what you feel when a cop finds your fingerprint on money you never handled.

"You're lying," I said. "Bluffing. Good effort, Targent. I'm not surprised to see that's what you've fallen back on."

"I'll have the computer image to show you. It's not just one print. We've got three fingers, showing up on five bills. More that are smudged."

"They were planted."

"You can plant a fingerprint?"

"Of course you can. There's a way. Take something I'd handled, use tape or some shit, some chemical . . . that can happen, Targent."

I felt like a liar as I reached for the explanation, clumsy and inept, Targent watching me with raised eyebrows.

"Really," he said. "Well, I look forward to hearing your defense attorney find a forensic expert to explain it."

"I didn't touch that money, Targent. I didn't send it, and I didn't touch it."

"Just like you didn't know Thor?"

"This is different."

"Sure it is. A different lie."

"I'm being set up. Can't you at least *consider* that as a truth? See it as a possibility? I've come to you trying to explain that Andy Doran is the guy—"

"That reminds me," he said. "Your story about Donny Ward? I checked it out. Called him this morning. He denied every word of it. Said you showed up at his house trying to put words in his mouth. He asked you to leave."

"He's lying."

"*He's* lying. Even though you have no proof of that, I'm supposed to believe it. But when I say *you're* lying, and I do present proof, you remain in denial."

"I've got proof of what I told you about Doran. We talked to the victim's family. Jefferson went into their house with someone he claimed was a retired cop. This guy sounds like the same person who visited Ward. The Heaths won't lie about it, either. Unlike Ward, they have nothing to hide."

He sighed but waved me on with his hand. "All right. Tell me."

I explained more about the cop who had gone with Jefferson to see the Heaths, about the five-year reference from the man who'd attacked me and the way it matched up with Doran's story, about the defense attorney who went to work with Jefferson. He actually took a notebook out and jotted down things as I talked. I was surprised. I'd expected nothing but that bored look, the wiseass skepticism he'd given off like a scent over the past few days.

"Your understanding, then, or your belief, is that Alex Jefferson was responsible for the way things played out in Doran's case," he said.

"Yes."

"Why?"

"Look at the situation, Targent. His son was the only witness to the murder, and then Jefferson swooped in and rigged the investigation. What do *you* think he was doing? I can't imagine he'd ever met Doran before, or that girl. His only connection is through his son. Who conveniently disappeared from the community while all this was going down."

"You suggest that the son was more than a witness."

"Yeah, that's what I suggest. The connection between Jefferson and this guy who visited Donny Ward is what we need to prove. Ward's reluctant to talk to you. Fine. He's scared of Doran, thinks he might be coming for him, the same way he did for Jefferson. I don't blame him for that fear, and it's the only thing that motivated him to talk to me. He thought I'd see Doran."

Targent nodded again and wrote some more in the notebook.

"Go out and verify everything I've just told you," I said.

"It'll hold up, Targent. I know you think it won't, but it's going to."

"Actually, I think it will." He stopped scribbling and closed the notebook. He hadn't shaved, and now he ran the back of his hand over the short stubble and looked at me. "What you've done here seems thorough. Seems solid, too. I mean, assuming the Heath couple tell me the same things they told you, well, this is pretty strong. And you're right—it looks like the sort of thing that can be easily verified."

I didn't like his tone, didn't like the calm acceptance.

"What else you got on your mind, Targent?"

"Just that this is some damn fine detective work," he said, "and fast. I mean, *shit,* Perry, you rolled this together in what, a couple days?"

"Yeah."

"And what got you started, exactly?"

"The comment about paying the price for five years. I already told you that. The way Doran—or whoever the guy was—referred to the phone call."

"Hmm. Damn fast work."

"I get the feeling that's not a genuine compliment, but I also don't care as long as you take this seriously enough to check out."

"Oh, I'll be looking into it."

"Good. Look into it and remove me from your investigation."

He frowned, tilting his head. "Well, that's the problem. I can't see why all this would remove you from the investigation."

"What are you talking about? If all this holds up with Doran—"

"Then I'll be *adding* him to the investigation. But removing you? Let's take a step back, Perry. Remember what seems to have gotten this started. Someone was extorting Alex Jefferson, correct? Made some money from the endeavor and has since refocused on Jefferson's widow. But what was that initial leverage? Tough to blackmail someone if you don't hold some trump cards. If you haven't uncovered a secret, some skeleton in the closet. And to really pull it off? To convince someone not only to play along but to play with big money? That takes a heavyweight secret. The sort of thing that can involve criminal activity, conspiracies, cover-ups. The sort of thing that you"—he tapped on his notebook—"just explained to me in such detail."

"You think I just looked into this months ago, of my own volition, and then decided to blackmail Jefferson?"

"Somebody blackmailed Jefferson," he said, "and so far, you're the first person to produce even an idea of what the blackmail material might have been. Interestingly, you're also the lead suspect. Your background lends itself to a deep investigation of the man's life, to uncovering things that amateurs might not find."

"I haven't had anything to do with Alex Jefferson since that night at his country club. It ended there, Targent. You have to believe that."

"Glad you brought that night up. I heard an interesting story the other day, from someone who was in the country club parking lot. Remember what you yelled at Jefferson that night, right before you swung on him?"

"I yelled a few things."

"You know the one I mean."

I met Targent's eyes. "I said I'd take his life apart."

"That's what I heard. Now the question is, is that what you *did*?"

Responses and rebuttals spun in my head, but I left them there. It wouldn't do any good. Targent was locked on to me now. There was no dissuading him, not until we had somebody else in handcuffs who was ready to confess. Maybe not even then.

"Targent," Joe said, "are you completely ignoring the fact that Doran is *out*? Don't you think the timing of that has significance?"

"Yes, I think it does. It could mean he's involved, or it could mean it gave somebody else an opportunity. If our killer was an intelligent guy, as intelligent as, say, Perry, he wouldn't go through with it unless he felt he had a cover story. A fall guy. The sort of story, the sort of guy, that's been presented today in the form of Andy Doran."

"So I'm still a murderer," I said, "but now I've been promoted to both opportunistic and intelligent."

"Explain the fingerprint, Perry."

"I can't. It had to have been planted."

"Five times. With three fingers."

"Maybe they stole money from me, I don't know."

"Stole a few fifties, but you didn't notice."

"I *don't know*, Targent. All I can tell you is that I didn't send money to that idiot in Indiana."

"But your fingerprints are on it."

"And Jefferson's aren't. You said that yourself. So you've got no proof—*none*—that the money is one and the same."

"I'm going to get it, though. You want to bet everything you've got on one sure thing, pick that one."

He was out of his chair, leaning on my desk, as aggressive as I'd ever seen him.

"I will go down to Jefferson's bank and stay there until I can prove it, Perry. I will drive those people out of their minds, make them show me every camera and every computer and every transaction record and serial number, and I will check and double-check and triple-check until I've got something that proves that was his money. You think that's impossible? You're kidding yourself. That money in Indiana was withdrawn by Alex Jefferson and given to you. I will prove it, and then I'll come down here and put you in handcuffs. When that happens, Perry? You better start telling the truth. You've lied your way through it so far, but that road's coming to an end. I'm sealing it off, understand?"

"The irony," I said, "is that you even believe you could recognize the truth if you found it."

He straightened up and moved back from my desk, his jaw set, and shot Joe a look as if daring him to step in. When Joe didn't say anything, he turned back to me.

"I'll see you soon, Perry. If I were you, I'd spend the rest of the day finding a good defense attorney. Got a feeling you're going to need one."

CHAPTER

29

A fingerprint is a fascinating thing. A small speck of residue left behind at each touch, marking your identity as you move through the world. A fingerprint, like your identity, is unique. It belongs only to you.

Mine was gone.

My fingerprint and my identity. With one went the other, and now a police detective had walked into my office and informed me that they were gone, missing, out of my control.

I had not touched that money. I had not sent it to an investigator in Indiana, had not handled, even seen it. But the facts—those irrefutable scientific facts—said that I had. The reality I knew had just been trumped. People are willing to believe words as the truth up to a point. That point, it seems, is when the facts—particularly those of hard science—dispute the words. Now all I had was the words. Targent had the facts.

It was just Joe and me in the office again, behind our respective desks, angled to face one another, the appearance of the afternoon just like a thousand that had preceded it. None of them had ever felt like this, though.

"You were right," Joe said after a few minutes of silence had passed. "The money isn't Jefferson's. If it was, it would have his prints, not yours. I don't know how they got the money, but—"

"It's his money."

He looked at me as if I'd confessed. "What?"

"It'll be his money, Joe. Targent will prove that. Maybe later today, maybe tomorrow. He'll find a way. It'll be Jefferson's money, and I won't be able to explain it. That's how this is going."

"He doesn't have as much as you think. Not as much as he thinks, either. That money isn't connected to the murder in any direct way. It wasn't recovered on Jefferson's body, doesn't have his blood on it. Even if they do find a way to show it was in that chunk he withdrew from the bank, that's no proof of guilt in a murder."

"Sure," I said, thinking that if Joe had suddenly become the office optimist, this thing was reaching dire straits, indeed.

"How did they get the fingerprint?" he said.

"I do the final money count each night in the gym. Touch a number of fifties. If they stole a few of those, or even one, and put it with the cash they had . . ."

"That would work. But how did they get in the gym office?"

"These guys? I don't think that would be much of a problem."

"Your cameras show the gym office, right? We can go back and look at the tapes and—"

"They don't show the office."

"What? You spend all that money on cameras, don't you want one on the money?"

"It was never about that. The cameras show the gym so people feel safer, and it helps with my insurance liability. I wasn't worried about security in the typical sense, someone breaking in and stealing a few dollars."

He studied me with uneasy eyes, then got to his feet and walked to the window and looked down on the street. He had his hands in his pockets, and his shoulders—good one and bad one alike—were stooped. Usually, he stood so damn straight you wanted to salute and break out into a goose step.

"It's not as bad as it looks, Lincoln."

"That's comforting. Because it looks damn bad."

He turned from the window. "We don't stop. Okay? We don't let this stop us, or even slow it down. We keep working, countering every one of Targent's moves with one of our own."

"He's the one countering, Joe. Each time we make a discovery, he does, too. And his seem to carry more weight."

"There are still things we can prove. Robert Walker, for one. That should be easy. Let's call the department and see if they've ever had a detective by that name. If they have, maybe that's even a bigger break. Maybe he's the one who can explain some of this."

I gave in on that, found the number for the CPD records division, and asked for a woman I'd known for years. She asked for ten minutes to check. It took her five.

"I've got no record of a Robert Walker in this department in the last twenty years," she said when she called back. "There have been seven Walkers, but none of them have Robert as the first or middle name, and the only one who was a detective is still here, and he's a black guy, first name Darryl. Not who you're looking for."

I thanked her, ended the phone call, and turned to Joe. "No Robert Walker. Jefferson brought in a fake cop, and one who matches the description of the guy who threatened Donny Ward."

He nodded, but there wasn't much excitement there. We'd both known Walker wasn't legitimate, so this wasn't news, just confirmation.

"Ward's killing me," I said. "If he'd be honest, if we could show Targent that the guy who threatened him and the guy who came with Jefferson to see the Heath family were one and the same . . ."

"So let's try it. Go out and see him again. Make him understand the importance."

"Whatever he says to us won't mean a damn thing, though. It'll only count if he actually goes through with it, talks to Targent."

"Let's try him," Joe said. "And this time, let's bring a tape recorder."

The tape recorder was a good idea, and maybe it would have paid off if we'd been able to find Donny Ward. He wasn't home, though. We stood on the porch beneath the sagging roof, water from the last rain still trickling through the breaks and cracks, dripping off ruined gutters, and pounded on the door, waited, pounded again. Nobody answered. We tried yelling for Donny, and the only response that provoked was a long, forlorn howl from one of the dogs.

"His truck's here," Joe said.

"Could be out in the woods. Could be someone drove him into work. If he actually works."

"Door locked?"

I tried the knob and nodded.

"Last thing we need to do is force the door, give Targent an excuse to arrest you."

"Probably not the best idea."

It was closing in on five now. The sky was already dark with the rain clouds, but now the day was disappearing, too. We could sit on Donny's porch all night. Maybe he'd show up, maybe he wouldn't. A neighbor came along in a wheezing Honda hatchback and gave us suspicious eyes and slowed before driving on.

"Hate to think we wasted another drive all the way out here," Joe said.

"Should we wait?"

He ran a hand along his jaw, staring at the shadows growing along the porch. "By the time we get back to Cleveland, it'll be late. That attorney should be home, or headed that way. Cole Hamilton."

"You think we should try him?"

"I think we should take a swing before Targent does. Once

he sets up a pattern of lying to the cops, he'll likely stick with it. If we can make him bend first, it would be a help."

"All right."

We walked off the porch, and the dogs milled around our feet, friendly now, even the one who'd growled at us on our first visit. Now we were familiar, or maybe they were just hungry, waiting on Donny's return. When we got into the car, they whimpered, as if they were sorry to see us go. The rain was opening up again, fat drops sprinkling the windshield, then a fast, fine rain by the time we got to the end of the rutted lane. The wind was a steady tug on the trees, peeling away the few leaves that remained on the branches and dusting them across the road. In another month, these heavy clouds would be dumping snow instead of rain, letting loose over Ashtabula County in the way they always did, the wind howling in off the lake, bending the pine boughs and snapping frozen power lines. This was the heart of the Snow Belt, recipient of more annual snowfall than anywhere else in the state. Those lakeside villages, so busy in the summer, would be long-since empty by the first snow, Ohio's version of Maine's south coast—visitors welcome in the summer, but you better be a hardy bastard to hang around in the winter.

We didn't talk much on the drive back, just watched the highway fill with headlights and tried not to think about fingerprints and stacks of fifty-dollar bills. Amy would be home by now, maybe. Be damn nice to pick her up for a proper dinner, share a relaxed evening, no worries of police or fugitives or the faceless associates who swirled around them. I thought of her, and my mind flashed on that picturesque gazebo in the Indiana orchard, cloaked in the smells of the autumn woods. What a gorgeous spot, right up until the blood had pooled on the deck boards and dripped into the shimmering dark water of the pond.

At least he has a reason. You've got nothing but greed.

The city was glowing when we got back, the downtown bridges lit with colorful floodlights. We drove past them and on to the west and got off the interstate at West 150th, headed for Lorain.

"Stopping by the office first?" I said.

"You got Cole Hamilton's address on you?"

"Nope."

"Then I guess we better."

The rain had stopped, at least temporarily, but when we got inside the building it was dark in the stairwell. The only glow was coming from the emergency lights in the jewelry store at street level and the exit sign over the door.

"Power outage," I said. "You write that guy's address down, or will we need to go somewhere else to use a computer?"

"I've got it on paper."

We made our way up the steps through familiarity rather than good vision. At the top of the steps, Joe reached for his keys, but I already had mine out, and I reached past him, got the key in the lock and turned it, stepped halfway inside, and reached for the light switch, sliding my hand along the wall.

"Power's out, remember," Joe said.

"Right. I'm an idiot."

I gave up on the light switch and dropped my hand from the wall just before I felt a hand on the back of my neck and tasted metal as someone pushed the barrel of a gun into my mouth.

CHAPTER
30

It was completely dark inside, and I banged against one of the filing cabinets, stumbling. I still had the gun in my mouth but couldn't see anything other than the silhouette of the man who held it.

"Come on in, Pritchard," he said, and then I knew it was the same man who'd attacked me on the street and called after obliterating most of my gym. "I'm sure you don't want me to pull this trigger any more than your partner does."

Joe stepped slowly into the office, and the door was kicked shut behind him. Then the gun slid away, the sight cutting a furrow through the roof of my mouth.

"Doran," I said.

"Excellent guess. Now, Pritchard, you want to walk across the room and sit down behind your desk, please? And don't worry, I already took the gun from your drawer."

Joe shuffled across the room and sat down. I was still standing, free for the moment, but Doran was right beside me, the gun close to my side. I had the Glock, but it was holstered at my spine. The doors to the building and to the office had been locked, but locks appeared not to be much of a problem for Doran.

My eyes were adjusting, and I could see Doran as more than just a dark shape. He was thinner than he'd been in the case file photographs, and he'd been thin in those. His face looked gaunt, and his body was wiry and tense, laden with a quality of speed. The military buzz cut had grown out into long light brown hair that hung across his forehead and over his ears. He was wearing boots and jeans and a fleece jacket.

"Here's how we're going to do this," he said. "Pritchard, sit behind that desk, stay there, don't make contact with anyone. Perry, you and I are going to take a ride. You're going to drive, and we're going to talk. If your partner does exactly what I told him to do, just sits here and shows some patience, then you're coming back here alive."

For a long moment, nobody spoke or moved.

"Sit tight, Joe," I said. "I'll be back in a bit."

Doran nodded. "What Perry knows is that I've had a couple of opportunities to kill him already, and passed. He's thinking that he'd rather trust me than test me."

"All right," Joe said. "I'll sit here, and I'll wait. For a little while, at least. And then, if he doesn't walk back through the door, I'll go out and find you and kill you, Doran."

Doran smiled at me as a passing headlight bathed his face with a white glow. "Loyal guy, your partner." He walked back to the door and pulled it open, then tilted his head. "You first. Down the steps, then out the back door and over to your truck."

I walked out the door, and a second later it closed behind me, Doran on my heels, Joe alone in the dark office. We went down the steps and out the back door and into the parking lot. Doran was walking close to me but a half step behind. We got into the truck, and I started the engine as he settled into the passenger seat with the gun, a big Colt Commander, resting in his lap, pointed at my stomach. His hands were covered by thin gloves.

"Go out of the parking lot and turn right and stay on that street," he said.

I turned onto Rocky River and drove north, as he'd requested. The radio had come on with the car, and Doran didn't turn it off. U2 was singing of a city of blinding lights. Maybe Doran was a Bono fan.

"You've been busy," he said. "Nice file you've put together.

I didn't bother going through the whole thing, though—it's pretty familiar to me."

"I'd imagine."

"How long have you been working on me?"

"A few days."

"Got to me fast." He nodded as if in approval. "Maybe this is good. Maybe you understand some new things, or understand them in new ways. You see my situation, don't you? I can't go away from this without some money, Lincoln. Got nowhere to go."

"You've got nowhere to go? I'm on my way to prison thanks to you."

"Looking to the wrong person for sympathy, Lincoln. I've *been* to prison thanks to Jefferson."

"So now you want to pull the same trick on somebody else?"

"Take the next street," was his answer.

I pulled off Rocky River and onto West Clifton, which continued north. We crossed Detroit and went over the old Norfolk Southern railroad tracks, and then West Clifton joined Clifton Boulevard, an east-west street running past beautiful old homes on tree-lined lots.

"Go right," Doran said, and I turned again, headed east.

We went a few blocks before he ordered a left, giving me an idea of where we were going. Lakewood Park was down here, a busy place on a summer evening but probably plenty desolate on a cold, rainy October night. Doran had me pull into the lot and then asked me to get out of the car. He hadn't checked me for a weapon, which seemed like a substantial oversight, but maybe he was just that confident in his ability to kill me if I went for it.

There was no one at the park. Doran ordered me to walk down toward the lake, past the picnic tables and shelters and swings. Then he moved me toward the edge of the tall fence that bordered the park, with strands of barbed wire across the top. There was a hole in the fence at this corner, probably cut open during the summer by kids who wanted to get down to the lake and drink or make out. Doran waved the gun at it.

"Go through."

I looked back at him as I reached for the loose section of fence. Ahead of us was a steep decline leading down to the jagged boulders that made up the breakwater along the lake's edge. Doran might have said he didn't intend to kill me, but he was taking me to a place where doing so would be convenient. It was isolated down there, and loud, with the water beating on the big rocks. Easy chore to kick a body into the lake, too.

"Go through," he repeated, his voice firmer, the gun raising a few inches. I pulled the loose fence back and stepped through the opening. He followed close behind, jamming the gun into my back. He put it up high, above my kidneys, so that it didn't touch my own weapon, but I was still afraid he might have seen the Glock's outline under my jacket.

There was a paved path down here that wound all the way to Edgewater Park. We walked along it for maybe two minutes before Doran ordered me to leave the path and walk across the large rocks that made up the breakwater. The huge blocks of stone were scattered at all angles, making for treacherous walking even during daylight hours. I went slowly and carefully, using my hands to help find balance as I worked my way down to the lake. Behind me, Doran moved nimbly, jumping from rock to rock without any hesitation.

The farther we got from the path, the closer to the lake, the worse I felt about it. I'd believed him back at the office when he'd told Joe he had no intention of killing me—why not take both Joe and me out if he wanted to kill, after all—but now I was losing that sense of security. He'd had no interaction with Joe; he'd given Joe no warnings. Maybe, in his twisted mind, that gave Joe a pass.

The rain had started again, light and cold, making the rocks slick. I was almost down to the lake's edge now, trying to use the sounds of Doran's footfalls on the rocks to place where he was behind me, and wondering if I had a chance of getting the Glock out before he shot me, remembering that brief struggle we'd had on the sidewalk on Chatfield, the astonishing speed he'd displayed.

"Stop," Doran said. The command didn't mean much, because to keep walking would have required plunging into the lake. I stood on the wide, flat rock at the water's edge and turned to face him. He was one rock above me, the gun held against his leg.

"There a reason we couldn't have this chat elsewhere?" I said.

He glanced down at the gun in his hand, then back at me. "I hadn't even planned this out yet, you know? Been thinking about it, but I wanted you alone. Then you two pulled up, and everything changed. I hit the circuit breaker and waited."

Great. All of this was a fly-by-the-seat-of-a-psycho's-pants outing, then. Made me feel even better about standing down here at the edge of the lake, nothing around us but rocks and rain.

"You understand things a little better now than when we last talked," he said.

"Which time? The time you shot up my gym or the time you knocked me out on the street?"

He raised the gun in a lazy arc and leaned forward, put the barrel against my forehead. The metal was cold and wet against my skin, and even in the darkness I could make out one raindrop resting on his gloved trigger finger.

"About six years ago," Doran said, "I came to this spot with Monica Heath. It was summer, and it was hot. Humid. Just walking down here from the park had my shirt stuck to my back. We brought down a two-liter bottle of Coke and a fifth of Captain Morgan and two paper cups. Had it all in a backpack. There were a couple of boats out in the bay, and one guy was water-skiing, pretty good at it, too. We sat here on these rocks and drank rum and Coke and watched the guy on the water skis and the sun went down and the whole lake glowed orange. Someone started a barbecue up at the park—I remember we could smell the smoke and the meat and hear the people laughing. They tossed a Frisbee over the fence and lost it. Thing fell all the way down here and got caught in the top of one of the trees. By the time the Captain was gone, we thought that

Frisbee in the tree was pretty damn hilarious. Then the sun went down, and the lake went from orange to black and the lights came on over at the Jake and we smoked a bowl and fell asleep on the rocks."

The gun snapped off my forehead and dropped, and I reminded myself I could breathe again.

"That," Andy Doran said, "is as much of a crime as I ever committed with Monica Heath."

The rain had increased a bit, speckling the lake behind me and falling silently through the bare limbs of the trees. Doran's hair was wet now, plastered against his forehead.

"Did Jefferson's son kill her?" I said.

He nodded. "Then his father rigged the investigation."

"How'd you find out?"

"Got a postcard from a friend. A friend who'd helped put me in, by lying to the cops."

"Donny Ward. He told us what happened."

"No shit? I haven't looked old Donny up. Figure if I see him, I might kill him. That's not something I want. He didn't drive the train, you know? Alex Jefferson did."

"How do you know?"

"I got that postcard, I decided I'd better contact my old lawyer, the guy who convinced me the plea was the way to go. Found out he was working with Alex Jefferson. I got to working it out pretty quick after that. Jefferson's son lied to the police. I could never understand why he did that unless he was involved in what happened. Found out they paid off my lawyer like that, and the rest of the math wasn't too hard."

"Once you learned all that, why not make an appeal? Get someone looking at your case."

"Because it would have given them time."

"What?"

"Think about it, Perry—I had to sit in prison and wait for people on the outside to look into it. As soon as the first call was made, Jefferson would have been back on it, pulling more of the same shit that got me locked up in the first place. I was supposed to trust another asshole attorney to do a better job than the first one had? Trust the cops? Not happening. It was *my* score to settle, in *my* way. You get that? It wasn't just about a prison sentence, it was about Monica."

Doran shifted on the rock above me, taking a few steps to the right, his footwork steady even on the slippery surface. The rain was still falling, and both of us were soaked. Every so often the wind off the lake would pick up and seem to drive the cold water right into me.

"I called Jefferson the day I broke out," Doran said. "Called him and told him I was coming for him. He denied everything, of course, pretended not to have any idea who I was, but the fear, Perry, the fear came off him and rolled right through that phone line, filled the booth I was in. Then I came for him and the son. The son got it. He understood what the end would be like. Believed me from the start. But not his father. I was ready to kill him, you know, ready to end his life, and the prick didn't even get that. Thought he'd handled it."

"He sent someone to kill you."

"And offered a disappointingly low price for such a wealthy man. Convincing his, uh, employee to change plans was not a difficult job, Perry."

My hand was high on my hip, inches from the Glock, and Doran didn't seem to notice. He was calm enough right now, and pointing the gun at the ground, but that didn't mean I should trust him to stay that way.

"You're setting me up," I said. "And it's working. That really what you want? To send another innocent person to jail? I'm the one telling the cops what happened to you, Doran. I'm trying to help."

"You were warned, you were given simple instructions, and you did not listen. That's not on me."

"How'd you get the fingerprints on that money?"

"Wasn't my idea."

"Wasn't your *idea*? Well, you did it, asshole. I'm supposed to think you're some sort of innocent in this, pushed along against your will?"

"Yeah, you should think that. It's the truth, my friend. It's what I *always* was. You want to thank somebody for your troubles, thank Jefferson."

"You got what you wanted," I said. "Killed Jefferson and scared his son to death. Walk away, then, Doran. The score's been settled."

He spread his hands, the gun now pointed up at the trees. "Walk away with *what*? Where can I go? Right back to prison, with more years tacked onto the sentence?"

"You've done a good job of staying out so far."

"I need the money. And taking it from Jefferson's bitch? I gotta be honest—that shit appeals to me."

"She's not going to pay."

He dropped his arms and looked at me with eyes that seemed almost sad. "Then people are going to die, Perry. People are going to die."

The menace that had been in his voice the last time we'd met was back in full force. He moved again on the big rock, turning away from me slightly to look down at his footing as he stepped. I hadn't even planned on going for my gun, but when he turned away like that, the opportunity was there, maybe the only good one I was going to get. The holster at the small of my back had a Velcro security flap instead of one that snapped, and a single, quick tug was all I needed to free the Glock. I drew it faster than I'd ever drawn a gun in my life, got it out of the holster and brought it around to bear on Doran's chest, and right then he said, "Got ya."

His back was still to me, his head turned so that his chin was against his left shoulder, looking back at me. The Colt Commander was pointed at my stomach, just off his right hip. It had been a staggeringly quick move; when instinct would have called for turning and facing me, he'd simply looked back over his shoulder and reversed the gun in his hand. Even standing there with his back to me, he'd beaten me.

"Feels like a tie," I said. That awkward position, calling for him to fire almost behind his back, should have given me a clear advantage. But when the distance between a gun and the target is about four feet, that advantage disappears. If he squeezed the trigger, he couldn't help but hit me.

"Gonna kill me, Perry?"

"Could be."

For a moment we were frozen there, our guns not wavering. Then Doran shrugged his shoulders and lowered the Commander.

"I took a big risk coming to find you. But I've been watching you. Got the idea you knew who I was, that you were getting a sense of the situation. Figured I owed you a real explanation. I've given that. Want to take me down, now's the time."

I took one step forward. "Put the gun on the rock, Doran."

He shook his head. "Nope. You want the gun, you better shoot me."

Another step forward, but Doran countered by moving away, sliding backward. "Not ready to take the shot?"

"I'll take it if I need to take it."

"Why?"

"Because you're a murderer, Doran."

"Killing a man who set me up for his son's crime, that's not murder—that's justice."

"Not in anyone's world but yours."

"Then take the shot!" He stuck the Commander in his waistband and held up his empty hands, spread them wide. "Take the shot, Perry. You think that Jefferson didn't deserve to die? Here's your chance to settle it up, then. I know you owe him a whole hell of a lot, right?"

"I don't owe him shit." I kept shuffling forward, closing the gap. He was higher than me, though, my head even with his chest as he stood on the rock, daring me to shoot him.

"But I did?"

"He deserved to go to jail, Doran. Not to die."

He threw back his head and laughed, and even as he did it he took another quick step backward, onto another, higher rock.

"You actually believe that could happen? That in this system we've got, this *justice* system, a millionaire attorney is going to go to jail and a poor guy with a record is going to walk? Bull*shit,* man. The way I look at it? Fate cut me a break and dealt Jefferson exactly what he'd earned when I rode that trash truck out of prison. That's justice, Perry, sweet as it gets."

"And extorting his wife? That's justice, too? Not enough you took her husband, you also have to take her money?"

"I did *five years*, man. That's not worth a few dollars to you? The fact that I did *five years* for another man's crime?"

"It wasn't Karen's crime."

"Wasn't her money, either. Not originally."

"Get on your knees and put your hands behind your head, Doran. You're going to jail tonight, and then you can tell the police and the jury what your vision of justice is. Because right now, I'm the best suspect they've got, and I am not willing to go to prison for your sorry ass."

A laugh bubbled out of his lips, the wild sound riding the wind just a pitch above the water thudding against the rocks at our feet.

"Here's the beautiful thing—you could run me into jail tonight, let me sit there for weeks, months, years, and it wouldn't help you. They could run every DNA test in the book at me, bring out the best detectives in the state, the FBI, the CIA, Sherlock Holmes, whoever the hell they got. They can run 'em all at me, and still your ass wouldn't be cleared."

My foot slipped on the rock and splashed into a shallow pool of trapped lake water, but I hardly noticed the chill. I was holding the gun on him, but he was still chuckling, looking at me as if I were the straight man in a comedy routine and didn't even realize it.

"What are you talking about?"

"If the cops get me, it won't help you. Know why?"

"No."

His smile widened. "Because I didn't kill him, Perry. I did not kill Alex Jefferson."

I could add a few ounces of pressure to the Glock's trigger and end this all right now. Call Targent to come down here and collect Doran's body and figure the rest of it out. But the longer I looked at Doran down the barrel of the gun, the more convinced I became that it wouldn't be the end of anything. He wasn't lying.

"You dragged me off the street and put that bag over my head and *bragged* about killing him," I said, the words coming slowly. "Told me why you'd done it, told me why it was justified."

"I know that. But it wasn't true."

"Why claim it, then?"

The deranged look of amusement left his face, replaced with anger.

"Because it should have been me. The son of a bitch sent me to jail, set me up, made me do five years for his son's murder. It should have been *me*."

Doran planted his feet firmly on the rock and looked down at me, the barrel of my gun pointed at his chest.

"Last chance, Perry. You want to finish this, go on and take the shot."

I kept the gun where it was, didn't say a word.

"All right." He lifted two fingers to his forehead in a salute. "See you around."

"You're not going anywhere."

"Then take the shot," he said again, and he began to run. He was gone from one rock and onto the next almost before I saw him move, running across the slick, uneven stones as if they were part of an indoor track, designed for speed and balance.

For a moment I stayed where I was, kept my feet planted and swung the gun after him. He was bouncing from rock to rock, though, moving horizontally and vertically at the same time.

"Shit!" I said, and then I lowered the gun and began to run after him.

He moved incredibly fast, considering the darkness and the treacherous footing. I was trying to match his pace and simply couldn't; he seemed to make decisions about which rocks to hit even before they came into view, barely touching the surface of one before leaping to the next. We'd gone maybe thirty yards when my foot came down on a smooth, wet rock that was like glass. My front leg slipped out from under me and I was falling backward and sideways. My ribs connected with the edge of a stone slab, all the air vanishing from my lungs in a burst of pain, and then I was on my back, the gun clattering to the ground somewhere behind me.

I sat up as quickly as I could, but for a few horrible seconds it seemed I wouldn't be able to draw a breath. Then the air came back in a long, shuddering gasp, and I struggled to my feet and looked for the Glock. It was wedged between two of the rocks behind me. I took a few painful steps over and picked it up, brushed off the dirt and rain, then looked ahead.

Doran was at least fifty yards in front of me now, and he'd climbed up to the edge of the breakwater, where the trees came in. He paused for a moment and turned and looked back at me. Then he lifted his hand, waved it once, and disappeared into the trees.

CHAPTER

31

By the time Targent arrived there were a half-dozen uniformed cops combing the breakwater and surrounding woods. I knew they wouldn't find Doran, but I'd made the call anyhow—after placing one to Joe. He'd beaten the police to the park and stood with me in the rain while I'd recounted my story to a sergeant who looked skeptical at best and seemed relieved to hear Targent was on his way, somebody to receive the baton.

I gave it all to Targent as he stood with his hands in his pockets, rain shedding off the baseball cap he wore.

"Six hours ago you wanted me to believe Doran killed Alex Jefferson," Targent said, watching the flashlight beams play across the wet grass around us, searchers looking for Doran. "Now you're telling me you were wrong. That he thoughtfully grabbed you and drove you down here to explain this?"

"It's one of the things he said."

"So who did kill Jefferson?"

"I don't know."

"He failed to mention that one? Too bad. But you say he did admit to being involved in this extortion attempt. Took the credit."

"Yes."

"While you were down here, he didn't happen to make a phone call?"

I wiped rain out of my eyes and shook my head, spraying water like a dog. "No. Why?"

Targent just nodded. "You want to get in my car for a second? Both of you? Get out of this rain."

We sat in his car, Joe in the back, Targent and I in the front. He turned the dome light on, then held up a small tape recorder.

"You say Doran was with you at 7:00 P.M.?"

"Yes."

"And he did not make a phone call."

"No."

"Karen Jefferson received a phone call tonight. We've got a trap on her line." He rolled the volume switch up with his thumb. "I want you to listen."

He pressed play. There was a momentary hiss of static, and then the first voice came on.

"Hello?" Karen.

"How's my money looking? Ready to move, or have you been too busy with the police?"

This voice meant nothing to me. It was deep and distorted, probably altered with some electronic device.

"I haven't been busy with the police."

"That's not true. You've spent a lot of time with them, despite clear instructions that you should not."

"They're investigating my husband's murder. They're going to be here. I can't stop that. I can't stop that." Karen's voice rising with frustration and fear.

"You're under a lot of pressure. That's too bad. But it's not my fault. I was promised my money. If you're upset about that, you should talk to Lincoln Perry. You've spent a lot of time with him, too."

"What about Lincoln?"

"Like I said, I was promised my money."

"By who? What's that have to do with Lincoln? Who promised you any money?" Karen's voice was balanced on a sharp edge, a scream on one side, tears on the other.

"Lincoln."

"What?"

"Lincoln promised me my money. I don't know what he's convinced you of, but he convinced me that I was going to be paid. I intend to see that happen. He won't stop it, and neither will you."

"Lincoln didn't promise you any money! Who are you? Why are you—"

The line had already gone dead. She stopped shouting only when the dial tone began to hum. The static hiss returned, and Targent shut off the tape, his eyes locked on my face.

"Comments?"

I didn't say anything. I stared at the tape recorder in his hand as if it were alive, a person who had done me harm.

"That's cute," Joe said, "but it doesn't make a damn bit of sense. If you think Lincoln made that call, why would he possibly implicate himself? If you think he's been working with someone to get that money, why would he be implicated now? It's clearly a weak attempt to set him up."

"It doesn't make a damn bit of sense? Fair enough, Pritchard, but I could repeat the phrase back to you for *everything* your partner has told me since this got started. You know why? Because when you stack lies on top of lies, *none* of it makes any sense."

"Can't you see that I'm being set up?" I said. "First the fingerprints, now this call, it's just a—"

"Speaking of fingerprints, you say he was in your truck?"

"Yes."

"So he should have left some of his own."

"He wore gloves."

"Of course he did. Maybe there's some other evidence. Fibers, a boot print, something."

"Maybe."

"Glad you're in agreement. For that reason, I'm going to impound the vehicle."

"Go for it."

"While I'm at it, maybe take a good look at those tires. See if they match with the plaster casts we made in that field where Alex Jefferson was found."

"They're not going to fit," I said, but by now I wasn't even sure of that. I was still hearing the voice on that tape using my name again and again, Karen's voice on the edge of hysteria.

"Maybe not," Targent said, "but I've stopped trusting your assurances."

"I'm going to see Karen. I know she can't believe any of this, but I need to see her."

Targent shook his head. "That's not happening."

"You can't stop it, Detective."

"My partner is still with Mrs. Jefferson. She is quite distraught. She has agreed, with our admitted encouragement, to request a formal protective order banning you from any further contact until this thing's settled. Until the court paperwork is done, that protective order will be enforced by police. You so much as call her, and I'll have your ass in jail within an hour."

"You can't do that, Targent. That's your idea, not hers. This son of a bitch calls and now you're trying to cut me off from her? Not happening. I'm going over there."

"Then you're going to jail. One phone call, and you're going to jail."

I looked at Joe and saw nothing but helplessness in his eyes. What was Karen doing right now? Listening to Daly nurture the ideas Targent had planted?

"We can make this go easier," Targent said, leaning toward me, half of his face lit by the dome light, his elbow propped against the steering wheel. "If you didn't kill the guy, now's the time to talk. Tell us who did. Tell us what you know. Do that, and things can be a lot less painful."

"I gave you every damn detail. Doran's the guy, and his partner was hired by Jefferson."

"I'm done listening to that shit, Perry. I've busted open some of your lies already, and I'll keep right on doing it, and the longer you sit there with your mouth shut, the more certain I am that you ran the whole show. That you killed Jefferson."

I didn't answer.

"Dwell on that," he said. "And get out of my car."

CHAPTER

32

They towed my truck out of the park, and Targent drove off and left me standing there in the rain. The same sergeant who'd been so eager to pass the buck to Targent took pity on me now; he offered me a jacket and asked if I needed a ride home. I told him Joe would take me.

By the time we left, Joe was rubbing his bad shoulder, water dripping down his scalp and out of his hair and beading up on already saturated clothes. He turned the engine on and cranked up the heater. We sat there while the vents blasted us with tepid air that soon warmed and fogged the windows.

"I had him," I said. "Could have shot him in the knee, dropped him, been done with this thing."

"You wouldn't have been done with it. Not if Doran didn't kill him."

"Maybe he knows who did. At the very least he could have cleared me for this phone call. I should have taken the shot, Joe."

"You think?"

I pictured Doran running across the breakwater, saw his back over the barrel of my gun again, and I shook my head. I wouldn't take the shot now for the same reason I hadn't then—I believed him. Believed him when he said he didn't kill Jefferson, and believed him when he said he'd been set up for the murder of Monica Heath. That didn't mean having him in custody wouldn't be a tremendous help to me. It just meant I wasn't ready to shoot him in the back.

"His partner is driving this," I said. "He must have made that phone call. I doubt Doran even knew about it."

"The invisible, nameless partner. No wonder Targent's not a fan of that explanation. Who the hell is this guy, Lincoln?"

"Whoever Jefferson hired to kill Doran. We know he tried to recruit Thor and failed. Clearly, he didn't give up there. Somewhere along the line he found someone who was willing to help, and that's the guy. He joined up with Doran, maybe even killed Jefferson."

"That doesn't make any sense."

"No?"

"This guy decides to partner with Doran for what purpose? Blackmailing Jefferson into a big-league payout, is what we've decided. So why kill him before the paycheck arrived?"

I sighed and ran my hands through my hair. Somehow the heater was making me more aware of how wet I was, intensifying the cold.

"I want to get out of here, Joe. Let's go home."

The cops were closing up when we drove out of the park, returning to patrol cars with nothing to show for their search but wet clothes and muddy boots. Below us, rain hammered the big slabs of stone on the breakwater. I tried to find the fence, to locate that hole where Andy Doran and Monica Heath had descended five years earlier with a bottle of rum. It was too dark, though, and the rain was falling too hard.

When Joe dropped me off outside of my building, my eyes went up the street and found a car parked in a space always vacant at night. Long and low, like a Crown Vic or a Taurus.

"Targent left somebody on me," I said.

Joe found the car without needing me to point it out. He stared at it for a long time. Then he said, "You want me to go somewhere else, see if they follow?"

"Let them sit."

I got out of the car and watched him drive out of sight, then went into my building. Upstairs, I took off my soaked clothes and threw them in a pile on top of the washing machine, then got in the shower and turned the water up hot.

When I was out of the shower and dressed in dry clothes, I stood in the living room with the lights off and looked out at the street. The car was still there, keeping watch. The longer I looked at it, the angrier I got. They'd searched my home and taken my truck, and now they watched me through the night.

I closed the blinds, leaving the apartment even darker, and called Amy. It was a nice normal-relationship move—come home and share a conversation about your day. In a normal relationship, though, that talk would probably involve board meetings and problems with the fax machine and maybe a dental appointment. With me, it was murder, the taste of a gun barrel, and police interrogation. At least I bring home a little color.

"It's Lincoln."

"You okay?" Her voice showed she'd either been asleep or close to it, the words thick and unfocused.

"Been better. You need to get back to bed?"

"No, no. I just called you a while ago." I could hear a rustle, probably as she sat up in bed. "What happened today?"

"My fingerprints were discovered on Alex Jefferson's money, Andy Doran stuck a gun in my mouth, and Karen fired me before agreeing to request a protective order."

There was a pause, and then she said, "I guess I won't bitch about all the trouble I had with my e-mail, and the flat Diet Coke I got at lunch."

"Hey, this isn't a competition over who had the toughest day. I'd be happy to listen to your woes."

"What a mature approach to communication."

"I learned it in relationship school. Been taking online classes for your benefit."

"You can use the help."

"Thanks."

"You want to come over here, as long as you woke me up anyhow?"

I started to say yes but stopped. "Probably not a good idea. A police surveillance team will follow me down there if I do, and I don't want these idiots to get involved in *your* life, too."

"The fingerprints . . . are those something they can use to actually . . ."

"Send me to jail? Maybe. Any chance you have a conjugal visit fantasy?"

"Eh, no. I guess I'd have to break you out."

"Just tell me where to find the tunnel when you dig it."

"No tunnels. I don't like dirt."

"Over the wall, then?"

"Oh, yeah. Much more style. I've got a grappling hook in the closet just begging for use."

The stupid jokes and silly conversation were helping me in a way nothing else could have, letting some of the tension out of my muscles, pushing that surveillance car on the street into the back of my mind.

"I can't tell you how much I've needed you this week," I said. "And, no, not as a surrogate Joe."

"I already apologized for that, Lincoln."

"I know. But you get what I'm saying."

"Yes. I'm glad."

"When this ends, let's go somewhere. Take a weekend. Be alone, and without cops parked outside the door."

"I hear Indiana's lovely this time of year."

"Bad joke."

"Yeah."

We talked for a long time, and then I realized that it was very late and she had to work in the morning, and I said goodbye and hung up the phone and walked back to the window to check on my watchers. They were still there, rain dancing off the roof of the car. Without the lights on they probably couldn't see me, but I showed them my middle finger anyhow, just in case, and then I went to sleep.

When the phone rang, I thought it was another call in the middle of the night. Then I opened my eyes and saw a gray light in the room. I checked the clock and found it was just past seven—ten more minutes and the alarm would have gone off anyhow. The phone was still ringing, and I reached for the handset before I realized it was my cell and grabbed that instead. The number was blocked. I answered and said hello, offering more of a croak than a clear word.

"Hate to wake you," an unfamiliar male voice said, "but this is the biggest day of your life, Lincoln, and it's probably a good idea to get an early start."

"What?" I sat up, trying to place the voice, knowing only that it wasn't Doran or Targent or anyone else I'd talked with recently.

"Payday, Lincoln. Payday. You're going to make that happen for me. Someone needs to convince Karen Jefferson to move that money. You volunteered for the job."

"She's not paying, and I can't talk to her, asshole. Thanks to everything you've done, she has a restraining order against me."

"You'll find a way to convince her how important this is, because I've certainly found a way to convince *you.*"

"Yeah?"

"Want to say good morning to your girlfriend?"

I got to my feet and stood beside the bed with the phone in my hand, every muscle suddenly very awake, every nerve very cold.

"You understand what that means? Or you want me to explain in detail? Okay, here goes—I've got your girlfriend, Perry. Right here with me. I'd let her talk, but she's not really in the mood right now."

"You son of a bitch. She's got nothing—"

"To do with this? No shit. Neither did you, but you decided

to join in. Well, now you're in. And since you made it so damn clear you'd like to be involved, we've decided to deal directly with you. The blond bitch here didn't think it was the best method, but I've assured her she's wrong. Now, tell us one more time that Jefferson's wife won't pay?"

"I can't get her to pay. I can't even *talk* to her. Cops are all over that house, waiting to arrest me if I show up."

"Sounds tough. You've got the rest of the day to figure it out. I'll find a way to keep myself occupied. Maybe with your girlfriend."

"If you touch her—"

"Shut up. She's fine, but you're in no position to make threats, either. We're going to get our money. Not in some meeting under the highway like this was a movie, either. You'll never see us, so don't worry about getting any opportunities to stop this. Your *only* opportunity is to follow instructions. You've got the rest of the day to convince Jefferson's wife to get the money ready to move. I'll be calling tonight with an account number and some simple instructions. She'll move the money to it herself, using a computer. When we're satisfied that we've got the money and that the transaction wasn't rigged, you'll have an opportunity to collect your girlfriend. That'll be on our terms, too. As of this moment, you've lost all control of the situation."

"You're the reason I can't talk to Karen. You set me up, then expect that I can convince her to pay you? That's not possible."

"You'll need to make it possible. Go ahead and make a decision on the police, too. You want to bring them in, you know the risk. I think you're smarter than that. Cops aren't going to work fast enough to give you a prayer. And, Perry? For all the work you've done on this, have you seen me yet? Even know my name? Think about that."

He hung up.

PART THREE

GUILTY MEN

CHAPTER

33

I lowered the phone and flipped it shut, my fingers moving from instinct, disconnected from my brain. For a moment I stood still; then I crossed the room to the window, spread the blinds with my hand, and looked out to see the unmarked car still parked on the street.

She'd wanted me to come to her apartment, and I'd declined because the police would have followed. Because the police would have been present and watching all through the night.

"She's not part of this," I said, and the apartment didn't answer. She was part of it now, though. Thanks to me.

There were decisions to be made, but I couldn't focus on them. The options slid in and out of my brain mixed with snapshots of her, the way she'd looked in that oversized T-shirt and her glasses, how she'd promised to break me out of jail with a grappling hook because it had more style.

It was seven twenty in the morning. Outside, traffic was picking up on Lorain, the day getting started, people who would deal with nothing more critical than a tax form or an oil change today already in motion as I stood frozen in my apartment, listening to them pass by.

"Move, Lincoln." I said it aloud again, and the words rang loud and foreign through the empty room. "Move."

I pulled on clothes and tied my shoes, fastened the holster

against my spine and dropped the gun inside. Nothing I touched felt real. Seven thirty now. Fifteen minutes since the call, and I was still at home, nothing accomplished. The desire for speed, for swift action, was building, and I had to make a conscious effort to push it back down. Speed without purpose was useless and would cause mistakes that I couldn't afford. Even leaving the apartment required pause for thought. If the police saw me leave, they would follow. I couldn't have that now. I went down the steps and out the back door and found no one waiting. That wasn't a surprise; to park with a clear view of my small parking lot would have been far too obvious. I crossed the lot and put my hands on the top of the board fence that ran behind my building, got my foot on one of the two-by-four braces, and hopped over, landing in the alley. Across that and over another fence and into a backyard, then out on Chatfield and moving for Joe's house at a jog.

He was awake, sitting at the kitchen table with coffee, newspaper spread in front of him, a normal morning until I arrived. He'd left the front door open when he went out for the paper, and when I stepped through it he looked up and half-rose from the table.

"Lincoln?"

"They have Amy."

"What?"

"They have Amy. Doran and his partner. I just got the phone call."

He started to shake his head, as if he could refuse my news.

"Karen's supposed to move the money tonight. I'm supposed to convince her to do that."

"You can't talk to her."

"Yeah. I tried to say that. Didn't help."

I told him the rest of it, recounting the phone call as completely as I could, and when I was done he shook his head again.

"Lincoln, we've got to get help. Call Targent. This is a kidnapping."

"They'll kill her, Joe."

"They may kill her anyhow."

I looked at him, and he held up a hand and said, "Sorry."

"No. You're right." The numbness that had been lodged inside me melted and turned to fear. "They could kill her anyhow. Even if Karen pays him, they might. The decision we have to make is which option will protect Amy. I don't think going to Targent is that option, Joe."

"So what is?"

"We have to at least preserve the idea that Karen will pay. The image that things are proceeding the way they want."

"This is someone else's life, Lincoln. This is *Amy*. You want responsibility for the way this works out? You want to go into this alone?"

I could feel the Glock against my back, a hard lump in its holster. The press of it teased and tormented me. I wanted to feel the weight of the gun in my hand, pull the trigger, and watch bullets explode out of the barrel and bury themselves in . . . who?

"It wasn't Doran," I said.

"On the phone?"

"Yeah. It was his partner, but not Doran."

"We don't even know who he is," Joe said. "We don't know who he is or where he is, and we don't have the time to look. We can get the FBI hostage people involved, have them ready when Karen's contacted, try to negotiate."

"Cops screw this up, and Amy . . ." I didn't say *and Amy dies*. I wasn't ready to put it that coldly and bluntly, not about her. It was that cold, though. That cold and that real.

"*We* screw this up, and it works out different?"

"I need to talk to Karen," I said. "That's where we start. They're going to contact her, and she needs to know what's changed before that happens. Needs to know that there's another life at stake."

"Will you ask her to pay?"

I didn't answer.

"Lincoln?"

"I don't know. It's easier to get money back than a human life, and Karen will understand that."

"They own you," he said. "You understand that? They've spent days laying the framework to show you're the one going after Karen, and now they've convinced you to actually do that. If you pressure her into paying, do you think that'll be the end? That Amy walks out unharmed and you sit down and explain the thing to Targent and it's all over? That won't happen. They'll have another play, one that finishes you off."

"We need to give them the image that things are moving the way they want. That buys us time."

"Time to do *what*? We don't have the first idea how to find these guys."

"I want to talk to her, Joe. They're going to contact her, and when they do, she needs to understand the situation."

"We go over there and find out they've got a cop watching her place, you're done. They'll arrest you for violating that protective order, and you'll have to try to explain this from jail."

"I'm going to try," I said. "Now do you want to drive me, or should I find a car?"

Joe's face was anguished. He wanted to go through the proper channels, wanted desperately to get the cops and the FBI involved, approach this the way he would tell anyone else to if it weren't Amy, if it weren't someone he knew and cared about deeply. Wanting that didn't mean he could ignore my point, though. He knew the risks on both sides.

"I'll take you over there, but you've got to promise me you aren't ruling out help, not yet. This is a hostage situation, Lincoln. Okay? We're not ready to deal with this, not alone. If you're hoping Karen will pay and we'll just play it straight up, that's one thing. But if she won't, I'm not going to go along with you. We'll need help, need the best team the police can get out there."

"Let's make that decision after we talk to Karen."

He didn't like that, but he was kept from responding when my phone began to ring again. In the second before I got it out of my pocket I think we were both sure it would be Doran or his partner. This time the number wasn't blocked, though.

"Targent," I said.

"You could answer. Tell him what's happening."

"Not yet."

"He might know something. Why call so early unless—"

"Not yet, Joe. I want to see Karen."

The long driveway was a problem. We drove the street twice, down and back, and saw no sign of a surveillance team. The driveway was hidden, though, blocked by the trees. If a cop was in the house, we wouldn't see his car until we were all the way up the drive.

"I don't think they'd leave someone with her around the clock," I said. "Twenty-four-hour protection isn't something CPD does often, and now that she's agreed to cut me off, they'll have less reason to watch."

"Hope you're right." He was approaching the driveway again, at slow speed.

"Make the turn," I said.

He took the driveway, and we rounded the bend and passed through the trees, and the house came into view. No car, no evidence of police. They could have left one guy inside and driven away, but I trusted my instinct. Without a hostage involved—and nobody else knew there was one—Karen's situation wouldn't have been elevated to that sort of police coverage. Not yet.

Joe parked, and I got out of the car fast and went up the steps. The protective order was Targent's idea, but that didn't mean Karen wouldn't take it seriously and call the police when she saw me. I was already knocking on the door when Joe got out of the car. The ornate windowpane beside the door gave a distorted view into the house, but through it I saw Karen approaching. She had the cordless phone in her hand.

"Shit," I said softly, and then louder, "Karen, it's Lincoln. You've got to talk to me for a few minutes."

She stopped short a few feet from the door, but she didn't lift the phone.

"No, Lincoln. You can't be here. I'm supposed to call the police if I even hear from you. Please leave."

"They've kidnapped another woman," I said. "It's bigger than either of us now, Karen. You've *got* to let us in and talk about this."

While I watched, she took another step back from the door, deeper into the hallway.

"I can't do that. You need to talk to the police, not me."

"Karen!"

"Leave now, Lincoln. I'm calling."

She lifted the phone and turned it so she could see the numbers to dial, and when she did I acted without pause for thought. I stepped back and lifted my foot and drove my heel into the center of the door with everything I had, splintered the wood in the frame and busted the spring lock but didn't get past the dead bolt. She screamed when I did it, and then I kicked again, and this time the dead bolt failed, tore out of its hasp, and I was across the threshold and into the house as the alarm began to shriek and Karen turned to run.

I caught her at the end of the hallway, grabbed the phone and took it out of her hand, and wrapped one arm around her waist and held her against me so she couldn't run. Joe stepped through the door then, and when I turned back and got a half-second glance at his face I felt like I was no longer myself. His expression was a mirror image of what he saw before him: I'd just kicked in a door to run down a woman who had a protective order against me, to stop her from calling the police. It was something he'd seen in nightmare situations of domestic violence, and now it was his partner.

"They kidnapped Amy Ambrose," I said, holding Karen tight against me as she tried to twist her way free. She was facing me, and the suspicion in her face that I'd seen when we were with Targent had been vanquished, replaced by terror. She was petrified of me. The look hit me harder than any of her physical struggles, and I loosened my grip and she stepped free and ran into the living room. I watched her go, then looked back at Joe standing in front of the shattered door, and I wondered what had happened to my life.

"Turn that off," I said. The alarm was still wailing, and soon it would summon police. Karen was standing in the middle of the living room, watching warily, waiting for me to move. "Turn it off and listen, Karen. Then call the police if you want to. But give me five minutes. The same people who killed your husband have an innocent woman now. You have to listen to me."

"Please," Joe said behind me, and her eyes went to him and found reassurance. She hesitated only a moment and then moved back down the hall—making a wide circle past me—and found the alarm box, punched buttons until it went quiet.

"I'm sorry," I said. "Karen, I'm sorry. But they've taken a woman who has nothing to do with this, taken her because she matters to me. This is how they intend to get their money."

"It's what they told me would happen. That you'd be the one to ask for the money."

"Karen, you can't believe I'm part of this."

She didn't say anything, just made another nervous step to the side, moving away from Joe, back toward the stairs.

"We were together for years, Karen. Remember that. Remember me. Then think about what they did to your husband. They *tortured* him, put tape on his mouth and—"

"I know what they did!"

"And you know *me!*" I shouted back at her, and for a few seconds it was silent, the three of us standing like separate points in a triangle, everyone afraid to close the gap.

"Do you believe I could have been involved?" I said. "Honestly, Karen, can you believe that?"

She was starting to cry, but she shook her head. "No."

"Then you've got to listen to what I'm saying. They will ask you for money today, and they'll tell you things about me, involve me somehow. I need to be able to talk to you. To communicate while we try to get Amy back. I'm going to need your help."

"The police—"

"If I go to them, it's a big risk for Amy."

"That's not what I meant. The police won't let me talk with you. They listen to the calls—"

"We'll leave you my cell phone, or Joe's, something I can use to talk to you."

"They'll be here, Lincoln. The police will be in the house all day. They're on their way now."

"What?"

Her chest was still rising and falling fast with fear, fear that I'd put there. She glanced at Joe and then back to me.

"You're going to be arrested. Detective Targent just called and told me. They're sending someone here to protect me until they get you."

"*Arrest* me?"

She nodded, but she also stepped back into the living room, closer to me.

"He told me a man named Donny Ward was murdered. The one you said told you those things about Andy Doran. They found his body last night. There was more money hidden in his house. It had your fingerprints on it." She paused, eyes locked on my own, and said, "And my husband's. It had both of your fingerprints on it."

I looked at Joe. Didn't say a word. What I'd predicted in our office had just come true. It was Jefferson's money, and my fingerprints were on it, and now they could arrest me.

"Donny Ward," he said. "Shit, Lincoln. We were at his house. He might have been inside then, dead. The neighbor saw us."

I turned back to Karen. I held her eyes and tried to see her as I'd known her once long before, tried to show her myself as she'd known me. I don't know if you can do that through a desperate look fogged with fear, but I tried.

"I did not do this. I did not kill your husband, or Donny Ward, or anybody else. They can put me in jail for it, though. Fine. I'll let them do that. Turn myself in. But not until Amy's safe."

"I believe you, Lincoln. I'm scared, okay? I'm scared,

and I'm confused, but I believe you. That's why I'm warning you."

I took a few steps across the living room without purpose. The numbness that settled in me at first after the morning's call returned as I thought about Donny Ward and a stack of cash covered with fingerprints from me and Alex Jefferson.

"We're on our own, Joe. We can't go to the police now. It's not even an option. They'll arrest me for murder when they see me, and my story about Amy is going to seem like a distraction, a smoke screen. By the time they confirm that she's really gone, too much time will have been wasted."

A car pulled up to the house then. We heard the tires and the engine, and then it went quiet and a door opened and closed. Joe was closest to the door, and he looked out and said, "Cop."

Karen's eyes didn't go to the door. Didn't leave mine.

"Detective Targent or someone else?" she asked.

"Patrol officer. Young one."

She moved then, a swift blur, walking past Joe to the open door. I watched her go and looked at the backyard and wondered if I should chance it. We wouldn't get Joe's car out of the driveway with the cop there, but if I made it out of the yard I could find another car, steal one if I had to, do what it took to stay out of a cell until Amy was safe.

"Hello," Karen said, and then the cop was inside the house and it was too late for me to move. I turned to face him, and he looked at Joe and me, and his eyes went guarded and his hand inched toward his gun.

"Mrs. Jefferson?" Still looking at me. He was very young, early twenties, just a patrol officer, and unless he'd been shown a photograph of Joe and me he would not know us. I watched him and knew that he did not. He was suspicious enough to indicate he'd heard a description at least, but he wasn't sure.

"Thank you for coming," Karen said. She stood close to the door frame, using her body to hide the damage I'd done. "Detective Targent told me he was sending someone."

"Uh-huh." The kid looked uncertain. He was watching

me as if ready to go for the gun, but Karen's calm didn't fit with what he'd thought of the situation, and now he was confused.

"This is John and David," she said, pointing at Joe and me. "Friends of my husband. I asked them to wait with me until you were here."

He squinted at her, trying to pick up on any sign of a lie, but she met him with a composed stare.

"You were fast, though," she said. "Thank you."

"Uh, yes, ma'am."

We had a chance. She'd given us that. Time to get moving.

I walked up to Joe and gave him a soft pat on the back, nodding at the door. "Probably should get out of here, let the officer do his job."

"Right."

We walked to the door, and I expected the cop to stop buying it at any second, go for the gun, and radio for backup. Instead, he stepped aside as we approached.

"Thanks for coming," Karen told us. "It meant a lot."

I leaned down and embraced her, put my face against hers, and whispered "Thank you" into her ear before stepping outside.

"Good luck today," she said, and she stood in the door, blocking the ruined trim around the frame until Joe drove us out of sight.

CHAPTER

34

We rode in tense silence for a few miles, both of us watching the mirrors and waiting for the sound of sirens. Nothing happened. If he'd seen the door frame, she'd provided him with a convincing excuse. It had been a hell of a thing for her to do after I'd just lost my mind like that, kicking my way into her house. She knew me, though. After everything else, she still knew me. It was a small thing, maybe, but it had been enough in that moment.

"Donny Ward," Joe said. "The poor son of a bitch. Do you think it was Doran? You told him about Donny."

"Doran already knew about him. I don't know who it was, and I can't worry about that now. It's about Amy, Joe. She's the only thing. I meant what I said back there—get Amy back, and I'll turn myself in and let it go the course. But I can't go to the police now. Not to turn myself in, or for help. That option was just eliminated."

"I know."

"More of that damn money," I said. "They're throwing away a lot of it just to set me up. Makes it seem they're pretty confident about the chance of success with Karen."

"This was supposed to be the trump card. I don't think Doran and his partner wanted to show it so early."

"What do you mean?"

"This is enough for the warrant, enough to put you in jail.

After they get their money, it's perfect—you command all the police attention, and they disappear. But to find Ward's body so early doesn't help them. It makes it impossible for you to maneuver with Karen, and they needed that."

"If they know that . . . If they find out how useless I just became . . ."

"They could panic."

We didn't need more discussion of what panic meant while Amy was with them.

"We've got to find them before that happens and before they go for the money," I said. "That's the time frame, Joe. It's that fast now."

"It's *too* fast, Lincoln, Marshals and cops have been looking for Doran for weeks. How are we going to find him in a few hours?"

"We'll get help."

"I agreed with that this morning, but if there's an arrest warrant for you, then going to the police—"

"Not that kind of help. Not the police."

"Then who are you thinking of?"

"Thor."

I had no idea where to find him. Guys like Thor don't list phone numbers in the book, and even if they did, I wasn't sure of his last name. I'd seen it written only one time, on an FBI report, and it wasn't the sort of name that you glanced at and remembered. Some bizarre collection of K's and V's and a dozen vowels, maybe? Without a full name, we'd have to go through his acquaintances, find someone who would be able to tell us how to locate him. Thor's acquaintances tended not to be the sort of people you sought out if you cared about your health.

"We'll try Belov," I told Joe. Dainius Belov had offered help to us once in the past. It was the sort of offer you never wanted to need, but right now it might be our best hope.

"That house on Lake?"

"Only place I know to find him."

He shook his head, not liking the idea.

"He can help, Joe," I said. "If he'll tell us how to find Thor, we can get the name of the man who put Jefferson in touch with him. The same person probably hooked Jefferson up with Doran's partner. We get that much, we'll find Doran's partner, and then we'll get Amy back."

"Assuming we can find Thor, and assuming he'll actually talk."

"It's what we've got. Maybe the only thing."

"You understand who you're counting on for help. He's a killer. An enforcer for one of the worst criminals in this city."

"We've got to get into this guy's world, Joe. It's also Thor's world."

Joe looked over his shoulder, made sure the lane was clear, and then accelerated onto 480 westbound. He didn't offer any argument, didn't say anything else for a long time.

I thought of her while Joe drove, the way she'd looked on the couch, how she slept with her hair over half of her face, breathing slow and deep. Was she awake now? Had they hurt her, knocked her out, drugged her? Was she bound and gagged, or was Doran sitting above her with his Colt Commander? I thought of the possibilities, and my chest tightened and my temples ached and things deep inside of me went cold.

An arrest warrant had been issued, a piece of paper that would send me to jail for murder, and that was somehow an afterthought in my mind. It caused me no fear when compared with Amy. If I could get her back from these bastards, the hell with the rest of it. Targent seemed like a good friend compared to Doran's partner, that voice on the phone.

Joe's driving—right at the speed limit—seemed impossibly slow, but I understood his reasoning. The last thing we could afford right now was to be pulled over for speeding. His car would soon be a risk anyhow. Targent would put Joe's plate out on the radio eventually.

He drove us into the city, then came back to the west down the Cleveland Memorial Shoreway until we hit Lake Avenue. We didn't have the address, but neither of us would struggle to locate the house, either. The only time we'd been inside, it had been in the company of Thor and another of Belov's enforcers. Visits like that tend to stand out in your memory.

The big Victorian house looked the same, the home and grounds immaculate. I wondered if the neighbors knew what Belov did, or if they guessed about it—real estate, commodities broker maybe?—while they ate dinner and looked out at his quiet estate and the stern-faced foreign men who visited.

We parked in the driveway and went up the walk and rang the bell. There wasn't a sound from inside. Joe rang the bell again, and we gave it a few more minutes, but nothing happened. No one was home.

"He's not here, and that means we're in trouble," Joe said. "I could go along with you on the idea that Belov might put us in touch with Thor. But without him?"

"We'll try the River Wild." I turned and walked down the steps and back to the car.

Joe was still standing at the door, looking down at me. "Just walk through the door, clear your throat, and ask for Thor? In that place?"

The River Wild was a Russian-mob-controlled bar in the Flats, a strip club where Dainius Belov's crew could often be found.

"You wearing a gun today?" I said.

"Yeah."

"Good."

The River Wild was on the east bank of the Flats—the old warehouse district that had been converted into an area of restaurants, clubs, and nightlife. Many of those once successful businesses were gone now, the Flats having fallen on hard times yet again. The River Wild hung on, but it's easier to do that when you're backed by mob dollars.

The building's windows were covered with faded gray boards so passersby wouldn't get a free glimpse of the dancers inside, and the door had a chain looped through the handle but not locked. I slid the chain off and pulled the door open and stepped into the dim interior.

I'd never been inside the bar before, but I'd seen it once through a grainy surveillance camera. A camera that had recorded a murder. We entered into the wide main room, looking out over rows of tables at the base of a tall stage with four brass poles mounted in the center. There was a bar on the left and another across the room. A wall clock shaped like a pair of breasts ticked over our heads. No one was in sight, but there were voices in the building.

"There's another room in back."

"Yeah." Joe didn't say anything else, but I imagined he was thinking exactly what I was: The room in back was where the surveillance camera had caught the murder.

We crossed the empty room and went past the stage and the rear bar and found a set of twin doors beside it. The voices were louder now. I let my hand drift back to check the Glock, then shoved through the doors with Joe behind me.

Three men at a table and one standing, everybody turning with hostile looks when we entered. There were decks of cards on the table, but nobody was playing; one cigar leaked a thin trail of smoke into the air. I didn't know any of the men by name, but the one on his feet—a shorter guy with the flat face and beefy shoulders of a small, muscular dog—was familiar. I'd seen his photograph during a briefing with the FBI a year earlier.

"You got business here?" one of the guys at the table said. He had a deep cleft in his chin and steel-colored hair that clung to his head as if he'd just climbed out of a pool. "Or you in the wrong place, want to excuse yourselves and get the hell out?"

Joe moved around beside me, and now a chair creaked as the only man with his back to us turned all the way around.

"Looking for Thor," I said, as if that were a perfectly normal thing for strangers to be doing in here.

The man on his feet said, "No Thor here, officers."

"We're not cops."

"No? Then I won't need to be polite again. Take off."

He had the heavy Russian accent that Thor spoke so carefully to avoid. His nose was crooked, and there were scars above his lips and beside his eye, a face that had taken plenty of beatings and probably enjoyed every one, seeking the violence out like an alcoholic who'll drive thirty miles to find an open bar for one more drink.

"We're not cops," I repeated, "and Thor knows us. So does Belov."

"If you're such good friends, you'd know how to find him."

"Call him," I said. "You get in touch with him, I'll tell you my name, and you can let him make the decision. But I need to speak with him."

"People who need to speak to Thor know how to find him, asshole. And if they don't, and Thor needs to speak to them? He finds them. You get the idea? Now get out. We aren't open yet, and this is a private room."

I shook my head. "Maybe I'm not making myself clear. This matter I need to discuss, it's the sort of thing that can get police involved. Thor finds out he could have avoided that, but then you screwed it up? I don't think that'll make him happy."

"Go get your police and tell them to blow me. You don't walk in here and make threats like you know somebody. You don't know anybody."

"Want to ask Thor about that?"

"Don't need to." He walked over, moving slowly as he shoved between us, letting his shoulder hit Joe's. Joe stifled a wince at the contact, trying not to show the pain. I caught it, though, and so did the Russian. He stood in front of Joe, his face level with Joe's chin, and smiled.

"Sore?" He reached out and delivered a short, chopping punch with the heel of his hand, catching Joe right on the damaged tendons of his shoulder. Joe grunted with pain and took a step back, and the Russian laughed.

"Do not come in here with a weak old man and give me orders," he said, and then he stopped talking when I punched him in the side of his jaw.

I heard chairs scraping on the floor as the men at the table got to their feet, but I didn't look at them. The one who'd hit Joe had taken my punch well and spun back to me. I met him with my right elbow, pivoting to generate the power, like a left-handed baseball swing. The elbow caught him on the side of his mouth, and I felt the sharp edges of his teeth against the bone. He staggered and then fell, and when he did I stepped clear and drew the Glock in time to stop the rush of the man who'd been seated with his back to us. He was almost on me, and when I turned my gun was a foot away from his face.

The two others were on their feet, the one with the cleft chin holding a chair in both hands, ready to swing it. Joe had his gun out, too. They looked at my gun and his, and then the chair hit the floor and they all took a few steps back. If any of them had a weapon, he hadn't cleared it in time, and now it was our show.

"Maybe you didn't understand me when I told you this was important," I said. "It'll be important to Thor, too. When we're gone, feel free to call your boss. You tell Belov that one of your dumb-ass buddies assaulted a man named Joe Pritchard today, and then you see how pleased he is."

None of them spoke. There was fury in their eyes, the look of violent men who'd just lost a confrontation and would not soon forget it.

"Now," I said. "I will ask again—how can I find Thor?"

There was a pause. The one on the floor had struggled back to his feet, blood streaming out of his mouth. He was feeling his teeth with his thumb. I hadn't looked at my arm, but there was a warm wetness of blood on my elbow, trickling down the forearm, a souvenir from those teeth he was checking on.

"You know Cujo's?"

This came from the one with the cleft chin. Cujo's was another bar, less than a mile away. I'd never been inside, but I could picture the sign, the face of a snarling dog.

"I know it."

"Go there."

"That's where Thor is?"

"Most likely."

"I'd like a phone number."

"For Cujo's?"

"For Thor."

"He does not use phones. Go to Cujo's."

I wasn't convinced that Thor didn't have a phone, but it wasn't impossible, either. He liked to keep a low profile.

"All right. We'll go to Cujo's. And if we don't find him there, we'll come back. With Belov."

It was an empty threat, since Joe and I had no idea how to locate Belov, but it was the best I had. I took a few steps back, moving toward the door without lowering my gun. There would be a weapon somewhere in this place, and I didn't want to give them the chance to move for it.

The Russian I'd hit suddenly sucked the blood off his lips, tilted his head back, and stepped forward to spit on me. Before he had the chance, Joe whipped his good arm around and drilled him in the center of the forehead. He still had the gun in his hand, and the sound of metal on bone made everyone in the room stiffen. Instead of bringing his head forward to spit, the Russian kept going backward and hit the floor for the second time. I had my back to the double doors by then and pushed through them, Joe stepping out with me. We moved quickly through the main room of the bar, guns out, but no one followed.

"You pop him because he hit your shoulder?" I said.

"No. That was for the weak old man comment."

It took us ten minutes to get to Cujo's. I'd remembered it being on Carter Road, but it was actually on West Fourth, tucked along the bend in the river. From the parking lot you could look up and see the Eagle Avenue lift bridge, and just beyond that the brick chimneys of the old waterfront firehouse, built decades earlier to deal with lumber fires. On another day, I would've stood there and taken it in, the little patch of cracked asphalt offering a perfect vantage point of the river that had allowed the city to thrive. Today, the only reason I scanned the area surrounding the parking lot was to look for cops.

Below the snarling dog sign, on a board decorated with red-tinged drops of saliva from the beast's jowls, were the bar's hours: OPEN 4:00 P.M. DAILY.

"Places around here seem to have private hours for Soviet nationals," Joe said.

"I've noticed that."

There were a couple of cars and an old truck in the parking lot, but no one was outside. I took my gun out of my holster as we approached the door and held it down against my leg.

"Going in a little strong, aren't you?" Joe said.

"I don't trust that guy at the River Wild. Maybe Thor's here, maybe he was setting us up."

"Same thing I was thinking. We go in here and get into the same situation we did in the last place, then what? Keep crashing into bars all day, waving guns and asking for Thor?"

"It's the way to get her back, Joe. The police are not going to know how to find Doran's partner, even if they believe my story. Thor will."

"Then we better hurry up and find him."

The door was unlocked, and I pushed it open and stepped inside. No overhead lights were on, but there were neon signs scattered around the walls, casting the room in a crazy variety of colored lights.

"No friendly faces," Joe said.

"No faces at all." I took three more steps into the bar and heard the door slam shut behind Joe just before someone looped a length of chain over my head and pulled it tight.

The immediate, jarring power of the man behind me lifted me onto my toes and yanked me backward. I got the fingers of my left hand between the chain and my throat, but it did no good; the metal links tightened into my flesh and I felt my air supply give out, the breath already in my lungs the last I would taste until the chain loosened.

The Glock was still in my hand, but when I lifted it and tried to turn it my attacker knocked it free in one easy blow. Then I clutched at the chain with both hands, gagging, as someone in a sleeveless T-shirt moved forward from behind the bar. I saw him wind up, pulling his fist back as he ran at me, and I had enough time to tighten my stomach muscles before he hit me. Even with that, the blow seemed to shatter my insides. His fist came up into my solar plexus, knocking breath I couldn't waste from my lungs. The forced reaction was to try and draw in a harsh gasp of air, but the chain around my neck kept me from doing that. I lost my breath and tried to take more in at the same time, and that pain was unlike anything I'd felt before, an internal tearing sensation that rode from my abdomen to my throat.

The room disappeared into a set of dancing diamonds, and then the chain loosened around my neck and I was thrown to the floor. I didn't even have a chance to gather myself before the chain connected with the side of my head, knocking me prone. My lips removed a smear of dust and grime from the floorboards as I slid across them.

I was only vaguely aware of a shaft of light passing in front of my face, feeling no pain in my skull yet because I was so focused on trying to bring some oxygen into my lungs. As soon as the shaft of light moved over the floor, though, the assault stopped. I heard voices I didn't understand, people talking in Russian, and I lay there on the floor and brought in slow, painful breaths. Dust and dirt filled my mouth each time I inhaled, but air had still never tasted so sweet.

Once I was sure I could breathe again, I rolled onto my side and propped myself up on my elbow. Blood was running down the side of my face from the spot where the chain had hit my head. I wiped at it with one hand and then sat up and looked around the room. Joe was back by the door, held by a powerful-looking man who had his arm wrapped around Joe's throat, a gun pressed to his head. The two men who'd attacked me were standing in the middle of the floor, chattering in frantic Russian with the man who'd just entered the bar, spilling the light into the room. I blinked a few times, trying to clear my vision, as the new man snapped something and a second later Joe was released. I still couldn't see him properly in the dark, but I knew the soft, steady voice, even when it was speaking Russian.

We'd found Thor.

CHAPTER
35

A moment later Thor was kneeling beside me, his fingers moving through my hair, studying the wound.

"Scalp always bleeds," he said. "It is not bad."

He turned and spoke in Russian, and the man in the sleeveless shirt hustled behind the bar and came back with a towel. Thor put it in my hand and pressed it to the side of my head.

"You can stand?"

"Yeah." I wet my lips with my tongue. "We tried to find you at the River Wild. Your boys down there set us up, I guess."

He nodded. "I was told what had happened and where they had sent you. I was close to this bar. You are lucky that was the case."

"I guess so."

"To go in there and do that . . . it was not wise."

"Didn't figure it was a particularly brilliant move, but I had to find you. It's bad, Thor. The—"

"Do not talk here." His voice left no room for argument. He straightened and then offered his hand to me. I took it, and he lifted me back to my feet.

"We will leave," he said. "You will drive, and then we will talk."

I followed him back to the front door. Joe looked unharmed.

They'd apparently held him so he could watch while they whipped my ass around the room. Maybe when that was done, he would've gotten to enjoy the same treatment. I could finally see the man who'd looped the chain around my throat—a pale ape with tattoos all over his arms and even on the sides of his neck. Thor guided me toward the door and then stepped away. He reached out and took the man's face in his hand, squeezing the sides of his jaw while he whispered something in Russian. He didn't seem to be exerting real force, but the muscles in his hand and arm had gone tight and the man with the chain was squinting, his eyes beginning to tear. He made no attempt to resist, though. Thor whispered to him for a long time. When he finally released him, the man kept his eyes on the floor. Thor opened the door and held it while Joe and I walked through and back into daylight.

"You all right?" Joe handed me my gun.

I took the towel away from my head and looked at the dark red stain.

"Yeah."

"Still bleeding pretty well."

"It'll stop."

It was late morning now. Amy had been gone for five, maybe six hours at the minimum. A lot could happen in that amount of time. They could have taken her out of the state, thrown her in the back of a truck and started to drive, be hundreds of miles away from us by now and still moving. That wasn't the worst scenario, either. Just the worst I could let myself consider.

The door opened again, and Thor joined us outside and pointed at Joe's Taurus.

"That is your car?"

"Yes."

"We will go in that. You will drive, and you will tell me what is happening that made you do such foolish things."

Joe got behind the wheel, and Thor motioned me into the passenger seat, then sat behind us. He was dressed in dark jeans and a black jacket, and I didn't have to study the jacket for any bulges to know that he was wearing a gun underneath it. He had gloves on, too, even though it wasn't nearly cold enough to warrant them. I could see Joe's eyes on the mirror, trying to look back at our passenger. I waited until we were out of the parking lot to speak.

"I know who was extorting Alex Jefferson. His name is Andy Doran, and he's working with whoever Jefferson hired after you turned him down. He was hired to kill Doran, to eliminate the problem for Jefferson, but instead this guy joined up with Doran. He saw more money in that, I guess."

The streetlight ahead went yellow, and Joe made a right turn to avoid it, driving without purpose but wanting to stay in motion.

"They kidnapped a woman today."

Thor slouched in the seat and watched the street go by. He did not react to my words. Did not look at me.

"She has nothing to do with this," I said. "Absolutely nothing, Thor. They kidnapped her because they know what she means to me. I've got to find out who Doran's partner is, and then I have to find him. This has to happen now."

"And you think I know who he is?"

I shook my head. "No, but you know the man who might. Whoever put Jefferson in contact with you, this attorney you told me about, he might know. It makes sense that if Jefferson relied upon him once, he would have gone back to him. I need to know who that man was, and I need to see him."

"I have told you before that I do not wish to be a part of this. The police found me over a mistake. I do not want to see more mistakes."

"You're more a part of it than you realize. Did you know there's a warrant out for my arrest? They think I killed Jefferson. Actually, they think I *arranged* the murder. You're the one they're looking at for the killing, Thor."

"This Doran, he is the one who killed him?"

"He says he didn't."

"Then who?"

"I don't know, and right now I don't care." I lowered the bloody towel from my head, the wound finally beginning to clot, and twisted so I could face him. He hadn't changed position, hadn't so much as shifted since settling into the seat, but I saw that his gloved hands were clenched against his knees.

"I've got to get Amy back. That's her name. Amy Ambrose. She's an innocent in this, Thor. Other than making the mistake of knowing me, she's got nothing to do with any of it. And they've got her right now."

I was trying to keep my voice even, calm, but it wasn't working. I knew Thor could hear the change, and when I looked back again his ice blue eyes searched mine.

"Help us find him, Thor."

It was quiet. I knew better than to say anything else. He was considering, and all we could do was wait. It was as I had told Joe earlier—we were operating in a darker world now, and Thor was the guide we needed.

"This will not be an interview, the sort of thing you do in your investigations," he said at last. "We will get the information that you want. But not in the way that you are used to getting it. And if we do get the name, if we do learn who is involved in this, he will not be the sort of adversary you have dealt with before. He will be a professional at his job, and his job will be killing. This is the situation."

"I understand that."

He held my eyes for a long time, so long that I had to look away. Then he told us where to go.

CHAPTER

36

The attorney's name was J. D. Reed. He was not, Thor explained, the sort of attorney you approached to draw up a will or defend you in a small claims lawsuit. He was a mob lawyer, a con who'd passed the bar. Reed's specialty wasn't criminal defense, as I'd imagined, but tax law, or actually tax fraud. He got his start cooking books for a small-time hustler who owned a few bars around Cleveland. One of the bars was the River Wild. That was where Reed fell in with Dainius Belov, who eventually bought the place. The attorney wasn't a member of the Russian mob by any stretch of the imagination, but he helped them, saved them dollars and eased them out of legal trouble at times. His contacts grew, and before long he was as connected to the organized crime scene as anyone in the city, a dirty lawyer who floated between the Russian mob and the Italians and any number of hustlers and cheats. The positive side about being so openly corrupt was that his network expanded easily. If you were dirty, and needed an attorney who was willing to help you along those lines, J. D. Reed was often the first name suggested. The criminal business world is not that different from the legitimate—word of mouth is key.

"He hides money," Thor said, "and he does that well. Do it well enough, and people will come to know you. A certain kind of people."

"He introduced Jefferson to you?"

"He arranged the meeting."

Thor directed us into the underground parking garage of an old brick warehouse that had been converted into offices, still downtown, maybe twelve blocks from where we'd been. As Joe shut off the engine, Thor leaned forward so he could see us both.

"Whatever happens today," he said, "will not be spoken of, to anyone. You understand the value of silence. You have proved that before. Do not forget its value today."

"I won't."

He turned to Joe. "You will wait for us."

"What?" Joe's face clouded.

Thor didn't respond, just gazed back at Joe, as if his silence were all the explanation he needed to provide. And it was. I understood, even if Joe did not. I'd been tested before, and passed. Joe had not seen the things that I had seen from Thor. He knew of them, but he had not seen them. As far as Thor was concerned, Joe had not proven himself yet. Not as I had.

Thor got out of the car and I followed, and we walked to the elevator. I touched the side of my head with my fingertips as we walked, and they came back flaked with dried blood. My head ached along the cut, but it was a dull pain.

When we got to the elevator, Thor pressed the button for the twelfth floor, the building's highest.

"Are you sure he'll be here?" I asked.

"He keeps his office and his apartment in the same building. They are connected. He is always here."

Thor was still wearing the jacket and the gloves, and his face was empty, expressionless. He'd told me about Reed in his usual voice, that careful English without contractions or inflection. He never displayed emotion, not in his speech or in his face. It was the way he went through the world, leaving barely a ripple behind. Looking at him, I had the sense that he could pass right through the wall if he wanted to, leave me standing alone in the elevator wondering if I'd imagined his presence the whole time. I knew the cops on the organized crime task force had the same opinion of him.

The elevator door slid open with a chime, and we stepped out into an empty hallway, facing one closed door. There was no number or name on the door.

"Penthouse," Thor said. He tried the handle and found it locked. There was a small intercom box beside the door. He pressed the button and waited. A few seconds later a disinterested voice came on.

"Yeah?"

"Thor."

Static on the box, and then the voice came back, sounding decidedly less relaxed than in the initial greeting.

"Oh, okay, man. Sure. Sure. Um, come on in."

There was a buzz, and then the lock ratcheted back and Thor pulled the handle and the door swung open. He stepped inside and I followed.

We were now standing in an open room that was half living quarters and half office. To my left was a U-shaped desk with two bookshelves and some filing cabinets behind it, plush leather chairs resting in front of the desk. A flat-screen television hung on the wall beside the bookshelves. On the other side of the desk was a small bar with a few bottles of wine and a crystal decanter filled with Scotch on top of it.

The office area then opened up into a sunken living room filled with more leather chairs, a sectional sofa, and a mammoth television. The far wall was composed of floor-to-ceiling windows looking out on the lift bridge over the Cuyahoga and the city beyond.

A short man with wet, curly black hair walked into the room. He had both hands clasped together and moved with the hurried steps of someone used to walking beside people with a much longer stride. He wore suit pants and a dress shirt with suspenders, the jacket missing. When he saw Thor, he picked up his pace even more, almost jogging across the living room with his hand extended. He saw me but didn't give me more than a quick, curious glance. Thor commanded all of his attention.

"Hey, man, don't get many surprise visits from you," he said as he reached us, still with his hand outstretched.

Thor took Reed's right hand in his own and yanked, hard. Reed stumbled, and then Thor put his left arm across the smaller man's back and swept him forward, straight into a set of glass shelves. The shelves clattered together and one fell off its supports and hit the floor, but the tempered glass did not break. A small onyx sculpture and an ornate ashtray tumbled free and rolled to a stop near my feet. Reed floundered in the mess, regaining his balance just in time for Thor to spin him around and knee him in the groin. He hit him so hard that Reed was lifted up onto his toes before he fell to the ground and curled into a gasping ball of pain.

I'd been about as surprised as Reed by the sudden attack. Thor had given no sense of aggression until the moment he threw him into the shelves. Now he stood over him, blank-faced, watching as Reed writhed on the thick carpet, eyes streaming and mouth agape in agony.

"You gave my name to Alex Jefferson," Thor said after a few minutes, when it looked like Reed's breathing was almost back to normal. "I met with him to hear his proposition, and I told him he was confused. That should have been the end of it. It was not the end. Do you know who I have had to talk with since then? Who I have had to deal with because of your stupidity?"

Reed pulled himself into a sitting position, staring up at Thor with the eyes of a misbehaving child steeling himself for punishment. He shook his head but did not speak.

"Police detectives," Thor said. "They have come to discuss Jefferson with me. They are very interested in my meeting with him. You can imagine that I do not appreciate the interest of these detectives. You can imagine that I do not appreciate you sending them to me."

"I didn't send them," Reed said. His voice was choked with spit, his eyes still leaking tears.

"Yes, you did. You brought me into it." Thor looked at me. "Tell him what is happening now."

I knelt beside Reed, and he pushed himself away with the heels of his hands.

"Whoever Jefferson hired instead of Thor has kidnapped

a woman. He kidnapped her to stop me from interfering. He's trying to extort millions of dollars from Alex Jefferson's wife. You sent Jefferson to him for help, but he turned on Jefferson."

"Do you hear this?" Thor said. "Kidnapping. Do you know who becomes involved with kidnappings?"

Reed was silent until he saw Thor wanted a response, and then he spoke in a whisper. "The police."

"The FBI," Thor said. "Federal agents may be involved in this soon. They will talk to the police, who will tell them that they should talk to me. All of this, because of you."

Reed was shaking his head again. "I don't even know what you're talking about. All I did was facilitate a meeting between you and Alex. I didn't know what he wanted. I just—"

Thor reached down and wrapped his fingers in Reed's shiny curls. He tightened his grip and lifted, and Reed hissed with pain and stumbled to his feet, trying to lessen the pressure. Thor's right hand slipped into his pocket and then came back out with the silver Buck hunting knife that he favored. His thumb flicked against it, and then the blade was open and at Reed's throat.

"I do not want to hear your excuses, your whining like a child. You have brought this to me, and now you will tell exactly what we want to hear, and nothing more. Do you agree with this?"

"Yes," Reed whispered. The knife blade had been pressed tight against his Adam's apple, but now Thor lifted it and rotated it so the point was pressed into the bottom of Reed's fleshy chin, the blade facing out.

"Nod your head if you agree," Thor said.

"I agree."

"I said nod your head."

Reed swallowed, looking at Thor's face. The knife blade was placed at the bottom of his chin, keeping him from moving his head, but he decided it was best to try to nod anyhow. He bobbed his head, Thor guiding the motion with the hand he still had wrapped in Reed's hair. When Reed nodded, the knife point slid up his chin and back down. For a second there was just a thin white imprint from the folds at the bottom of his chin to his lower lip. Then it opened up and blood seeped through it.

"Good," Thor said. "First question." He looked at me. For a moment I just stared back at him. Then I realized he was waiting.

"Did Jefferson come back to you after Thor turned him down?" I asked.

Reed's small brown eyes tightened as he stared back at me. He didn't know me, but he blamed me for his current position, standing there with blood oozing down his chin and a Russian killer's hand tearing his hair out at the roots. He answered the question, though.

"Yes."

"Did you send him to someone else? Another person to help him with his problem?"

Reed hesitated this time, and Thor tightened his finger and pressed the tip of the knife into his chin, puncturing a deeper hole through his flesh.

"No," Reed said, and he dropped his eyes as far as he could, trying to look down at the knife.

"You're lying," I said. "Who did you send him to?"

"I didn't send him anywhere."

"Give us the name."

"I just told you that I didn't send him to anyone else."

Thor was watching me while he held Reed. Now he dropped his hand, snapped the knife shut, and put it back into his pocket. He stepped away from Reed.

"You think he is lying?" he asked me.

"Yes."

"I'm not lying, you asshole. I don't even know what the hell you guys are doing here." Reed wiped at his chin with his palm and smeared the blood, a hint of the bravado coming back as soon as the knife was gone from his face.

Thor walked away from us as if he'd lost interest in the discussion, went down the hallway, and disappeared into a room on the left. A second later a faucet squeaked and water began to run. Reed decided to take advantage of the momentary freedom and, casting a wary glance down the hall, hurried toward an end table with a telephone.

"I can call someone to remove you psychotics," he said, reaching for the phone, "or you can leave on your own."

He had the phone in his hand when I crossed my right fist into the back of his head, driving him forward, into the couch. I had his arm up and wrenched behind his back before he got his balance back, and I took the phone from his hand while I shoved him against the wall.

"You're going to give me the name," I said. "Until that happens, nobody is called, and nobody leaves. You know who Jefferson went to, you son of a bitch. Now tell me."

"Bring him here."

Thor spoke from behind us, and I turned to see him standing at the top of the sunken living room, gesturing me forward with one gloved hand. I pulled Reed upright and shoved him forward, toward Thor. Thor reached under his jacket and brought out a pistol, a Glock 9 mm very similar to my own. Reed began to tremble against me. Thor pointed the gun at his forehead and said, "Walk him into the bathroom."

I pushed Reed down the hall, Thor walking backward in front of us, the gun trained on Reed.

"Let me go, unless you want me to start shouting," Reed said, twisting against me but not making any headway. "There's a security guard right underneath us. He'll hear."

"No, he will not," Thor said. "And you will not shout."

A door opened up to my left, and I forced Reed through it. We were standing in front of a large bathtub, scalding water cascading into it. Steam rose off the tub and clouded the mirror behind us. Reed was shaking now, his knees hammering.

"No, don't . . . You've got to understand. I do *finances*. That's all! I don't know anything about this woman."

Thor stepped in beside me, placing his hand near my own, so that he was holding Reed's arm behind his back. He twisted it upward, and Reed gasped in pain as his shoulder tendons pulled to their limits. I let go and stepped back.

"Take off his clothes," Thor said.

"What?"

He'd placed the Glock back in its holster and had the knife out again. Now, in a quick flourish, he whipped the blade along Reed's pinned arm, and the shirtsleeve parted and fell away. Two more quick cuts, and the suspenders flapped against his legs.

"Get his shirt off first," Thor said. "Then the pants."

I didn't move, and he looked up at me, his blue eyes seeming to catch the light in the room and hold it. "The shirt first," he repeated.

I stepped forward and grabbed Reed's shirt at the collar. He put up his free arm to ward me off, but Thor grabbed it and jerked it behind his back and pinned both of his hands, holding him easily. For a thin man, Thor was remarkably strong. I tore the buttons loose and then ripped the shirt away from Reed's chest. Thor cut the fabric free from the arms until the shirt dropped to the bathroom floor. Reed's fat, pale chest and belly appeared. He was still shaking, and the rolls at his sides quivered, the white skin coated with sweat.

"Stop it," he said. "Stop it. Don't." His words came out in ragged gasps.

"We will take your clothes off and you will step into the water," Thor said. "You will have one last opportunity to be truthful. If you do not take it, I will cut your wrists, wait for you to die, then clean every trace of us from this apartment and leave you in the water."

Reed bucked against him and then lunged forward, but Thor held on. A stream of urine ran down Reed's leg, soaking his pants and trickling out around his ankle. Without looking down, Thor moved his foot out of the way.

"Take off his pants," he said. "The pants and the shoes, and then we will put him in the water."

"*Stop!*" Reed shouted. He sagged, and Thor had to lift to

keep him from falling to his knees. Reed's face was wet with tears and the steam from the bathtub.

"Tommy Gaglionci," he said, his voice thick and choked. "I think that's who he went back to."

I looked at Thor, and for the first time since he'd walked into Cujo's I saw some sort of reaction in his face. His eyes showed recognition of the name, and something more. Something that seemed akin to alarm.

"You know who he's talking about?" I said.

Thor was looking down at Reed, and now he lifted his head and met my eyes. Whatever I'd seen in his face folded beneath the usual empty expression, and he nodded once.

"Used to work with the Italians. His family was connected, when that still mattered. He works alone now. Does not like partnerships. He is an intelligent man, and violent, and unpredictable. I do not know where to find him."

I dropped to one knee so I could look up at Reed, full into his face. His hair hung wet against his forehead, blood and water a pink smudge across his chin and mouth.

"You said you thought that's who Jefferson went *back* to. Clarify, Reed."

"I arranged for Gaglionci to help Jefferson with some things a long time ago. I don't know what it was, Jefferson just came to me, and I put him in touch with Gaglionci. That's why—"

"Wait," I said. "How long ago? When was this, Reed?"

"I don't know, maybe five years."

"No—you *do* know, and you're going to think about it and give me the right answer. When was it?"

He sniffed back tears and mucus and considered it.

"It would be, well, about five years."

"More specific."

"Summer. I know it was the middle of summer."

"And he's Italian. A dark-looking guy, muscular?"

"Yes."

Son of a bitch. Donny Ward's description of the man who'd shot his dog and Jerry Heath's description of the fake cop who'd arrived with Jefferson and Fenton Brooks spun through my head. Summer, five years ago. When Doran was arrested, before he'd been pressured into the plea bargain. Jefferson hadn't wanted to go back to Gaglionci, but he was out of options. Now I saw Doran on the breakwater, telling me that his partner was the same man Jefferson had hired to kill him. Didn't seem likely Doran understood what role Gaglionci had played when he went to prison.

"It's the same guy," I said. "This prick is working with Doran now, but he sent him to prison before. Whoever waves the biggest handful of money wins. Doran convinced him they could get more out of Jefferson than Gaglionci would get for killing him. He just doesn't understand who the guy is, what he did."

Reed didn't follow a word of that, and the confusion seemed to scare him more.

"You said Jefferson went back to him, but he didn't want to," I said. "Explain that."

"He told me he needed someone again, but not Gaglionci. He didn't trust him. Seemed scared of him. I told him I didn't know who to send him to, but he kept asking, insisting. I told him to talk to"—Reed shot a fast, nervous glance over my shoulder—"Thor."

"So you don't know that he went back to Gaglionci? You're guessing?"

"He went back to him. He told me he didn't like the idea of it, but I didn't have anyone else to offer and he kept saying he was running out of time."

"How do we find Gaglionci?"

His lips opened and closed, a string of spit appearing in the corner of his mouth, but he didn't say anything.

"Reed," I said, "we could kill you today. You already know that. We could leave you in that bathtub to be found in a day or two, your body sitting in water gone cold and bloody. That's your option. That's all you can gain from silence."

"He has a town house somewhere on the east side. I don't know the address. All I have is a cell phone number."

"He has an abducted woman with him. You think he'd take her back to his home?"

His tongue slid out and wiped over his lips. "Probably not."

Probably not. I drew back my fist, ready to hit him, but stopped myself. I turned away and looked into the mirror and saw my own face, distorted through steam but with the fear still obvious. We'd made progress, but not enough. Even if Gaglionci had Amy, he wouldn't have taken her back to his own home. If we checked it out, it would be empty. I was sure of that. He was a pro, and he'd have a safe house somewhere.

Thor dropped Reed. He fell onto the bathroom floor and scrambled over to the toilet, tried to shove himself between it and the wall. I looked at him and felt overwhelmed with anger and disgust. His life was devoted to making money off the crimes of others, people like Gaglionci and Doran. They hid the bodies; he hid the money.

Hid the money. That was what Thor had said—*he hides money, and he does that well.* And what was it Reed himself had whined as we'd brought him in here? *I do finances. That's all! I don't know anything about this woman.*

"They're going to move millions with computers," I said. "And not just move the money—make it disappear. An untraceable transaction that even trained professionals won't be able to follow."

Reed's eyes were on the floor. He'd wedged himself as far behind the toilet as possible. I pointed at him and turned to Thor.

"Could he make that happen?"

Thor looked almost impressed as he nodded. "Yes. He could do it."

Reed tried to move but couldn't. He had nowhere to go. It was just him and us, trapped in that bathroom. He began to weep.

"I didn't know about this. *I didn't know about the woman.* I just said I'd help with the money. That's all I knew about— the money. *That's all!*"

His voice was wet with spit and tears. I nodded as he talked, and I thought my expression must be calm, because it seemed to reassure him. The sobs stopped, although his face was still streaked with tears, and he repeated what he'd already said—all he knew about was the money.

"That's fine," I said. "That's really quite good, Reed. I'm glad you're helping him with the money. But I think you're about to have a problem with the transaction. And you're going to need to see him in person."

CHAPTER

37

It was Joe who came up with the scenario we needed.

He'd joined us in the apartment after Thor dragged Reed back out to the living room. I said I wanted Joe with us, and Thor didn't object. When Joe came through the door his eyes went right to Reed, sitting there in his underwear, his body still damp with sweat and steam, his face dripping blood. Joe looked at him for a long time and then at me.

"We've got the name," I said.

Joe didn't say anything. He walked down into the sunken living room to join us, and he kept his face away from Reed. I knew what he was thinking—that he'd gotten a lot of information out of a lot of suspects over the years without putting any of them in Reed's sort of condition. This was a different game, though, and that was why I'd gone to Thor. We were in a darker world now, and the clock was running. The time for rules was gone.

Joe sat down, and I told him that Reed was in charge of the money transaction, that I wanted to use him against Gaglionci and Doran.

"If we can get them here, we're halfway done. To do that, we need a reason for them to see Reed in person. They're going to call me in a few hours with instructions on how to move the money. We need a change in that plan, something that seems like it came from Reed but will disrupt them enough that one of them will actually come here."

Joe frowned. "Gaglionci's got a kidnapped woman with him. It's not going to be easy to convince him to come in without making the trap obvious."

"He wants that money, Joe. Wants it bad. He'll come in if he feels like he has no other choice. All we need is an excuse to bring one of them down here, but everything I've thought of is too simple—signing a transaction document or some shit like that. That won't work. Not for a computer transfer like this."

If Reed had any ideas, he wasn't volunteering them. Thor was silent, watching us with his gun in his hand, and I didn't know the first damn thing about money transfers.

"How will you do this, Reed? Once the money is ready to go, how do you make it disappear?"

Reed was sitting on the floor, holding what was left of his shirt against his chin to stop the blood. He took the shirt down when I spoke and looked at the crimson stain on it as if reminding himself why candor was the way to go.

"I'll ricochet it."

"Excuse me?"

"Ricochet—that's the term we use. When the money moves into the account I've designated, I cycle it out immediately, keep doing that through a series of accounts. I use numbered accounts, offshore banks . . . there are a million ways to do it with computers. It's called a ricochet because it bounces off a number of accounts before finally landing. That makes it harder to trace."

"These accounts exist only for the ricochet?"

He nodded. "They're dummy accounts. I've already got them set up."

"What's a reason you'd need to see these guys in person? It doesn't have to be real, it just has to *sound* real."

"I don't know."

"Well, you'd better start thinking, asshole. Because either we get them to come here, or—"

"Fingerprints," Joe said.

I turned to him. "What?"

"I saw something on TV . . . maybe it was in the paper, I don't remember. About computer security. How there's a move to use fingerprints for identification now. They've got these readers, fingerprint scanners, that you can hook up to your home computer. There's a whole brand of laptops that have them built in."

I looked back at Reed, who was nodding.

"Biometrics," he said. "That's what it's called. A lot of off-shore banks are using biometric security for computer transactions now."

"That's what it was," Joe said and then turned to me. "They used fingerprints to burn you. Let's throw it back at them."

"That's good," I said. "Better than anything else I have, at least. Reed calls Gaglionci and tells him he needs a print for one of the accounts. Convinces him it's added security."

"Gaglionci won't want to use one, obviously," Joe said. "So we have Reed tell him he needs somebody's print, and maybe Gaglionci will offer up Doran. I'm guessing he'll like that idea—it attaches Doran to the money, and not him."

"But I don't have a fingerprint reader."

"They don't know that, Reed," I said. "All they need is to *believe* you have one. Think you can make them do that?"

He looked unconvincing as he nodded.

I made him use the speakerphone on his desk. That way we could hear both ends of the conversation and know for certain whether Gaglionci was buying his pitch.

"You screw this up," I said, "and they'll know we got to you. They'll know we've got Gaglionci's name. Then they'll panic, and innocent people will get hurt. If that happens, I will hold you responsible, Reed."

He was sitting in the big chair behind his desk. When he leaned forward, his fat back peeled off the leather and left a moisture stain behind. He was still in his underwear, and there were dried drops of blood on his pale, hairy chest. I reached over and hit the speakerphone button. The dial tone hummed.

"Call him."

Reed punched in the numbers and sat hunched over the phone, the rest of us standing above him. Thor had his Glock out, hanging against his leg right in Reed's field of vision.

"What do you need?" The voice that answered after the third ring was not Doran's but that of the man who'd told me they had Amy. I looked at Thor, and he nodded once. Gaglionci.

"Um, hey, look, had a little bit of a problem," Reed said, and his voice was too high, too fast. Thor moved the gun maybe a fraction of an inch, and Reed's eyes went to it and he got himself under control.

"It's not a big deal," he continued. "I've got this thing almost set up the way we want it, but I—"

"Problem? There's a *problem*?"

Gaglionci's change in tone seemed to unnerve Reed more than Thor's gun, but he swallowed and pushed on.

"No, no problem. It's just that . . . I've got a system here that I think is perfect for what you want to do. A system that will let us bounce right into a South American bank. We can move money from that into a numbered account in another country. Makes it tough to trace, and American law enforcement doesn't have the same access."

"Good." Gaglionci bit the word off, heavy with intimidation. "So make it happen."

"Right, that's what I'm going to . . . I mean, yeah, we'll get it done, but this system, see, to start it off with the first account, I need a fingerprint."

A long pause. "Fingerprint."

"Yeah. I've got a scanner that's hooked right into the computer. You press your thumb on it, I click a few buttons, and we've got an account set up on this thing. It's the perfect way to start this move. Increases our protection level right away."

"I don't want to use a fingerprint. Are you kidding me with this shit? A *fingerprint*?"

Reed looked up at me, then back at the phone. There was sweat on his brow, and he had his hands clasped together, squeezing his fingers.

"Okay. You don't want to use it, okay, but what I'm telling

you is, this helps. It's the safest way to do this. The fingerprin
lets us set up with a safer account, and the money will just floa
through and disappear. The banks look at the fingerprint a
added security, so the accounts are actually better protected."

"And I'm attached to them. I don't want that."

"I need a fingerprint from someone. I'm not using my
own. Find somebody else to give me one." Reed's voice was
rising in pitch.

"You moved half a million for me and didn't need one
then. What the hell changed in a week?"

I'd been watching Reed, but now I turned to Joe and saw
the same look in his face I felt in my own. Half a million? A
week ago?

"This is more money," Reed said, and I refocused on him
"A lot more, man. At least that's what you told me. I'm trying to help *you*, that's all. This much cash, it's harder. And
you said the cops could be tracing it, or trying to. I'm not going to jail for you. If I move this, I'm going to do it as safely
as possible. That takes the fingerprint."

He was doing better now, his voice edging away from nervous and toward argumentative, the way it should have been.

"You use a fingerprint to get it started, and then it ends up
in the same account we've discussed?" Gaglionci said. "Is
that it?"

"Yes. Yes, that's exactly what I mean. Using the fingerprint
lets us set up a different sort of account to get everything moving. A more secure account. They feel protected, but it really
helps us."

Gaglionci was silent. The speakerphone hissed softly,
and Reed licked his lips and stared at the glowing blue light
on the display as if it might come to life.

"You need one thumbprint," Gaglionci said. "Mine or
anybody else's, and then we're ready. Then we can make this
happen."

"Yeah. Yeah, man, absolutely. We'll be all set then."

"All right. You stay there."

The blue light blinked off.

CHAPTER

38

"Half a million," I said once Reed had turned off the phone and pushed back from the desk, wiping at his sweaty forehead with his hand. "You moved half a million for him a week ago?"

Reed's face immediately crumpled. For a moment I thought he was actually going to try to lie, even though we'd all stood there and heard it, but finally he just nodded and said, "Yeah."

"Where'd it come from?"

"I don't know."

"Reed . . ."

"Honestly, I can't tell you that. The originating account was anonymous to me, just a number."

"Is that common? For Gaglionci to move that much money?"

He shook his head. "I've never seen any amount close to that from him."

"What day did the money come in?"

He licked his lips and looked at the floor, was silent for maybe thirty seconds, reviewing a mental calendar, then said, "October twentieth."

October twentieth.

"You get it?" I said to Joe. "That's the day—"

"Jefferson was murdered."

"No. Day *after* Jefferson was murdered. Gaglionci killed him. Gaglionci murdered Alex Jefferson, and someone paid him to do it."

Joe frowned. "Maybe not. Could be they got more money out of Jefferson than the fifty grand."

"No way, Joe. Jefferson isn't so rich that half a million would disappear and nobody notice. Think about how hard the cops have been going over his accounts. If they noticed fifty missing, they'd sure as shit notice five hundred thousand."

"But Jefferson hired Gaglionci."

I nodded. "Yeah, and it seems somebody outbid him. Doran thought it was him, promising to get more cash from Jefferson. Maybe that wasn't the truth of it, though."

A half million dollars, paid out the day after Jefferson was murdered. And Doran didn't know about it. Couldn't know. He'd stood there on the breakwater and spread his hands and said *on what money?* when I'd told him to run. Five hundred grand was a decent chunk. I couldn't imagine Doran hanging around, risking capture and a trip back to prison just to bump the dollar figure a little higher.

"He's using Doran just like he's using me," I said. "Hasn't shown his face yet to anybody, but Doran has. He's taking the risk, and that's how Gaglionci wanted it."

"Donny Ward could identify him," Joe said. "Connect him to what happened to Doran. Then we sent the cops out there, and you told Doran—"

"That I knew about Ward. Gaglionci must have killed him. When he took him out, he eliminated one thread while tying me to it with the money."

The more I thought about it, the greater the implication of what Reed had just told us became. I'd been worried about Doran at first, then Doran and his partner, but this revelation made it clear that I'd been unaware of another player. There was someone else involved, and Gaglionci was operating on his orders.

"Who paid him?" I said.

Joe didn't have an answer, and I didn't, either. For a while we just stood there, Reed watching us with apprehension and Thor silent as always. Eventually, Joe shook his head.

"We need to get ready. He's sending somebody. One of us should be down in the garage or out on the street, watch to see who shows and tip the people up here."

"Will you do that?" Thor said.

"Yeah. I'll move my car out of that garage, too. They'll probably recognize it by now. It shouldn't be close. I'll park it somewhere else and walk back down."

"Good."

Joe took his keys out of his pocket, turned on his heel, and walked for the door. He was reaching for the knob when I stopped him.

"Gaglionci came into the Heaths' house with Alex Jefferson and Fenton Brooks," I said. "Jefferson told police he was acting as a liaison between Brooks and the Heath family. Liability reasons."

"Yeah. And Fenton's dead now."

"His son isn't. How much money do you think that family is worth?"

"Brooks Biomedical has to be worth, what, hundreds of millions? Maybe a billion? It's a huge figure."

"Right."

He stood with his hand on the doorknob and stared back at me across the open apartment.

"Gaglionci taking down half a million the day after Jefferson was killed isn't a coincidence," I said. "I don't see how that's possible. That payout is connected to what happened with Doran and Jefferson, and the Brooks family is, too. They're the only ones involved with that sort of money."

"You're thinking Fenton helped protect Matt Jefferson?"

"Maybe. Matt was a family friend and the son of his top attorney. Fenton was the first person Alex Jefferson called."

Joe dropped his hand from the door and turned all the way around, his face thoughtful.

"I could go with that," he said, "if all we had was the past. That makes some sense. It's a stretch, but it makes some sense. Until you get to the present. Why would Paul Brooks hire someone to take Jefferson out? If he knew what happened with Doran, he'd own Jefferson. Not the other way around. Jefferson wouldn't be a threat to him."

No, he wouldn't. If Fenton Brooks had knowingly helped Jefferson cover up a murder, that revelation could tarnish his legacy and embarrass the family. Jefferson would never bring it forward, though. To tarnish Fenton's legacy would be to indict himself for the same crime and to identify his son as a murderer. So what did Jefferson know that scared Paul Brooks?

"We had the wrong damn rich kid," I said.

"What?"

"Paul Brooks, Joe. What if he killed her?"

"I don't see how you're getting there."

"The night that girl was killed, Matt Jefferson called his father, who called Fenton Brooks."

"To check on the kid's story. To see what was happening."

"Who told us that?"

He made a nod of concession. "Paul Brooks did."

"Right. And a day after those phone calls, Matt changed his story and implicated Doran. Maybe that wasn't about clearing himself. Maybe he did see somebody up there, but it wasn't Doran. It was the son of his dad's richest client."

"That's a big jump."

"Matt wrote the prosecutor and told him he was refusing to come back and testify. Why do that, why risk attracting that sort of attention, if he'd killed her? His dad would have coached him better than that. If it was just about saving his own ass, he would have waited quietly and with his fingers crossed that the plea bargain bid would work. When he moved back to Indiana, he cut off communication with his dad. Maybe he wasn't running away, though. Not from what we thought. Maybe he was running away from the guilt and cut off his dad because of what he'd convinced him to do."

"A *big* jump," Joe said again, and then, when I didn't respond, "but they'd have the money. No doubt about that. Paul Brooks would have that sort of money."

"And Gaglionci was tied into everything that happened with Doran. He was a key player in that. If anyone could have figured out how to work Brooks against Jefferson and make money off it, he'd be the guy."

The room went quiet again. Thor was impassive, but Reed watched us with interest, some of the fear replaced with fascination.

"Get out of here," I told Joe. "Go move the car, and watch for one of them to show. You won't recognize Gaglionci, but let us know if you see anyone who even looks close. We can deal with the rest of this after we get Amy back."

He opened the door and went out and then it was just Thor, Reed, and me in the apartment. I walked up to the door and sat on the floor beside it with my back against the wall and my gun in my lap, feeling the way you do after everything you've known to be true is shattered.

An hour passed, then two, and nobody showed. Joe called three times with false alarms. I began to wonder if we'd blown it, if Gaglionci had smelled the trap and pulled out. I stayed against the wall, shifting position occasionally, but always close to the door. Reed—now dressed and with the blood washed off his face in case we needed him to show himself— was still down in the living room, where we could see him clearly. Thor was standing on the other side of the door. He didn't sit, didn't pace, didn't even stretch. Just stood there.

The wait was brutal for me. Throughout the day, I'd found temporary solace in moments of confrontation, of action, the tasks at hand allowing me to stop thinking about what could happen if I failed. Amy had always been in my mind, even as I lay on the floor at Cujo's with a chain whipping down at my head, but in the pressure of those moments she existed as a goal, a reminder of why I had to get back up off the floor. During the waiting, though, she became a fear again. The empty minutes ticked by, and I began to imagine things I did not want to consider, to see all the awful possibilities that disappeared in the immediacy of action.

It had been nearly two and a half hours when Joe called again.

"There's another one pulling into the garage. Little sports car. A Mazda, I think."

"All right."

I disconnected, went back into the apartment, and repeated the information to Thor, who didn't so much as nod in response. Several minutes passed, and just when I'd begun to think that the Mazda visitor was another false alarm, Thor said, "Elevator."

I frowned at him and rose to a crouch, listening. I hadn't heard anything. A few seconds went by, and then there was a chime as the elevator reached the penthouse floor. I don't know what Thor had heard before that, but he was right.

The intercom buzzed, and I pointed at Reed. He hurried across the floor, his feet slapping off the ceramic tiles, and punched a button on the intercom.

"Yes?"

"Let me in." The voice was garbled; maybe Gaglionci again, maybe not. Reed looked at me, and I nodded. He hit another button, and I heard the lock slide back in the door in the hall. I'd decided—at Thor's recommendation—to leave the entryway empty and wait for them inside the apartment.

I was kneeling against the wall, Thor standing opposite me, when the knob turned and the door swung open. Thor stepped around it in a combat stance, and Andy Doran walked into the room, saw the Glock pistol pointed at his heart, and said, "Well, *shit,*" just before I rose up behind him and hit him in the back of the head with the butt of my gun.

CHAPTER
39

"Nowhere to go, Doran," I said. "Might as well relax, get comfortable."

He'd landed on the tile floor on his face and stayed down, his body still but his feet shuffling as if they were trying to move away from the rest of him. I leaned down and found his gun in the shoulder holster under his jacket, took it out, and handed it to Thor, who stuck it in his waistband. It took Doran a few seconds, but he rolled over, his eyes tight with pain, and stared at us, groggy but sizing the situation up. He got into a sitting position with an effort, then slipped a hand up to his head and felt the spot behind his ear where I'd hit him with the gun.

"I owed you one," I said. "More than one."

He moved his arm against his body, and I knew he was feeling for the Colt Commander, noting its absence. Nodding to himself, he slid backward until he was supported by the wall. We didn't stop him. There was blood on his lip, a souvenir from bouncing his face off the floor, and he tasted it with the tip of his tongue.

"Where is she?" I said.

He tasted the blood and didn't answer. Thor was standing quietly, flicking his knife blade open and shut with his thumb. It made that soft *snick* noise over and over, and Doran had trouble keeping his eyes off it.

"You're not walking out of this room unless you tell us, Doran. You really ready to make that sort of sacrifice for a guy like Tommy Gaglionci?"

Doran turned to look at me. The soft flesh under his eye was already red and starting to swell. He didn't speak.

"Give me one honest answer," I said. "Just one, Doran. You give me this, and I think I can explain some things that you're going to be damn interested in. Did Gaglionci kill Jefferson?"

He rubbed the back of his skull and turned to Thor, watched that knife blade slipping open and closed, open and closed. Didn't say a word.

"All right," I said. "So you're loyal to him. That's nice, man. I'll throw a different one at you. Did Gaglionci kill Donny Ward?"

His eyes came up fast and sharp, looked at me but he stayed silent.

"Yeah, Doran, Ward was murdered. Last night. There's a warrant out right now for the guy who the police think killed him. That guy is me. Problem is, I didn't kill Donny. I don't think you did, either. I'm pretty sure your partner did. Got an idea why he did that, other than taking the opportunity to set me up?"

Doran just returned his stare to Thor's knife and licked at the blood on his lips.

"Because the cops had already been to see Donny, and Gaglionci couldn't let that continue," I said. "Donny Ward could identify him as the guy who sent you to prison. Gaglionci went to see Donny, shot his dog and threatened his daughter and offered him a stack of cash, all to make sure he denied your alibi."

That one got his eyes off Thor's knife and back on me. He tilted his head, and the blood that dripped off his lip was forgotten for the moment.

"The summer you were arrested, Alex Jefferson came to him," I pointed at Reed, "and asked for someone to help him handle some unpleasant tasks. Sort of tasks the police tend to be interested in. This guy hooked him up with Gaglionci, who then went to see Donny Ward and came into the Heath family's house masquerading as a detective the day before cops found the girl's underwear in your trailer. When you broke out and put the pressure on Jefferson, he went right back to Gaglionci. And you're right—he hired him to kill you. But Gaglionci's not your partner, Doran. He sent you to prison once, and he's probably hoping to do it again."

I pointed at Reed. "Tell him how much money you moved for Gaglionci on October twentieth."

"Five hundred thousand." Reed looked sick. He'd just taken the least pleasant of gambles—giving up a killer like Gaglionci to keep one like Thor happy.

"You hear that?" I said, turning back to Doran. "Half a million. That's how much your *partner* is sitting on. How many dollars of that have you seen, huh? How many?"

"Not one dime."

"That's what I imagined. And it came in the day after Jefferson died. The day after *he* killed Jefferson."

"Who paid him?"

"I'm not sure yet, but I've got an idea. If I'm right, then the guy who paid him is the one who should have done your prison sentence."

"Jefferson's kid."

I shook my head.

"*Who?*"

"I'll give you that when you give me Amy. But it's obvious that *somebody* paid him to do it. You didn't see the cash, you didn't get your revenge. You just got suckered. Throughout all of this, when has he taken a risk? He's put you out there, made you take the heat, and if he can't make me go down for all of this, he'll see that you do. That's the only reason you're still around. You gave him someone to put into the field, to deal with me and watch the cops and now to put *your* fingerprint on *his* money. That's how it's going to work out. He's kidnapped a woman and sent you into a trap because of it. Still feel like covering for him?"

Doran was looking at the floor, quiet, taking it all in. I didn't have time to let him think, though. It was too late for that.

"This is the guy you're protecting," I said. "He sent you to prison. You don't have to believe me, don't have to buy a word of it. But I do have to get Amy back."

I held my hand out to Thor and pointed at his knife. He gave me a curious glance, then passed the knife to me. The grip was warm from his hand. No trace of Reed's blood left on the blade, though. He'd wiped it clean.

"We'll stay here a long time if we have to, Doran. I'll do all the things to you that you wanted to do to Jefferson. I'll do those things, and I'll tell myself it's justified because of Amy, the same way you told yourself it was justified because of Monica Heath. I'll convince myself, easy as you did, and maybe it'll work out better for me."

Doran raised his head. "We'll get her out, and then you'll tell me."

"What?"

"We'll get your girlfriend back, I'll deal with Gaglionci, and then you'll tell me who paid him. I need to know that. I *will* know that. Because if this thing is ending tonight, I'm going to be the one who finishes it."

We left the apartment with Doran walking free. Before he opened the door, Thor folded his knife and put it in his pocket, scratched the side of his nose with a gloved finger, and stared at Reed.

"You made good decisions today," he said. "Better than the other decisions you have made recently. You will have to make another one now. We are leaving, and you have many choices of recourse over what happened today. I would recommend choosing to forget I ever walked through your door."

Reed nodded.

"I do not want to see you again," Thor said. "I do not want you to even speak my name."

"I won't."

"Another good decision," Thor said.

Joe was waiting for us in the garage. He had the Taurus back inside, watched us approach with Doran, and nodded at the car next to my truck, a little Mazda RX-8 sports car.

"This is what he drove in. He was alone, too."

"Good."

"You know where she is?"

"With Gaglionci. Somewhere out by Geneva. Doran's going to take us there."

He'd told us that much up in Reed's apartment—that Gaglionci waited for him near Geneva, in a place he'd found weeks earlier. He refused to offer more, saying only that he would show us himself.

Joe frowned. "Why doesn't he *tell* us where she is first?"

"He won't."

"I'm not going to tell you now, have you on the phone getting a hundred cops down here," Doran said. "You want to do that, you can, but you're going to waste time. You don't have a lot of time, either. Gaglionci knows how long it should take me to get back. Waste an hour or two, he'll know something's gone wrong, and he'll react. He's not the sort of guy you want to force into reactions."

I nodded. Doran wasn't lying about the risk of panicking Gaglionci.

"All right. You'll take us there. Joe will drive, and you're going to sit behind him."

I pointed at Thor. I'd been careful never to use his name in front of Doran.

"He'll be beside you. Move one inch more than he wants to see, and you'll find it to be a very painful experience."

Thor was frowning.

"What?" I asked.

He nodded at the RX-8. "Gaglionci is expecting this car to return. He will not look at it the same way as your car. It is not a threatening vehicle to him."

A damn fine point.

"Okay," I said. "Okay, we'll take the car. It may let us get closer."

"He will go with you and your partner," Thor said, pointing at Doran. "I will take this car and follow. If we are all in the same vehicle, he may try to cause an accident. By following, I will make sure that if he does that, he dies."

Doran looked at Thor as if he were impressed. Doran had been a soldier, but he'd probably never had a sergeant who was more coldly efficient than Thor.

"You heard him," I said to Doran. "Give him the keys."

He took the keys out of his pocket, tossed them to Thor, and then got into the passenger seat of Joe's car when I waved my gun at him. I holstered my gun, and Joe withdrew his Smith & Wesson with one hand and his keys with the other.

"You drive," he said. "I'll get in back and watch him."

I was surprised for a moment, and then I understood: He had one good arm, and if Doran attempted to disrupt anyone's driving, it would be easier with Joe than with me. Neither Joe nor Thor had any trust in Doran's good intentions. I got behind the wheel of the Taurus, and Joe climbed in the backseat, sitting behind Doran, with his gun out. We left the garage with Thor following in Gaglionci's car.

"This place you're taking us," I said to Doran. "You've been there since you broke out?"

"Yes."

"Pretty secure place, then."

"Empty place. Has been for years. A sort of campground for motor homes. It's been closed a long time. There are some old cabins. Used to be a lake there, but the state breached the dam because it was going to fail. That's been years ago."

I was surprised he'd offered that much, but it didn't help me a whole lot. I could get on the phone and tell the cops to find an old RV camp near Geneva and blanket it with a SWAT team, but before they got that in place, I'd be there.

"How'd you find Gaglionci?" I asked.

"Jefferson sent him to do the first money drop. He told me what the real deal was, that Jefferson had paid him to kill me. Said he thought Jefferson was too rich for me to settle for just fifty grand anyhow."

"That's what you asked for?"

"I told him fifty grand would buy his son one extra week of life."

"You were serious? You would have killed his son?"

Doran was quiet for a moment.

"Maybe," he said. "I thought about it a lot. All the time. I mean, I did his sentence, you know? And he killed Monica. End of the day, that's what it was really about. Nobody had answered for her yet. But would I have killed him, really, if Jefferson had done what I asked, not brought Gaglionci into it? Maybe not. I think if I had that money in my pocket . . . maybe not."

"It was Gaglionci's idea to partner up and go for more?"

"Yeah. I didn't know how much Jefferson was worth. He did."

"You ever see any of that fifty grand?"

"None. He told me it was what he'd been paid to kill me and that he was keeping it. Told me we'd get a hell of a lot more than that."

"*He* did. Left you out, though, and all that fifty grand went to was setting me up. How'd he get my prints on it?"

"I did that. The night I grabbed you off the street. He'd told me what to do, just put the bills in your hands and work them around once you were out. Easy trick."

Easy trick, easy answer, and somehow I still hadn't thought of it.

"Who is that guy, anyhow?" Doran said, pointing in the rearview mirror at Thor.

"Someone I've worked with, time to time."

He chuckled and shook his head. "Sure, Perry. You're a PI. That guy's a *warrior*. I've seen a few before."

"And Gaglionci?" I said.

His eyes moved to me, then back to the dark road unfolding ahead of us.

"Yeah."

CHAPTER

40

I told Doran I wanted to stop a mile or two before we reached the place where Gaglionci waited. For the remainder of the drive, off the highway and down winding country roads lined with trees, I worried that he wouldn't tell me where to stop—that the story about the campground had been a lie, that he'd approach Gaglionci and signal him somehow, and we'd be exposed before we even knew we'd arrived. Instead, Doran instructed me to pull off the road in a gravel turnaround circle that seemed to be part of a farm.

"It's maybe another half mile. There's a gravel road off to the left. Big sign in front, and a gate, made up to look like some sort of a ranch, something Wild West. There's an old trailer that was the office, and then a bunch of concrete pads where people parked the motor homes."

"Is he in the trailer?"

"No. There are five or six cabins where the lake used to be. He's in one of them."

A knuckle rapped on my window. Thor. I opened the door and got out to join him, and Joe and Doran followed as I told Thor the situation. He didn't say a word.

"You were right about him expecting the car," Joe said. "The question is how to use it best. We can have Doran drive us inside the camp. Use him to get Gaglionci out somehow."

Thor shook his head. "We should not all be in the car. Something goes wrong, we are all trapped in one spot."

"Okay. What's your suggestion, then?"

Thor leaned away from the car and studied the pine trees waving above.

"Is there a way into this camp from the rear? Through the woods maybe, or around the lake?"

We all looked at Doran, and he nodded. "Some old train tracks run up against it. There's a fence between the tracks and the edge of the camp, but it's been torn down in places. If you find the tracks somewhere else, you can probably use them to walk up there."

This pleased Thor. He gave one short nod. "I will drive the car. We will find these tracks, and you and he will walk up to the camp together."

I frowned. "I should probably be the one to drive in. The driver's going to be the most likely to have to deal with Gaglionci and—"

"And I am better at that than you," Thor said. His pale eyes looked dark, but they were fastened on mine. It was not his battle to fight, but he'd come here to help me, and he was right—he was better than me. I thought about objecting, but that flat gaze of his quelled it. We were here to get Amy. If this gave us the best chance, then this was how we would approach it.

"All right," I said.

"I go with them, or with you?" Joe asked.

"Neither," Thor answered.

Joe looked angry. He'd been left in the garage when we'd gone to see Reed, and now Thor was ordering him to stay behind again. He didn't like being told to sit it out.

"There is one way to drive out of that camp," Thor said. "Supposing things do not go well, and Gaglionci leaves, perhaps with the woman, who will be here to stop them? Take your car and block the exit onto the road after I drive in. Nobody leaves without going through you. That is necessary."

"Fine." Joe's expression changed, and he nodded. Thor

was right, of course. In this sort of discussion, Thor would always be right.

"Okay," I said. "I'll take Doran and go up the tracks. How do we time it, though? You shouldn't drive in until we're up there, and we don't know how long the walk will take."

Thor pointed at Doran, who shrugged. "Depends where you find the tracks," he said. "Only place I know is where they crossed the road a little ways back. Probably take, what, fifteen minutes to walk in from there."

"I will wait twenty," Thor said. "Once I am inside the camp, where is he?"

"There are some cabins around the lake. He's in the third one, right side. So is Perry's girl."

We drove back to the spot where the tracks crossed the road, maybe a quarter mile behind us. Thor put the RX-8 off on the shoulder, resting in a cluster of dead weeds, and I pulled in behind him. Doran and I got out of the Taurus, and I turned to Joe and passed him the keys.

"We'll see you soon."

"Yeah," he said. "You watch your back with Doran, Lincoln."

"I will."

Thor looked at me. "Twenty minutes."

"Okay."

Doran and I started to walk ahead down the tracks, a winding path of white gravel and old wooden ties that disappeared into blackness. It didn't take long to round the first bend and leave Thor and Joe out of sight behind us.

The tracks clearly hadn't been in use for years, because they'd actually pulled the rails. All that was left behind was the gravel bed and the wooden ties. An occasional rusted spike rolled underfoot, but other than that it was easy enough to move along at a good pace. Doran walked ahead of me, moving effortlessly, without even looking at the ground. The rain was gone, but it had left the air chill. My breath fogged in front of me for the first few minutes, and then either it cooled enough to stop reacting with the air or it grew too dark to notice.

The air smelled of wet earth and leaves and water, the scent reminding me of the winery where Joe and I sat on the deck with Paul Brooks, listening as he lied smoothly and successfully. We'd swallowed his story and moved on, wasting days that had culminated in this: Amy trapped with a professional killer who had his eye on the clock. Now the cost of that delay . . . I shook my head and quickened my pace. I couldn't let myself think of the potential cost.

Fifteen minutes after we'd started down the tracks, Doran said, "We're close."

"How do you know?"

"Fence up ahead. On the left."

I squinted and stared ahead and saw nothing. The last time I'd had my vision tested they'd told me it was actually better than twenty-twenty, and still I had no idea what Doran was seeing up there. We were a good thirty paces farther along before I could finally make it out: a sagging wire fence, knocked down in many places, strung along the edge of the tracks, separating them from the trees on the other side.

We stepped off the tracks and through the tall, dead grass. Despite the dampness, it crackled and rustled underfoot, the woods seeming too silent, our steps too loud. I imagined Gaglionci sitting inside one of those cabins, tilting his head at the sound of our approach and reaching for his gun.

The chain-link fence had been beaten down, breaking and sagging until it was only two feet off the ground. Doran stepped over it, and I followed. I could see the lake basin to our right, tall reeds and grasses growing where the water belonged. The dark shapes of the cabins began to show themselves on the opposite bank. We were moving around the lake basin toward the cabins, and the gravel road inside the camp was visible now, a light band in the dark grass.

We made it around the edge of the lake and behind the cabins. Doran had said Gaglionci was in the third cabin, and there were six of them that I could see, with small docks protruding into the lake basin behind them, the wood probably rotten by now, unused in many years. I turned once, walking backward for a few steps, and looked back up the gravel road. I could see the shape of the trailer Doran had spoken of up near the entrance, but then everything faded in shadows. No sign of Thor yet.

The first cabin was beside us, dark and empty, old trash and debris scattered behind it. I stepped over a discarded propane tank as I made my way along the narrow strip of grass between the cabin and the dock. I was ahead of Doran by a few steps and couldn't even hear him. It seemed each breath I took was impossibly loud, but he didn't make a sound. A cluster of pines separated the first and second cabins. I pushed the branches aside to step through them; Doran simply ducked his head and bobbed through. The needles left a sticky sap residue on my hands. We were behind the second cabin when the light inside the next building became visible.

"Is that it?"

Doran didn't respond. He'd stopped where he was, staring at the cabin as if he didn't trust it.

"What?" I said, my voice a harsh whisper.

"He knows."

"Gaglionci?"

Doran nodded and ducked, got low to the ground and stared back up the road at the trailer, then swiveled his head to look at the rest of the cabins. I knelt beside him.

"What are you talking about?"

"The lights. He wouldn't have left lights on in the cabin. We had the windows blacked out with cloth. He wouldn't have taken it down unless he wanted someone to think he was there. He's setting a trap in case I didn't come back alone."

Light showed on the road behind us. It was Thor. I could tell that from the look of the headlights and how low they were, trademarks of the small car. Doran had underestimated the time it would take to walk up here along the tracks. We'd gone at a good pace and barely arrived ahead of Thor.

"Shit," I whispered. "This is too fast."

Doran said nothing. Staying low to the ground, I moved along the wall of the second cabin after the RX-8's headlights passed over it. Thor was driving slowly. I came around the edge of the building and knelt beside it. A few shingles, blown off the old roof, lay around my feet. I swept them out of the way and planted my left foot, brought the gun up with both hands, and rested my forearms on my knee. Thor had stopped the RX-8 at the third cabin but hadn't gotten out yet, leaving the engine idling. The headlights lit up the outside of the cabin, and I leaned forward and stared at it. Nothing changed. The door stayed closed, the light stayed on. If Doran was right, and Gaglionci wasn't inside, then we were in trouble. Any hope of a surprise was gone now—Gaglionci wouldn't have missed that car.

"Where would he go?" I said and spun in time to see that Doran was twenty feet away, moving toward the tall reeds that filled the lake basin. I stood to go after him, but in that moment I heard the engine of the RX-8 roar and gravel spin under the tires as Thor hammered the accelerator, and I turned back to see what was happening.

He kept the car in reverse—screamed it backward about ten feet and then cut the wheel, spinning it around to face the trailer. As the car spun he hit the brights, and the beams caught Tommy Gaglionci full in the face as he stepped out of the trees just up the gravel road and lifted a shotgun.

The brights had been a good idea, a last-ditch attempt to disorient Gaglionci, but he still pumped a shell into the chamber and got off a shot that blew a cloud of fiberglass and metal off the front end of the RX-8.

I lifted my Glock and fired, but it was a long distance for a handgun, and I missed wide and low. He heard the shot, saw it kick into the gravel by his feet, and spun and fired the shotgun in my direction, showering wood chips from the cabin wall around me.

I stumbled to the nearest tree, just a few feet away, fell against it, and looked out on the dark road. The RX-8 was motionless, smoke rising off the engine compartment.

Maybe the last shot had damaged something critical and frozen the car. I watched and waited for a door to open and Thor to step out, or at least return fire. Instead there was nothing but the thin stream of smoke. The car's windshield was shattered, Thor nowhere to be found.

I rolled onto my shoulder and looked up the road, searching for Gaglionci. A shadow moved in the trees, but then it was gone. He was working his way down to me through the trees, and I couldn't see a damn thing. It was a bad position, backed up against the cabin wall with just the one tree offering shelter. I could either move forward, deeper into the trees and toward Gaglionci, or try to get behind the cabin, where Doran had gone.

I'd just made the decision to retreat and move behind the cabin when the RX-8's engine howled. I looked back in time to see the tires find purchase on the loose gravel road and send the car roaring toward the trees where Gaglionci had been moving. No driver was visible behind the wheel. Thor must be lying beneath the dash, using the car for protection, and driving blind.

Gaglionci spun around a tree no more than thirty feet in front of me and fired the shotgun once more, blowing the remaining shards of the windshield away, but the car didn't slow. He hesitated for one second before diving back into the trees, and then Thor cut the wheel again and the car hit the pines broadside.

For a few brief seconds everything was quiet and still. There was more smoke rising out of the engine compartment of the car, the radiator probably leaking steam from one of the shotgun blasts, and the headlights cut a crooked swath through the trees, one of them pointed up now, into the sky. Nobody moved near the car. I could see the airbag filling the driver's window. I stepped around the tree and moved cautiously into the open, looking for Gaglionci and wondering if Thor was dead. Almost at that moment, they both reappeared.

Gaglionci had hit the ground and rolled when he saw the car accelerating toward him. Now he rose again and stepped toward the RX-8 with his shotgun leveled. I lifted my own gun and tried to draw an accurate line on him while he pumped the shotgun, and as he did that Thor rose up in the wrecked car and fired out of the back window, the only one that didn't have a pine tree in the way.

He took two shots but missed with both, and Gaglionci swung the shotgun back around toward the car and got off another blast that hit the trunk and back window. Then he was stumbling back, sliding down the ditch behind him and into the grass.

I put three rounds into the weeds where he'd disappeared, and then it was quiet again. There had been no sound from Doran, who was probably hiding in the woods somewhere or moving away from the camp. He'd chosen escape at the first possible opportunity. I started up the road at a jog, watching the tall grass and trees where I'd last seen Gaglionci. He didn't fire at me, but I could hear the rustling and breaking branches as he moved through the woods. I fired blind into the trees again, two shots that had no hope of hitting him. Then the sounds of his retreat were farther away, and he was out of range and lost to the darkness.

I pulled up alongside the RX-8 just as the passenger door popped open and Thor fell out onto the grass. There was blood on his face and on his arms, but he was alive and moving. I knelt to help him up, but he waved me off and used the car as a support while he got back on his feet. He never let his Glock out of his hand. The blood appeared to be from a collection of shallow cuts, not from a gunshot.

"Are you hit?"

He shook his head and wiped at his face with the back of one gloved hand. "Not badly. He was firing buckshot. I took a few pellets, maybe."

Looking closer, I could see where his jacket was tattered on his left side, blood saturating the fabric along his ribs. He glanced at it, too, but didn't seem concerned; he was ready to speak when he was cut off by a scream from up the gravel road.

"*I'm gonna kill her!*"

Gaglionci had reemerged from the trees, now fifty or sixty yards up the road, beside the trailer. We could see his silhouette against the shape of the building. I started to run as Thor turned and laid his wrist over the roof of the RX-8, and I'd made it only a few steps when I heard the report of his Glock three times, shots that came closer than they should have, firing at that distance in the dark. None of them connected, though, and Gaglionci turned for the trailer, the shotgun rising again. I didn't even bother to lift my own gun, just kept running, knowing the only chance I had was to make it there before he got inside, knowing also that it wasn't a real chance, that he was too far ahead, that I would be too late.

Gaglionci opened the door and stepped inside the trailer and fired. I heard the gunshot and shouted as if it had struck me, still running, stumbling now, my feet going too fast for the rest of me. In the same instant as I realized the sound of the shot had been wrong—a harsh crack instead of the throaty roar of the shotgun—Gaglionci tumbled back through the door and hit the ground. The shotgun fell free, and I got my balance back on the loose gravel and ran harder until I was standing above him, my gun pointed at his forehead as he twisted in pain.

"It's probably a good thing," Andy Doran said from inside the trailer, "that I was here."

He was leaning against the door, a revolver in his hand that was aimed at my chest.

CHAPTER

41

"Come see your girl," Doran said.

I stepped inside the trailer. There was a dim light on, but I saw immediately why it hadn't been visible from outside: The windows were covered with a thick black cloth. Doran had probably purchased a few bolts at some fabric store for ten dollars, but it did the job. The light died on the cloth, leaving the trailer looking empty at night to anyone who had happened by.

Doran led me around the corner and through a tiny kitchen as Thor entered the trailer behind us. The place reeked of sour garbage and mold. Dirt covered the floor, and there were puddles where rain had leaked through the roof. Doran had lived here for nearly a month, waiting for his windfall. I passed through the kitchen, and then a bedroom opened up on the right and I saw Amy.

She was on the floor, lying on an old blanket. Her hands and feet were handcuffed, and there was duct tape over her mouth, but her eyes were wide and bright even in a room dark with shadows. I dropped my gun and fell on my knees and reached for her, and Andy Doran leaned down and laid his revolver to her forehead.

"She's alive, Perry. As promised. Pay attention to me and she may stay that way."

My own gun was on the floor beside my hand, where I'd

dropped it when I reached for Amy. Thor was in the doorway now, and without looking at him I knew he had his gun out and drawn on Doran, who was smiling up at him over my shoulder.

"Easy, man. Easy. No need for a lot of excitement here. You start pulling triggers, and I will, too. You know that drill. Way I'm holding this gun, and where it's pointed? She's likely to die if you go for it. Can't guarantee she will, but you can't guarantee she won't, either."

Thor didn't say a word. I was only a few feet from Doran, separated from him by Amy's body, but I didn't even consider a move. Not with the way he held that gun against her skull, finger tight on the trigger. My eyes were fastened on Amy's. She looked unharmed. Scared, yes, but unharmed.

"Tell your buddy to put that gun on the floor," Doran said.

Thor didn't move. I looked at him and then shook my head at Doran.

"He's not going to put his gun on the floor."

"Well, he better. You tell him—"

"No," I said. "Nobody can tell him to give up his gun. He won't do it."

"Holster it, then," Doran told Thor. "You as damn fast as I think you are, that shouldn't be so much of a problem."

Thor lowered the Glock, slowly, and slipped it back into its holster. His body seemed to hum with readiness.

"Okay." Doran slid around Amy, keeping the gun against her head but moving closer to me. Then, in one quick motion, he raised the gun and pointed it at my head instead of hers. Thor tensed when he did it but didn't reach for his weapon.

Doran collected my gun, then showed me where the keys to the handcuffs were. He let me undo the cuffs at Amy's feet but not her hands. He also refused to let me take the tape off her mouth. Once her feet were free, I helped her upright. She stood on wavering legs, and I held her, feeling a crush of relief move through my body at the warmth of hers, and then Doran banged his gun off my skull, not gently, and told me to step back.

"I promised you her, and there she is," he said. "Now you've got your end of the bargain to live up to, Perry. You come with me. Bring her along."

Doran pushed me forward, into the hall, then shoved Amy. Her legs started to buckle, but he caught her and kept her upright and guided her through the trailer and out into the yard with that gun pressed into her side.

Gaglionci had crawled maybe thirty feet since we'd entered the trailer, leaving a swath of blood behind him. Doran had thrown the shotgun into the trailer, leaving Gaglionci unarmed. Now Doran shoved Amy back to the ground and knelt between her and Gaglionci.

"Stand back a bit, Perry. Get too close and more people might get shot. That doesn't need to happen."

He rolled Gaglionci over, onto his back, and I looked down, seeing him clearly for the first time, a man of medium build and height with a dark complexion, dark hair combed straight back off his forehead, opaque eyes staring at a starless sky. There was blood around him, soaking the grass and forming little pools and rivulets as it ran away from his body and melted into the wet earth. I could see a ragged hole punched through the top of his chest, near the collarbone.

"How you doing, buddy?" Doran said. "Looking a little rough."

Thor was standing in the doorway of the trailer but coming no closer. His gun was still holstered. Amy lay on the grass behind Doran. I tried not to look at her. Each time I did, I wanted to move for her, and that would only invite Doran into a dangerous reaction.

Gaglionci used his elbows to slide backward across the dirt.

"You know how many times I thought about killing you?" he said to Doran. His voice was a graveyard whisper, but it took a lot of effort just to manage that.

"Too bad you passed on the chance. Perry tells me you collected a nice check for killing Jefferson. Half a million, was it?" Doran made a displeased sound with his mouth, like a scolding mother. "A cut of that could have made me long gone. It's a shame that didn't work out. I'm going to need to know who paid you."

Gaglionci's jaw muscles were working even though he wasn't speaking, and his right hand opened and closed around a small mound of dirt he'd gathered in his fist.

"Who was it?" Doran laid the gun against Gaglionci's skull. "You're not dead yet, man. That little hole in your chest? Shit ain't gonna kill you, trust me. Seen a lot worse than that in guys who were running miles a few months later. But where the gun is now? *That* is going to kill you. And I will pull the trigger if you do not tell me the truth."

"Paul Brooks."

He said it without hesitation, as I knew he would. Gaglionci was no sort of stand-up guy, just a killer and a hustler whose decisions were motivated only by guns and cash. Brooks had used the latter to motivate him, and now Doran trumped with the former. In Gaglionci's world, that's the way it would always play out.

Doran looked over his shoulder at me.

"You said you had a guess. You said you weren't sure, but you could make a guess. Is Brooks it?"

"Yeah. He's it."

"Paul Brooks." Doran said the name slowly. "Son of the guy who owned the winery where Monica was killed, isn't he?"

"Yes."

"If he paid you . . . if he killed Monica, then what the hell was Jefferson doing in it to begin with?" This to Gaglionci, not me.

Gaglionci drew another breath and pushed it out slow, each one taking concentration. His eyes kept sliding down, trying to see his chest. He didn't answer, and after a few seconds Doran reached forward and shoved the barrel of his gun into the wound.

Gaglionci howled. He pulled his lips back and screamed and tried to push away, but Doran held him. I'd felt no pity for him until then—he'd kidnapped Amy, had been on his way to kill her when Doran shot him—but the sound and the look on his face made my stomach recoil, and I turned my head.

"We were waiting on an answer," Doran said. His voice was soft.

Gaglionci breathed for a long time, fighting the pain back, waiting until he could talk.

"I didn't know he killed her. Not at first. Night Jefferson sent me to kill you, I asked what you had on him. You told me about his son. That you thought he'd killed the girl, because there was no reason to frame you if that wasn't the case. That was a surprise to me."

"But you were in Monica Heath's house with them," I said. "Brooks and Jefferson both. You had to know who you were protecting."

"No. Jefferson said . . . well, he made it sound like it had been someone at the party that night. A friend or someone who worked with Brooks, along those lines. Told me I didn't need to know the details and gave me enough money to make me agree."

That much explanation took a lot from him, and he bit down on his tongue and squeezed his eyes shut as the pain rode at him harder and faster.

"You aren't done," Doran said. "Keep talking."

After a moment, Gaglionci spoke again, but he kept his eyes shut.

"I went back to Jefferson and said I knew about his son, and now he'd be paying a lot more than the fifty. He went crazy. Said his son hadn't killed the girl. He thought you were coming after him because he framed you, and going after his kid because he helped. But when he found out what you really thought . . . that you believed his son murdered the girl, it changed things. He told me he was going to the police, explain what had happened, give himself up for what he did. He wanted me to go back to you one more time, give you the fifty you wanted and tell him he was going in, that you'd be cleared. I said I didn't like that idea . . . he went to the cops, cops would come for me."

Gaglionci coughed, and although his eyes went wide with pain I didn't see any blood in his mouth, no sign of critical internal injury. Doran gave him a few seconds, then lifted the gun and moved it back toward Gaglionci's chest. That got him talking again.

"I told him I thought he was lying, that his son killed her, and he wouldn't have spent so much money otherwise. He laughed, said it was never his money and that anything he gave me was pennies to the guy who killed her. I'd gone to see that girl's family with Jefferson and Brooks's father. I knew how rich he was. So I went to Paul Brooks."

"Told him that Jefferson was talking about going to the police," Doran said.

"It was a gamble. Worked out."

"You killed Jefferson and got rich and still went after his wife for money. Wanted to turn your half million into three and a half. Let Perry deal with the cops."

Gaglionci didn't respond, just watched Doran. His wound wasn't bleeding badly anymore, and Doran was right—I'd seen worse. Gaglionci wasn't going to die tonight. Not from that, at least.

Doran stared at nothing, the gun in his hand. He sat that way for a while, and then he shook his head slightly and looked at Thor, making sure he was still just standing there, no weapon in view. When he stood, it was with the slow, unsteady motion of an old man who'd sat for too long. The gun barrel lifted off Gaglionci's chest and came around to me. Doran used his free hand to toss me the handcuffs he'd removed from Amy's ankles.

"Put those on him."

I walked around Doran, knelt over Gaglionci, took his wrists, and fastened the cuffs. Gaglionci didn't try to fight me, didn't take his eyes off Doran.

"All right," Doran said. "We're going to take that van and get out of here. You drive, Perry. Me and my buddy here will ride." He tapped Gaglionci with his foot.

"You go wherever you want with that piece of shit, but I'm not going along. I'm taking Amy out of here."

"He'll take her." Doran nodded at Thor. "I got no problem with that. Walk her down to meet your partner, and then they can take her to the cops or the hospital or wherever the hell they want. But you and me, we got a trip to take."

"Where?"

"To see Paul Brooks. I wasn't kidding when I said I'd finish this tonight, and either you go with me now, or people start shooting again. I don't know how that would turn out, but I do know your girl's safe now. Be a shame to jeopardize that again so soon."

Amy sat between them, right where the crossfire would be if anyone pulled a trigger. It wasn't worth it to challenge him. Not now, when Amy was safe and the danger—at least here, in this spot, in this moment—was done.

"Get her out of here," I said to Thor. "Get her someplace safe. I'll go with him."

CHAPTER

42

There was an old van parked behind the trailer, set back on a dirt access path cut into the trees, screened from sight. Doran had keys for it. I drove down the gravel road, Doran in the seat beside me with a gun, everything just as it had been on our trip to the lake except for the addition of Gaglionci bleeding all over the backseat of the van. Doran sat with his back pressed against the door and the gun aimed at my head. We drove past the trailer down the rutted gravel road and came to a stop where Joe's car was parked sideways, blocking the exit. Joe was not inside.

"Step forward and put your gun down," Doran called loudly. He had both windows down, the gun pressed in the soft tissue under my chin. "I'll count to five, and then your partner dies."

There was a movement in the trees to the left, and Joe stepped forward. He hadn't lowered his gun, but I was a hell of a lot more confident that he wouldn't take the shot than I had been with Thor.

"Go on and holster it, Joe," I said. The pressure from Doran's gun under my jaw made it difficult to talk loud enough. "Amy's safe. She's in the trailer with Thor. Let us pass and then get her out of here. That's what matters."

Joe holstered his gun. His face was pale in the glow from the headlights, his thin gray hair damp and windblown.

"Get her out of here," I repeated.

"I will."

"Move the car," Doran said. "Then go somewhere and wait. We're almost done here, but don't get stupid. Any cops show up behind us, your partner will die. That's not just talk, Pritchard."

Joe walked back to the Taurus and started the engine, backed it out of the way, and sat with the motor running while I drove us past. I looked in the rearview mirror as we pulled away and saw the taillights of the car moving toward the trailer where Thor and Amy waited. She was safe.

"Brooks still in the winery?" Doran said.

"I don't know."

"Don't lie. He lives out there. I remember there was a house. Big, fancy-ass house. That's where he lives, isn't it?"

I didn't answer.

"Your woman is fine," Doran said. "You got that? You saw her, Perry. She's fine, and you can thank me for that."

"Thank you," I said, and I was serious. Regardless of whether he held a gun on me now, he'd been ready for Gaglionci in a moment when I had not.

"Shooting Gaglionci was my pleasure, Perry. My absolute pleasure. I may well do it again before the end of the night."

Behind us, Gaglionci was quiet. I could see his face when I looked in the mirror, though, the shine that showed his eyes were open and watching us. Even unarmed and injured, with handcuffs on, he still seemed like a threat.

"When you took off, I thought you were gone," I told Doran. "Headed for the highway or something."

He shook his head. "Only two buildings in that entire camp are still solid. The third cabin and the trailer. Once I figured out he wasn't in the cabin, I knew they had to have moved to the trailer. It made more sense, being closest to the road and I knew he wouldn't have left her alone."

"Where'd you get the gun?"

"Inside the trailer. That's where I'd been staying for the last few weeks. I knew where the gun was, but he didn't." Doran shifted in the seat and lowered the revolver. "Point is, your girl is safe now, so you can just relax, all right? Shit's done, as far as you're concerned. Me, I got a little left to handle. You just got lucky enough to go along for the show." He cocked his head at me. "Jefferson's kid—why'd he kill himself? If he wasn't responsible, why'd he do that?"

There was regret in his voice, and it surprised me. I looked back at him for a moment, then away.

"You told him you were going to kill him, Doran. Torture him and kill him. I think he believed you."

"Why let it come to that, though? Why not go to the cops, give Brooks up? If he'd done that . . ."

"Giving Brooks up would mean giving himself up, too. And his father. His father would have gone to jail. They might have been estranged, but I don't think he was ready to do that. By the time he guessed that his father was already dead, I was standing in front of him, and he assumed you weren't far away."

"I wish he'd gone to the cops," Doran said. "Could've changed some things."

I looked at him, saw his face lined with shadows. "Let me out of the van, and you take over. Only don't go to see Brooks. Go north, south, west, wherever. But don't go there, Doran. It won't end well."

"Just shut up, Perry."

For a while neither of us spoke. We were the only car on the road, nobody coming in the opposite direction, just us in that musty old van listening to the wind and the tires on the pavement.

"There was a time," Doran said, "right before Monica got killed and I got arrested, that I about had my shit together. Be the first to admit it had been a long time coming, but, man, I was getting it together. Cutting back on the booze, cutting back on the pot, working steady hours, honest hours. It was that place in Geneva that did it, you know? Out there with the trees. Not even an hour from where I grew up, but *damn*, it was good to be out of the city. I liked those trees. I was happy out there. Had a savings account, even. Putting some dollars in there when I could, thinking about upgrading to a better place after winter."

I saw it in my mind: a trailer in the woods, tall trees surrounding it. I saw that, and then I saw Alex Jefferson's sprawling house by the country club, Paul Brooks's winery and estate just off the lake.

"I was doing all right," Doran continued, "and Monica, she was good for me. Knew it wouldn't last, she and I both knew that, but she was good for me. Her friends and her parents didn't like me, but they didn't know me, either. All kinds of rumors going around about me being violent and shit, but that was done. That was in the past, and Monica got it. Nobody else did, maybe, but she got it. When we split up, I remember sitting outside that night and smoking a cigarette and thinking that I was going to be clean by spring. I mean, really living solid. I'd have a new place by then, be done with the drugs and the drinking and the rest of it. I was close. All I had to do was make it through winter."

His voice changed, went soft and almost musical. "Just make it through winter."

We reached a four-way stop, and Doran motioned for me to go right, toward the winery. The wind picked up and shook water from the trees.

"You had to know somebody was setting you up," I said. "Why take the plea?"

"Because someone *had* set me up, Perry. They'd done it well, too. It's one thing to fight a charge when you're sure of the facts, but I wasn't anymore. I didn't know what the hell they'd find, and that attorney, that paid-off prick, he was in my ear every damn day telling me I'd better think about the plea. Said I could always appeal, get out early, but that I was done if we did a trial in that county. Case was too big, my reputation too bad, I had no chance. Told me he couldn't get a new venue, either. So take the plea and then think about an appeal, he said. The safe bet."

"Did you have any ideas about who set you up?" I said. "Just blame the cops?"

"Had a million ideas, and none of them were close. I thought the cops were a part of it, but who killed her? At first I wondered about her father. He never liked me. But he never seemed like a psychotic, either. So why me? Who picked Andy Doran for the fall? I thought about that every day and every night and never got close. You know I honestly considered the Army? Can you believe that shit? I'd been kicked out, and I thought, hell, maybe those boys take things more personally than you realized. That's how far off I was."

"You didn't know Paul Brooks?"

"Never seen the man. Still haven't. We're about to fix that."

"I'll get you some money, Doran. Somehow. Get you a nice amount of cash, and then you take off. Go wherever you can go and just fade out. Forget Brooks. Joe and I will see that he goes down. You can watch it on TV, read about it in the papers, from someplace safe and far away."

Doran's face was turned away from me, staring out at the dark countryside. "You were a cop. You've been in some prisons."

"Yeah. Several times."

He nodded. "Then you know what they feel like."

I thought of the hollow sound the door had made banging shut and locked behind me in the jail in Indiana, the way it had reminded me of a submarine hatch, that sense of finality.

"Yes," I said. "I've got an idea."

"And you know what goes on in there, when those doors close."

I didn't answer that one.

He turned back to face me. "I did five years inside, Perry. Something like that? You don't forgive it, you don't forget it, you don't walk away from it. You take it back in blood."

CHAPTER

43

Brooks was home. That was obvious as soon as we cleared the pines and the illuminated windows of his big log home became visible. There were no cars in the driveway. I parked in front of the garage, watching the house and wondering if Brooks had seen us arrive or if he'd missed us entirely and was sitting there in front of his television feeling at peace with the world, any memory of murder cast aside.

"Get out," Doran said, opening his own door. I got out and stood beside the van as Doran came around and slid the back door open. He looked up the drive and then back at me. "Get him up. He's coming in, too."

I reached in the van while Doran held the gun at my back, got my hands under Gaglionci's arms, and lifted him clear of the seat. He got his feet down and stood under his own power, breathing hard, staring at Doran.

"We could be counting money right now," he said. "Instead you're—"

He stopped talking when Doran laid the barrel of the gun against his lips.

We walked up to the house, Doran a half step behind me, with the gun in one hand and the other wrapped in Gaglionci's hair, shoving him along. At the front door, he told me to knock. I dropped the brass knocker on the heavy wood, and we waited. Footsteps moved inside. The door swung open, and Paul Brooks stood before us in a bathrobe, a curious expression on his face until he recognized Gaglionci and saw the blood on his chest.

"What in the hell?" Brooks lifted his hands, palms out, and stepped away from the door, and that was when Doran shoved past Gaglionci and pointed his gun at Brooks.

"This him?"

"Yeah." I nodded, and Brooks looked at me and frowned. His face, with the hard jawline and smooth skin, made me think of an aftershave commercial.

"Can I ask what you think you're doing?" he said.

"Shut up." Doran stepped all the way into the house, shoving Gaglionci in with him, and kicked the front door shut. Brooks was backpedaling, and Doran followed him.

"You recognize me, asshole? You know who I am?"

Brooks hesitated, not because he was trying to place Doran, but because he was trying to decide whether to tell the truth.

"You're Andy Doran," he said. "The murderer."

Doran let go of Gaglionci and hit Brooks in the face with the gun, a loud, vicious smack, and Brooks stumbled and caught the banister at the foot of the stairs to keep from going down. I'd moved maybe a foot toward them before Doran spun and put the gun to my forehead.

"Stand down, Perry. Like I said, you're here for the show. You're a spectator now, all right?"

We were standing in the long entryway of the house, the kitchen looming dark behind us, the stairs heading up to our left. A wide loft hung just above us, a bank of skylights reflecting the light from the open room below. Brooks clung to the banister and stared at Doran as blood dripped out of his nose and splashed onto the shining hardwood floor. Gaglionci had fallen to the floor when Doran let go of him, and stayed there now. Doran pivoted and pointed the gun at him.

"This is your boss, right? Guy who paid you?"

Gaglionci nodded.

"You tell me," Doran said, "you tell me here, in front of him, why he had you kill Jefferson."

Gaglionci fought his handcuffs, trying to sit upright. "Because he killed that girl. The one you went to prison for."

As soon as Gaglionci spoke, Doran hit Brooks again. He was ready this time and turned his head in time to take the blow above his ear instead of flush in the face. He moved up one step, trying to put himself behind the banister and use it as a shield. Doran was in front of me now, and I took one small step backward. I wanted to be out of his field of vision if I saw an opportunity to make a move.

"Is that true?" Doran said. "You kill her?"

"No."

"Wrong answer."

Brooks tried to avoid the blow entirely this time, stumbling backward up the steps, but Doran grabbed him and pulled him down and cuffed him twice across the back of the head before shoving him to the floor. There was hair on the barrel of Doran's gun now, and a ragged line of blood began to show along the base of Brooks's skull.

"Perry here agrees with your boy. Thinks you killed her."

Brooks shifted his eyes to me, trying for shock but offering only anger. "Are you insane?"

Even on the floor, with blood on his perfect aftershave-commercial face, he oozed a haughty arrogance.

"Probably be best to tell the truth tonight," I said.

"I have no idea—"

Doran swung on him again, and Brooks moved with surprising speed, ducking the blow and scrambling free. He was on his feet, halfway back to the kitchen, hands held up to ward Doran off.

"*Admit it!*" Doran screamed. "Say you did it. *Say it!*" He sprayed spit when he screamed, and his knuckles were white against the stock of the gun, his whole body trembling with fury.

"I didn't—"

Doran fired. The gun, that big revolver he'd had at the trailer, bucked in his hand, and the bullet buried itself in the wall just behind Brooks, who shouted at the sound and ducked.

"Admit it," Doran said, his voice calm again, as if the shot had soothed him.

Brooks was cowering. He'd backed up against the wall but still had his hands lifted as if he thought they might be able to protect him if Doran fired again.

"I did it," he said. His voice was a whisper, so soft I wasn't sure he'd actually spoken at first, even though I'd watched him say it.

"What?" Doran said.

"I did it." Louder this time. "I killed the girl. Monica Heath."

It was almost a full minute until Doran spoke, and then it was just a single word. "Why?"

Brooks cocked his head, his mahogany hair flopping across his forehead.

"It wasn't intentional. I mean, I didn't want to . . . she'd started fighting me. We'd been fooling around a little. We were out on the deck. I reached under her skirt and pulled her underwear down and she started to fight me. Then she got loud. She was almost shouting, really. And there were all those people outside of the house, my father and all of those . . ."

Doran stood with the gun lifted, still aimed at Brooks, but he seemed not to breathe. He reminded me of a statue from a war memorial I'd seen somewhere, a frozen moment of imminent violence.

Brooks broke the silence. "I didn't want to kill her, I just wanted her to *shut up*. She was trying to walk away from me, and I grabbed that towel and just came up from behind and took it and used it to quiet her down. I didn't want to kill . . ."

He stopped again.

"You sent me to prison," Doran said. "I did five years for you. Five years because you didn't want to be *embarrassed* by a girl who didn't want to have sex with you."

Brooks didn't say anything.

"Why me?" Doran asked.

"I don't know. I didn't *pick* you."

"Why me?"

When he said it again, Brooks paused, mouth open. Then he said, "Because you were there. It wasn't personal. You were just there."

"I was just there. I was just there, and it wasn't personal," Doran echoed. "Good. That means a lot. Those five years I did inside, they weren't personal."

"You want money?" Brooks said. "All of you? Fine. Name a price. Anything. You pick a figure, and I'll make it yours."

I actually moved toward Doran when Brooks said it, I was so sure he was going to fire. So sure that he wouldn't be able to bear what Brooks had just done, trying to quell Doran with money, to control this situation in the same way he had the murder of Monica Heath, the way Doran had ended up in prison. Doran didn't fire, though. He smiled.

"Money," he said. Rolled the word out slow, as if he were enjoying its flavor. "You can give me some of your money?"

Brooks nodded. His nose was still bleeding, splattering the blue robe. "I can give you more money than you've ever imagined. More money than you can believe."

Doran looked down at Gaglionci, still on the floor, then back up to me. I couldn't read his eyes. They didn't seem to be seeing me, or anything in the room.

"How much money can you give me tonight?"

Brooks frowned. "You mean cash?"

Doran tilted his head and studied Brooks, still with that remote expression on his face. Then he shook his head. "A check. I think I'd like a check."

Brooks stared at him. Then he nodded. "Okay. A check. All right. Yeah, I can write one. As a down payment, right? And then we can get you more. We can get you more later."

"Sure," Doran said. "As a down payment."

For a moment Brooks just stood there, still nodding, and then he pointed down the hall to his right. "In my office. The checkbook is in my office."

"Then we should go there," Doran said. His voice wasn't his own anymore. It was relaxed, almost amused, as if he were on a different plane of the conversation and we couldn't follow it. The voice bothered me.

Brooks started down the hall, and Doran looked back at me and waved his gun. "Come on, Perry."

"Leave," I said.

"What?"

"Get out of here, Doran. Take the van and go."

He smiled at me. The blood on his lips was dry now. "I don't think so."

I walked down the hall behind Brooks, and Doran followed. Nobody said a word to Gaglionci; we just left him bleeding on the fancy hardwood floors with the handcuffs on. Brooks hadn't turned a light on, and it was dim in the hall. There was an extravagant wine rack along the wall, probably fifty or sixty bottles in it, the white wines reflecting the faint light and the reds blending into the shadows along the wall. Brooks was walking fast, hands at his sides. He turned into the first door on the right and hit a light switch. We were in his office now, an expansive room with windows that would look out on the deck and the trees and lake beyond during the day. Now, at night, the dark glass simply showed the room.

Doran stepped past me and stood in front of the desk while Brooks sat down in the chair. He didn't look away from Doran while he pulled a black checkbook across the top of the desk and set it in front of him. He flipped it open and found a blank check, then reached out and patted his chest just over his heart, searching for a pen. I tensed when he did it. It wasn't a genuine gesture, there was something heavy and false about it, but I didn't understand why.

"Now just let me get a pen," he said, and he pulled open the drawer on the right side of the desk.

"Don't," Doran said, but Brooks already had his hand inside the drawer, and Doran fired.

The shot hit Brooks, shattered his collarbone and blew through his body and the chair behind it, but he'd gotten his hand on the gun in the drawer and he pulled the trigger. A hole opened in the desk with a cloud of splinters and then its twin bloomed red in the center of Doran's stomach.

Doran got off one more shot, and this time the bullet caught Brooks in the middle of the throat, tore a bloody fissure through his neck and slammed his head back against the chair. Blood burbled in the open wound as he tried to take one last breath that never came.

I started to move toward Doran, who was still standing, and he made a wavering turn to point the gun at me. I stopped where I was and held my hands out. For a second he looked right into my eyes. There was an expression of great concern in his face. Blood welled out of his stomach and spread across his shirt. He dropped the gun and sat down on the floor and looked at the wound for the first time.

"I wanted to kill him with his checkbook out. I wanted to kill him while he wrote the check," he said, and then he died.

CHAPTER

44

Rain was falling again, drumming on the big window behind Brooks, keeping me company as I sat with two dead men. I stayed in that office watching Doran long after I knew he was dead. The only sound was the rain at first, and blood dripping off Brooks's chair to the floor, but then I began to hear things from out in the main body of the house. It took me a minute to remember Gaglionci. Best not to leave him to his own devices.

I stood up and walked out of the office and down the dim hall, came around the corner, and found the front door open, Gaglionci gone, a trail of blood splatters leading out into the dark, rainy night.

Go after him, or stay here and call the police? It should have been an easy decision, but my brain was cloudy, unconcerned, as if none of this mattered anymore. Sit in a room with two corpses long enough, that's the way it starts to feel.

I went through the door and stood on the porch, watching the rain splash into puddles in the driveway and pound off the roof of Doran's rusted van, and then I heard footsteps from up by the road and a silhouette appeared, moving slowly. For a moment I thought of the guns back with Doran and Brooks and considered going for one of them. Then I saw it was Thor.

He had Gaglionci, now unconscious, draped over his arm, feet dragging along the wet pavement. Thor hauled him up onto the porch and dumped him at my feet.

"Thought you would want him back."

"Yes. Yes, that's good."

Thor stood on the porch and peered in at the house, saw the blood on the polished floors and heard the silence.

"It is done," he said. It was somewhere between a question and a statement of fact. He believed it to be true but was asking for verification.

"They're dead," I said.

He didn't respond. I realized that it was exactly what he'd meant.

"I didn't kill either one of them. They shot each other."

Still silent. I supposed it really didn't mean a damn thing to him one way or the other.

"Where are Amy and Joe?" I asked.

"Going for help. To the police. I thought it would be best if I went after you. It seems that was unnecessary. Your partner told me how to get here."

"I'll need to call the police now," I said. "You probably shouldn't be here when they come."

"No."

"I'll try to keep you out of it, Thor. I'll do my best."

He didn't say anything.

"You got her back," I said. "It wouldn't have happened if I'd been on my own. Thank you."

He made a slight bow. It was the motion of a professional performer thanking the grateful audience that had appreciated his talents, and I thought it was damn appropriate.

"Do you need to go to a hospital?" I looked at his side, where the blood was still not dry.

"I know a man who can help with that."

"I bet you do."

"I will leave now," he said. "You make your calls."

"How are you getting back to the city?"

"That is not a problem," he said, and then he turned and walked off the porch and into the woods.

* * *

I gave him five minutes before I called the police. By then, Gaglionci was conscious again. I passed on 911 and called Targent. He answered on the first ring, and he recognized the number.

"Perry, you are about twelve hours late with this call, you son of a bitch, and you'd better be ready to come in."

"You want to close your investigation?"

"I doubt you say that because you're offering to confess."

"Good guess."

"What do you have for me?"

"I've got two bodies in a house by Geneva," I said. "I've got a woman who was abducted today and is now safe and ready to explain some things to you. I've got the man who killed Alex Jefferson and Donny Ward in handcuffs."

"Tell me where you are," was all he said.

CHAPTER

45

They held me for three days. The warrant for Donny Ward's murder was still plenty valid when police arrived at the winery, and nobody was so impressed with my explanation that they wanted to tear it up and cut me loose. Tommy Gaglionci wasn't offering a confession, either. I'd been arrested on a Friday night, which gave the police—or maybe me—a break, because it postponed arraignment until Monday morning, giving them forty-eight hours to plunge into the stories Amy and Joe and I had to offer. On Monday morning my attorney learned there would be no arraignment.

By then, my claims had some evidence behind them. Along with Amy's story of how Gaglionci had abducted her, breaking into her apartment and covering her mouth with a sweet-smelling rag, the evidence techs had matched prints left in Donny Ward's yard with the boots on Gaglionci's feet.

They finally kicked me loose slightly after noon on Monday. Targent came to take me out of the jail himself. Joe was waiting to drive me home, but Targent held the door of a small interview room open and asked me to give him a minute. I went in and sat behind the table, enjoying the absence of handcuffs.

"Listen," Targent said, "maybe you're wanting an apology from me."

"I'm wanting to go home. That's it."

"Maybe you deserve one," he said as if I hadn't spoken. "I thought about that a lot last night. We still don't have all the details of this thing worked out, but if it holds up the way it looks now . . . My point is, you think I tried to force this onto you. That's not true. The things that happened to increase my suspicion, I didn't imagine those, Perry. I wouldn't have been doing a good job if I didn't try to explain them, right? And that's all I was doing. I was just trying to explain—"

"I've got it, Targent. I understand. No, you didn't imagine those things. You didn't need to believe them so completely, or at least *dis*believe me so completely, but I know what your job was, and I do understand that you were trying to get it done."

"A case like this," he said, "somebody actively trying to frame a guy . . . You don't see that much. It's tough to believe even when it's in your face."

"Your approach, while unimpressive, was no worse than what I brought to the table."

He tilted his head, looked at me curiously. "Yeah?"

The better part of three days spent in jail, I'd had a long time to consider it. Liked myself less as each day passed.

"You got a taste of some evidence against me and shut out the rest of the possibilities," I said. "Because you wanted me to be guilty. You didn't like me. You wanted to take me down. All of that? Same thing I did with Alex Jefferson. I railroaded a suspect, him and the son both. Decided they were guilty because I didn't like them. I didn't go out to find the truth, I went out to prove they were guilty. Even while I was ripping you for that approach with me, I was doing the same thing to Alex Jefferson and his son. At least you had the dignity to railroad somebody who was still alive."

He'd kept his eyes moving around the room when he'd talked, but now they were full on mine. Neither of us said anything for a while. Eventually, he stood up.

"Go home, Perry. Go home."

Amy and Joe met me outside of the jail. Amy got out of the car when she saw me approaching. She reached for me and

I caught her and held her and for the first time I felt like it was done. The worst of it was done. She was here, and she was safe, and I was with her. Tommy Gaglionci and Paul Brooks and the rest of them be damned. They hadn't done as much damage as they could have.

When Amy stepped back, her eyes were bright with tears that didn't fall.

"About damn time," she said.

"Yeah. Long weekend. The accommodations in there aren't nearly as nice as what I was treated to in Indiana."

"Write a guidebook," Joe said. *"Around the Midwest in Fifty Jails."*

He shook my hand and opened the passenger door for me, as if I were a visiting celebrity.

"No red carpet?" I said.

"Thought it might piss the cops off. You know, rubbing it in their faces?" He got in and started the car.

Still standing on the sidewalk, I turned back to Amy. "Are you all right? Did anything—"

"I'm fine. As fine as I could be, at least. I'm okay."

"When I saw you in that trailer . . . saw you were alive . . ."

I stopped talking then, and she looked away, and I knew we were both thinking about Andy Doran and the shot that dropped Gaglionci as he'd kicked the door open and stepped inside with his shotgun, going for Amy.

"Can I drive us somewhere?" Joe said. "Longer Lincoln stands on the sidewalk in front of the jail, more likely it is someone will think he escaped, throw him back in."

We got in the car. While Joe drove, he and Amy caught me up on what the police hadn't.

"I haven't heard anything about Thor," I said.

Joe looked at Amy in the rearview mirror. "Hopefully, you won't. We made a decision not to volunteer anything about him. It looks like you did the same."

"But Gaglionci and Reed?"

"Gaglionci hasn't spoken at all. Not yet. We'll see what happens with him. As for Reed, cops have interviewed him probably ten times, and he hasn't mentioned Thor once. Says you and I came in and threatened him, alone."

"Good."

"Reed's rolling on Gaglionci now, says the only reason he ever helped him was because Gaglionci had threatened to kill him."

"No surprise there. Reed's the type who'll do plenty of talking when he sees charges ahead."

"Should help you, though. He'll seal some things up with Gaglionci. Who was, I might add, arraigned this morning on one charge of kidnapping, two of murder. There's a team doing background on Paul Brooks, too. Found out he was arrested for sexual assault out east, during college. The girl backed out on her accusation, and charges were never filed. About the same time that happened, the girl started driving a new Lexus, and Brooks came home to Cleveland."

"Fenton's heavy hand."

"You got it. He'd already been diagnosed with his cancer by the time Monica Heath was killed. Knew he was dying."

"Seems he was willing to go pretty far to protect the legacy."

"I wonder how many times Jefferson's son thought about what might have happened if he'd just called the cops instead of his dad," Amy said. "Told them the truth."

"I'm pretty sure," I said, "he thought of it the night I met him. I left that damn note on the kid's door, and he expected Gaglionci and Doran were in town to finish the job. Yeah, I'd say he thought about it then."

I woke up in Amy's apartment the next morning, with her hair soft on my shoulder. I watched her for a long time, following the slow rise and fall of her chest as she breathed, relieved to see that she'd found sleep. We'd remained awake well into the night, and she'd told me the things she had not told the police, the things she'd felt and feared when she woke up in the van, the things she'd thought when Doran crawled back into the trailer with the sound of gunfire echoing outside. She told me that Gaglionci had hummed to himself while he cleaned his gun, waiting for Doran to get back, that he'd smelled of cologne and smiled at her in a way that made her go cold with fear, that even when I'd entered the trailer she'd felt hopeless because Doran was there, and when Thor holstered his gun she knew it was over.

She told me all of those things, and I told her some others, and at some point we slept. It was nearly nine now. I forced myself out of bed and onto my feet. Amy didn't wake when I moved. I went into the bathroom and took a shower and came out and brewed a pot of coffee.

Thirty minutes passed, and Amy didn't wake. I hoped that she would, that she'd come out and talk and we could waste the morning and delay the visit I had ahead. That wasn't going to happen, though. Amy needed sleep, and I needed to deal with a conversation I'd hungered for once and wanted nothing to do with now.

The day was clean and crisp after the rain, a cold sun still putting up a hell of a fight to work its way past the clouds and through the bare branches that surrounded Alex Jefferson's house. Karen came out into the driveway when I pulled up. When I got out of the truck, she came over and put her hands on my shoulders and looked me in the eyes.

"I'm sorry."

"Don't need to be, Karen."

"I've talked to the police. I've heard about most of it, although I'm sure there are a thousand details I don't know or don't understand. What I *do* know is that it's over, and that you made that happen. And I'm so sorry, Lincoln. I never wanted to believe any of the things that were being said about you, but every day it seemed like there was something new, and I just—"

"You just responded like they hoped you would," I said. "They wanted to play with your emotions. Targent and Gaglionci both. They wanted to turn you against me, and they did a damn good job of it. You don't need to apologize for that. In the moment when it mattered most, when that cop showed up, you trusted me. Enough to let me leave, at least. Without that . . ."

"They told me about your friend," she said. "Amy Ambrose. I'm so glad she's safe."

"She's doing fine. You helped let that happen."

"Okay." She took her hands off my shoulders and stepped back. The wind picked up and blew her hair over her face, temporarily obscuring the fear and the fatigue and the pain that were in it. I ached for her in that moment, thinking of the memory I'd held of her on the day we'd rented that boat in the Bass Islands, the smile she'd been capable of back then. A smile like that wouldn't come to her again after all of this, or at least it wouldn't come easily.

"When all of this got started," she said, "when Alex was killed and the police couldn't tell me why, I called you."

"Yes."

"I called you because this family had too many secrets. Or at least it felt like that to me. The breach between Alex and his son . . . it was something I always wanted to understand. When Alex was murdered, that changed. I *had* to understand it."

I didn't want to meet her eyes anymore. There was such a sense of bracing in them, of preparing for fresh anguish.

"Now I know you can do that," she said. "You can help me understand. And all of a sudden, I don't think I want to anymore. I don't think I want to at all."

She forced out a laugh that was on the edge of tears and shook her head.

"But I need to know. I've heard some of it from the police, and I need to know the rest."

We stayed outside while we talked. Sat on the steps in front of the house, side by side.

"If what the police think is true," she said, "then Alex always knew that Andy Doran was innocent."

I held her eyes for a moment before I looked down.

"Here is what I can tell you, Karen. Paul Brooks killed Monica Heath. He confessed to it in front of me. Andy Doran thought your husband's son killed her. So did I, for a while. We were both wrong."

"But they knew," she said. "Alex and Matthew, they knew what had happened."

"Yes," I said, and a swell of sorrow passed through me when I saw the look on her face.

"Alex helped," she said. It was not a question. "He helped put Doran in prison when he knew who had really killed that girl."

"It cost him a lot. He lost his son, Karen. Saved his client's son from the proper punishment and lost his own."

"Lost his son," she echoed. "Yes, he did. And when his son committed suicide . . . when his son *shot himself in the head* because he thought someone else was going to do worse, he blamed Alex for that. Didn't he? He thought Alex was the reason it was happening."

"I think he blamed himself, too. He wasn't a child, Karen. He was encouraged to identify Doran, yes, but the decision was his own."

She was quiet for a few minutes, then said, "You think Alex was evil, don't you? How could you not? He helped send this innocent man to jail, made a profit from it. You think he was evil."

I shook my head. "No, Karen. I don't. I think he deferred to money and power on that night, and once he'd deferred, he felt trapped. I don't think he envisioned what would happen as it continued, and once it got rolling he didn't know how to get out of it. And he paid dearly for what he did. More than he should have. More than anyone should have."

She sat with head bowed, silent.

"Have they told you why he died?" I said.

"Paul Brooks was afraid of him. Afraid he'd tell people what he knew."

"He was *going* to do that, Karen. He told Gaglionci he was ready to talk to the police and tried to convince him to do the same. He wanted to send Gaglionci back to find Doran and give him his money and assure him that he'd be cleared. He just needed a few days to prepare for it, I guess. To talk to you, I'm sure. He might have gone to jail. Probably would have. Even in the best case, his career would have been over, and he would have been shamed in a way that's tough to imagine. He was willing to let that happen to get his honor back, Karen. To protect his son, to set right what he'd made wrong."

She was crying.

"I think when he found you, it helped him," I said. "Gave him an escape, almost. You were young and good and so far from being in his world, and I'm quite sure that he needed to be with someone who was all of those things."

I was thinking of her on the boat again, the smile she'd had that I would never forget, the overwhelming sense of youth and energy and joy she gave off back then, like a pulse. I imagined Alex Jefferson meeting her in the aftermath of his greatest sin, and I understood what she would have done to him. I understood it very well.

She used her fingertips to wipe tears from her eyes. I reached out and rubbed her back, squeezed her shoulder until she ran out of tears. When they'd stopped, I put my hand on her neck and turned her face to mine.

"You told me that Alex said you healed him. That when he said that, you felt like he needed you in a way you couldn't fully understand."

She nodded.

"That," I said, "was probably as true a statement as you'll ever hear, Karen. And it should matter to you."

We sat there for a while, and then I got to my feet. She stood with me, and I hugged her and held her and then it had gone on too long and was accomplishing too little, and I walked to my truck and drove away and left her there with her grief. Sometimes, that's all you can do.

CHAPTER

46

I didn't talk to her again in the weeks that followed, but I saw plenty of her. Unplugged the television so I wouldn't have to stumble across another picture of her on the screen, listen to the commentators explain her husband's actions, tell the sad story of Andy Doran.

Soon the newspaper was reporting she'd left town, gone to stay with family. Two weeks after Doran and Paul Brooks were killed, movers were taking furniture out of her house, loading it into trucks. A real estate agency had control of the home, but the word was they'd wait a few months before putting it on the market. Tough to sell a place that has news crews camped out on the lawn.

Sometimes, I thought about calling. The day Cole Hamilton was arrested on charges of conspiracy was one. The day traces of Alex Jefferson's blood were found in Tommy Gaglionci's van was another. Gaglionci had washed the van with bleach and water, but that's the thing about blood—it'll find places to hide, crevices perfect for disappearing, and just when you think it's washed out of your life, it makes another appearance.

I never called, though. Lacked the words, and without them the telephone's pretty damn useless. Maybe a call around Christmas, I thought. Maybe a card. Maybe she'd call me. Maybe there was nothing to say.

* * *

The media coverage was relentless. I had to change my un-
listed home number, then my cell number. The more enter-
prising reporters took to waiting in the parking lot beneath
my apartment, but they didn't get any quotes, either. Nobody
did. My involvement was the subject of endless questioning in
the newspaper, my relationship with Karen became a fifteen-
minute feature on one of the morning news shows, and
numerous mentions were made of the arrest warrant for murder even though I'd never been charged. My attorney called to
suggest a lawsuit against Targent and the department for
wrongful arrest. I told him not to call again. If I required his
services, I'd let him know.

Since I ignored the phones, reporters took to sending letters requesting interviews. Going through a stack of them one
day, I found a postcard from Indiana. On the front was a photograph of a covered bridge in autumn, surrounded by crimson trees. I flipped it over and read the short note.

> *Mr. Perry—*
> *It appears I was wrong about you. Please*
> *accept this admission, and my apology. Also,*
> *please do not ever return to my county.*
> *Best Wishes,*
> *Lt. Roger Brewer*

I flipped the card back over and moved my hand to cover
the bridge, so all I could see were the trees. It was easy to
imagine they stood above a pond and gazebo, an orchard
nearby. The leaves would all be gone by now, just bare limbs
watching over cold water.

I went to Indiana for the money. That's what I told Joe
and Amy. If not for the money, just because I wanted to help.
An honorable thing. I'd wanted to help. In my more dishon-
est moments, I could try to leave it there. Not anymore,
though. Not with Karen gone and Matt Jefferson and Andy
Doran dead.

What took me to Indiana was the Jefferson family secret. I wanted to have it before Karen had it. Wanted to know why the son cut Alex Jefferson off, what evil he'd seen in his father. He was supposed to tell me, and I'd get to tell her. I'd be the one to explain what a bastard her husband had been. Validation, the nice word. Revenge, the true one.

I'd wanted Matt Jefferson to tell me what his father had done that was so wrong. Now, both of them dead, I wanted ten seconds to tell him what his father had been about to do that was right.

I found a magnet and put the postcard on my refrigerator. Isn't that what you're supposed to do with the things you need to remember?

The office was closed for three weeks while I spent time with Amy, hiding from the media. Being a member of that obnoxious little militia, Amy has great expertise in how to avoid them. While I was gone, clients got nothing but a voice mail saying the absence was indefinite. Joe came by my apartment on the third Monday after I'd closed the office to tell me I needed to get down and open the place again.

"You stay shut down for another week and you may not recover, LP. When a client takes his business somewhere else, it's likely to stay there."

I nodded. "You're right. But it's been a hell of a few weeks, Joe. I couldn't work. You know that."

"I know that. And now I'm telling you it's time to start again."

He was standing in my living room, using his index finger to turn a lampshade that he'd decided was crooked. He wouldn't look at me.

"Time to start again," I said. "Yeah, I guess it is. Does that go for you, too?"

He stopped playing with the lampshade. "No, LP. I'm afraid it doesn't."

I sat and stared at him. He looked sad but resolved. He stepped away from the lamp and paced across the room.

"I'm going to take the winter off. Get out of town, go somewhere warm. I can't do another winter in this town. Not right now. You know I've never been gone from Cleveland in the winter? You believe that? All those trips I took with Ruth, they were always in summer or fall. Maybe one in the spring. But I've always been here for winter, and, shit, I need a break. I'm thinking Florida, maybe Texas, somewhere down along the Gulf."

It took me a minute to say anything. When I did speak, all I could say was "Okay."

He finally stopped walking and sat down on the chair across from me, ran his hand over his jaw and studied the carpet.

"I just need a break, Lincoln. Don't know for how long, exactly, but I know I need to get out of here for a while. You can handle it without me."

"Yeah," I said, "but it's not going to be a whole lot of fun."

He snorted. "Damn, almost like a real job. You know, a lot of guys haven't had the luxury of working with someone like me. Now you'll have to appreciate it for the treat that it is."

I managed a smile. "Okay, Joe. But don't go down there and get lost. Spring comes and it starts to warm up around here, you damn well better be on your way north."

"I will be."

He left on the first Sunday of December. His arm was improving all the time, but he still needed help packing the car, and I went down and loaded the Taurus up as well as I could, Joe growling out irritated instructions from over my shoulder. Finally, I wedged the trunk lid shut and stepped back. He handed me his house keys.

"Don't forget to water the plants. And remember—no parties."

"Right."

Amy came out of the house and walked down to join us. "Is that it? You're really leaving now?"

"I'm leaving, my dear. And, yes, I know that you'll miss me."

She hugged him and kissed him on the cheek. A brisk wind was blowing, and the broad gray clouds overhead promised snow. The forecasts said it could be heavy. Joe zipped up his jacket and smiled.

"A few hours, and I'm ditching this thing for a polo shirt and a seat by the pool."

"Rub it in," I said. "Nice."

It was quiet for a minute, and then I said, "Be in touch, Joe."

"Absolutely." He put out his hand, and I shook it, and then he got in the car. By the time he hit Tennessee he'd probably have doubled the total miles on that damn Taurus. He started the engine, and I thumped my hand on the trunk and then stepped back and waved. He turned out of the driveway and went down Chatfield toward the interstate ramp at West 150th. I watched him go, and out of nowhere Andy Doran's voice was in my head. *All I had to do was make it through the winter. Just make it through the winter.*

Amy stepped close to me and wrapped her arm around my waist. "I'm going to miss him."

"Me, too."

She squeezed me and then stepped back. "No sense being sad about it all day, though. I've got plans for us."

"Browns game," I said. "Right. We can watch that."

"Christmas decorations at my apartment," she said. "They don't hang themselves."

I looked at her in horror, then back out at Chatfield. "If I run really fast, do you think I can catch him?"

We locked Joe's house and got into my truck and drove away. Snowflakes were falling now, remaining as crystals for a few seconds on the windshield before the heat from the truck reduced them to water. On the radio, the announcers were predicting six inches by nightfall. Joe would beat the storm on his way south, and I was glad for him. Amy and I were here for the duration, but that was fine, too. The snow would melt. It always does.

ENVY THE NIGHT

It was a Big Brother kind of thing, no doubt about it, but Grady Morgan had kept an active monitor on Frank Temple III for seven years. It wasn't proper, or even really legal, because Frank had no role whatsoever in anything that could still be considered an active investigation for Grady. But nobody had noticed or cared or commented yet, and as long as they didn't, he'd keep watching. Without a touch of remorse. He owed the kid at least this much.

The feelers Grady had out there in the world, computers that ran daily checks on Frank's fingerprints and Social Security number, had been quiet for a long time. As had the phone lines and the e-mails and the mailbox. No word from Frank in quite a while, and there were times when Grady ached to speak to him, check in, but he didn't. He just went to work every day and eyed the calendar that showed retirement was not far away and hoped that Frank would continue to stay off the radar screen. Grady didn't want to see a blip.

Here was one. The wrong kind of blip, too, an arrest in Indiana, and when it first came through to his computer Grady felt an immediate sick swirl go through his stomach, and he actually looked away from the screen for a moment, not wanting to read the details.

"Shit, Frank," he muttered. "Don't do this to me."

Then he sighed and rubbed a forehead that was always

growing, chasing the gray hair right off his skull, and he turned back to the computer screen and read the details of the arrest. When he got through, he let out a breath of relief.

Public intoxication. That was it. The second arrest in seven years, the second time Grady had felt this chill of sorrow, and the second time he could roll his eyes and chalk it up as No Big Deal, Kids Being Kids.

He hoped.

As he pushed back from his desk and walked to the window and looked out at the Chicago skyline, he sent a silent request to Frank Temple III somewhere out there across the miles.

Tell me it was just fun. Tell me, Frank, that you were out with some buddies having beers and chasing girls and laughing like idiots, like happy, happy idiots. Tell me that there was no fight involved, no temper, no violence, not even a closed fist. You've made it a long way.

A long, *long* way.

Frank III had been eighteen years old when Grady met him. A slender, good-looking kid with dark features contrasted by bright blue eyes, and a maturity that Grady hadn't seen in a boy of that age before, so utterly cool that Grady actually asked a psychologist for advice on talking to him. *He's showing nothing,* Grady had said. *Every report we've got says he was closer to his father than anyone, and he is showing nothing.*

He showed something in the third interview. It had been just him and Grady sitting in the Temple living room, and Grady, desperate for some way to get the kid talking, had pointed at a framed photograph of father and son on a basketball court and said, *Did he teach you how to play?*

The kid had sat there and looked at him and seemed almost amused. Then he'd said, *You want to know what he taught me? Stand up.*

So Grady stood up. When the kid said, *Take that pen and try it to touch to my heart. Hell, try to touch it anywhere. Pretend it's a knife,* Grady hadn't wanted to. All of a sudden this was seeming like a real bad idea, but the kid's eyes were intense, and so Grady said what the hell and made one quick thrust, thinking he'd lay the pen against the kid's chest and be done with it.

The speed. Oh, man, the speed. The kid's hands had moved faster than anybody's Grady had ever seen, trapped his wrist and rolled it back and the pen was pointing at Grady's throat in a heartbeat's time.

Half-assed effort, Frank Temple III had said. *Try again. For real this time.*

So he'd tried again. And again, and again, and by the end he was working into a sweat and no longer fooling around, was beginning to feel the flush of shame because this was a *child,* damn it, and Grady had done eight years in the Army and another fifteen in the Bureau and he ran twenty miles a week and lifted weights and he could beat this kid . . .

But he couldn't. When he finally gave up, the kid had smiled at him, this horribly genuine smile, and said, *Want to see me shoot?*

Yes, Grady said.

What he saw at the range later that afternoon—a tight and perfect cluster of bullets—no longer surprised him.

Seven years later, he was thinking about that day while he stared out of the window and told himself that it was nothing but a public intox charge, a silly misdemeanor, and that there was nothing to worry about with Frank. Frank was a good kid, always had been, and he'd be absolutely fine as long as he stayed away from a certain kind of trouble.

That was all he needed to do. Stay away from that kind of trouble.

CHAPTER

2

Frank woke to the grinding of a big diesel motor pulling away, sat up, and saw gray light filling the sky. When he opened the door and tried to get out of the Jeep his cramped muscles protested, and he felt a quick razor of pain along the left side of his stiff neck. He was hungry now, the alcohol long since vanished from his cells and the Gatorade calories burned up. He took the edge off with a Snickers bar and a bottle of orange juice from the vending machines, ate while he studied the big map on the wall. He'd come closer last night than he'd realized; Tomahawk was only one hundred miles ahead.

The closer he got, the more his resolve wavered. Maybe it would be best to pretend he'd never gotten that message from Ezra, didn't even know Devin was on his way back. Maybe he'd just spend a little time in the cabin, stay for a weekend, catch some fish. It would be fine as long as he didn't see Devin Matteson. If he stayed away from Devin, if it was just Frank and Ezra and the woods and the lake, this could end up being a good trip, the sort of trip he'd needed to take for a while now. But if he *did* see Devin . . .

What are you doing here, then, if it's not about Devin? he thought. *You really think this is some sort of vacation?*

Whatever part of his brain was supposed to rise to that argument remained silent. He drove with the windows down as the gray light turned golden and the cold morning air began to warm on his right side. Past Wausau the smell of the place began to change—pine needles and wood smoke and, even though there wasn't a lake in sight, water. There would be a half-dozen lakes within a mile of the highway by now. He knew that both by the change in the air and from the map in the rest stop, this portion of the state freckled with blue.

The smells were triggering a memory parade, but Frank wasn't sure if he wanted to sit back and watch. It was that sort of place for him now. The deeper he got into the tall pines, the faster the memories flooded toward him, and he was struck by just how much he'd loved this place. It was one thing to recall it from somewhere hundreds of miles away, and another to really be here, seeing the forests and the sky and smelling the air. Maybe he'd stay for a while. The summer stretched ahead of him, and the money wouldn't run out. Blood money, sure, and spending it while hating the methods that had earned it made Frank a hypocrite at best and something far darker at worst, but it was there.

The first few times he and his father had made the trip, the highway had been two-lane this far north. Then the tourism dollars began to knock on the right doors down in Madison, and soon the four-lane was extending. Frank's mind was on the cabin, and he blew right past the Tomahawk exits before remembering that he had nothing in the way of food or supplies. He'd have to come back down after he'd unpacked, grab some lunch and buy groceries and then head back to the lake.

He exited at an intersection with County Y, a narrow road slashing through the pines, and had gone about a mile down it when someone in a silver Lexus SUV appeared behind him. From the way it came on in the rearview mirror Frank knew it was really eating up the road, had to be doing seventy at least. As the car approached, it shifted into the oncoming lane, the driver planning to pass Frank without breaking stride. Had to be a tourist, driving like that. The locals had more class.

It was that thought that made him look at the license plate. He probably wouldn't have done it otherwise, but now he wanted to prove his theory correct, so his eyes went to the plate.

Florida.

The car was gone in a silver flash then, swerving in ahead of him and pulling away. The muscles at the base of his neck had gone cold and tight and his breath seemed trapped.

Florida.

It didn't mean anything. A strange little touch of déjà vu, sure, but it didn't mean anything. Yes, the Willow Flowage was an isolated place and a damn long drive from Florida, but there were several million cars with Florida license plates. There wasn't even a *chance* that Devin Matteson was driving that car.

"Not a chance," Frank said aloud, but then that message from Ezra filled his head again—*I got a call from Florida . . . he's coming back*—and he pressed hard on the gas pedal and closed the gap on the silver Lexus. A closer look was all he needed. Just that minor reassurance, enough that he could go on to the cabin laughing at himself for this reaction.

He kept accelerating, closed until he was only a car length behind. Now he was leaning forward, his chest almost against the steering wheel, peering into the tinted rear window of the Lexus as if he'd actually be able to tell who the driver was.

There was only one person in the car, and it was a male. He could tell that much, but nothing else. He pulled a little closer, almost on top of the Lexus now, staring hard at the silhouette of the driver's head.

"It's him." He said it softly, exhaled the words, no justification for them at all but somehow he was *positive*—

Brake lights. A flash of red, one quick blink that he saw too late because he was too close, and then he hammered the brake pedal and slammed the wheel left and hit the back corner of the Lexus at fifty miles an hour.

"*Shit!*"

The back of the Jeep swung right with the impact, then came back to the left and sent the front end sliding, a fishtail that was threatening to turn into a full three-sixty. Even as the skid started Frank could hear his father's voice—*turn into it, turn into it, your instinct will tell you to turn away, but you've got to turn into it.* He heard it, recalled those old lessons in the half second that it took him to lose control of the car, and still he turned away from it. It had happened too fast and the instinct was too strong. He turned away from the skid, the tires shrieked on the pavement, and then any hope of getting the car back was gone.

Frank was saved by bald tires. He'd lectured himself on the tires a dozen times, thinking they'd kill him someday if he didn't get them replaced, but instead they saved him. The pavement was dry, the Jeep was a top-heavy vehicle, and if the tires had been able to grab the road well he probably would have rolled. Instead, because there was hardly a trace of traction left on the worn rubber, he slid. He saw whirling trees and sky and then the Jeep spun off the shoulder and into the pines. He heard a crunch and shatter just as the airbags blew out and obscured his vision and then he came to a stop.

The airbag deflated and fell away, leaving his face tingling, and for a few seconds he sat where he was, hands still locked on the steering wheel, foot still pressed hard against the brake, blood hammering through his veins. It was amazing how fast the body could respond—you'd spend an hour just trying to wake up on a normal morning, but throw a crisis out there and the body was ready for a marathon in a split second. He reached over and beat the airbags aside with his hands and saw spiderwebbed glass on the passenger window, the door panel bent in against the seat. Bad, but nothing terrible. He could probably drive away.

What about the Lexus? Devin Matteson's Lexus. He was sure of it again, absolutely certain, and without any pause for thought he turned and reached behind his seat, found the metal case, flicked the latch and opened it and then he was sitting behind the wheel with a gun in his hand.

Reality caught up to him then. *Sanity* caught up to him.

"What are you doing?" he said, staring at the gun. "What the hell are you doing?"

He slid the gun back into the case and closed it and opened the door—after a glance in the sideview mirror to make sure he wasn't going to step out in front of a truck, survive the accident only to get squashed when he was on foot—and then got out of the car. He walked around to the front and saw that he wouldn't be driving anywhere. The right front tire was blown out and the wheel bent inward, crunched down beneath the mangled front quarter panel. If he'd handled it right, turned into the skid instead of away, he might've been able to keep the Jeep straight enough to avoid the trees. Then he'd be left with a dent and a drivable car, instead of this mess.

He'd lost track of the Lexus at the moment of impact, and now he was surprised to see how far behind him the car was, a good hundred feet at least. The driver had made the shoulder as well, but the car was facing the wrong direction and angled against the trees that lined the road.

Looking up at the car made his previous suspicion come on again, and again he thought of the gun, had to shake his head and move away from the Jeep before the urge to go for it got any stronger.

"It's not him," he said. "It's not him."

At that moment the driver's door on the Lexus opened and Frank's breath caught and held for a second until the driver stepped out onto the road.

It was not Devin Matteson. Not by a long shot. Even from this far away he could tell exactly how ludicrous the idea had been, could tell that he'd just caused a dangerous accident over an utterly absurd moment of paranoia.

He walked toward the Lexus as the driver began to survey the damage to his vehicle. Frank's first thought, watching him—*the dude's on speed.*

The guy, tall and thin with a shock of gray hair that stuck out in every direction, was dancing around the Lexus. Literally dancing. He'd skip for a few steps, twirl, lift both hands to his face and then prance back around the other side. He was talking to himself, too, a chattering whisper that Frank couldn't make out, and he seemed completely oblivious to the fact that there'd been another car involved in the collision.

"Hey." Frank got no response and walked closer. "Hey! You okay?"

The guy stopped moving then and stared at Frank in total confusion. Then he looked up at the Jeep and nodded once, figuring it out. Up close, Frank saw that he wasn't too old, maybe forty, the gray hair premature. He had a long nose that hooked at the end and small, nervous eyes set above purple rings that suggested it had been a while since he'd had a full night's sleep. His hands were still moving, too, fingers rippling the air as if he were playing a piano.

"Yes," he said. "I'm okay. Yes, everything's fine. You don't need to worry about me. I'll just call Triple-A. You can go on now."

Frank raised his eyebrows. "Just call Triple-A? I hit *you,* man. You're going to want to hang around and get this worked out for insurance."

The guy was shaking his head. "No, no, I hit my brakes, just slammed on my brakes, not your fault at all."

Not his fault at all? What the hell was he talking about? Frank had been tailgating so bad he'd slammed into him as soon as the guy slowed. It was clearly Frank's fault. The guy must be nervous, that's all. Shaken up. Collision like that, at nearly highway speeds, who wouldn't be?

"What I'm saying is, we need to call the police," Frank said. "Get an accident report made, so we can make this square with the insurance company, right?"

The gray-haired guy winced and rubbed his forehead as if a pain had developed there. He probably had a bad driving record. Maybe a few accidents, and driving a car like that Lexus, his insurance rate already had to be high. He was worried about the money. Didn't understand that Frank was liable for all the damage.

"Tell you what," the guy said. "It'd be a big help to me— a *big* help—if we didn't get an accident report made."

So he'd been right—bad driving record. Unless it was something more serious. Hell, maybe the guy *was* on drugs. Frank frowned, studying him closer, looking for the signs. He just seemed amped-up, that was all. Buzzing. His eyes were clear, and he was cogent enough in conversation. A Starbucks addict, maybe.

"I'll pay for your damage," the gray-haired man continued. "I know what you're thinking—as soon as I can, I'll take off and stiff you on the bill. But I promise that won't happen. We can take care of it right now. Find a repair shop, and I'll take care of the bill beforehand."

"I hit *you*," Frank said again.

"Don't worry about that. It was my fault, my responsibility, and I don't want an accident report made, okay?"

Frank shook his head and walked a few steps away, looking at the Lexus. It was even more beat to shit than his Jeep. The front end was crumpled, there was a gash, maybe three feet long, across the passenger side of the car from the contact with the trees, and steam was leaking out of the hood.

"Please," the man said, and there was a desperate quality to his voice that made Frank look back with surprise. Whatever trouble this guy had with his driver's license—if he even had one—was serious. Frank stood there on the shoulder as two cars buzzed past them, nobody stopping, and looked at this weird guy with the nervous hands and panicked eyes. Why not give him a break? It was Frank's fault, so it was only fair to let this guy handle it in whatever way he wanted.

"All right," he said, and the look on the gray-haired man's face, the way it broke with relief, was enough to convince him he'd made the right call.

"Thank you. Oh, man, *thank* you. I'll call a tow truck. The car's got a navigation system, you can find anything with it, we can pick any repair shop you want, I'll show you the choices . . ."

CHAPTER

3

Jerry was staring at Nora's ass again, in that way he had where his eyes seemed to bug right out of his head, nothing subtle about it, but she wondered if she was allowed to care today—she'd done the same thing that morning as she got dressed, looking her butt over in the mirror like some sort of sorority girl instead of a woman with wrench calluses on her palms. You did something like that, could you get upset when a guy allowed himself a stare? Maybe she'd earned the leer. Karma.

The glance in the mirror was important, though, a morning reminder that Nora was still very much a woman. This before putting on the jeans and the heavy work shirt, tucking her hair into a baseball cap so it wouldn't hang free and invite a painful accident. She'd learned that lesson one afternoon when she'd used the creeper to check up on Jerry's work and rolled right over her own hair. Stafford Collision and Custom was open by seven thirty, and from then until six or six thirty when she shut the doors and turned the locks, Nora would interact with few females. It was a man's business, always had been, but she liked the touch she brought to it and thought the customers did, too. Granted, they were her father's customers and probably kept returning more out of loyalty—and pity—for Bud Stafford than for his daughter, but the shop still did good work. On those rare afternoons when a particularly difficult job was done and the car driven out of the shop, Nora might even let herself believe they did a better job now. She wouldn't admit it to anyone else, of course, but she did have an eye for detail that her father couldn't touch. Too bad an eye for detail wasn't enough to keep the bills paid.

The phone rang out in the office, and Nora straightened up and looked back at Jerry, who promptly flushed and averted his eyes. Even when you *didn't* catch Jerry, he thought you had. Jerry would've made a piss-poor criminal.

"I'd like you to take another pass over that front quarter panel," Nora said.

"Huh?"

"There are waves in the paint, Jerry. Ripples. I know you can see them, and *you* know how I feel about waves. Doesn't matter if they disappear in the shadows, you can see them in the sun, and that's when people care about their cars looking the best. They go home and the first sunny Saturday morning they wash the car and wax it and see those waves. And then you know what happens? They don't come back. Now get rid of the waves."

She walked away from him, got into the office just in time to grab the phone before it rang over to voice mail. She was always forgetting to take the cordless handset out into the shop with her, and she knew they'd lost business because of it. When a body shop doesn't answer, people just call the next one in the phone book; they don't wait and try again. She'd been one ring away from losing this call.

"Stafford Collision and Custom, this is Nora Stafford."

She sat on the edge of the desk and took notes on one of the old pads that still had Bud Stafford's name across the top. The caller wanted a tow truck for two cars that had wrecked up on County Y. Her last tow driver, who'd also been a prep man and part-time painter, had picked up a drunk driving charge three months back and to keep him would have required bearing an insurance rate spike that she simply couldn't handle. In reality it was a welcome break— the shop's financial situation was going to dictate firing somebody anyhow, and the drunk driving charge gave her an excuse. She'd let him go and couldn't afford to hire a replacement. But two cars—including a Lexus—that was business she couldn't turn down, either. Jerry could drive the tow truck, but he wasn't covered by the insurance policy, and she needed him to finish repainting that Mazda this morning. She'd have to handle this one herself.

She got the details of the wreck's position and promised to be out within twenty minutes, then went back into the shop and told Jerry where she was going. He just grunted in response, not looking at her.

"What's the problem, Jerry?"

"Problem?" He dropped the rag that was in his hands. "Problem should be pretty obvious. You got me wasting all my time *re*painting work I shouldn't have had to *paint* in the first place."

She waved a hand at him, tired already, the argument by now just like the dying water heater in her house—too familiar, too annoying, too expensive to fix.

Jerry was a body man, a fine body man, none better in town. Didn't have the eyes for a top-quality paint job, but that wasn't the problem so much as the way he felt disrespected when asked to paint. If she could afford to bring someone else on board, she would, but that explanation hadn't appeased him.

"Jerry, this is not a big deal. If you'd done it right the first time, I wouldn't have asked you to repaint it. Instead, you half-assed the job and then tried to make up for it with the buffer, like usual."

"Damn it, Nora, last time I painted cars it was with—"

"Single-stage lacquer, spray it on, buff it pretty, don't have to mess with no damn clear coat . . ."

Nora mocked his voice perfectly, capturing the drawl so dead-on that Jerry pulled back in anger and grabbed his rag again, tightened his fist around it. He was a small man, only a few inches taller than she was, but strong in the wiry way that comes from years of physical labor. What was left of his hair was thin and brown and damp with sweat.

"All right," he said. "So I've told you before, if you remember all that. Think you're clever saying it back to me, I 'spose. But if you was clever you'd understand, instead of using it to make fun of me. Your daddy understood. I'm not a combination man. I do body work. Been doing it since back when you was playing with dolls and putting on training bras and learning to paint your nails."

Same old shit. He'd start bitching about his workload, then begin with his what-a-pretty-little-girl-you-are routine, slighting her gender either directly or with what he thought passed as slick humor.

"Tell you something, Jerry? When I was learning to paint my nails, I was also learning how to paint a *car*. Now it's time that you do."

She turned and walked away from him, heard the *bitch* muttered under his breath and kept on going, out of the shop and into the tow truck. Sat behind the wheel and let the engine warm and lifted her hands to her face and thought, *I would've cried about this. A year ago, maybe even six months ago, I would've cried.*

Not any more, though. No way. But was that entirely a good thing?

She wasn't going to think about it. Pointless exercise. What she needed to think about was the cars waiting for her up on County Y. Two cars with substantial damage, body work and painting needed, one a Jeep and the other a Lexus. That was more than a pleasant surprise—it was salvation. She'd spent the morning trying to determine which bills she could be late on. It was down to that now, down to creating a rotating schedule of missed payments because she simply could not pay them all and keep the doors open. Now here was a phone call offering two cars, enough work to keep those wolves distracted, if not completely at bay. And to think, she'd been one ring away from missing it altogether.